No Broken Hearts

A LAUREN ATWILL MYSTERY

No Broken Hearts

Sheila York

FIVE STAR

A part of Gale, Cengage Learning

GALE
CENGAGE Learning

Farmington Hills, Mich • San Francisco • New York • Waterville, Maine
Meriden, Conn • Mason, Ohio • Chicago

GALE
CENGAGE Learning®

LIBRARY OF CONGRESS CATALOGING-IN-PUBLICATION DATA

York, Sheila.
    No broken hearts / Sheila York.
        pages cm. — (A Lauren Atwill mystery)–First edition.
    ISBN 978-1-4328-2914-8 (hardcover) — ISBN 1-4328-2914-9
(hardcover) — ISBN 978-1-4328-2909-4 (ebook)
    1. Women screenwriters—Fiction. 2. Motion picture industry—
Fiction. 3. Murder—Fiction. 4. Hollywood (Los Angeles, Calif.)—
Fiction. 5. Mystery fiction. I. Title.
PS3625.O755N6 2014
813'.6—dc23   2014018202

First Edition. First Printing: September 2014
Find us on Facebook– https://www.facebook.com/FiveStarCengage
Visit our website– http://www.gale.cengage.com/fivestar/
Contact Five Star™ Publishing at FiveStar@cengage.com

Printed in the United States of America
1 2 3 4 5 6 7 18 17 16 15 14

No Broken Hearts

CHAPTER 1

March 1947

Normally, when I get really angry, I'll throw a few unbreakable things around my study.

Not this time.

I snatched up another ashtray and flung it into the fireplace. The green glass exploded against the firebox, the emerald shards showering the flames and joining the layer already under the grate.

But now I'd run out of ashtrays. I yanked open another cabinet in the bookcase, grabbed a couple of ceramic candlesticks and slung them in, one after the other.

"You could try swearing, save some china," Peter Winslow suggested, calmly. But then, he'd been shot at all over the Pacific during the war, and since then a few times on the streets of Los Angeles, so he wasn't likely to be intimidated by ricochet, from temper or tableware.

Nevertheless, he stayed where he was, in the chair behind my desk, his hat still in his hands.

But I wasn't taking orders from anybody right now, not me, so I grabbed another candlestick and whipped it into the fire. Then I prowled the hearth rug, glaring at the painted rosebuds on the candlestick as they slowly curled and melted in the heat.

Peter just sat there. He didn't tell me to calm down, didn't tell me to stop acting like a hysterical female, didn't ask who the hell I was so mad at. Didn't ask what the hell he'd walked into when he'd come all the way out to Pasadena for a quiet dinner. He waited.

Finally, I threw myself down on the sofa and slung my arms across my chest, holding my hands in check because they were still twitching to find something to throw. Like a punch.

But the object of my fury was twelve miles away, in Hollywood.

It was my boss, Sol Noble, head of Marathon Studios.

"I just got a call from the studio," I said. "I've been loaned out. Loaned out! To *Epic*! Sol Noble promises me my first screen credit in years, then he sends me to Epic to crank out another Mary Ann McDowell picture. My first screen credit in three years is going to be on a Mary Ann McDowell picture. Take a look. There, there on the floor." I released one hand long enough to jab a finger at the copy of the *Los Angeles Eagle* lying where I'd thrown it, along with a few other unbreakable items, before I'd moved on to bigger game.

"Page eight," I said. "Savannah Masters's column. Look at what it says about her latest picture. 'A coed romp,' that's what she calls it." I had it memorized. " 'Miss McDowell is flirtatious and charming as always in this coed romp, a feather-light amusement about three lovelies out to win degrees and husbands.' That's the best she could do. I know what this is. Sol Noble's a superstitious bastard. He's loaning me out to do a coed romp, for which Marathon will get paid more than he's paying me. Meanwhile, he gets to find out if it's true that whenever Lauren Atwill signs on to a picture, somebody gets killed."

Peter slid his fedora onto the blotter, rose slowly to his six-two, and walked over to the table under the window where Juanita, my housekeeper, had laid out a bar for us. He mixed me a stout gin and tonic, scooped ice into it from the bucket, then twisted the lime while I thought about twisting Sol Noble's neck.

He poured himself a bourbon and came over to the sofa. He handed me my glass.

"Is that the word?" he asked, looking down at me with his hard, dark eyes. "How far has it gone?"

I shrugged. "A couple of cracks lately, around Marathon. Maybe not too far because most people have no idea how true it is."

"Most people have no idea because when you find a body, you go ahead and find out who left it there. Then you let the cops take the credit, and that's a secret they're glad to keep." He sat down beside me. "You know that whatever the latest thing is going around the Hollywood track, it's lucky to make the backstretch before the next thing overtakes it."

"You're going to keep being rational, aren't you?"

He smiled. And, as always, it did remarkable things to those eyes.

I decided to calm down. None of this was Peter's fault. He was an innocent bystander. Which can't often be said about Peter Winslow.

"I guess you talked to Ross," he said.

Sam Ross was a producer at Marathon, where I'd done most of my work as a screenwriter. He and his wife, Helen, were also my friends.

"They're in Hawaii," I said. "I'm not ruining a second honeymoon. Besides, there's nothing Sam can do." I took a healthy sip of my drink. "Juanita's making that roasted pork for you."

"Tell her I had nothing to do with this mess in here."

Juanita didn't care too much for men, believing they were, by and large, swine. But she liked Peter. Of course, she had reason. He'd saved my life, twice, while he and I had solved some cases in which people had left bodies lying around.

"I'll clean it all up," I said. "Usually, I just throw pillows."

"You had a half-dozen ashtrays in that cabinet all set to go, and you don't smoke."

"You're a pretty good detective, aren't you?"

"Enough to keep the license."

"All right, I keep some cheap, breakable stuff. Just in case." I kicked off my shoes and drew my legs onto the sofa. "You're not scared of me, are you?"

"I'm scared of Juanita."

I laid my head on his shoulder. It's a nice shoulder. He shifted his drink to the other hand, put his arm around me and kissed my hair. I snuggled against him. Since I was on his right side, there was no gun to get in the way, and I took full advantage. He didn't seem to mind.

"So what are you going to do?" he asked.

"Go work for Epic."

"How bad will it be?"

"Twenty years ago, they were a major studio, but they almost went bankrupt in the Depression. For a while, seven, eight years ago, they were one step up from Poverty Row. A boss at a major could keep a star in line by threatening to loan him to Epic. Just before the war, they got a new boss, Ben Bracker. He merged them with a couple of small studios, built up their B picture thrillers, turned out more A pictures, branched out into musicals. Still, their budgets are low." I lifted my cheek and repositioned it against his lapel. "It's been a long time since I had a screen credit. Longer since I had anything I was proud of. That story treatment I wrote. It's pretty damned good. I'm afraid Sol liked it so much he'll give it to someone else while I'm gone, off writing the coed romp. And if he does, I've got nothing to say about it. The story belongs to the studio. Maybe I should have read the fine print."

"It wouldn't have made any difference."

It was true. Not many of even the biggest Hollywood stars got to call their shots. And I certainly didn't qualify as anyone's star. I'd had something of a career before the war, then cut back my work, confined myself mostly to fixing up other writers' work anonymously, in an attempt to save a crumbling marriage. I'd been sure that, if I just spent more time being a proper wife to my movie star husband, he wouldn't have so many affairs. I'd actually been aiming for no affairs at all, which shows you how little I'd learned about Hollywood in over a dozen years of working there. I turned out to be a very good script doctor, a complete failure at saving the marriage.

Peter said, "What do you say we have a couple of drinks, eat dinner, and then I'll spend a long time taking your mind off Sol Noble."

"How did you know that was exactly what I was thinking? You *are* a good detective."

He pressed his lips into my hair, then whispered, "Don't worry. Nobody's going to die."

CHAPTER 2

The next morning, I drove over to my office at Marathon Studios, which is out on Melrose. I pulled through the tall, wrought iron gates, waved in by the guard. Now that I was a regular, I didn't have to stop and remind him who I was. At least *someone* knew I was a writer.

The main avenue stretched back to the sound stages, lined with Spanish-style buildings of heavy-cream stucco, red tile roofs, and narrow balconies. The first set belonged to the people who help keep the studio running and hardly ever get any credit for it: accountants, bookkeepers, and the art, research, and advertising departments. Then, suddenly on the right, appeared an expanse of sparkling lawn and glistening palms. Glaring at you from the center of it was the executive office building, known to most of those who don't labor inside it as the Ice House. It's a white box in a style someone with more power than taste had considered the latest thing a decade ago, cut down the center with a wall of glass to give you a full view of the white-white-white lobby, so you could be sure its interior ugliness did indeed match the inspiration of the exterior design.

Past that, we returned abruptly to Spanish and the offices of the cinematographers, art directors, and set designers. Then just opposite a sound stage, the Tate Building, where most of the studio's writers are housed behind chipped desks and doors with rattling hardware in offices reached by a groaning elevator.

It's old and cranky, pretty much the way I was feeling.

Not that Peter hadn't kept his promise, but a man's skill can only distract a woman for so long, then she has to go back to work. And sometimes she has to do it after soothing her ego with too many gin and tonics the night before. As I'd left my house in Pasadena, I'd pressed a pair of sunglasses to my face and snapped down the visor on my Lincoln convertible. I'd driven into Hollywood with the top up, despite the glorious late-winter sunshine.

I parked in the Tate's narrow lot and went up to what is now my regular office, on the fifth floor. Before I even took off my hat, I cranked the awnings out to cut down on the glare.

I sat down in the sprung desk chair, still in my sunglasses, opened the desk's middle drawer, and pulled out a bottle of aspirin. I unscrewed the lid and tapped out a few tablets, as the ones I'd taken at home seemed to have had little effect. I washed them down with a cup of strong coffee I'd purchased from the wagon downstairs, which was on its start-of-day rounds. It was well supplied. It had to be, given the number of writers who regularly showed up at work in my condition.

"Atwill!" Eleanor Hawkins stood in my doorway, her shoulder leaned against its frame. She tapped her forehead in a salute.

"Hawkins," I said, blearily. If you wanted Hawkins to think well of you, you called her by her last name.

"I thought I heard your tread. The news is out around here, about the loan-out. I've come to offer condolence and to ask a favor if you're in the mood to grant one."

"As long as it doesn't involve clear thinking. I had a late night of not celebrating."

I took off the sunglasses. She flinched, then dropped onto my sofa. It was a comfortable old thing, its cushions swayed and frayed from long years of writers throwing their legs up and lounging until an idea struck them, or the writer they'd come to visit bailed them out with the loan of one. Most ideas in

Hollywood are only on loan.

Hawkins sported her usual attire: high-waisted pleated slacks and a blouse styled like a man's shirt and tailored for her. Today, she had a long scarf under the open collar, knotted at her throat. Often she wore a waistcoat, but today it was a thick, amber-colored shawl-collared cardigan. The Tate Building holds the morning chill extremely well. Her short black hair was sharply parted on the side and smoothed with a bit of hair oil.

Hawkins writes melodramas, often costume melodramas, that set audiences weeping at the sacrifice or cheering for the triumph over adversity of the star. When an actress needs to rebuild her image with the public after a divorce, Hawkins is often the first writer at Marathon to be asked for an idea.

Reclined, she crossed her ankles and shoved her hands into the sweater's pockets. She said, "I do believe all the bathtub gin they drank in their misspent youth rendered every future studio magnate an imbecile. Alas, the condition only reveals itself in the high fever of power."

"At least Sol didn't have his secretary call me."

"I heard it was Mickels. That's not an improvement."

Mickels is the assistant to one of Marathon's vice presidents, and his sole mission seems to be harassing writers into appearing to be hard at work, which to him means hunched over a typewriter. When an artist is actually working, it can result in long periods of thinking, something with which Mickels is not well acquainted and therefore could not recognize.

Hawkins said, "Want some whiskey for that coffee, to help take the edge off?"

"No, thanks. I should probably be sober for whatever lies ahead. I might have something on that very subject right here." I opened my handbag and pulled out a folded message slip I'd retrieved from my mailbox beside the switchboard desk in the lobby. I unfolded it. I read it. I stared at it.

"What's wrong?" Hawkins asked.

"It's from Ben Bracker."

"Himself?" She pulled her hands from her pockets and sat up.

I turned it over as if the answer could lie on the other side. "I didn't look at it when I picked it up. It would seem so." I held it out for her inspection.

"Well, well."

"It has to be from someone who works for him," I said. "This can't be his number."

I dialed 0, and when the switchboard operator downstairs answered, I asked her to give me an outside line, which she had to do, as none of the Tate Building phones allow dialing beyond the studio lot otherwise. I got the line and dialed the number on the message slip. After two rings, the secretary to Benjamin Bracker, the head of Epic Pictures, answered. I took a second, then told her who I was and that I was returning Mr. Bracker's call, fully expecting her to huffily connect me to some Epic Pictures version of Mickels. But she politely asked if I could meet with Mr. Bracker at noon.

I said of course, repeated the time, thanked her, and set down the phone. Hawkins's eyebrows were halfway up her forehead.

"Help me," I said. "I've seen *one* Mary Ann McDowell picture. What are her strengths, do you know?"

"She's cute."

"Oh, dear God."

"She's a nice kid," Hawkins said. "I met her at a party last month. But I don't think she knows yet how much work acting should be. She's just done what she's told through all her bobby-soxer flicks, which, though you and I might scorn them, are very popular. She has some talent, which I'm sure you'll mine expertly. Bracker won't expect you to talk. All you have to do is smile, nod, and let him look at your legs. It's not every day

the size of sound stages. And if those buildings were booked, you could always shoot interior scenes outdoors if you filtered the sun properly. Traffic, blaring horns, the barks of directors or canine actors made no difference. When Epic finally needed sound stages, the land around them had been scooped up by speculators at the end of the twenties' boom, so Epic—rather than borrow to pay the exorbitant prices—ended up filling most of the lot's remaining open land. That had required clearing trees, including all the Washington Palms, the only indigenous palm to Los Angeles, while the rest of LA was madly planting palms in all varieties. Their decision not to borrow probably kept them from going bankrupt after the crash, but I'd heard that, outside of a couple of the back-lot streets, there wasn't a single tree left on the entire lot.

Palms remained out along the public sidewalk, providing fingers of shade to the passersby and casting shadows on the front wall, which Epic used for a series of billboards. Flanking the gate were huge posters of the two newest releases: Mary Ann McDowell's *The Girls Can't Wait* and Len Manning's new musical, *Swing Through the Night*.

Although not on par with MGM, Epic had managed to build a solid reputation for musicals, and Len had a strong masculine style that audiences now seemed to prefer over the society sophistication of dancers like Fred Astaire. And as long as MGM continued to alternate Gene Kelly's dancing roles with straight roles in B pictures, Len had a chance to become a very big star.

Further along, posters trumpeted Epic's three most successful short subjects—shorter films that led off double or triple bills, were filmed cheaply, and therefore cranked out steady profits. Their children's dog-hero series, Pepper and His Pals; the Rough and Ready Boys, a gang of delinquents whose smart, tough talk always ended in grudging good deeds; and the detective series, Blaze Bannister.

Epic was fond of alliteration.

Even in the name of the head of the studio.

Now sitting outside Ben Bracker's office, I unfolded the *Eagle*. Above the fold on the front page, there was a story about a prominent religious group whose members had voted to pass a public resolution declaring their loyalty to the United States. The foundations of American life were being shaken to their core by the threat of Communism, the statement said. They proclaimed themselves to be in accord with Congress's view that Hollywood and trade unions were "bastions of foreign thought" and applauded its seeking to expel this dangerous presence.

Apparently, the men and women who worked hard to produce the wealth of this nation should have no say at all in the wages they received for doing it. Apparently, employers were always fair and generous. Apparently, I was a bastion of foreign thought.

The buzzer sounded twice, two short bursts, and the secretary got up and went into Bracker's office. In ten seconds, the door opened again, two men came out, then the secretary. She closed the door and went back to her desk.

I knew the men weren't from Epic. Because the secretary had escorted them out. Because they were carrying hats, which they wouldn't have bothered with for a meeting on their own lot. And because I knew one of them.

He was about fifty, beefy, with thick brows and sharply blue intelligent eyes. He saw me immediately and paused as he put on his fedora. He nodded, touched the brim to me, a simple gesture of politeness, nothing more. I could have ignored him, if I'd wanted to. He gave me the option.

"Sergeant Barty," I said.

The man ahead of him turned around. He was a tall, long-chinned number with a naturally suspicious scowl. Barty walked over to me.

"It's good to see you again," I said. "I'm on loan-out to Epic. That's why I'm here. I know that's your first question."

"Glad to hear you got something else to pass your time." Phil Barty had been part of two cases I'd been involved in. He didn't appreciate civilians sticking their noses in, but he was a good cop.

The tall one watched me intently.

The secretary glanced his way, then over to Barty and said to him, "Detective, could I get you that cup of coffee now, if you have time? It's fresh and it won't take a minute."

"That would be nice. Black. Thanks." She picked up her phone and whispered into it. I'd noted throughout my career that the volume of secretaries' voices tended to be inversely proportional to that of their bosses. I hoped this didn't mean Bracker was a screamer.

Sergeant Barty went over to the other man, rumbled something to him. The other man slipped on his hat and went away, casting a final, dour glance at me before the elevator door opened. As Barty sat down in the chair beside me, a china cup and saucer with a small china pot of coffee appeared on a tray in the hands of a serious-faced young woman. She set it down on the table between us and disappeared as efficiently as she had come.

Barty poured, sipped, sipped again. The secretary went back to typing, the clacking covering our conversation. Barty said, "Studios always treat us well. Nowhere else do I ever get offered good coffee. Except your house."

"You were on the verge of arresting me."

"It was still good coffee."

"Was that your new partner?" I asked.

"Yeah. That's Loomis."

I dropped my voice. "Is something going on?"

His sharp eyes held mine. "What makes you say that?"

"I'm getting a reputation for bodies showing up when *I* do. I'd like to be prepared if it's happening again."

"Nothing like that. Just a courtesy call. The chief likes to keep the studios happy. We give them a report from time to time. Which of their employees might be headed for trouble. Drunk driving, bar fights, domestic fights, that sort of thing." He glanced away, examining nothing out in the hall.

A courtesy call from Los Angeles detectives?

I'd learned a lot about police corruption in the last year. No report to the studios would come without strings attached. Like a fat envelope of cash to the chief and his staff as gratitude for the reports about who might be headed for a vice arrest, and for not arresting stars who plowed their cars into lampposts while drunk. You could be a good cop and you still had to pick up the payoff if your bosses told you to.

I was saved by the intercom buzzer. Again, no voice came from it, but the secretary got up and said to me, "Mr. Bracker will see you now."

I said to Barty, "Peter's fine, by the way. I know you'd want to give him your regards."

He chuckled, which sounded like a series of grunts, but I could tell the difference. "Tell him I don't want to see his footprints in anything."

I shook hands with him, and the secretary ushered me into the office.

It was impressive. If you're trying to shoulder your way in among the big boys, you want an office that at least matches theirs. A thick carpet of burnished gold, a fireplace with a carved overmantel, wing chairs of chocolate leather, a sofa of burnt umber that no one had ever lounged on, especially not a writer.

Bracker stood up on the other side of his desk. It wasn't so big that I had to crawl onto it to reach his extended hand.

Then I took one of the chairs opposite and regarded him across the expanse.

Hawkins had been right. When I crossed my legs, of which I am justly proud, he took a good look at them. To be fair, I appraised him too. Tall. That is, a couple of inches taller than me in my heels, which would make him about six feet, taller than most studio executives. He was also better looking, although that wouldn't be particularly high praise. Somewhere in his late forties. A bit stocky. Thinning dark hair immaculately cut and combed, smoothed straight against his head, more like a twenties silent film star. He smiled, with perfect white teeth, so white, so perfect, I expected them to twinkle at me any second.

He sat and leaned back in his chair. "I've heard good things about you. You work fast, and you know how to write for the ladies."

Somehow, I'd got myself a reputation for being a woman's writer. Which was not generally a compliment.

I said, "I write for both men and women, but I keep female stars happy. They don't get shortchanged."

"And *that's* why you're here, to make one of my stars happy. We're looking for something to break Miss McDowell out of school, you might say. She needs to grow up."

Was he saying I might be able to avoid the coed romp?

While I was digesting this unexpected bit of luck, he went on. "She's nineteen," he said, "same age as Bacall when she made *To Have and Have Not*. Bacall's what everybody wants to see, even though she's only made three pictures, and that second one was crap."

I agreed *Confidential Agent* had been a mistake, but hardly Bacall's. Studios put their actresses into projects, and the actresses have little choice, especially when they're new to the game. These decisions are too often made by studio executives who don't really understand acting. If the camera likes a girl, the studio will sign her, try to train her, then hope the director, cinematographer, and editor can do the rest. In addition, the major studios own their distribution—their own chains of theaters—so audiences who want to go to the movies go to see what the studios put on the screen. Too often, the bosses think they can just put the pieces together—actors who are popular, no matter whether the roles make sense—and audiences will come, and magic will happen. Because sometimes it does.

I said, "No one knew Bacall when they first saw her. The audience knows Miss McDowell. I think an overtly sensual character might be dangerous for her."

He popped his fist onto his blotter. "Exactly. That's exactly what I was thinking. But I don't want to see her too old."

"Of course. Nothing domestic."

"I'm thinking about a mystery. I've seen your work on those."

"Her character would need a career, to get her into the action. She can't be an heiress. Unless it's an heiress who goes to work."

"Sort of like you?"

He'd done a bit of checking up.

I said, "My uncle was generous in his will, but that was only a few years ago, long after I started writing." In truth, my family had always been comfortable, especially after my uncle, Bennett Lauren, made a fortune in oil in the forest of rigs that carpeted parts of Los Angeles County. He'd made sure his sister's family was taken care of. But he'd done far more than pay for my education. He encouraged me when I was a near-changeling to my parents, a girl who showed far too much interest in a career and far too little in vying for men and marrying well. My uncle listened to me, guided me, loved me, and made the difference in my life.

Bracker picked up a book from his desk and slid it over to

me. James G. Burkett's *The Hard Fold.* "You ever read that?"

"Ten years ago, when it came out. Are you thinking of this for Miss McDowell?" I asked, shoving down creeping panic. "They tried to make this over at Marathon before the war. Mr. Breen wasn't about to let that happen." Joe Breen is the administrator of the Motion Picture Production Code, the rules by which Hollywood studios have agreed to live, to assure "clean" movies. That helps ensure a studio's film wouldn't be cut to ribbons by American cities' local censors or condemned by the Catholic Legion of Decency. Your script and your movie's final cut has to be approved by Mr. Breen's office. If the final cut doesn't get that approval, there aren't more than a few dozen theaters in the entire country in which you might be able to show it. If the communities would let you. And the studios aren't going to risk the bad publicity or the expense of a rejected film.

Bracker said, "Times have changed, all the GIs coming back. People want something more like real life."

"So you want to take a popular young star and turn her into a metaphor for America."

Bracker laughed and popped the desk again. "People who sit there don't usually tell me I'm full of crap. I heard you could be scrappy."

"I've been known to be blunt."

"It's something I'm thinking about. I want something for a woman, not a girl."

"Mr. Bracker, have you *read* this book? You'd have to gut it to get it past the censors."

It was the story of a jaded newspaper man, cut low by alcohol and unsavory habits. His one last shot is covering a wife-murder. He starts out savagely, like all his fellow reporters, determined to make good copy, no matter how, and convict the husband, but he gradually decides maybe the guy is innocent after all and that he's being railroaded by politicians, prosecutors, and even his own attorney, who don't give a damn if the guy did it, as long as their own careers prosper.

I said, "All the women are schemers or prostitutes, often both. Who would Miss McDowell play?" I flipped into the book to remind myself of the name of the character. "Ruby?"

The closest there was to a nice girl was a young woman who was being kept by a wealthy man and whom the hero visited from time to time.

Bracker said, "We got some notes from the Code Office. Yeah, they pointed that out, about the women."

"First off, the prostitutes would have to come out, which means a lot of scenes are going to take place in dance parlors."

He laughed. It was the standard script trick. Women of ill repute ended up as girls in taxi-dance halls. Ten cents a dance, and your movie gets made.

Bracker said, "We'd create a new character for her. *You* would. It's been done. You know it's a good book."

"I recall its being quite powerful, and the public would eat up stories about Epic trying to make this picture. But the Code Office will fight you."

"Here's a copy of their letter. You can read it." I knew he didn't mean right now, so I left it folded on the desk.

I said, "And who would play the reporter—the hero—opposite Miss McDowell?"

"We're thinking about Jack Stanley. He's one of our—What? You don't think so?"

"Fans of the book will pillory you if he's a pretty boy, and Mr. Stanley is frankly a bit callow on screen for this. Miss McDowell needs a strong actor. And you're more likely to get the script approved if you have a prestige actor in the role. You have Roland Neale signed for a second picture, don't you?"

"Don't you think he's a bit old for her?"

"He can still play forty. I've heard he's a generous actor, willing to share the spotlight. If Miss McDowell can play mid-twenties, a romance could work, as long as she does the chasing. But like I said, she needs a reason to be in the action. Off the top of my head, we could make her a reporter, too. Maybe the reporter who begins to suspect the accused is innocent. I have no idea if it could be made to work. And it would change the plot."

"That's been done, too, plenty of times. I'd have to think about Roland. He's just finished his first picture for us. We've had some test audiences in, and it's done well, but it's tricky, his age."

Trickier than taking a young woman who's played sweet schoolgirls and putting her in a Jim Burkett book?

"Of course," I said.

Roland Neale was one of the few silent-film stars who'd successfully made the transition to sound. First because he'd been gifted with a beautiful, masculine, recordable voice, and, two, he was talented enough to move out of the dashing adventure roles that made him a star when he was young and into other, more mature, roles. Unfortunately, he was now the victim of age. For women, it's thirty. For men, forty. Studios begin to look at you differently, look harder at box office grosses. They were less willing to sign long contracts. To keep the studio happy, an older actor will take roles he might have resisted more strongly at the height of his career, which sometimes means doing pictures that couldn't be saved by all the talent he could put into them. Paramount hadn't renewed Roland Neale's contract, then he'd freelanced and ended up with one mediocre picture at Warners. Now, he'd signed with Epic. Two pictures.

Bracker jotted down a note with a gold retractable pencil. Without binoculars, I couldn't be sure, but I thought it said "Roland Neale."

"One thing." Bracker laid down the pencil. "Before you come to work here, I have to make sure there won't be any problems."

"I'm sorry?"

"We don't want Epic all over the papers."

"People can be very superstitious," I said.

"Not what I'd call it."

"I didn't mean you. I meant, well, it *is* just coincidence after all."

"What is?" he asked.

"The rumors. What you've heard. They're really just jokes."

"People aren't joking about commies."

"I beg your pardon? I'm sorry, Mr. Bracker. I misunderstood you. I thought you were talking about something else."

"We can't have any politics, that's what the lawyers tell me." He stood up and opened the door next to the fireplace. I caught a glimpse of a small conference table. He signaled, and two men came in.

One of them was short, with a face like a sour hawk. "This is Joe Gettleman; he's a big-wig lawyer around here," Bracker said.

The other was broad-shouldered with a lot of chin and the eyes of a man who knew your secrets. He knew some of mine.

"This is Mack Pace," Bracker said, "our chief of security. Do you two know each other? He used to work over at Marathon."

I said, "Yes, we met once or twice over there."

The last time I'd seen Mack Pace, back in December on the Marathon lot, he had a nice set of bruises from Peter's having put him headfirst into a file cabinet because Pace had put me in some danger, and Peter thought it was a good idea to make sure he understood he should never do that again.

I shook hands with Gettleman before he sat down in the chair next to me. Pace occupied himself by pulling a side chair a few inches from the wall. He sat. I nodded to him. He looked at me.

Gettleman said, "My responsibility at Epic is to see the studio is protected legally."

"For cripes sake, Joe," Bracker said. "She knows what a lawyer does. Let's get on with it. We know how you screenwriters are, full of opinions. And we need to make sure you aren't getting your marching orders from Moscow, about what to write."

There were screenwriters who'd thrown their sympathies in with the Communist Party during the Depression and who are periodically called on the carpet, so to speak, by their local party leaders and in print by the party newspapers for not writing about real life and workers' struggles. As if Hollywood writers have the choice.

I said, "Directors, producers *and* studio bosses tell me what to write. It's about all I can handle."

Bracker laughed.

Gettleman said, "Mr. Bracker doesn't care what you do on your own time, but I have to. Epic will not be dragged into this investigation by Congress by any of our employees, even temporary ones."

"Of course," I said.

From the inside pocket of his suit jacket, he extracted a sheet of paper, folded in half vertically. "I want you to look at this list and tell me honestly whether you have ever been a member of any of these organizations or attended meetings."

"Attended meetings?" I asked.

"Please read it," Gettleman said.

I did. There were a couple of dozen names. The first was the Communist Party. I kept going. Workers Party, Civil Rights Congress, Hollywood Writers Anti-Nazi Refugee Committee, California Book Store Alliance. Halfway down, The Hollywood Helping Hand Society, which had been organized back in the mid-thirties by some people whose politics could certainly, and truthfully, be described as Socialist to help refugees from Europe to resettle in the United States.

I said, "I did volunteer work for The Helping Hand. I donated money. I helped find apartments, helped children get registered in school, set up English lessons. So did lots of people in Hollywood."

"That doesn't really matter," Gettleman said. "What others, please?"

"None. That's the only one."

"You're sure. You would swear to that?"

Bracker tossed down his pencil. "Joe, if she was lying, she wouldn't have qualms about swearing. It's not like it's illegal for her to lie to *you*. Mack probably knows all there is to know about her, the way he's checking up on everybody these days. So, does she pass?"

Gettleman glanced at Pace, who nodded. It was the most grudging nod I'd ever seen. Then Gettleman said, "While you're working for Epic, you will not attend any meetings of a political nature."

"Unless it's the Republican Ladies Club," Bracker said.

"I think it's best if Miss Atwill were to confine her activities to writing," Gettleman said. "No meetings, no opinions expressed in public, and certainly not for attribution. No politics while you're here."

"I understand," I said.

"Good. Very well, thank you for your time."

Gettleman took his list back, and the men went out the way they came. Pace returned the chair to its place before he did. He didn't look back, didn't say good-bye.

I was longing to give Peter another shot at him. The bastard had set me up. He'd put one organization in there that would pass muster, knowing full well I'd worked with it. He wanted me to lie, to say I hadn't worked with any of them. Wanted to be able to tell Bracker and Gettleman I lied.

While I was sure Pace was capable of making something up to get me thrown out of Epic, a couple of things would stand in his way. Peter might introduce his head to another file cabinet. And, more importantly, Julie Scarza, the gangster for whom Pace used to run hookers in and out of Marathon, might not like it. A few months ago, I'd found the killer of someone he cared about. Nobody wanted Julie Scarza mad at them.

Bracker said, "What were *you* talking about?"

"I'm sorry?"

"Before. What you thought I meant about you getting into trouble."

"There are some jokes going around. Not jokes really, more like wisecracks. About police cases involving Marathon. That when I sign on to a film, things happen."

"You got tribes in Africa, never seen civilization, not half as superstitious as this town. What do you say to a whiskey?"

"Gin?"

"Sure thing. Tonic? We'll need to set you up to meet Miss McDowell, soon as possible. What are you doing tonight? Jean and I got a little party. Jean's my wife. You could drop on by. Mary Ann'll be there. Starts about six. Cocktails, buffet, who knows when it'll end."

"I'd be happy to come. Evening gown?"

Bracker looked baffled.

I said, "Will the ladies be wearing evening gowns? Long skirts?"

"No, no, don't think so."

It was no use pressing him. I'd have to find another source of information. "I could make it by seven."

"Grace'll give you the address, and she'll set you up with a place to write while you're with us. Not as fancy as Marathon, but we'll take care of you. Let's see if we can do anything with that book. Keep that copy."

Deftly, he mixed my drink at the black-glass bar cart. "I read about that thing over at Marathon back in December, that guy who got killed. You involved in that?"

"I was working on the movie."

"That all?"

"Yes."

He handed me my drink. "It's a good thing you write better than you lie."

CHAPTER 4

Grace, Bracker's secretary, gave me her boss's address for the party. I asked her what to wear. A nice dinner dress would be fine, she said. Then she called in a bald-headed minion named Herb in a sharply starched shirt and a bow tie to escort me to my bungalow.

Just off one of the back-lot streets—a block of gritty brownstone facades—was a one-story strip of white stucco with a tin-roofed porch running its length. Off the porch opened a series of rooms, with windows front and back, rooms that probably all looked the same as the one my minion unlocked. A square, roughly fifteen feet a side, with a desk, three hard chairs, a short file cabinet, a small bookcase, and a sink in the corner with a towel rack beside it. Next to the sink, along the shared wall, a narrow door opened to a tiny room with a chain-pull toilet on one side and a coat closet on the other. You'd have to wait for one visitor to finish using the bathroom before you could fetch another one his coat.

They were old dressing rooms, patched up and passed on to whoever needed a temporary office on the crowded Epic lot.

My escort handed me my new office's key and a laminated card with my name on it, which I could show the guard at the gate every day till he got used to who I was. He told me my best bet for parking was a lot down the street. There wasn't enough room inside the studio walls. Show the parking attendant my card.

There was a knock on the open door. Standing in the doorway was a young man of about thirty, short, muscular, with hot, appraising eyes and the assured smile of a man entitled to—and determined to get—better things. His clothes had cost money. I pegged him for the relative of one of the executives.

He said, "Hi. I'm Arky Kulpa. K-u-l-p-a. There are a lot of Catholics around here; they think it's a *C*. Like mea culpa. If I'm guilty of anything, I'm not admitting to it."

Herb set his lips so tightly, they disappeared.

I smiled and told Arky my name.

He handed me a card with the number of the studio's messenger office on it. "If you need somebody to run your pages over to the typists, pick up your laundry, get your smokes, your lunch, anything at all, I'm your guy. You can check for messages by calling the switchboard, but we bring copies of them down regularly, just in case, pin them up on the corkboard right here on your door if you're not in. Packages, we leave in the wicker basket out there. I wrote my name and a little reminder on the back of the card."

I thanked him.

"Sure," he said. "I'll take good care of you. Nice to meet you." He gave me a little salute and stopped short of a leer before he departed.

Herb thawed his lips, then said, "I'm sorry, but we don't have keys for the desk or the file cabinet."

"That's all right." It didn't matter, but not for the reason he thought—that I was being gracious. I could lock and unlock them myself. Once, years ago in my foolish writing youth, I was determined to show a real lock-picking in a script—not the ever-present but inaccurate single "skeleton key" the movies liked to give detectives. The retired locksmith who'd humored me made me a present of a set of picks, knowing probably better than I that no actor would ever get his hands on them. I found out quickly that the Code Office would never allow anything on the screen that might look like advice to criminals. But the picks had helped me mightily in my script-doctor career as I bounced from office to office, bungalow to bungalow. Or, in this case, from office to bathroom with a desk in it.

"That number," Herb said, "the number he gave you, you can find someone there to run an errand for you, if you need it. It doesn't have to be that guy, if you don't want him. He works here, he doesn't run the place."

"Is he related to somebody?"

"Every studio's got a few of those. The guy who's got a job and nobody knows how he got it, but he gets paid, and nobody says anything if he does what he wants, makes his own rules. I don't gamble, but some of these Joes around here, they might as well set fire to their paychecks. Arky's got the matches, if you know what I mean."

I promised not to be led astray, then said, "Could you find me another copy of this book?" I held up *The Hard Fold*. "And some glue, another few hundred sheets of typing paper, an art knife, and a ring binder. Do you know what an art knife is? One of those blades on a stick, so you can cut things out without bending or cutting the rest of the paper?"

"I can get everything but the book right away. Maybe tomorrow for the book."

"Tomorrow would be fine for all of it."

"If you're not here, I'll leave it all in a package, in that basket by the door."

"An old copy of the book will do, as long as all the pages are there. I'm going to cut it up." I opened my handbag to reach in for a tip.

"That's all right, ma'am. It's my job. They'll give me petty cash to cover the book. They'll send over a voucher you'll have to sign."

"Of course." I handed him fifty cents anyway. "But they'll make you go on your own time to get the book, so let me at least pay for the buses and your lunch tomorrow."

He accepted the coins. I asked him where the research department was, as I thought I might get to know something about Mary Ann McDowell before the party. Epic's research department would have clippings and biographical information, some of which might even be true. He offered to walk me there, but I said I needed to make some phone calls. He told me where to find the research department and the typing pool when I needed a typist. Then he left me, apologizing once again for the lack of keys to the desk and file cabinet.

I opened the windows, as the office appeared to have been regularly used by cigar smokers. Then I sat down and called Juanita and asked if she'd bring my black taffeta dinner dress, evening sandals, stockings, organza wrap, gloves, bag, handkerchief, jewelry, and whatever else I'd need, including my makeup case, over to my Marathon office and leave it all there for me. I told her I wouldn't be home till late and not to bother about dinner. To this, she would pay no attention whatsoever, and there would be something in the refrigerator ready to heat up whenever I got home.

I'd had the dress made during the war, when shorter skirts for evening wear became fashionable because fabric was rationed. It had a deep square neck and shorter sleeves, also the result of rationing. The bias-cut skirt gave it a soft sway when I moved.

Now I had a dress, and I had a plan.

I phoned Peter's office, but he was out. He almost always was. He worked for the Paxton Agency, and they were popular with lawyers—criminal, civil, and domestic. Ed Paxton had given Peter his own group of men to run, and they specialized in locating witnesses and verifying testimony. He was particularly good at digging up anything a witness might be trying to hide. It was hard to keep secrets from Peter.

I left a message for him to call my Marathon office between four thirty and five if he could. Hawkins had said she'd come pick me up at five to go to Madison's, for whatever it was she needed to talk about. I didn't include in the message that I intended to invite Peter to finally go out publicly with me, to Ben Bracker's party.

Since we began our affair, Peter had been diligent in assuring that no divorce lawyer could threaten to charge me with adultery to get my husband a big portion of my uncle's money as a settlement. Peter would come to my house, but whatever we did in my bedroom, he ended up either sleeping in the guest room or going home. Juanita would never have to perjure herself. She could say he was a dinner guest. That's all she knew. He slept in the guest room. That's all she knew.

We'd been seen in public, but only as client and bodyguard. We'd never gone out as a couple. Never to a dinner, never to a club. With the result, of course, that his protecting my reputation occasionally made me feel like a back-alley romance. In my gloomier moments, I imagined all kinds of things he was getting up to on the nights he didn't come see me. I had some idea of what his romantic life had been before he met me.

But now my divorce papers had been drawn up. The agreements, reached and signed.

Perhaps we could drop by the Brackers, spend an hour. Then go on to dinner. This could be my first night out in public in Los Angeles with the man I loved.

I was grinning as I rolled paper into the typewriter and tested it. It was a Corona, an office model, not a portable: sturdy, heavy. It was far from new but had been well oiled, bedecked with a new ribbon, and I didn't have to punch the keys.

I typed out the names of every suspect organization I could

recall from the list Gettleman had presented me in Bracker's office. Carefully, I tucked it away into my handbag. It was a list I might want to share with other writers. Then I typed out the off-the-top-of-my-head ideas I'd had in Bracker's office.

Epic had bought rights to *The Hard Fold* because they'd seen the kind of money that could be made in *Double Indemnity* and *The Postman Always Rings Twice*. Those movies had managed to keep something of the cynicism and sordidness of the original books despite the Code Office. These were the kinds of books that shocked sensibilities, got banned in Boston and condemned by decency committees. And made a bundle of money. But to be turned into movies, they had to be cleaned up for the "general audience," which meant they had to pass muster with some of the most conservative organizations in the country.

How did one keep the jaded, seamy, even prurient sensibilities of *The Hard Fold* and add a character who could be played by Mary Ann McDowell?

I cursed Sol Noble once again for being a superstitious bastard and sending me into this. I could see it now. I'd work for six months on the story, then the script, re-writing and re-writing till the Code Office was happy. By then, the soul of the book would have disappeared. My first screen credit in years—on a disaster.

Nevertheless, I picked up the copy Bracker had given me and started reading.

After an hour, I was convinced Mary Ann would have to be a reporter to give her a starring role. Adapting any of the actual female characters would be ludicrous. They were no more than stopovers for the men. God, I hoped Mary Ann could handle snappy patter. We were going to need some to make the romantic tension work.

I'd have to explain how a woman that young ended up covering a crime beat. In Bracker's office, I'd dismissed the idea of her having inherited money. But maybe she *could* be an heiress who goes to work, has family connections to the publisher and the publisher's social set. That would make the hero mistrust her, resist her, dislike her. She wants to stop writing "women's stories" and get to the nitty-gritty of real reporting. He thinks she's a phony. Class and sex conflicts? It might work.

I opened my handbag and took out the copy of the Code Office's letter Bracker had given me. It was not encouraging.

The office had deep reservations about the book and could not on any account approve it if the script followed along the lines of the novel. In summary, they said, "The prostitution, general portrayal of the justice system, the excessive use of alcohol, the profane language, the overtly sexual content, and the suggestions of sexual deviance are all completely unacceptable." It was signed "Very cordially yours" by Joseph I. Breen.

I rolled fresh paper into the typewriter and began making notes about a woman reporter and how she might be fit into the book.

For over an hour, I typed and started over, cursed and started over, yanked out pages, circled a few portions, decided they were crap, threw them out, rolled in fresh paper, started over.

I resisted the temptation to set the trash can on fire.

There was a knock on the door.

"Yes?" I called out sharply and kept typing.

The door opened.

The man I fell in love with when I was sixteen walked into the room.

Roland Neale.

Twenty years later, you still couldn't take your eyes off him. I couldn't anyway. The brooding brown eyes, the aquiline nose, the pristine jaw, the profile. Lord, the profile.

The tousled black locks he'd worn as Captain Demar in *In Service of the Queen* when I was that sixteen-year-old had thinned a bit and were now brushed into behaving. He still sported the moustache, which only made his sensual lips more prominent. He was a bit thicker about the middle than in the days of his epic sword fights, which almost always managed to occur in a flowing shirt open halfway down his chest—the chest that set a standard by which a generation of schoolgirls would judge all others.

I have no idea how long I stared at him.

"Hello," he said, with his warm baritone. "I'm Roland Neale."

I managed my name. I'm pretty sure I got it right. It wouldn't have mattered, as he knew who I was.

Roland Neale had come calling on me.

I stood up. "Mr. Neale. What a pleasure. I'm such a fan. Please, sit down. I'm sorry, the place smells like cigars. The windows were all closed. I'm afraid I don't have anything to offer you. I just moved in. I need to get something to brew tea or make coffee. But I don't know where I'd keep the milk." I snapped my lips together before I actually babbled.

He waited till I sat back down, then picked up one of the chairs and placed it at the end of my desk. He crossed his legs and laid his elegant hands across his thigh. He wore a sports jacket of gold and brown tweed, a turtleneck sweater underneath. The slacks were knife-creased and didn't look as if a knee had ever pressured the fabric before. "The trimmings are a bit spare at Epic," he said. "But we're all troupers. You might try the tank in the water closet."

"I'm sorry?"

"For the milk. Put the bottle in the water tank. The water's usually quite cold in them. We used to do that backstage when I was a very young man, touring. Quite sanitary, I assure you. I was just meeting with Ben Bracker, and he said he might have a picture for me, a mystery, and you'd be writing it. I thought I'd stop over. Hope you don't mind."

"Not at all." Stars rarely paid calls on writers. At least not actors as famous as Roland Neale on writers as unknown as me.

He said, "And please call me Roland."

"I was sorry to hear about your aunt's death. I met her, doing charity work on a few committees during the war. She was a fine lady."

"She was a crusty little martinet, but I loved her dearly. However did you get on a committee with her?"

"Standards have become shockingly lax. Of course, my mother's Bennett Lauren's sister. And my father's a respected writer, Martin Tanner."

"Ah, so the talent runs in the family."

"Thank you. I'm—I'm sorry. With you sitting here, I'm a little intimidated."

He regarded me steadily with his eyes of hot coffee. "The last two years, whenever I've heard flattery, it's usually been a prelude to suggesting I consider retiring. I'm not going to be the professor, am I, who gets the young people together?"

"Didn't Mr. Bracker tell you? I'm—I'm not sure how much I can say at this point. It's all a bit up in the air. But he wants me to take a crack at a story based on this." I slid the book forward. "You'd play the reporter, the narrator."

"Intriguing. And he thinks he can get that past Mr. Breen?"

"Not without changing the plot a bit. And he wants to add a romantic interest."

"One the hero doesn't have to pay by the hour."

I laughed. "We'd have to make the woman a reporter, I think."

He touched the book's cover lightly. "I'd love to try something like this. Something rough. And real. Who'd be the girl?"

"Mary Ann McDowell."

He looked horrified. "She's a child."

"If she can play twenty-five, it could work. And the romance would be subtle. Just tension between you. The man in the book wouldn't fall for a woman easily. I think we could present it to the censors as the redeeming moral lesson, about love and ideals, to offset some of what we'd want to stay in the film. At the end when it's all resolved—and I think you should save her life along the way—you'd thank her for her help, you'd wish her well, you'd look at her, just look at her, then walk away. Back to your lonely world. Then she follows you. She refuses to leave. She could sit down on your front steps and tell you she's learned how to be patient, now that you've taught her to be a real reporter. I think that's an ending corny enough to please Mr. Breen."

He said, "I won't make myself ridiculous."

"Of course. I wouldn't let that happen if you decide to take the role."

"If it's offered to me. I know you're busy, but I'd certainly like to discuss this some more, if you wouldn't mind. A project like this would be—Well, I'm very interested. Do you have time this evening?"

"I'm going to Mr. Bracker's party."

"What a pleasant coincidence, so am I. It will be packed; they always are. Poor Jean Bracker. Ben does love a houseful of worshippers. I don't live far from him, a few houses. If you have time, why don't you drop over after? Just to talk. I promise to leave all the doors open for easy escape. We can sit on the porch of my cabana and listen to the night. I like to do that, sit outdoors late and listen to the solitude."

He took a sheet of my script paper, wrote down his address, and sketched a little map to show where he lived in relation to Ben Bracker. Their backyards were nearly adjoined. "There's a lane behind the houses, built originally for golf carts I believe; we're not far from the golf course. My house is behind his, two houses down. You could just walk on over, if you want, the back gate's never locked. Say, about nine o'clock? If you have a date, bring him, of course, although I'm sure he'll be bored by the shop talk. If you can't come, I understand. Another night." He stood.

I did too, and put out my hand. He took it and held it. "It was very nice to meet you, Lauren."

And then he left, closing the door softly after him.

I worked on, and, with my new inspiration, the pile of pages on the desk began to exceed the pile in the trash can. Then I spent a half hour in the Epic Pictures research department finding out more about Mary Ann McDowell before going back to my Marathon Studios office to wait for Peter to call.

He didn't call.

CHAPTER 5

Classy bars are ambivalent about women. They know the men who patronize bars sometimes like to be with women, but they also know they don't want to encourage the kind of women that men sometimes like to be with.

Fortunately, Madison's wasn't classy enough to have such concerns.

Madison's sits across the street from Marathon's front gate, the de facto studio bar and grill, with strong drinks and good food. It has a large rear dining room, which is far quieter and less smoky than the bar, and because it's patronized mostly by movie people, a couple of women can have a drink there together in the evening, and if they don't happen to have a male escort handy to come along with them after work, nobody will think they're the kind of women the classy bars wanted to keep out.

But even at Madison's, most women wouldn't be comfortable sitting by themselves while they waited for a friend to arrive. So I met Hawkins at her office, and we walked over together, joined by another writer who was meeting a group of friends. So I had to wait till Hawkins and I were settled comfortably into a small booth before I could fill her in on my meeting with Ben Bracker. She particularly enjoyed the part in which I'd been forced, because of my misunderstanding him, to tell him about the rumors that, when I showed up, so did a body. Her laugh, which consists of a series of husky barks, drew a bit of attention. Despite the early hour, the back room was catching overflow from the bar.

I waited till the patrons went back to their drinks, then lowered my voice and told her about the lawyer Joe Gettleman and the list that Epic's security chief, Mack Pace, had created of suspect organizations.

She said, "I'm lucky I never joined anything, even the Brownies."

"If Epic has a list like that," I said, "other studios do too."

"For all we know, that bastard Pace made the whole thing up," she said.

"What if he knows someone on the congressional investigators' staff? Or the Department of Justice? You know they have lists, even if they're secret. The government's already firing employees for being on them."

A couple settled in at the table beside us. I thought maybe it was time to stop talking about lists. We signaled the waiter and ordered drinks. He snapped a couple of dinner menus down on our table and left. Madison's waiters always leave menus for the ladies, so it looks like we're there for dinner, even if the waiters know full well we're only there to drink.

I didn't tell Hawkins about meeting Roland Neale. It still felt as if the prince had paid a call, and I wanted to hold on to that feeling. Instead, I asked, "So what did you want to talk about?"

"Actually, it's somebody else who wanted to talk. I hope you don't mind. She wanted to meet you, but maybe she won't show."

"Meet me?"

"Look, if she doesn't show, I'll buy you a steak some night, and we forget it."

"And you can't tell me who?"

But an actress knows her cues. And there she was. Mary Ann McDowell, pausing just a step inside the arch from the bar to scan for us. And maybe to wait for a few heads to turn in her direction.

A lot of pretty women come to Madison's. But not all of them were leggy nineteen-year-olds with large blue eyes and glistening auburn hair. And wearing a body-hugging dress of cobalt blue that made the eyes, the hair—and other details—stand out.

I'd never seen Mary Ann McDowell in person, so I didn't know if she always wore that kind of dress off-screen or if the studio was now picking her clothes to make her look like a woman. As she crossed the room, I thought if they were, they were doing a damn good job.

She offered her hand to me. "Nice to meet you," she said, a little breathlessly.

"And you."

She slid in beside Hawkins. She had quite a few freckles, which I hadn't noticed in the one movie of hers I'd seen or in any of her photos. But then actresses generally wore heavy makeup for the camera. And false eyelashes. But Mary Ann had plenty of her own; she didn't need fake ones off-screen. Some of the heads in the room were still turned our way.

"Did Hawkins tell you I was coming?" she asked. "She said she might not, in case I changed my mind."

"I'm glad you came," I said.

I knew why Hawkins hadn't told me it was Mary Ann who wanted to see me. If the meeting hadn't come off, I would have wondered why she ditched it.

"I hope you don't mind meeting here," she said.

"Not at all."

We couldn't have met at my office or Hawkins's. Mary Ann didn't work at Marathon, and as she was a star, she wouldn't be the one to visit the writer. Here, it could be a casual meeting. Drinks, a half hour.

"As it turns out," I said, "Mr. Bracker invited me to a cocktail party tonight to meet you. We're just getting an early start."

"We'll have to pretend we've just met at the party," she said. "Mr. Bracker likes it when what he plans comes off the way he planned it."

Another woman strode in, shorter, with plump curves under a leaf-green evening suit whose jacket might have been cut a bit too low for her age. She had her henna-rinsed hair pinned up and curled above her forehead. Behind the curls sat a hat with a high, sharp peak in front and a large velvet bow at the back.

"Why didn't you wait?" she demanded of Mary Ann. "I was checking our coats. I'm not your servant."

"You said I should go see if they were here."

"I didn't mean you should let men think you were in a bar by yourself."

Hawkins said, "What a nice surprise. You brought your mother."

"My daughter doesn't go out alone at night unescorted, especially not to bars." Mary Ann's mother deposited herself into the booth beside me. I got a strong whiff of alcohol despite the cloud of cologne.

Hawkins said, "She doesn't need an escort here. It's all right."

"You don't count as a man, much as you might like to think you do."

I opened my mouth. Hawkins laid her foot hard on my toes.

"Mama!" Mary Ann whispered urgently.

"That photographer's in the bar," her mother said. "I saw him just now."

"He is?" Mary Ann said, glancing over her shoulder.

"Don't let him see you looking. Every step you take, someone could see you; don't I tell you that? My girl has some little weasel with a camera following her around. I tell her, she has to watch every step."

"Lauren Atwill, by the way," I said to the woman.

"Vera McDowell," she said. "You're writing a movie for my girl."

"I'm writing the treatment—the first step—and maybe the script, too."

"I never heard of you till today."

"That makes us even," I said.

Hawkins trod on my toes again.

"Don't be thin-skinned," Vera said. "I'm not insulting you. It's just a fact. Like her wearing pants all the time. What have you done I might have seen? You afraid to blow your own horn?"

Mary Ann said, "Mama, why don't we order something, and you leave Lauren alone? We just came to get to know each other."

"She'll have to talk if we're going to do that."

The waiter came with my drink and Hawkins's. Vera ordered a martini and Mary Ann, a gimlet.

Vera said, "I believe in facing things head on. I don't pull punches."

I said, "Let's hope it doesn't come to punches. I'm going to take my gloves off now. It doesn't mean anything."

She laughed, a few sharp little whoops, then sat back and pulled her gloves off as well. She said, "Epic's got gold in my Mary Ann, and I want to make sure she's in good hands."

"Of course," I said. "I was over there today, at Mr. Bracker's office."

"Who'd you talk to over there?"

"Mr. Bracker himself. He's the one who requested me from Marathon. If you're worried about his decision, you should speak with him." I said it pleasantly, as if it were possible for Vera McDowell to pick up the phone and lay down the law to Ben Bracker.

"So what's he got in mind?" she asked.

"We're in the early stages." I wasn't sharing any of the

conversation with Vera. "I understand you play tennis," I said to Mary Ann. It was one of the bits of information I'd picked up in Epic's research department. "Maybe we could work that in." I thought it would give her a chance to show off her woman's body without its being obvious. It was also a sport that could point up the class difference I wanted to give her and the hero.

I had no idea whether she had much acting talent. The only one of her movies I'd seen hadn't required much, just onscreen charm, of which she had plenty. If she didn't have much talent, or much training, it would be best to give the character as many of Mary Ann's attributes as possible. However, if she was going to play an independent career girl, we'd have to keep Vera off the set. Somehow, I didn't think Epic would mind that.

"Mama thinks I should do a musical," Mary Ann said, "but I don't dance that well."

"You dance plenty good enough," Vera said. The waiter came. Vera hardly gave the glass a chance to touch the table. "We thought the studio was teaming her up with Len Manning. They introduced them a few months ago, said they were thinking about it. Then suddenly her agent says the picture might be a mystery. I don't know if I like that."

"Perhaps the studio's thinking more in terms of a mature role for you." I said it to Mary Ann. I wasn't here to get her mother's approval.

"Len Manning's a big box office draw," Vera insisted. "He likes my girl. Doesn't he, honey?"

"Mama, we've only been out a half-dozen times."

She was dating Len Manning? I glanced at Hawkins, then said, "He's a very talented young man."

"And very attentive to my girl," Vera said. "It would be a good thing, to get her settled. You're married." She glanced at my left hand. I still wore my wedding and engagement rings when I went out. Not, of course, when Peter came over.

48

"I am," I said. It was none of her business that, if the lawyers put their minds to it, I'd be divorced in a month, just in time for my thirty-seventh birthday.

"You tell her," Vera said, "it's good to be settled, especially a girl in a career. Time passes and, suddenly, there are no men worth having. And you know how people talk when a woman's not married."

I kept speaking to Mary Ann. "It would make Epic's publicity department happy, but you'll have a lot on your mind, if you're moving into more mature roles."

"That's what I've been telling Mama. I don't have to rush into anything."

I said, "And what does 'settled' mean in Hollywood? One would like it to be love." Of course, I'd waited for love, till I was twenty-seven to marry, and still it hadn't worked out.

We chatted some more, through the drinks. I asked Mary Ann what she liked most about acting, about her movies, steered the conversation away from whatever Vera stuck in. There was nothing I could do about what she wanted.

Then Vera announced they had to go. Mary Ann had to get home and freshen up before the Brackers' party. As Vera pulled on her gloves, she said to me, "You see what a treasure my girl is. This is going to be good for you, working with her."

"Mama!"

I said to Mary Ann, "I'll see you later, then, at the party."

When they were gone, Hawkins said, "She reminds me of my kid sister: too naïve for this world, certainly for Hollywood." She raised her hand for another round.

"I'll get that." Birdie Hitts slid into the booth. "On me," he said to the waiter. "What are you having?" he asked me. Birdie had small, excited eyes behind thick, round glasses, and he had a habit of licking the corner of his mouth like a lizard with a very short tongue.

"Thanks, I'm fine," I said.

Birdie Hitts specialized in mayhem and scandal. There wasn't a woman murdered in all Los Angeles County he couldn't get a picture of, and often, I'd heard, he'd pay off the cops or morgue attendants to lift skirts and open dresses to make the shot worth more to a certain kind of rag.

In his more artistic moments, he worked for *Inside Scoop*, which trafficked heavily in sex scandal, especially among the wealthy and famous but more recently was adding articles alleging to unmask communists in government, trade unions, and Hollywood. Rumor had it that *Scoop* had new investors, men with big bankrolls and a big interest in getting rid of trade unions. Manufacturers, mining companies, studio bosses. The candidates' list would be fairly long.

Birdie had to be the photographer Vera had mentioned, the "weasel" who'd been following Mary Ann.

"How you doing?" he said to me. He stuck out a dry, callused hand. Years of working with developing chemicals had left the skin cracked. I took the hand. Briefly. "Hey there, Hawkins," he said and grinned at her. "Nice little tomato, that girl, huh?" He jerked another nod in the direction Mary Ann had gone.

Hawkins said, "Why do you always talk like a B movie?"

"Maybe I need a better writer, doll."

I said, "Maybe it's because if you went down to the morgue talking any other way, the attendant might start feeling guilty about what he's doing."

He chuckled. "Hey, I like you. I heard Marathon sent you over to Epic."

"I'm on loan, yes."

"Writing for the tomato?"

"No." I had no compunction about lying to him.

"Come on, she's here, you're here. You can tell me. What am I going to do with that? I haven't seen you around in a while.

Haven't *heard* much about you, publicly. That's not good in Hollywood, people got a short memory. Here's something, maybe I can fix that. Just something, you think it over. I got this idea, when I saw you pass by. I'm doing a layout, might interest you. Gorgeous gams of Hollywood. I'm getting some girls people don't know so well, match their gams against Grable. Could be some nice publicity for you. It'd be very classy, you don't have to worry. *Scoop*'s got money now."

Hawkins said, "She can buy her own publicity if she wants it and not take off her dignity to do it. She's got a fortune, Birdie."

"She didn't get all of it, I hear." He turned to me. His eyes said he knew why so much of my uncle's fortune had gone to someone else.

"That story's not worth your time," I said.

His tongue whipped out and back. "You're right, old news, old news. Look, I didn't mean anything. It's a bad habit. You're a dame a guy in my line of work wants to stay in good with. Everywhere you go, things happen. A guy's got to make a living, so if you hear anything over at Epic, maybe you could push it my way."

"What could I hear? Nobody talks to writers, except to order them around."

"I'm thinking maybe you're not going over there just to write."

Anthony came over, the titular bartender, in his starched white shirt and tailored black vest. Anthony was in fact co-owner of Madison's, but that didn't get spread around too far. Anthony was Negro, and there were still some customers who'd be happy to let him mix the best gin and tonic in Los Angeles but wouldn't like it if he owned the bar in which he mixed it, not in this neighborhood.

"Hey there, Mr. Hitts," he said. "What do you say to a couple of rounds on me, at the bar?"

Some customers would especially not like being told by him

to leave the white ladies alone.

Birdie took no umbrage. "You think I've lost my charm?"

"I think Miss Lauren could find a guy who could kill you before midnight."

Hawkins said, "I'll do it for free."

Hitts laughed with great pleasure. "You're my kind of dames." He got up and threw a five on the table, not exactly like it was a nightstand. He said to me, "You should think about that layout." He went off with Anthony, slapping him on the back like they were old friends.

Hawkins said, "Sorry I brought up the money. If he does anything with that story, I *will* kill him."

She knew about my estrangement from my parents, and so I didn't have to explain Birdie's crack. Before my uncle died, he'd given away a chunk of his fortune in stock, art, and property to his last lover, the love of his life. My parents had thought everything that wasn't coming to me or going to charity was going to them. Plenty of it did, but not nearly as much as they thought. They threatened to sue, to declare in public that my uncle had been unduly influenced during his illness, taken advantage of by a ruthless gold digger. I'd sided with the lover. My parents and I hadn't spoken since.

Hawkins said, "I was afraid he was going to ask about Mary Ann and Len. Epic's publicity's been pushing that, the fan mags are all excited. America's favorite coed and the handsome musical star."

"Does Mary Ann know? About Len?"

"It's hardly the sort of thing I can bring up in conversation."

Len Manning was born Lester Frobish and had a contract with Marathon a few years ago when Marathon had thought, briefly, that it could crank out musicals like MGM. That's where I first heard the quip that Len had been "manning" long before he changed his name from Frobish.

"What do you expect *me* to do?" I asked.

"Be Aunt Lauren when you can. She doesn't want to get married. I think she knows not too deep down that husbands inside the business can be dangerous commodities. They have a way of not wanting you to be as successful as they are."

"I'd almost rather advise her to marry Len and get away from Vera."

"Somebody'd have to kill Vera. Maybe you can help out with that."

CHAPTER 6

I returned to my Marathon office and took everything Juanita had brought me into the ladies' room, which, unlike most ladies' rooms in buildings occupied mostly by men, had decent lighting, a good mirror, and a tap that didn't spray water all over you. I brushed my teeth, changed into my dress, and pinned up my hair, doing it so badly I promptly took it down again. When I try to pin up my hair in evening high fashion, I usually end up looking like I'm ready to scrub floors. Fortunately, Juanita, who was long familiar with my lack of skill, had sent along my diamond-studded hair combs, so I used them to fold the hair back from my face and let the rest fall, tucked under, on my shoulders. I put on a fresh round of makeup, clipped on earrings. I didn't look nineteen. But I didn't look bad.

I called Peter's office again. He'd picked up his messages, the answering service told me. He'd left one for me: Call him at home after seven.

I had a new plan.

I'd drive over to Peter's. It would be pretty damned hard for him to resist going out with me in this dress, especially if I mentioned I was going to a party where there would be men. Hollywood men. Like Roland Neale, who had asked me to stop by his house afterward for a drink.

Even if Peter were tied up for the evening, working on a job, I could still show him what he was missing, and maybe it would

54

induce him to make plans for the weekend. Sooner or later, mister, you're going to have to take me out in public.

Peter lived in a small pale-gray bungalow on one of the rising, dipping labyrinthine streets east of Cahuenga. His front porch light was on; there were lights inside. He was home. I pulled to the curb at the end of his short driveway and checked my lipstick.

I left the organza shawl in the car. I didn't want to cover the dress.

I strutted down the drive and up the sidewalk, through the rectangle of light thrown by the open living room drapes. My heart was suddenly drumming. I breathed deeply of the honeysuckle that grew thick on the fence of the house next door. Then I stepped carefully onto the porch, straightened my skirt, reached for the doorbell.

Before I could ring, Peter came out of the kitchen carrying a drink. He was in shirtsleeves, no tie, the first buttons undone, casual, tall, lean, handsome. He was smiling slightly, the sort of smile one gets in fond recollection. Maybe he was thinking about me. Anticipating my call. It was almost seven.

Then, through the glass panel beside the door, I saw a woman come down the hallway to his bedroom, touching her hair at the neck, putting in the last pin. She wore a red taffeta blouse and a slim black skirt. She had a showgirl's figure and walked like she knew it.

Lily Graham.

I'd met her once, on a set. Her sixteen-year-old daughter was working as a stand-in for a popular Marathon actress for whom I'd done some script work. Lily manages the coat check and cigarette girls at Ramon Elizondo's nightclub. Peter's a friend of her boss. He'd worked for Ray Elizondo back in the day, rum-running during Prohibition.

Lily walked over to Peter, held his face in her hands. He put his free arm around her.

I stumbled off the porch. I tried to run back down the sidewalk, but it was suddenly so steep, and the driveway so far away. It seemed to take forever to get to the car, and then every move required so much effort: opening the door, climbing into the car, finding the handle, closing the door, finding the ignition, remembering how to turn the key.

Then I was at a stoplight on Franklin with no memory of how I got there.

The light had changed, and the car behind me complained loudly. I pulled slowly forward and turned into the first side street I came to. I drove past the streetlight, into the hard darkness. I parked, scraping the curb, shut off my lights, and fumbled for the hand brake, my hand was shaking so badly.

I found my wrap in the dark, pulled it around me, held it close, turned on the car's heat as high as it would go.

Why couldn't I do what I was told? Call him at seven. *Call him.*

I *knew* what his life had been like. Did I think he was going to change suddenly because of *me*? A man who looked like that, with a strong sexual appetite, who'd reached his mid-thirties and wasn't married. Why did I think this time it would be different?

All the compromises I made in my marriage, pretending I didn't know, didn't see. The agitated energy when my husband started a new affair, the high-strung effort to be normal. The extra attention he paid to me that should have made me happy, but instead made me feel the fool. And then when there was no avoiding it, years of "She doesn't mean anything to me."

Why do men say that? Why do they declare the most intimate of acts means nothing to them and then use that act to try to show how much they love *you*?

It means nothing. It won't last. A week, a night, till the picture wraps. She means nothing. Why do men say that? As if that would mend your heart.

What would Peter say? What *could* he say? That he knew women, and sometimes he might sleep with one of them. It might happen. But it didn't mean he didn't love me.

Love me. Had he ever said he loved me?

Would I confront him? Would it make any difference? Would he stop because I knew? Or would he simply pretend? Could *I* stand pretending all over again? Suspecting every woman he knew. Every woman I introduced him to. I'd already spent years doing that.

I couldn't go home. I couldn't sit there all night, thinking. I couldn't have him call me, wondering why I hadn't phoned. I couldn't talk to him, and I couldn't tell Juanita I didn't want to talk to him.

I opened my bag, my fingers still trembling, and pulled out the folded notepaper with Ben Bracker's address on it, set it on the passenger seat, tucked under my evening bag in easy reach. I turned on the headlights, released the brake, and shifted into drive. I'd go to the party. I'd spend the evening with strangers, talking about business, about gossip, about anything that wouldn't hurt, and not thinking about what I couldn't bear to face right now.

And then, by God, I'd go have a drink with Roland Neale.

CHAPTER 7

Ben Bracker lived in Holmby Hills, north of the country club, in a French country–style house, with a mansard roof and a horseshoe drive not quite wide enough for a tank division to turn around.

The house was ablaze in light.

A jacketed attendant took my key and gestured me up the front steps. A butler opened the door before I could ring the bell. I stepped into the front hall, which soared two stories. The legions of crystals in the chandelier threw prismatic light on the sweeping staircase, the marble floor, and the gold-flocked wallpaper.

I gave the man my name, and soberly he examined a list on the table by the door. He frowned and ran down it again, begging my pardon.

"What is it, Lionel?" a woman asked.

She was coming down the stairs, one bejeweled hand gliding along the railing, the other holding a martini. She wore a square-necked, floor-length hostess gown in apricot. Her brunette hair had been pinned up by hands infinitely more talented than my own.

I said, "I'm Lauren Atwill. My name isn't on the guest list. Mr. Bracker invited me this afternoon. I'm a writer, on loan to Epic."

"Just like him. Half the people here he forgot to tell me were coming. Jean Bracker. Welcome." She had a bright, healthy face, well tanned, with the sorts of lines around her eyes one gets living outdoors. "Give Lizzie your wrap, if you want, she'll keep up with it." A maid in a black uniform and white apron took charge of my wrap and disappeared up the stairs with it. A party this size, she was getting a lot of exercise.

"Lionel," Jean said, "how are we? Did the dancers arrive?"

"Yes, ma'am. All of them, and all appropriately attired."

"Good." She turned to me. "We invited a group of girls out from Epic. Pretty girls who get to meet people as long as they promise to dance with the guests. Are you all right? You look a bit pale."

"I think I should have eaten more lunch," I said.

"Then let's get you some food and a sit-down."

"Before you go, ma'am," Lionel said, "I believe some of the guests have begun a tennis match, and articles of clothing have been discarded to allow for greater movement."

"Oh dear. How much?"

"We are keeping an eye on the situation, ma'am, so to speak."

"Thanks. Let me know if I need to go have a word with them." Jean took my elbow and led me into the living room.

I wouldn't get a sit-down in there. It was enormous and designed for entertaining, with what they call conversation areas: sofas and chairs arranged in groups. But by now, the guests who needed to get off their feet had taken it over, so even the arms of the furniture and the floor around the coffee tables were full. I didn't know any of the loungers. I hadn't been to many parties since my husband and I separated, now almost two years ago. The names of people who got invited to Hollywood parties could change ruthlessly in two years.

A broad arch at the far end led into a wide corridor that ran the width of the house, dark despite a parade of sconces. Across the corridor, a garden room stretched away between the wings of the house, its peaked glass sky full of the clear night. From the room poured cigarette smoke and the raucous squawk of conversation above the music of an ensemble out on the terrace.

"Oh, God," Jean said, "what a mob. You don't want to go in there." She raised her hand, and a young man in a short white coat materialized. "Would you get a plate of sandwiches and some cake from the buffet. What else would you like?" she asked me. "Coffee? Tea? Whiskey?"

I told her coffee would be nice.

"Bring the food to the study," she told the waiter. Then she turned to me. "Let's go find you a quiet place. There's a powder room to freshen up in, down here, on the right. Across from that, there's a study. Let me show you. We'll put the food in here."

She opened the door.

"You stupid, stupid girl!" It was Vera McDowell.

I could only see about half the room. Mary Ann McDowell sat in a wing chair by the fireplace, her hand to her face as if she'd just been slapped. Vera stood over her on the hearth, with a face full of fury.

"That's enough!" Len Manning, Epic's musical star, stormed over to Vera.

Then she saw us. Then the other two did. All movement in the room ceased.

For a second, I thought someone else was in there, in the corner on my right, hidden from me by the open door, a shadow cast across the floor.

"You might want to use the key," Jean said to them. She said it with a smile, but her brows arched. "It locks the door."

She closed it again. There were footsteps, and the key turned.

"There's the powder room, just there. I'll have your food put upstairs in the morning room, top of the stairs. It's a place for the ladies when they need to take off their shoes. Oh, and be careful in the stairwell. We tore out a room down here and had the stairs built last year. The servants were running their legs off. But I'm not sure I did any of us a favor. It's even darker than the hallway. See you later."

The powder room had a velvet slipper chair in the corner; I locked the door and sat down, suddenly weak, my thighs trembling. I bent forward and put my head between my knees. Maybe coming here had been a bad idea. We'd see. Some food, some conversation I didn't have to stand up to have, then we'd see.

After a couple of minutes, I got up and looked in the mirror.

Jean had been gracious about my looks. I had no color at all, and every line on my face stood out. I dabbed a bit of lipstick on my cheeks, heated my chilled hands under water, then smoothed the color evenly with my warm fingers. I added a bit of powder, then reapplied the lipstick to my lips, blotting it afterward to take away some of the starkness against my still-pale face.

It was an improvement. But anything would have been.

I took a deep breath and opened the door. The waiter came striding down the hall, balancing a laden tray. He said, "They were just bringing out fresh sandwiches, sorry to be late."

"Not at all," I said. "I'm afraid someone's in the study. Mrs. Bracker said something about the morning room."

"Of course. This way." He led me to the small switchback stairwell and started up. "It's this way. Careful, it's a bit—"

Suddenly, there was a muffled thump, impossible to confuse with anything other than someone falling down, and hard.

He had a tray, so I dashed around him and onto the landing.

Jean Bracker lay flat on her stomach, about halfway up the next flight, her feet toward me. She'd lost a shoe.

She rolled onto her side. "I think," she said, "he was going to tell you it's a bit dark. Got my damned shoe caught in the hem."

Her skirt had rucked up a bit, to her knees where she'd slid down a step or two. I went up, gently pulled it down and helped her sit up. The waiter quickly set down the tray on the landing carpet and came forward to help.

"I'm fine," she said to him. "Go put the food in the morning room. I don't want to be fussed over."

The waiter scooped up the martini glass Jean had dropped, retrieved his tray, and slipped past us into the upper hall.

She said, "Please, go have your food."

"I think you might be more shaken than you know," I said.

"I was just—Being everywhere at once sometimes requires you to run when people aren't looking. I'm not used to this dress."

I sat down on the step below her. "Then let's just sit here a moment. There's a mark on your—Did you hit your chin?"

"No. I guess so. That *is* sore. You'd think I'd get used to it. Parties, I meant, not falling down."

I laughed. "More than ten guests, and I'm a nervous wreck."

"I love small dinner parties. Eight people. Conversation about things other than Hollywood, and music for dancing after. But Ben loves a crowd. Always has to be a crowd. I'm sorry, how do you know Ben?"

"I'm a writer. I'm on loan from Marathon," I said.

"Of course, you said before."

"No reason you should recall."

She stretched her arms in front of her and flexed her hands. She gave her head a few vigorous shakes. "All better now."

"Are you sure you're all right?"

"Of course. I'll be fine. Carry on. Always do. Don't let me spoil your evening. Come on, let's go find that food." She got up carefully and, lifting her skirt, made her way up the last few stairs.

Her morning room was a large sitting room with a desk that, while feminine, was meant for work. This was the room in which she'd answer all her letters, organize her household and her and her husband's social commitments every day after breakfast. I recalled the demands made on me as the wife of a prominent man, when my husband and I were still together. Some people, who like Vera McDowell had never heard of me, would assume that since my last name was Atwill, I'd married into Hollywood and was not part of it myself. They had no idea I'd been so deeply in love with my husband I'd even changed my professional name.

They'd expected me to join committees as Mrs. Frank Atwill, to help plan charity balls and political dinners, to do the grueling private work that would permit my busy husband to maintain a public reputation for good works.

As the wife of the head of a studio, Jean would hardly have a moment to herself, especially if she had children to care for as well.

She said, "If you need the powder room again, there's one just through here. I think I'll go take a look at my face." She slipped in, the tap came on. "No damage done," she announced when she came out a couple of minutes later, touching her lipstick. "Come see me later. We'll find someone you know. God knows there are enough to choose from."

The waiter had deposited the tray on the ottoman of a roomy armchair. I sat down. On a plate under a damp cloth, there were small sandwiches, the bread sliced thin. Coffee in a small, hot silver pot. A warmed cup. Warmed milk and small glass dish of sugar. A generous number of cocktail napkins, a wedge of chocolate cake, and a short glass of dark liquid that turned out to be brandy.

There was paper-thin roast beef pleated onto rye bread with horseradish sauce. Seafood salad on white. Cream cheese on brown raisin bread.

And in white rounds, peanut butter and jelly. Amused, I bit into one of those and was stricken by a sudden, nearly overwhelming urge to weep.

Flooding over me, uncontrollably, memories of all those sandwiches I'd shared with my uncle when I'd bicycle to his house on Saturdays, the ones he made with his own hands, the jelly always dripping over the sides. All those Saturdays when I would come to him, after another week had more firmly convinced me I was a mysterious disappointment to my parents. I'd never measure up to Marty, my poor brother who'd died when he was only three, only a few months before I was born, too soon into their grief. Marty would forever be the bright, open, happy, joyously loving child, who would always be full of promise, never grow up, never prove himself imperfect. And I'd hated myself for being packed with jealousy.

Now my uncle was gone. My marriage was gone. I had no children. My body was incapable of having children. I was growing old, alone, and what the hell did I have to show for my life?

I hurried into the powder room, closed the door, grabbed one of the small folded guest towels, and soaked the end in icy water. I pressed it lightly under my eyes.

Enough. Enough.

The doorknob rattled, the door opened. "Oh, sorry," a woman said.

"I'll be out in a minute."

"Don't worry. I'll go across the hall." She left. Silence.

I locked the door and took another few minutes, blotting under my eyes carefully with the icy cloth to remove all traces of the sudden tears. Then I hung the towel on a rack and turned on the tap again to wash my hands.

I wondered if Jean had any makeup in this room. While I had lipstick and a small powder compact in my evening bag, replacing a bit of mascara wouldn't do me any harm.

The sink had a small vanity. I opened the drawer, lifted aside a pair of folded handkerchiefs. A comb and brush, a box of hairpins. A nail brush. And a bottle of pills, with a trace of fresh water on the cap, a prescription label glued on.

I didn't read it. I shut the drawer. Half of Hollywood had pills in their bathrooms. It was no business of mine. If they helped her get through the party, she was welcome to them.

I washed my hands and returned to my chair. I considered the brandy, but drinking sure as hell wasn't going to improve my state of mind. I helped myself instead to a roast beef and then another one. Then a couple of the seafood salads. Nothing mawkish and self-pitying in any of them. I felt better. I really had needed some food. I sipped the coffee and finished off the cream cheese sandwiches and the cake.

Much better.

I moved my tongue over my front teeth to check for bread. There was a long, oval mirror hanging between the windows. I went over to it and pulled my lips back like a horse. Of course, someone came in.

She wore a silver-gray dress, a bit tight for her figure. Her dark hair was folded back from her face, carefully if severely, gathered onto her neck, and topped with an evening hat, a velvet cap with a veil that could be brought down over the eyes.

Savannah Masters, columnist for the *Eagle*, whose brief review of Mary Ann's new movie I'd recited to Peter just last night.

We nodded. She went into the powder room. When she returned she asked, "Can you see your seams in that mirror?"

"Not very well."

She stood in the middle of the room and tried to see the lines up the back of her stockings.

"They're fine," I said.

She gave her girdle a tug through her skirt. "Don't I know you?"

"Lauren Atwill. I read your column religiously."

"And I hope irreligiously now and then. I *do* know you. You're Frank Atwill's wife. First, I hear you're getting back together, then I hear there's a divorce."

"We're good friends, and I wish him all the best, but we won't be getting back together."

"Can I quote you? How about if I say, 'Looking spectacular at a chic soiree tossed by Epic chief Ben Bracker, Frank Atwill's wife, Lauren, tells me she wishes him all the best, but it won't be with her.' Got a new interest? I remember that hunk of a bodyguard you had last year, the private detective. What was his name?"

"I'm taking a rest from romance for a while."

"That won't do. Fix your lipstick, and let's go see if we can find you some trouble. Anybody you spotted look interesting?"

"I met Roland Neale earlier today. He said he might come."

"Oh, honey, you do like a challenge. He might still be around, but he's not fond of crowds, unless they're adoring him."

"He seemed very nice."

"But you were adoring him, right?"

I laughed. "Maybe a little."

"Jean practically had to whip out the smelling salts when he showed up. You can always tell if a woman's lying about her age when he walks in the room. Anybody who's reduced to a simpering fool, you can bet she's pushing forty, probably from the other side. Are you ready for some trouble?"

"Sure, what the hell."

She yanked both legs of her girdle, and we headed for the main stairs. She said nothing about my having a reputation for increasing the murder rate at a studio, so maybe the gossipy cracks hadn't gone as far as I feared. Or maybe it wasn't worth her trying to get a quote about it. Marathon would howl to her publisher if she printed anything that reminded the public of scandals that hadn't been the studio's fault. And Epic wouldn't be too pleased either. Better to be nice to me in case I might give her an exclusive interview about my marriage and divorce, which I assumed was why she'd attached herself to me.

We met two pairs of women coming up, one chatting and laughing. The other was Vera and Mary Ann McDowell. I nodded and smiled. Mary Ann did her best. Vera stopped momentarily as we passed. I felt her gaze hot on my back.

"What are you doing at an Epic party?" Savannah asked me.

"I'm on loan. I might be working on Mary Ann's new picture, but please speak to Mr. Bracker for anything official."

"You going to write a musical?"

"It won't be a musical," I said.

"I heard they were pairing her with Len Manning."

"Please talk to Mr. Bracker."

"Is that why the battle-ax was giving you the eye?"

"What?"

"Honey, I'm paid to notice things," Savannah said. "Vera McDowell. She wasn't giving *me* the hard eye a second ago."

"Does she chaperone Mary Ann to cocktail parties?"

"She likes to be *everywhere* in that poor girl's life. What do you hear about Mary Ann and Len?"

"I hardly know her. I don't know him at all."

"I'd love to get their engagement scoop. You hear anything, let me know. Come on, let's go find Rolly Neale for you."

The living room was even more crowded than before. A maid circulated with a silent butler, discreetly dumping cigarette butts into the small hinge-lidded brass pan. None of the occupants was Roland.

As we moved through the room, the guests smiled hard at Savannah and spoke. And then they eyed me, the smiles fading, trying to figure out who I was. She greeted them, sometimes a nod, sometimes a few words. Sometimes a touch on the shoulder for the specially chosen. But we kept moving, on through the garden room and out into the fresh air of the terrace, where some of the guests had begun dancing to the ensemble's romantic sway. Jean would be glad to see that.

The night air was settling fast, with a light breeze fanning the scent of the bougainvillea and fresh-mown grass. Soon, it would be too chilly to be outside without a wrap, but bougainvillea trumped cigarettes every time. We filled our lungs.

The lawn was a sweep of intense green, bordered on one side by trees pruned to match. The other side had been built up as a sort of terrace, which extended from that wing of the house—a formal walking garden, the pool, and the cabana.

"I know the first place to look for Rolly." Savannah led me into the trees, and we followed the flagged path that wound through them down the right side of the lawn to the tennis courts, which had attracted a small, but enthusiastic, standing crowd. Barefoot young women were lobbing balls back and forth, with sufficient skill not to spill their drinks. They had discarded their dresses and stockings and were playing in their slips, which they'd hiked up somehow till they were short as tennis togs. None of them wore a girdle. One of them still sported her garter belt.

A group of guests—warmed by liquor and the thrill of bad behavior—cheered them on. Roland Neale was not among them. On the far side, however, seated on one in a row of benches, was a man who at first glance looked a bit like him: the shape of the shoulders, the nose, the well-tended moustache. But the hair was wrong. It was too black for his age. And there were pouches under the eyes. He was leaned into intent conversation with a buxom little bottle blonde in a black slip. He put his hand on her knee.

"My old man," Savannah commented, following my gaze. She marched over and planted herself in front of them. "Hey there," she said amiably to the girl. "Savannah Masters. That's my husband."

The girl yipped sharply and jerked her slip down, knocking his hand away.

"Pet," the man said in a bored voice. "We were only talking."

"With sign language?"

He sat back with a jaded sigh and languidly took out a gold cigarette case, opened it, offered it to the girl. She looked at it as if it were another stray hand aiming where it didn't belong. He offered it to me. I declined. Slowly he took a cigarette, returned the case to his jacket, took out a lighter and lit the cigarette, smiling at me over the flame.

Savannah said to the girl, "You might think you have to let him do some things because he might put in a good word for you with someone around here, maybe even me. You might even think anybody here gives a tinker's damn what he thinks."

The girl gulped, her eyes enormous.

"But," Savannah said, "I think you're cute. What's your name?"

"Mimi. Mimi Delacourt," the girl said.

"You made that one up, didn't you? What was your name when it was at home?"

"Ida Smoody. I'm really sorry. I didn't know who he was."

"Come on. Let's go get your clothes, then you can tell me all about your Hollywood dreams. And no one will try to put a hand up your skirt while you're doing it."

The girl gulped again, then got up meekly.

"Sorry," Savannah tossed to me. "If I see Rolly, I'll steer him your way." They went off, the girl's back stiff.

The man draped an arm onto the back of the bench and crossed his legs. He let out a long whisper-cloud of cigarette smoke. "I saw Rolly a moment ago. He came down to watch the show, but he stalked off almost at once. Nobody was noticing him, I suppose. I'm Kentwood Grantlin, Dr. Grantlin."

"Lauren Atwill."

"Why don't you sit down?"

"Thanks, but I need to find my escort."

"Who is it? Maybe I've seen him."

"I'm sure you don't know him. He's not one for parties. I think I'll check over by the pool."

I made a hasty retreat. He didn't pursue. He was smoking and watching his wife.

CHAPTER 8

I hiked over to the pool. It wasn't quite far enough to need a native guide. Guests were reclined on loungers and enjoying refreshment brought to them from the portable bar. I found a few people I knew and chatted awhile, though the conversations never got deep enough that I wanted to sit down and stay, nor did they ask me to.

The ensemble on the terrace broke into some hot swing music. The dancers whooped. The piano was pounding. More couples flowed out of the garden room. I strolled back up and watched them for a while, admiring their enthusiasm, their joy at being together—even if some of it was created by liquor—before my envy took over.

Sometimes when Peter came over, we'd turn on the radio and dance in the study. But never publicly. I wondered if he'd taken other women out to dance from time to time, at some club where he'd be unlikely to run into anyone I knew. "Oh, Lauren, hey, last night I was out at a roadhouse. I saw that bodyguard you used to have, he was with a real dish. You know who she is? He serious about her, do you know? She up for grabs?"

I retreated down the lawn. I didn't want anybody to see my face. On the tennis courts, the barefoot, slip-clad girls had been joined by young men who had stripped to trousers and undershirts. The party would probably be over before the competition for attention reached the point of naked bathing in the pool. Probably. I had no idea how the Brackers' parties generally ended.

Behind the courts, set into the tall, thick yew hedge that ran along the foot of the lawn, was an iron gate. I lifted the latch, which first stubbornly resisted; the hinges creaked. With my well-honed detective skills, I deduced the gate wasn't used too often.

I stuck my head out. Beyond was the lane Roland had told me about. The tennis courts threw some light on it, but further down, the trees and tall border shrubs blocked much of whatever there might be from the other houses and yards. The moon sat at the end of the lane, cupped on the horizon, still rising.

Was it possible the builders had created this lane solely for residents to drive their golf carts to the country club, as Roland had said? I hoped it wasn't used as a horse trail, for the sake of my shoes. Should I walk down to Roland's? His backyard, according to his drawing, wasn't more than a hundred yards. Should I go get my car? Why was I reluctant to park in his driveway? It wasn't as if my being seen calling on Roland Neale at night would create a scandal. No one was watching me like Birdie Hitts—and scandal photographers like him—watched stars like Mary Ann, hoping to unearth some secret shame to sell to the highest bidder. Nobody cared what I did.

It wasn't as if word would get back to Peter. And if it did, so the hell what?

"Hey there."

I jumped about a foot.

"Sorry," Mary Ann said.

"It's all right. I was thinking about something else."

"Making a getaway?" She wore the same body-hugging cobalt blue dress she'd had on at Madison's, touched up for the party with a rhinestone pin, bracelet, and earrings. There was a cocktail hat, hugging the right side of her head, with feathers curved across to the other cheek. She'd changed shoes into black evening slippers with a diamante strap.

I said, "Roland Neale lives just down there, on the left. He invited me over for a drink later. Stupidly, I've been thinking about sneaking over rather than driving."

"Would your husband get jealous if he knew?"

"My husband and I are getting a divorce."

"You have a boyfriend? Would he be jealous?" she asked.

"Maybe."

"You should do it," she said. "And make sure he finds out it was Roland Neale. Sometimes men don't pay enough attention till they think somebody else is after you."

This sounded like advice she'd gleaned from reading romance columns in cheap magazines while waiting for the cameras to be re-set. Or from her mother.

"Could I have a word?" she asked. "Just a few minutes."

"Sure."

"Do you mind if we go back inside? It's a little cold out here, and I have to use the ladies'."

The first floor was even more crowded than before, and the powder room near the study was occupied. "Let's go on up," I said. I took her up the back stairs.

In the morning room, Savannah Masters was sitting on the ottoman. Jean Bracker had the armchair.

"Excuse me," Mary Ann said and slipped into the powder room.

"You should lie down," Savannah said to Jean.

"I just need a couple of minutes to get my second wind. I'm fine," Jean said.

"The hell you are. Where's Ben? I'll go tell him he can run his own damned party for a while."

"He's tied up," Jean said.

"What on earth is he up to? He threw this party, and I haven't seen him all night."

"He and Joe Gettleman are still in the study," Jean said. "He can just lock himself up when he feels like it."

"I'll go warm his britches for him, as my mother used to say." She patted Jean's hand. "Go lie down. Just a few minutes." She turned to me. "Talk some sense into her."

Jean did indeed look shaky, pale. There was a taut nervousness in her eyes. She kept sucking in on her lips.

"Maybe you should," I said. "Just a few."

"You go rest, and I'll tell Ben to get his ass out of the study," Savannah said.

Mary Ann came out of the powder room. "Let me just say good-bye then; I'm going soon." She went over to Jean. "Thank you for inviting me. It's such a lovely home. I can't wait till I have one as comfortable and welcoming."

"I'm sorry. What did you say?" Jean just looked at her.

"Come on, that's it. Up, up," Savannah said. "You're going to your room. No excuses." She led Jean out.

"She doesn't look very well," Mary Ann whispered.

"She's tired."

"I think it would be fun to throw parties like this."

"Not if you had to plan them and keep everybody happy." Ah, the enthusiastic naïveté of youth.

A couple of other women arrived, to kick off their shoes and have a rest.

"Come on," I said to her. "I have an idea."

I led her back into the stairwell, and we sat down about halfway between the landing and the first floor in what passed for solitude at the moment. "Here we go," I said.

Ben Bracker was indeed still in the study. I could hear the rumbling of his voice, though not the exact words, through the wall as I leaned my shoulder on it. The builders who'd cut out the space for the new stairwell hadn't bothered to re-plaster the wall properly. Of course, it wasn't like people would press their ears to the paint to hear what was going on.

Mary Ann smoothed her skirt and tucked her legs to the side. "I wanted to explain, about what you saw earlier, in the study, between me and mama."

"You don't need to do that."

"I do. Mama means well. She just wants me settled."

"Of course." I wasn't sure that allowed her to slap her daughter. "But she has to know you can't force your heart, to fall in love or fall out. God, I sound like a Victorian novel. Is Len pressuring you that hard for an answer?"

"No, he's very nice. Mama's afraid—Well, you know, men change their minds."

"You're nineteen, and you're delightful. I can't imagine a man who'd fallen for you changing his mind just because you didn't answer right away. What kind of husband would he be? But I might not be the best one to hand out romantic advice."

"And the studio set us up."

"That doesn't mean you have to marry the guy. They're putting you into mature roles. You have a career to think about. Tell them—all of them—that you need time, and you remind the studio that a girl like you—whose reputation is very, very important—cannot risk a divorce. You tell them that, in three months, you'll have a better idea of how you feel. About everything."

"I sound stupid, don't I?"

"Not at all."

"I do. You're just kind. But, yes, I like that. Tell them I need to think about my career. And that if they want me to be happy, they should want me to have a marriage to the man I love."

"There you go, not stupid at all."

She glanced at her watch. It was just after eight o'clock. "I have to get to sleep early," she said. "I have to have some pictures taken in the morning, and it always takes at least an hour for the puffiness around my eyes to go down." I imagined it was Vera who had continually pointed that out to her. "I'm tempted to just take Mama's car—I know where it's parked, I could sneak out the back gate—and let Len take her on home. I guess that would be the wrong thing to do."

"Yes. But I don't blame you for wanting to."

She laughed, thanked me, and went off down the stairs.

I recalled being her age, half rebellious and half terrified of displeasing anyone.

I hauled myself to my middle-aged feet just as Savannah came down the stairs, and we walked together toward the foyer. "Jean's lying down. She takes so much on herself. Since the last boy went off to school, she's been—Well, never mind. You find Rolly?"

"Not yet."

"I've got to make a few more rounds, then I think I'll call it a night."

She promptly deserted me. A naughty-boy actor had made a grand entrance, sweeping off the coat that had been draped over his shoulders. He spotted Savannah and gave her a wicked glance. "My love," he said and opened his arms.

I might as well have disappeared.

I had about an hour to kill before going over to Roland's. He'd said nine o'clock. I needed someone to talk to. I hadn't planned on it being Bob Philby, a producer at Warners. A cigar in his hand, he pinned me to the hallway wall and told me about this terrific comedy he had ready to shoot over there, wanting to know if I'd be interested in punching up the dialogue a bit. No credit, of course. I told him I was on loan to Epic and working on a story for them. Yeah, he said, he'd heard that. He spent awhile trying to find out what the Epic project was. I told him we were in early days. I could take a look at his script, if Epic and Marathon cleared it. I asked about money. He said maybe he could go to eight.

I said he should talk to Mr. Bracker, then we could talk more. I managed to get myself off the wallpaper. He grinned, patted my shoulder with his cigar hand, and strutted off.

Eight hundred a week to fix dialogue in a comedy that needed help and help fast? Is this what happened when you got loaned out to Epic? Your price suddenly plummeted?

I dusted a bit of ash off my skirt and headed down to one of the sconces to get some more light on it. If he'd burned a hole in my favorite dinner dress . . .

There was a thud-thudding on the carpet of the back stairs, and a maid in uniform shot out of the stairwell. She knocked frantically on the study door, then tried to open it. It was locked. "Mr. Bracker, are you there, please?"

Bracker opened it.

"It's Mrs. Bracker," the woman gulped out. "She's collapsed! I found her in her room!"

Bracker rushed past her into the stairwell, and she followed. Joe Gettleman, the studio lawyer, was right behind them, but then he saw me. "Go get a doctor! Can you try to find a doctor, please? Do you know anyone?"

"Dr. Grantlin is here. I saw him—"

"Yes, please get him. Quietly."

"Of course."

I had no idea where Kentwood Grantlin was. Maybe he was still out by the tennis courts. I squeezed through the garden room, craning the crowd as I went. I found him out on the terrace, near its portable bar, watching the dancers.

"I'm sorry to interrupt," I said to him, "but Mr. Bracker asked if you could come see him a moment."

When I got him into the corridor and out of earshot of the

guests, I told him what had happened. He reached into his pocket and pulled out a ring of keys. "I'll go get my bag. It's not far. I always park in the driveway. Tell Ben I'll be right up."

I went to deliver the message, taking the back stairs. But the corridor above was empty. I had no idea where Jean's bedroom was. I went along the hall, listening at the closed doors for the sound of voices. Then a door opened toward the other end. Joe Gettleman came out, his face very grim.

I told him I'd found Dr. Grantlin. But I needn't have bothered. Kentwood was already back with his bag and striding toward us. Joe opened the door just enough for Kentwood to slip in.

Gettleman said to me, "Mrs. Bracker suffers from a nervous condition for which she gets medical treatment."

"Of course, I understand."

"Thank you for your help. And your discretion."

I nodded. I left. I went on downstairs, squeezed my way to the garden room bar, and ordered a gin and tonic.

There was still no sign of Roland.

I did manage to run into the director Gilbert DeNewell and his wife, Estelle, who was nicknamed Slim. They were drunkenly arguing politics with D. B. Roscoe and another writer, whose name I never caught. But you could tell he was a writer: he wore tweed to a party.

"Lauren," Slim said, "these idiots, both of them, are trying to tell me that if there are commies in the State Department, we should just let them stay there and spy for the Bolshies."

"And I was telling this Nazi," D. B. said, "that you don't throw a guy out of his job because when he was a kid, he thought maybe, with a few million starving in this country, capitalism hadn't turned out so hot."

"Slim has a point," her husband said. "Now, she's got a point."

"And a damned stupid one," D. B. said. His cohort was satisfied with nodding vigorously.

"You think a commie ought to be handling secrets?" Slim asked.

"Jesus Christ, Slim, a commie to you is anybody who voted for Roosevelt."

"Oh, that's ridiculous. You lefties can't stop exaggerating. I say that if you joined one of those organizations on their list, you don't belong in the State Department."

"Doesn't matter whether it's true," he said.

"What's true?" Slim said.

"That you were a member. Maybe somebody lied, somebody with a grudge. Or maybe some investigator wants to impress his boss and makes it up. And good luck finding another job after getting fired for being a fellow traveler."

Slim said, "Oh, for God's sake, there'll be a panel. If it was a mistake, you appeal. If you're innocent, you get your job back."

"A panel of who?" D. B. asked. "Guys who think Catholics are traitors because they answer to the Pope?"

"That's stupid, that's just stupid," Slim declared. "I can't talk to you."

"Going to throw me out of a job, Slim, because I'm Catholic?"

"I'd never throw anybody out of work who'd let me drink while I'm praying. Just don't make me eat those damn wafers."

D. B. threw his head back and laughed. "You're a goddamn danger to the country."

"And you want to turn it over to lunatics. Bartender, another drink for this Bolshie. Well, hell, Lauren," she said and turned to me, "what have you been up to?"

I told them the parts of the last several months that didn't include murders. Which made my last several months sound pretty damn dull.

Len stared.
Vera said "Uh."

CHAPTER 9

Graciously, I said good-bye—telling Len it had been nice to meet him, and Vera, once again, that I was looking forward to working with her daughter. I waited till I was in the hallway, alone, unnoticed in the gloom, before I burst into a grin and a short "so there!" shimmy. Then, recovering my regal bearing, I weaved my way—elegantly, of course, as befitted a woman held in high regard—through the living room crowd, imagining they all knew exactly who I was.

Out in the drive, I asked the attendant for my keys and the location of my car. He offered to bring it around immediately, in a tone that implied I had impugned his reputation. I told him the truth, well, some of it: I'd been invited to another house just down the street for a drink and wasn't sure when I'd be back. Mollified, he handed over the keys and the location, a half block away, around the corner, near the top of that golf-cart lane. I thanked him and tucked the keys into my bag.

I retrieved my wrap from the maid, then dropped it over the back of a chair in the living room. I'd find some people I knew, chat for a while, then head on over to Roland's.

I found five. I knew them all only slightly. They were pleasant, but it was Hollywood cocktail talk, and after the "How are you?" and "What are you working on?" there wasn't much else to say except "Nice to see you again."

I didn't find anyone who might influence me not to make a ninny of myself by going over to Roland Neale's because Peter

Winslow was on his way to breaking my heart. I didn't meet anyone who dissuaded me. But then, I didn't really want to.

The rising moon cast webs of light onto the lane through the branches. Maybe this was a stupid idea. I risked ruining my shoes and looking like an idiot trying to force his gate or wiggle through a hedge. And all because I didn't want my car parked in his driveway?

Roland's gate was wood, the wall of brick. The brass plate on the gate proclaimed NEALE. The latch cooperated; the hinges protested, but not much.

On the other side was a flourishing stand of banana plants. A path of gray-green paving stone led through them, but the fronds overwhelmed it. Even though I ducked and lifted some aside, others welcomed me with cheerful pats on the head.

I came out near one end of the pool, which ran horizontally across the bottom of the lawn. The cabana sat at the other end, gleaming white. Its broad, deep porch was hung with summer lanterns and diaphanous curtains, loosely caught back. In my Epic office, Roland had told me he loved to sit there in the evening, enjoying the solitude. I could understand why. The curtains, released, would glitter in the rose pink of sunset. Then, as darkness fell, their undulations in the soft breeze would break and reform the pattern of the lantern light.

He wasn't there, but a lamp was lit in the cabana's center room.

The paving widened as it led around the pool, and I followed it, skirting the lawn chairs and the tables with furled umbrellas. I turned the corner.

A shadow moved in the light thrown from the half-open door. "Hello?" I called out.

As I approached the base of the cabana steps, I saw wet shoe-prints in the moonlight on the pale gray paving, coming toward me, from the other direction. I wouldn't have thought the grass was that wet. It hadn't been damp at all at the Brackers'. The gardener must have watered the lawn.

The shoe prints turned before they reached me and went up the cabana steps. And onto the glossy white paint. They went into the lamplight.

They were wet. But not from water.

Then I heard a moan.

"Roland?"

Slowly, I climbed. I followed the prints to the door. I edged my fingers forward, pushed it fully open.

Roland Neale sat in a rattan chair, in light tan slacks and a thick cardigan over a white shirt, different clothes than he'd been wearing earlier at the Brackers'. He was bent forward, his hands in fists pressed to his face. His breathing was shallow, suffering.

There was blood on the floor, not full prints anymore, but smeared bits across the painted planks. They led right to his feet, to the stained soles of his shoes.

He's fallen, he's cut himself. I told myself that was what had happened. Why else would he have blood on his shoes?

"Roland?" I said, softly.

His head jerked up; he stared at me without comprehension.

"It's Lauren." I eased toward him, stiff-kneed. "You're hurt. Did you cut yourself?"

He said, "You have to go away."

I stopped. "What?" I took a step back. "What happened?"

"I don't know." He unclenched one hand and thrust it out to me, pleading. "Please. I would never have hurt her. Never."

"Who else is here?"

"I never would have hurt her."

"Of course not. Is there a phone in here?"

"What?"

85

I took another step back, turned, and, as if I were wading through sand, I made it to the door. I had to get to a phone. The house. It would be unlocked. Nobody would lock their doors in this neighborhood. I stood in the doorway. The lawn stretching up to the house looked black and terrifying.

"You have to go," he said, behind me, low and agonized.

"Yes, I'm leaving now."

I took a step onto the porch, three more, another, reached the top of the steps. The shoe prints were stark on the white planks below me. I stood there, looking at the prints. They came from the opposite direction I had, the other end of the cabana. I turned to my right, forced myself along the porch to the far railing, and looked over. The paving became a sort of small patio dotted with flowering plants in large wooden pots. A woman lay crumpled on her side between two of them. I could see a bit of the blue hem of her dress, her slender legs, and her black evening shoes, their soles facing me, with their narrow diamante straps.

I staggered back, dropping my bag, my hands thrown up over my mouth. I fell against the cabana wall, slipped, began to slide. I clutched at the wall, caught the sill of a window, steadied myself. Pushed myself back up. I had to get out of here. Now. Go back to the lane. Back to the Brackers' and people. And safety.

Move. Run.

I rounded the corner. And collided with the tall, hard shape of a man.

He grabbed my arm. I punched him with my other hand, hard in the face. I tried to scream. He whipped me around, threw one brutal hand over my mouth and the other around my waist. He dragged me back into the cabana and kicked the door shut.

CHAPTER 10

"Shut up, and you don't get hurt," he snarled in my ear. "You hear me? I mean it!" I jerked a couple of nods.

After a moment, he slowly let go of my mouth and, when I didn't scream, my waist. I spun away from him and backed across the floor, as if there were safety behind a rattan sofa.

"Jesus Christ!" he exclaimed. "You!"

It was Mack Pace, the head of Epic security.

"What the hell are you doing here?" he demanded.

"I was invited," I snapped.

"Christ!"

"I just came from the Brackers' party. Peter Winslow's on his way over."

"Like hell he is."

"You don't think I have to tell him everywhere I go, everybody I'm with? You've seen his temper."

"You're sneaking around in the dark because your boyfriend's coming? I don't think so. I think it's just going to be us. Sit down."

There was no reason Mack Pace was here, and not letting me go, except that he'd come to fix this. I'd heard plenty of stories about how far studios would go to protect themselves and their stars. From the murder case last Christmas, I had some idea those stories weren't all just rumors.

Had he come to make this all disappear?

Pace might not think too much about another body. If that

body were me.

"Sit down!" he shouted.

I decided it was better to let the adrenaline wash out of me. Regain the strength in my legs that the fear had leached out. I had to get my breath back. It would give me the chance to sneak my shoes off, plan a way out. Find something to use as a weapon?

On each side of the room were two doors, both closed, probably leading to bedrooms and changing rooms, rooms that would have locks on the doors and windows big enough to crawl through. But I was too weak to make a dash for them yet.

If I told Pace that others were coming over, guests from the party, would he believe me? If he did, would it only make him more determined to act quickly?

"How long have you been here?" he asked.

Could the answer get me killed? The less I'd seen and heard, the better.

"I just got here."

"What did he tell you?"

"Nothing."

"He told you something, or you wouldn't have gone out there!"

"For God's sake, I saw the footprints!" I stabbed my finger at them. "They led to the path. He said he'd never hurt her. That's all he said."

My chance of survival might well depend on Roland Neale, on his making clear he wouldn't stand for murder to protect himself.

"Are you all right?" I asked him, quietly. "Roland?"

He dragged his gaze up from the floor. The skin under his eyes had gone gray, the lines around them, deep.

"He's in shock," I said to Pace. "He needs help. I should get him something to drink." On the bar, behind Roland's chair, bottles, one of which would make a nice club.

"Sit down!" Pace said. "You think that's going to make him lucid? You fucking movie people. You're all fucking idiots!"

"Stop it," Roland murmured. "Stop it. Please."

Pace said, "Mr. Neale, you need to pay attention to me. I can't help you if you don't pay attention." He stayed where he was, between me and the door.

"I hear you, I do," Roland said. "I don't know what happened."

"Who else did you invite over here?"

"What? Nobody."

"You sure?"

I said, "He has no idea what he's saying. I heard him asking people to drop over."

"Shut up! Mr. Neale, you're not going to say anything else, you understand? Not to me, not to her, not to anybody, unless your lawyer says so. We're going to do what we can to help you, you understand, but I need you to listen to me. Now."

"And the police?" Roland asked.

"Did you call the police?" Pace shot glances around the room. There was a phone on the bar. I hadn't seen it earlier. There were smears of bloody prints leading to it. "Did you call the police?"

"Just Joe. Joe Gettleman. Is he coming?"

Pace knew I hadn't called the police. I would have said so by now.

"She should go," Roland said.

"She needs to stay right here. She's the only person who's seen anything."

"I don't understand," Roland said. "She should go. There's no sense dragging her into this."

"She's dragged herself into it. It's a habit she's got. She's not going anywhere. We're going to sort this out, see what we can do for you."

Roland turned to me. "You don't have to do that. Please go on home."

"That's not what he means," I said. Carefully, I slipped out of my shoes and stood up. "I would be glad to help you, Roland, because I don't think you did this."

"I don't know what happened. I would never have hurt her."

"I believe you." I went over and laid a hand gently on his shoulder. "I believe you."

There was a knock on the door. It was too late. It was probably one of Pace's men, ready to help him clean this up, even if it meant moving one more body, before Roland Neale was capable of understanding what was happening. I was ready to scream and scream and pray I'd be heard. "Help me," I whispered to Roland.

"Open up please. It's the police."

"I'm coming!" I shouted and rushed for the door.

As I fumbled with the knob, I thought it might be a joke, something Pace's men always said to their boss when they arrived to clean up a mess.

But I flung the door open all the way, throwing the room's light onto the man on the porch. He wore a brown overcoat and a fedora pulled low over his heavy features and steady, cautious eyes, which quickly examined my face, my stockinged feet, then the two men behind me. Then his focused gaze was back on me.

Beyond him, down in the dark at the bottom of the steps, stood another man in an overcoat. In one hand, he had a flashlight; the other was poised to reach inside his jacket for his gun.

The man in front of me held up his badge.

"Detective," I said, and my voice caught.

"Costello. Who are—?"

"There's a dead woman over there, in the yard, on the pavement," I blurted and pointed toward the end of the porch.

The other man took a step in that direction. "Wait a minute," Costello said to him. "Ma'am, who are you, and who's in there with you?"

"I'm Lauren Atwill. This is Mr. Roland Neale, who owns the house. And this is Mack Pace. He works for Epic Pictures."

"Who else?"

"Nobody. I don't think so. I just got here."

"Sir," he said to Roland, "I'm going to ask you to stay right where you are. You, sir, if you'd sit down over there. Now, ma'am, where did you say the body was?"

I told him, and he signaled for the other detective to go have a look. The man wasn't gone long.

"She's just over there," he reported. "Looks like somebody shot her. In the face, close range. It's not pretty."

Costello went to the end of the porch and looked over the railing much as I had done. "Jesus," he whispered, then returned. "If you'd step back into the room, ma'am." I did. He gestured the other detective to stay where he was and came inside. He examined the other rooms, apparently satisfying himself no one else was there.

"So, who's going to tell me what happened?" Costello asked.

Pace said, "Mr. Neale won't have anything to say till he's talked to his lawyer."

"How'd you end up here?"

"I drove."

"You think that's funny?" Costello said. "There's a dead woman out there, and a live one in here, who looks scared out of her mind."

"I won't be saying anything either," Pace said glumly.

"Suit yourself. I always like a good suspect right off the bat. Makes my job a lot easier. Ma'am, who's the woman out there, do you know?"

"Mary Ann McDowell. She's an actress."

"Why don't you come and sit down?"

From the bottom of the steps, the other man was still able to watch Roland and Pace, so Costello gestured me into a small changing room, and I sat down on the padded bench. He closed the door.

He said, "He threaten you, the smart one out there?"

"He grabbed me out on the porch, forced me in here. He's the head of security for Epic. I don't know what he had in mind. I don't know how long he's been here. Not too long, I think, because he wanted to know how long *I'd* been here. Did Joe Gettleman call you?"

"Who?"

"He's a lawyer for Epic. I think Mr. Neale called him, and he sent Mr. Pace."

He said, "One of the neighbors called in, heard some commotion over here. We were on our way back from a call, so we said we'd drive on by. We didn't expect to find anything, in a neighborhood like this."

I told him who I was and how I'd got there, then said, "I looked over the side of the porch, the same as you did. That's when he grabbed me. I don't know where he came from. I didn't hear him. I only saw Mr. Neale."

"What did Mr. Neale say?"

"He's in shock, I think. But he said he didn't know what happened, and that he wouldn't have hurt her."

"You know they all say that. What was she to him?" Costello asked.

"I didn't know they'd ever met." I explained about seeing both of them at the Brackers' party, but not together.

"Tell me how you ended up here, everything you did and saw."

I did. Then he asked, "Did you hear anything on the way over, like maybe a gunshot?"

"No. Mr. Gettleman isn't Mr. Neale's attorney. He works for the studio. He shouldn't be giving Mr. Neale legal advice right now."

"I think we should let them worry about that. And maybe they should worry about how they didn't call the police. Where is this Mr. Gettleman now?"

"Still at the Brackers', I guess." I gave him the address. "It's just over there, not far at all."

"How well do you know Mr. Neale?" Costello asked.

"I only met him today, but I've been a fan for years. I don't want to think he did this."

"Neither would I, ma'am, but it doesn't look good."

"Do you know Sergeant Phil Barty?" I asked.

"No."

"He works in Homicide. He could vouch for me, if you need vouching. Assistant DA Betts, too."

"I'm going to need to take a look at your clothes, ma'am. You don't have to take anything off," Costello said.

"Of course."

He did. He took at good look at the dress, for any signs of splattered blood, and my skin, fingernails, hair. He retrieved my shoes and examined the soles, ran his fingers over the fabric. Nothing red came off on his hands.

He gave them back to me. I stared at them.

"What is it?" Costello asked.

"Maybe he didn't do it," I said, hushed.

"I'm sorry?"

"I know what it looks like. Especially since Mr. Neale didn't call the police."

"And called a lawyer first, who sent someone here to mess with my evidence, if I had to guess."

"It's the blood."

"On his shoes," Costello said.

"It's only on the soles. I didn't see anything on the tops. You're examining me for blood. Mr. Neale is wearing pale slacks. A white shirt. There's no blood on him."

"Are those the clothes he was wearing at the party?" Costello asked.

"No."

"He could have changed out of the bloody ones."

"Then why not change shoes?" I asked. "And if he did change shoes, why would he go back to the body and step in the blood."

"You said he's in shock."

"I'm sorry, detective, I don't mean to be difficult, but if he was rational enough to change clothes and wash away all traces of blood, would he have gone back and stepped in the blood?"

"Kirby's not an expert," Costello said. "He could be wrong about the distance between the shooter and the lady."

"Of course. I'm sorry."

"So how do you know the assistant DA?"

I told him about the case we'd been involved in. He'd heard of it.

He said, "I don't want to take you downtown, with what you've been through. But you'll have to promise to keep this under your hat tonight. I don't think you want reporters."

"No."

"And I don't want every good citizen around here to come running over, trampling my crime scene, to tell me how to do my job and how I ought to leave Mr. Neale alone because he's an important person. Besides, we don't know what happened yet. My boss won't be happy if this hits the papers and I let you go spread it around, especially if it turns out Mr. Neale didn't do anything after all."

"But you don't think that's likely."

"I don't know. What you said about the shoes, there might be something there. Despite what you might think, we don't always hang it on the first guy we see."

"Joe Gettleman will have told Mr. Bracker, who runs Epic. They'll be waiting for Pace to call them. When he doesn't, you might get visitors."

"Thanks. I'll be prepared. Somebody'll call you tomorrow to get a statement. You okay to drive?"

"Yes. My car's not far. Over in the next street."

"Why don't I walk you?"

He found my bag and wrap on the porch. He examined them, then my driver's license, and took down my address and phone number. He handed everything back. He walked me to my car, down the lane, past the Brackers' backyard. Through the narrow gaps in the yew hedge, I could see the staff moving around the lawn, collecting rubbish. The chill had moved the party inside. Jean would probably have got up from her bed to entertain them because Ben Bracker and Joe Gettleman would be closeted in Bracker's study, figuring out what to do. Epic's publicity director would be on the way over. Mary Ann was dead. Tomorrow, Roland Neale would be all over the news, detained on suspicion of murder.

And, once again, I'd signed on to a job, and someone had died.

We found my car parked on the street near the end of the lane. Costello opened the door for me. "That Pace fellow, you want me to rough him up a little?"

"I have a boyfriend who'll be glad to do that."

"But I can't get arrested for it. How about I make sure he falls down a few times when nobody's looking?"

"I'd appreciate that."

I had to drive all the way back to Sunset to find a phone. There were no stores in the Brackers' neighborhood, no corner phone booths. And even for a stretch after I reached Sunset, the drugstores and shops had long since closed. Finally, I spotted a booth outside a gas station open late. As I pulled in, the green-uniformed attendant hustled out, rag in hand, ready to fill it up and check my oil. I waved him off, pulled past and up to the booth. I slipped into it, closed the door, and sat down. I took a nickel out of my change purse, dropped it into the slot, and dialed. Peter answered on the first ring.

"Where are you?" he demanded the second he heard my voice. "I heard a car pull away, I saw your car. Are you at home?"

"I need to talk to you."

"I'll come there," he said.

"I'm not at home. I have to talk to you. But if there's someone there—"

"There won't be anyone here."

CHAPTER 11

As I pulled into the driveway, he came out onto the porch and stood under its light, waiting for me. He was in shirtsleeves, the same clothes I'd seen earlier. I walked silently past him and under the wide flat arch into his living room. I'd expected it to smell like perfume. More precisely, cheap perfume.

"You want a drink?" he asked.

"That would be all right," I said, crisply, not looking at him. "A brandy, something warm."

He went through the small dining room and into the kitchen. In my peripheral vision, I saw him glance back at me.

The living room was plain, well kept, not much lived in. There was a sofa of beige and green Tattersall. A coffee table. A wood-trimmed side chair upholstered in a nubby brown, with a magazine rack on one side, a lamp table on the other. A bookcase with horizontal framed-glass doors, the kind lawyers use. A floor model radio. A sturdy desk.

He returned from the kitchen, carrying the brandy.

"Sit down." He nodded toward the sofa.

I sat down in the chair.

"Why'd you drive off?" he said.

"What was I supposed to do, barge in here and humiliate myself? No, thank you. I have to talk to you. And it's not about that."

His shoulders moved back. Just an inch. How attuned I was to him, to what he was thinking that I could tell he wasn't responding to the tone of my voice but to what he was seeing in my face. He knew something bad had happened.

He set the brandy on the side table, dragged over the ottoman and sat down in front of me.

"What is it?" he said, quietly. His hand moved instinctively, hovered over mine. When I didn't pull mine back, he gathered it in both of his. And with his touch, I started to cry in jerking, brittle sobs.

"Take a breath. Nice and slow." He picked up the brandy and gave it to me, holding on till he was sure I had a firm grip. He kept my other hand in his. "Take a sip, let it settle. Okay. One more, slowly. Good. A few more breaths."

"Mary Ann McDowell's dead. I saw her. She's dead. The police said she was shot in the face."

"They shouldn't have let you see that."

"They didn't."

"Take a few more breaths, then tell me what happened. I called your house. Juanita said you were at a party."

"At Ben Bracker's. He's the head of Epic. I had a meeting with him today."

"Take a little more, then when you're ready, start at the beginning."

I went back and told him about my entire day, my meeting with Bracker, my visit from Roland Neale at my Epic bungalow, my meeting with Mary Ann and her mother at Madison's. I skipped over my trip to his house and told him about the party, about going to Roland's, the trail of smeared blood from his shoes, what he said, then about my going out onto the porch and seeing the body, Mack Pace grabbing me, and the police showing up before he could do anything. "I was afraid he was there to clean everything up, and that it meant me, too."

"That's a long way to go, even for him. It's one thing to get rid of evidence, even move a body, but another to kill a witness.

What time does Costello want to see you tomorrow?"

"Someone's going to call my house." I glanced at the clock on the bookcase. It was just past eleven. It seemed much, much later. I pulled my hand from his. "I have to go to the studio in the morning and pick up the work I did on the script. They won't need it now. I don't want to leave it there."

"You should stay here tonight."

"I'm all right to drive."

He didn't move. I couldn't get up unless he did. He said, "If you go home, I'll follow you, and I'll stay there. You're not going to be alone."

"I won't sleep in that bed."

"Nothing happened," he said.

"She came out of your bedroom."

"She came out of the *bathroom*. She'd been crying, and she was fixing herself up. She's seeing some guy. He's got a good job, a factory foreman, and he treats her well. Not all the men she's known have done that. But she's worried maybe he's too good to be true. Maybe he's got a wife and five kids somewhere. She asked me if I could find out, before she gets her heart broken. She doesn't know who else to ask."

"She couldn't ask her boss to help?"

"He'd just ask me to do it. You've seen the men who work for Ray Elizondo. Most of what they do, they don't need to be subtle. If you were the guy, and you found out some gangsters were asking questions about you, it might change your mind about Lily. She doesn't want to risk that."

He took my hand again, and I let him.

"I've been with a lot of women, you've known that all along. Lily was one of them. I think you knew that too. From the beginning, I knew what kind of woman you were, what you'd expect. I didn't know if I could toe the line. But if I wasn't going to try, I wasn't going to lie to you. I wouldn't have started this. Have I looked at women since I met you? Yes. Have I had thoughts? Yes. Tonight, I thought about it. But it was a thought, that's all. We're a long shot, you and me. I'm not going to do anything to make the odds longer."

He pressed my hand to his lips.

"I only went there for a drink," I said.

"But maybe thinking about a little revenge with Roland Neale?"

"It was just a thought. I had a crush on him when I was sixteen. After what I saw in here, I wanted a man to pay attention to me, a lot of attention. Anything else, though, I wouldn't have felt better, I knew that."

"You should get some rest. If you'd rather go home, I'll follow you out."

"I'll call Juanita, tell her I'll be here. I have clothes in the car, what I was wearing today. I'll need to wash out some things."

"You can hang them in the bathroom, they should dry. If they don't, there's a heater in there you can use tomorrow. I don't have a spare toothbrush."

"That's good."

"No nightgowns either. I could loan you pajamas."

CHAPTER 12

They were cotton flannel, blue with a light-gray stripe, laid out on the taut chenille bedspread, next to a burgundy bathrobe, a winter one of lightweight wool. I took off my dress and hung it away in his well-ordered closet on the wooden hanger he'd given me. I took off my slip, then sat down on the bed and rolled off my stockings, unclipped the garter belt, the bra. I could hear him moving around in the kitchen, the refrigerator door opening, maybe checking to see if he had enough eggs, bacon, and bread to feed two people in the morning.

I slipped into his robe and went down the hall to the bathroom. I cleaned my teeth with his brush, then washed out my stockings and panties with the tablet of soap from the bathtub dish while my bath ran. I rolled them in a towel and squeezed the water out, then hung them over the towel bar. I removed my makeup with a warm cloth and a bit of soap.

There was no night cream, so I made do with a few dots of the Basswood men's hand cream I found in the cabinet. Peter sometimes needed to pass himself off as a man who'd never worked with his hands, after spending much of his youth loading crates of illegal booze and doing other manual labor jobs for Ramon Elizondo during the tail end of Prohibition. Work he did so he could feed four sisters and a brother. I was at Vassar, the niece of a wealthy man.

We were a long shot.

I slipped out of the robe and tied up my hair in its belt, since there was no shower cap. I sank into the bathwater and soaped and rinsed and soaped again, washing away all traces of the sweat of fear. I sipped the rest of the brandy, then dried off and padded barefoot back to the bedroom. He'd brought in my clothes and makeup case from my car. The clothes were hung away, the case on the dresser. I slipped into the pajama top and climbed into the bed, which he'd turned down while I was bathing. I took the left side, the one I always took when I was with him.

He came in, dressed now in his pajamas. "You want the window open?"

"Yes." I liked a cool room when I slept. We both did.

"It might go down to the forties. There's a blanket here, if you want it. If you need anything else, just let me know."

"Aren't you staying in here?" I asked.

"Do you want me to?"

"Yes."

"You should sleep."

"She was only nineteen."

He slipped in beside me, switched off the light, and held me till I slept.

I woke up just after eight to the smell of coffee and bacon. Sometime during the night, Peter had spread the blanket over me. The chilled morning air lifted the curtains and wafted over the room. My nose was cold.

On my night table, Peter had set out a pair of white socks, the sort men wear when they exercise. I pulled them on and folded them down around my ankles before putting my feet on the floor. I slipped into his wool robe, closed the window, shuffled to the bathroom, and turned on the heater set in the wall by the door. The coils began to glow. They were too late to heat the toilet seat.

My panties and stockings were almost dry. I found a ladder-back chair in the second bedroom, draped the items over it, and set it a safe distance from the heater. I brushed my teeth, combed my hair, and went into the kitchen.

Sun streamed over the black and white tiles and glass-covered cabinets. Peter stood at the stove, taking bacon from an iron frying pan, still in pajamas and robe.

I poured a cup of coffee from the percolator and watched him finish making breakfast, frying me an egg over easy and two scrambled for him, then adding the bacon and a couple of slices of toast fresh from the oven to each plate.

"There's nothing on the radio yet," he said as he set my plate in front of me.

"Maybe they decided he could be innocent."

He sat down. "The Chief's letting Epic get their publicity together before they announce anything. This is a company town. They'll give them a few daylight hours. But not many, or the reporters will get it themselves, and the Chief will have to explain why." He scraped butter over his toast, then cleaned his knife by inserting it into the side of the slice. "I'll follow you over to Epic. You're not going by yourself, not if there's a chance Pace could be there. I don't want them trying to get you to adjust your testimony. We'll get the script and be on our way."

"It's not a script. It's just a bunch of ideas. A script would belong to them. Ideas belong to me. They don't have to see them. I don't know what's going to happen. The whole loan-out might be cancelled."

"We'll get what you need, then find out where the cops want you to go for your statement, probably downtown to Homicide. I don't know how long they'll keep you." He speared a bit of egg and bacon, chewed, then swallowed some coffee.

"If he's innocent, he needs help," I said.

"I couldn't work for Neale's lawyer, if that's what you mean.

My job would be to help Neale, even if I ended up believing the guy was guilty. How would you feel if I helped get him off, and he killed her? The cops might not be able to charge Pace with anything. He was found at the scene, but they probably can't prove he destroyed evidence. Epic will ask you not to press charges against him for roughing you up."

"I wouldn't anyway. It would just get my name in the papers."

Reporters from all over the country would be swarming over town, looking for a part of this story no one else had. Would someone tip them? Lauren Atwill was there. Wasn't she working on some other movies when people died? It would take just one story—The Unlucky Lady—even if it was tucked inside.

"Eventually," he said, "I'll have a talk with Pace about what he did to you last night."

It gave me some comfort that Pace would spend weeks, maybe months, looking over his shoulder.

We took both our cars and parked them in the lot down the street from Epic and walked back to the gate.

There was no crowd of grieving fans yet with flowers or Bibles in hand. No slow parade of cars being waved along by police officers, the cars stopping long enough to disgorge flocks of girls with their Brownie cameras, rushing to get a shot of Mary Ann's smiling face on the poster by the gate. The guard hadn't been told either. He still had his wide grin in place as he waved us through.

It was a crisp, brilliant day, with a stiff steady breeze down from the mountains. I thought I could smell the mountain laurel. We walked to my bungalow through the teeming activity of a studio morning, just like any other. Racks of costumes, bars of lights, and loaded hand trucks being rolled to their destinations. Flocks of extras, scurrying errand boys, and script girls. Men in suits, heads bent in serious conversation. The sea parted for the famous ones. Not for us.

There was only one sign that the studio was about to be shaken by scandal: in front of my bungalow stood Herb, the bald-headed minion who'd shown it to me the day before. His shirt was as crisp as yesterday. He wore a different bowtie. Mr. Gettleman would like me to call him right away, he said. It was urgent. I said I would. He handed me a brown-paper-wrapped package. I stared at it stupidly, then he reminded me I'd asked him to get me a second copy of *The Hard Fold* and some other items. Of course, thank you, I said. He nodded and left.

I unlocked my bungalow. The chair Roland Neale had used still sat at the end of my desk. But the janitor had been in during the night; my trash can was empty.

Peter glanced around, stuck his head into the tiny bathroom. Force of habit. Always check the layout.

I sat down and unlocked the desk drawer with my lock pick. It took the blink of an eye. It wasn't much of a lock, but I was also a pretty good lock-picker. Even better than Peter, by his own admission. I gathered the pages I'd worked on yesterday and tucked them into my pocketbook. I slipped the pick in after them. There was a rough outline and several snatches of possible dialogue. The studio would consider it all their property, if they knew it existed. Bracker might want me to finish the story idea, to see if he could tailor it to another couple. I might end up writing the picture for someone else. If he didn't, and the loan-out was cancelled, the story was mine, the way I figured it.

There was a knock on the door. Quickly, I put my handbag on the floor.

"Come in," I said.

"Oh, hi there! You're here!"

Mary Ann McDowell stood beaming at me in the doorway.

CHAPTER 13

I just sat there, staring and snatching shallow breaths.

She said, "Grace gave me your bungalow number. Mr. Bracker's secretary. I thought I'd take a chance you were—What's wrong?"

Peter stepped forward. "You must be Miss McDowell," he said smoothly. "I'm Peter Winslow. We're glad you're all right."

"I'm sorry?" she said.

"Someone called Mrs. Atwill this morning and said they'd heard you were in an accident last night, in your car."

"I'm fine. Why would anyone say that?"

"You know Hollywood. Nothing stops a rumor, not even the truth." He glanced at me. By that time, I'd recovered somewhat. "Please, sit down," he said to her.

"Thanks, but I just dropped by for a second. I have to get some pictures taken today. Look, no puffiness," she said to me, and raised her eyebrows, making her eyes even larger and more luminous. And comical. "I got a good night's sleep."

"Good for you," I said, smiling. I could still hear faint rasping in my breathing.

"Mr. Bracker told me about the script this morning. Such a scandalous book. Mama will go crazy when she finds out."

"I'll have to write a new character for you."

"Yes, he said. Goodness, I hope so. I've got to run. Nice to meet you, Mr. Winslow."

And she was gone. Peter closed the door.

I said, "I was so sure."

I reached for the phone to call Gettleman.

"Don't call anybody," Peter said. "Get your things. Let's go."

From Epic, Holmby Hills was ten minutes away in late-morning traffic. More like five, the way Peter normally drives. We took my car, because a Lincoln would be less likely to attract attention parked on the curb in that neighborhood. Peter parked at the end of the walking lane, not far from where my car had been parked the night before. We got out and headed down the gray-dust lane, past the backyards, then the Brackers' gate. No one stopped us. Certainly not the police.

Even Roland Neale's back gate didn't resist.

Peter went in first. We ducked beneath the fronds of the banana plants and waited before stepping out of their shelter. Nothing stirred. There was no sound at all except for the soft rustle of the breeze in the high branches and a distant wicking of sprinklers in someone else's yard.

Then we followed the paving around to the cabana, just as I had done the night before.

There were no shoe prints. Not on the paving, not on the steps. The white planks were pristine.

We continued around to the far side of the cabana, to the small patio. There was no body between the pots of flowers and no sign there ever had been.

My heart began to beat sharply. My upper arms tingled painfully with electricity.

"Where was she?" Peter asked.

I pointed to the spot. He crouched on the paving and inspected the gray-green stone, then stood up and dug in the soil of the pots with his fingers, examining the dirt. Then he went over and studied the banana plants and the grass at the edge of the paving.

He took out a handkerchief, wiped his hands.

My legs shivered. I couldn't catch my breath.

He looked over at me, then shoved the handkerchief into his pocket. He grabbed my arm. "Lauren."

"I know what I saw," I said.

"Come here. Look at this. The grass is wet, you see that? Flooded. Somebody washed down the pavement and used a lot of water to do it. And these flowers: this pot's soaked but not the ones further back. And these branches are about a foot shorter than the others. Freshly pruned. All they needed was a garden hose and some time. And something to wrap the body in. You didn't imagine it, and I never thought you did. Come on. We're getting out of here."

He held onto my arm tightly, all the way back to the car. He climbed behind the wheel and shoved the key into the ignition. At the next intersection, he U-turned sharply, driving back the way we'd come, curving north, past the golf course, his eyes keeping close watch on the rear-view mirror, till we reached Sunset.

He said, "You feeling better?"

"A little. I couldn't stop it."

"But you did, look at you." He glanced down at my hands. They weren't shaking anymore. There was still a soft tremor moving through my body, but there was no outward sign.

He ran a yellow light, signaled, changed lanes, and gunned past a car that made the mistake of obeying the speed limit.

I said, "It was like last night. Almost as bad."

He said, "I'm surprised it hasn't happened before, the things you've seen the last few months."

"So it could happen again?"

"It could. You'll be in a place like it, or it might just be a smell, a sound, and it'll come back on you. But after a while, you'll understand what's happening and why. And once you do, you can be ready for it. You can't stop it, but you'll figure out how to handle it."

The late-morning traffic suddenly clogged the way, and we slowed down. I dropped my visor, rolled down my window all the way, and took a few breaths of the settling smog. The mid-day air was growing heavy, holding close to the ground, and the wind was carrying the acrid scent from east of town. Some people said it was the refineries; some, the factories, the meat packing plants; some said the cars. Some said it was topography. If LA didn't have so many canyons, we wouldn't have smog.

It had never occurred to me what I'd dragged Peter back into, beginning last summer. He wasn't a policeman, never had been. It wasn't his job to step over the horror lying in a doorway, the sprawled reminder of what human beings could do to each other, to get into a room where there was even worse. Not till the war.

I could only begin to imagine what he'd seen during four years in the Pacific, what he'd done, what he'd had to do. He'd never tell me. For the first time, I wondered if his eyes had looked like that before the war.

He'd come home, a decorated hero, and gone back to his life. Then he met me, and it started again.

"Those bastards," I said. "A woman died, and Gettleman shows up with a sack full of cash, and it all just goes away."

"It would have to be a lot of cash for cops to take the risk, knowing a witness had seen it all, and she might not be as easy to buy off as Mack Pace. A witness who knows the Assistant DA. They might rearrange evidence, invent a story for Neale, but get rid of the body?"

"They did it."

"Were they cops?"

"What? Costello had to be—The way he talked. And his badge. Is it crazier that cops would take a bribe than that two men would show up out of nowhere pretending to be cops and sweep it all away?"

"I don't know what happened except you saw a dead woman, and now she's gone."

"We know she was shot, and in the head," I said. "The other cop said she was, and at that point he had no idea I hadn't seen the body up close."

"I have to go talk to Pace," he said.

"I want to go with you. I promise to do what you tell me. Unless it would put you in danger, I'd like to go with you."

"He'll be expecting us."

"I know."

The guard at Epic directed us to Pace's office, in a stucco building with striped awnings just inside the front gate. The reception area was a tight square, with four wooden armchairs, two on each side, each pair separated by a small table with a couple of dog-eared magazines. There was a tall metal ash can, the sand undisturbed. Straight ahead, behind a varnished counter, was a switchboard cabinet with a row of message boxes above it.

The girl behind the front desk looked up as Peter cleared the door. She wasn't a girl, really. She had stern gray hair finger-waved in precise rows all the way back to a thin, neat bun on her neck. Not a hair had been twisted out of place by her switchboard headset.

"Mr. Winslow?" she said before Peter could open his mouth.

Peter said he was indeed Mr. Winslow. He didn't take off his hat. He needed both hands free.

"I'll tell Mr. Pace you're here." She pulled a cord from the switchboard base and plugged it into the hole for the destination phone. She whispered Peter's name into the mouthpiece of her headset.

"Straight back," she said, "all the way at the end of the hall."

The hallway had new green linoleum, smelling of wax. Pace's door had a pebbled glass panel with his name painted on it, in the lower right corner. Peter put me behind him and knocked. Then he turned the knob and pushed the door fully open. He stayed where he was, tucked to the frame, his right shoulder leaned on it, left shoulder back, his hand inside his jacket.

Pace was in.

His gun was out.

Over Peter's right shoulder, I could see him. He had a revolver, holding it lightly, not pointing it at us, just letting Peter know it was there.

"If I wanted to ambush you," Peter said, "I could have done that somewhere else. And I wouldn't bring Mrs. Atwill along."

"She here?" He craned his neck to see me.

"Not till that goes in the desk," Peter said.

"Why don't we give it some company?" said Pace.

Peter went in, took his gun out of his shoulder holster, and laid it in the open desk drawer. Pace added his revolver and closed the drawer.

I came in then and shut the door. Peter motioned me to one of the chairs, took the other one, pulling it around the side of the desk so he could watch Pace's hands.

Pace said, "I didn't rough her up, whatever she's telling you."

I said, "It might be a good idea to hear what I told him first, especially since, as you know, Mr. Winslow's likely to take my word over anyone else's anyway. I told him you grabbed me, put me in the cabana, and wouldn't let me leave."

Pace's top lip curled up sourly. He was angrier at me than Peter about what had happened months ago, even though Peter's putting his head into a file cabinet hadn't been my idea. I'd been there, and if there was ever trouble and a woman was around, she usually ended up getting blamed for it.

"I had no idea who she was till I got her inside," he said to

Peter. "It was dark. I got there, I saw something that looked like blood on the steps. I heard something down the porch, around the corner. I go to take a look, and some dame runs right into me. It's dark. She could have had a gun for all I knew."

"Once you knew who it was," Peter said, "you didn't encourage her to leave."

"I had a job to do, and that was to find out what the hell was going on and make sure Roland Neale didn't talk to anybody. That meant finding out what he'd told *her* before I got there. Then the cops showed up."

"But they weren't cops, were they?" Peter said.

"They looked real enough to me. Real enough to her, too. You can get the hell out of here. I got no idea who they were."

"I'm inclined to believe you," Peter said.

"I don't give a damn." He glared at Peter a moment longer, then rolled his shoulders and leaned back in his chair. But he kept his hands on the arms, elbows squared, as if ready to jump up for a fight. He said, "I was here, right here, last night, working late. You can ask the night guard on the gate what time I left if you want. Joe Gettleman called me. He told me to get over to Roland Neale's fast. Something had happened. Some girl might be dead out in his backyard. I did. I saw the light on down in the cabana, I went down there, I saw the blood on the porch. That's when I heard *her.*" He jerked his head toward me.

I said, "Mr. Gettleman was at the party. Why didn't *he* come over?"

He ignored me. "That guy, Costello," he said to Peter. "After she left, he put me up in the house, locked me in a room, told me I'd be lucky if I didn't end up in jail, and that I should sit and think that over. He comes back after a while, gives me some coffee, says maybe it's not so bad as he thought. It might be a suicide. I drink the coffee, it's got brandy in it. I figure I know what he's up to: get me drunk enough to talk. Next thing

I know, the room's spinning, then I wake up on the floor breathing carpet dust.

"I find Roland Neale, passed out, too, in the kitchen, in his socks. They took his shoes. I wake him up. I found a flashlight, and we went down to the cabana. It's empty. The steps are clean. I throw some light around, go down to that little patio because that's where *she* said the body was. Nothing. I call Joe. Before I can say a word, Joe starts screaming about why I hadn't called him, why the *police* had to call him to tell him it's all some practical joke."

Peter said, "It wasn't cops who called him."

"I told him that. It only made him madder. He said the next time somebody plays a fucking practical joke on one of Epic's stars, he wants me to pull their balls right up their throat. Hey, she didn't have to come, so if she doesn't like my language, she can go sit with Edna."

I said, "I'm fine where I am."

"Did you ask Roland Neale who the girl was?" Peter said.

"My boss told me it was a practical joke. You been over there?"

"Yes."

"You see anything? A single trace of anything? Roland Neale's been around a long time, and he's not been all that careful about the women he plays around with. For all I know, maybe there's a husband out there with enough money that he can spend some of it on revenge. I wouldn't put it past some of the bastards in this town. For all I know it was some sick, fucking prank." He shoved the phone at Peter. "Why don't *you* call the cops? Why doesn't *she*? Because she's got nothing. Except a reputation for being around when people die. If she causes trouble for Roland Neale and this studio, she'll never get another job. She knows that. *You* know that. Take your damn gun, and get the fuck out of my office!" Pace yanked open the drawer and shoved his chair back. "Take it!"

Peter stood up, slowly, pulled the Colt from the drawer and slipped it into his holster.

"You two want to get into this," Pace said, "be my guest, but I like working. I like breathing. So keep me the hell out of it. But if it *wasn't* some sick prank, maybe you ought to think about this: they know who you are, Mrs. Atwill. And if they know you, they know him. And they'll be ready for both of you."

CHAPTER 14

Edna watched us all the way out. It wasn't often her boss's meetings ended with him yelling at his visitors to get out and take their gun with them.

When we hit the pavement, Peter said, "We need to talk, and not around here."

"Swell. You've got more bad news and want me sitting down."

"After we talk, I have to go back to work."

"Me, too, since the leading lady is still alive."

"I meant I can't do anything about this today. You have to leave it alone."

"I knew what you meant."

"Okay, then, let's go." He offered his arm, and I took it. It was the first time I'd ever held his arm in Hollywood. One of the many little things we never did in public.

"Where are we going?" I asked.

He said, "The sort of place I go. It's called Rocco's."

We reclaimed his car from the lot and headed east. But I figured we weren't going all the way downtown just so Peter could show me the sort of thing I'd be in for when we started going out in public.

I didn't know how much money Peter made. I knew what his agency charged for his investigation services—as I'd paid a couple of their whopping bills. But how much of that he got to keep, I had no idea. He had frugal habits, a small house, a nice, though not extravagant, car and wore good suits. But I had a million dollars in stocks and bonds, and more in some properties, all set up to keep earning tax-free money till I had to touch it, which I rarely had since my husband and I separated. When I wasn't paying detective bills to help solve murders, I too, was frugal. At least frugal by Hollywood standards.

Rocco's was on Vine, maybe a five-minute drive from Peter's house—the way Peter drove—a place he probably stopped to eat dinner a few nights a week and maybe got some breakfast, when he didn't have the time or inclination to cook.

It had two wide front windows, fairly clean, with faded, red-checked cafe curtains hanging in them from brass rings. The wall beneath the windows still had spaces in the brick where rubber tiles had been removed to use in making military tires during the war. In one of the windows hung a neon sign, announcing *Rocco's.* There were hand-printed signs in the corner of the window. One said BREAKFAST ANYTIME; the other, MUSICA ITALIANA OGNI SABATO NOTTE.

We went in. To the left was the kitchen pass-through, from which poured the clatter of metal pans and the commands of someone in charge, in spirited Italian. In front of the pass-through, a counter ran to the back wall. A few patrons, all in coverall uniforms, were hitched on the counter stools. A waitress in a blue cotton dress and bibbed apron was filling their coffee cups. Next to the pass-through a metal-framed black felt-board hung on the wall. Another waitress was working on the lunch specials, using white, stick-in plastic letters she was picking out of a shallow, sectioned cardboard box.

The walls were paneled in pine, aged in years of cigarette smoke, frying oils, and garlic and decorated with photographs of ancient cities, breathtaking countryside, and famous Italian entertainers. The pressed tin ceiling had caught everything that hadn't soaked into the wood. Around the warped wooden floor was a horseshoe of booths fitted with wrought iron sconces of rippled, yellow-tinted glass; in the center, a couple of rows of stout wooden tables. It was only just after eleven. We were early for lunch, so a booth was free. Peter hung his hat on a hook on the rack at the end of the booth.

The plump little brunette working on the specials board stopped sticking in letters to give me the eye before she picked up two glasses of water and headed our way. She set down the glasses and glanced at my left hand. I realized she was looking at my wedding ring. Peter had no ring, but a lot of married men didn't wear bands. Was she wondering if I was his wife? I could imagine Peter had created plenty of interest among the waitresses, as a regular customer. A good-looking guy without a wedding ring and with a steady job that paid enough for him to wear nice suits. He wasn't Italian, maybe not Catholic, but he was almost certainly an American citizen.

Peter ordered coffee for both of us, and she brought two mugs.

I didn't really want any more coffee, but I poured in some milk from the little stainless steel pitcher. The color in the mug hardly changed. I took a sip. It was far stronger than what I normally would make. Than what Juanita would normally make *for* me.

Without looking at the menu in the rack beneath the sconce, Peter ordered an Italian ham sandwich, extra peppers. And could she wrap it up for him to take with him. She was happy to do that. He looked over at me, to see what he should order for me. "Nothing right now," I said to him.

When she had gone, I said, "I'll go back to Marathon and work in my office there today. I can get something quick, from Madison's, but later. I'm not hungry."

"It's okay," he said. "I didn't think you were turning up your nose at the food."

"Good, because I don't really want the coffee either." I slid the mug away. "Am I going to need bodyguards again? Is that what you sat me down to tell me?"

"Costello didn't get rid of witnesses last night, when he had the chance. And, by now, you could have gone to the real police, and they'd have a sketch of him. Still, I'd feel better if you were over at Marathon and you didn't drive around alone."

He pulled a cigarette case from inside his jacket. Then he took a look at his hands, at the dirt still under his nails from digging in Roland's flower pot, and set the case down. "I'll be right back." He went off through a door just to the right of the counter.

While he was gone, I did some more thinking about why Costello would show his face and not care. Maybe because, with the kind of work he did, the people he ran into were more than willing to keep their mouths shut. The kind of work he did was usually done by gangsters.

Could he be a real detective, doing a little work on the side for gangsters? The Los Angeles police department's reputation was none too clean, and I'd had some personal experience with how dirty it was. But I'd also seen plenty of character and, in the case of one detective, even a willingness to put a career on the line.

When Peter came back, I said, "Maybe I should go talk to Sergeant Barty."

"There's no such thing as telling a cop about a killing unofficially."

"I still have to call Joe Gettleman, return his call. By now, he'll know his message to call him was delivered, in person. What do I say?"

"Pietro! My friend, how are you?" A man came toward us from the swinging door to the kitchen, both arms outstretched. He was short, with a proud crop of dark hair, immaculately groomed, a cook's hat perched on top of it. He had a good-sized, high-bridged nose and a good-sized middle under his apron.

Peter stood up. "Sir," he said.

"Two weeks, I don't see you. Carmine is making you best sandwich. Ah, who is beautiful lady?"

Peter introduced us. "Mrs. Atwill, this is Rocco Spinelli."

The man bowed over my hand, his dark eyes glowing. It was always refreshing to run into Italian men of a certain age. They had no compunction about admiring women past thirty-five, but they didn't make pests of themselves.

He said, "Come back tonight, and I make you sausage and peppers, come fresh today from cousin's farm."

"That would be lovely," I said, "but I'm not sure I'm free."

"Good. You try. I will not disturb you more. It was good to meet you, beautiful lady." He gave Peter a hearty slap on the shoulder, then said softly, "Pauly's good, good. Chin is up."

And he was gone.

Peter sat down. Quickly, he took a cigarette out of his case and lit it, using the matchbook in the tray. He tossed the match in the tray and took a pull on the cigarette, turned aside and blew the smoke in a long exhale while he stared out the window.

Then he said, "Pauly Spinelli. That's his son. Paul Spinelli. Ring a bell?"

"No."

"He's doing five to seven in San Quentin." He continued to stare out the window. "He'd been in some trouble: skipping school, he and some friends stole a couple of cars for some joyriding. A few break-ins, but never any rough stuff. New Year's Eve, a year ago, a patrol cop spotted him running out of an alley downtown and stopped him. The kid was scared, but not just of the cop. And he didn't have a very good story for where he'd been. The cop called in another car, and just up the alley, they found a broken rear window to a doctor's office. Inside,

119

they found the doctor shot dead at his desk. All the cabinets were opened, drugs gone. The kid's fingerprints were inside, though not on the cabinets or around the dead man. Still, the DA had himself an open-and-shut case, plenty of good publicity. A dirty little Italian thief who'd killed a doctor. Plenty of jury sympathy there.

"Rocco hired a lawyer, and the lawyer hired me. I found out the good doctor had been dead a few hours. The ambulance guys couldn't get him out of his chair, because of the rigor. They had to call the fire department to come cut the chair. The fire department was glad to hand over copies of their report to me. What the hell? That was before anybody told them to keep their mouths shut.

"We started asking for things, like to get the jacket tested to see if the kid had fired a gun, and the jacket disappeared. It wasn't on the evidence sheet. It was a nice, clean, fresh form, with the neatest handwriting I'd ever seen on an evidence sheet. It was an easy case, and they weren't going to lose it. Even if the grieving widow had a boyfriend with a pretty flimsy alibi. She was rich, her father knew the right people. But the cops couldn't get rid of everything. I found a photographer, one of those guys who troll crime scenes. He was the first guy there after the cops. He had a picture of Pauly wearing his jacket. In all the others, they'd already taken it, for evidence.

"Once Pauly's lawyer had the picture, the prosecutor offered five to seven for involuntary manslaughter. Otherwise, he'd go to trial. They'd ask for the death penalty, and Pauly was scared to take his chances. Maybe they'd find that jacket. You can bet it would have gun powder on it if it reappeared. The coroner would say the fire department didn't know a damned thing about rigor.

"Pauly's lawyer promised the prosecutors not to make anything I found public if the prosecutors agreed to parole at three years. The kid'll settle down, work for his father or a family friend. I couldn't get him off, but Rocco knows his boy's innocent. His family knows, his friends. It's something." He threw some more ash toward the tray. "Unlike you, I don't always catch the bad guy."

"You can't control the prosecutor, the police."

"If you go to the cops, even if you could get them to go out there to Roland Neale's house, what are they going to find? And Epic will make sure Pace's story makes it sound like a sick prank. You think Neale's going to admit there was a dead woman in his backyard? Besides, you said yourself he might be innocent. You said the blood was only on the soles of his shoes. We got no idea who did this."

A tableful of girls came in—maybe shop girls, maybe typists—and shimmied into chairs at the table beside us. They couldn't have been much out of high school, but their lips had been refreshed in bright red before they left wherever they worked. One of them spotted Peter, and then all four spent some time sneaking peeks over their menus and giggling at their subterfuge.

I dropped my voice, although I doubted they were paying any attention at all to me. "We know Roland didn't kill her after I saw him leave the party. There wasn't enough time between his leaving and my finding the body for anyone to have put that whole charade together. And he couldn't have killed her before he came to the party or during the party. If he was cold-blooded enough to behave like nothing happened, he wouldn't have forgotten to tell me not to come over. He wouldn't have fallen apart when he got back home, he wouldn't have stepped in the blood, and he wouldn't have got Gettleman and Pace involved. But he knew her. He said, 'I wouldn't have hurt her.' Not something you say about a stranger."

"No," Peter said.

"Why would the killer arrange to move the body when he could frame Roland?"

"It's not that easy to frame people who have money. But I think the answer is, whoever she was, the killer didn't want her body found. Not in the yard, not anywhere. She's someone who could be traced to the killer."

"If she's from Holmby Hills or if she was a guest at the Brackers' party, she'll be reported missing. We have to talk to Roland."

Suddenly, Peter crushed his cigarette. "No, we don't. Asking him who that girl was isn't going to help anybody, especially not you. We've got no idea what this is. The killer can find a guy like Costello and make a body disappear. You think he hasn't done it before? You think he won't do it again, if he has to? Goddamn it, leave it alone! You don't have to risk your life because you found another body!"

I stared at the table top, my cheeks flushing. A bit of ash from his cigarette had flown out of the tray with the force of his crushing the butt. One spark glowed hotly in front of me, then died. The girls at the next table stopped giggling. They couldn't have heard what he said, but his expression was enough.

He paid the check, and we left. I didn't take his arm on the way to the car, and I yanked open my own door and slammed it shut. When he'd settled under the wheel, I said, "I won't be ordered around in public."

"Nobody heard me."

"They *saw* you."

"Damn it, Lauren. The first thing you do is try to fix it, whatever it is. Not everything can be fixed. And it sure as hell isn't worth your life trying to prove it can." He shoved the key into the ignition and turned the engine over. He gripped the knob of the gear shift. "We're not going to fight about this. You're going to leave it alone. You're going to call Gettleman back, and whatever story he tells you, you let him tell it."

He drove to his house, and I called Gettleman. I held the receiver from my ear, enough for Peter to hear, with our heads nearly together.

"Forgive me, Mrs. Atwill," Gettleman said stiffly when his secretary put me through, "but I believe the boy made clear my request for you to call me was urgent."

"I thought it best if I returned your call from a place where I was sure I wouldn't be overheard. I didn't know how thin the walls are at Epic, or whether the operators listen in. Perhaps I was overly cautious."

"Well, yes, then, that was the proper thing to do. Yes. Well, let me say Mr. Bracker and I are appalled by what happened last night. Apparently, this was some sort of vicious trick. We attempted to telephone you this morning, but you were not at home. Mr. Pace has told me that he has since seen you and informed you of this. No one was actually injured. And those men were not from the police."

"Yes," I said, "I understood that from Mr. Pace."

"He said there was someone with you today. A man. A private detective."

"The man is a friend," I said. "You can imagine after last night, my nerves were a bit shaken. Such a horrible joke for someone to play. Mr. Neale must be devastated. Is he all right?"

I raised a hand before Peter could give me a glare of warning.

Gettleman said, "He's going to be away for a while, to recover."

"Of course. I hope he's with loved ones who can take care of him."

"Yes, yes. I'm sure they will. You understand not a word of this must ever reach the public."

"Absolutely." I said. "It would be awful for everyone."

"This man . . ."

"He wouldn't do anything that would get me into the newspapers, Mr. Gettleman. I'm absolutely certain of that."

"And you must not say anything to anyone else, not even to friends. You never know whom they might tell, and it might be someone with no honor, who would offer the story to the gutter press for pay. This was an appalling thing, and we do not want it spread around."

"Of course."

He said good-bye. I was amazed how easily he thought a woman could be convinced she was wrong.

CHAPTER 15

Peter said, "I want to get a sketch of Costello. How about the other man, the other guy playing detective with him?"

"No, I didn't get a good enough look at his face. Now that I think about it, he stayed down on the steps, out of the light."

Peter flipped into an address book on his desk and called a number. Whoever answered was able to make an appointment, but not till seven. Peter said seven would be fine, at his office. He didn't consult me. He did say he'd pick me up at Marathon at six thirty and drive me downtown to his office.

He drove me to the Epic parking lot, where I picked up my car, then he followed me to Marathon Studios' gate. Once I was safely inside, he drove off, headed for his office downtown. He hadn't given me any more orders. But he hadn't apologized for his public temper either.

I didn't want to be disturbed. I locked my office door against visitors and laid out my script notes on the desk, along with everything else I'd gathered up hurriedly from my Epic bungalow. I unwrapped the package Herb had presented me but left everything lying on the brown paper: the art knife (with a small cork on the end to cover the blade), glue, ring binder, and a second copy of *The Hard Fold*. It was a second-hand copy, with dog-eared pages. That wouldn't matter. I was going to cut it up.

I put away my hat and handbag into the desk drawer. I sat down and rolled paper into the typewriter.

I wasn't going to get anything done.

A woman was dead, and I had to act like nothing had happened.

Her life had ended in terror and maybe pain. What if she hadn't died instantly? Perhaps she'd bled to death in horrible pain, only her killer with her, waiting for her to die. I had no idea what the dead woman looked like, how old she was. She was slim enough to make me think it could be Mary Ann, but that only meant she was probably under thirty. I'd seen her shoes, but how many pairs of evening slippers with diamante straps might have been sold since the end of the war, when such things were manufactured again?

Roland Neale knew her, had seemed to care about her. Still, he was so frightened of being accused of her murder that he didn't call the police. Despite his contention he would never have hurt her, he let others throw her away.

He had plenty to answer for. But I was inclined to think murder wasn't one of them.

Whoever she was, her disappearance was unlikely to get any public attention. Peter was right. If the killer didn't leave the body there to frame Roland, it was because the dead woman had some traceable connection to the killer. Yet she was somebody unlikely to be reported missing, or, if she were, it wouldn't make the papers. That meant she wasn't well-to-do or well connected.

She was probably one of the eager legion of young women who came to Hollywood for the glamour and fame and ended up as disposable as a movie poster.

She could be thrown away, and nobody would do anything.

Don't worry about the Atwill dame: she'll keep her mouth shut, if she knows what's good for her. There's nothing to find, and if she makes a stink, nobody'll ever hire her again, and she knows it.

Hollywood was the most superstitious town in America. There

was a reason psychics and mediums flourished here. Superstition always flourished where people were least in control of their fates. Where everything you had could be lost on the whim of the gods.

Or a studio boss.

Get a reputation for trouble. Never work again. Especially if you were a woman.

I picked up the copy of the novel. I started reading where I'd left off. I'd turned a few pages before I realized I couldn't recall a thing I'd just read.

I tried to imagine the next time I saw Roland Neale. What would I say? Hello, Roland. How nice to see you again. I'm so glad you liked the story treatment.

Loved ones.

When I asked Gettleman if Roland was all right, I'd chosen my words carefully. I hope he's with "loved ones," I'd said, not "friends." "Friends" could be the staff of his favorite hotel or a sanitarium, but you wouldn't call them "loved ones." Gettleman's response might well mean nothing. He might not have been paying any attention to my words, concentrating on convincing me to keep quiet. But maybe Roland was with "loved ones," although that could mean anything from a brother in Boston to a mother in Dubuque.

Most places east of Oklahoma would take four to six days by train round-trip. It was possible he'd flown somewhere—although it baffled me why anyone would get on an airplane for any reason. By now, he could be in New York, headed for Paris. He could be on his way to Argentina.

But Roland knew the woman was dead. He knew it was no prank. Wouldn't he want to be able to find out quickly whether his secret remained safe, without having to wait for the vagaries of newspapers, long-distance calling, or telegrams?

Maybe he was still in California.

Peter had told me to leave it alone. And he was right. Anyone who could summon Costello was dangerous indeed.

I'd talk this over with Peter first. I'd wait.

And I might have, too, except that Mickels, the scourge of the screenwriter, came calling.

Mickels never walked, he charged, so I recognized his shadow as it flew past the pebbled glass of my door. He rapped sharply on the glass of the door at the end of the hall and, without waiting for an answer, opened it. Then the door closed, and he charged back to mine. In the same motion, he rapped and turned the knob. And rammed the door with his face when it didn't open.

"One minute," I called out pleasantly, as if I hadn't seen his cheek splayed on the glass. I got up and unlocked the door. An assistant to the head of production, Mickels was square-shouldered, square-faced, and squarely determined that writers never waste a minute of the studio's money.

"I was looking for Linden," he announced. Bill Linden. The man to whom I owed my career. It was his office down the hall.

Time was Bill Linden might indeed have been in my office, lounging on my sofa, tossing out ideas or the latest gossip until he was ready to go back to work. But since the murder case at Christmas, things had been uneasy between us.

Mickels looked past me to my desk, perhaps searching for evidence of my toil—or lack of it. But I'd been loaned out, so he had nothing to say to me.

"I'm headed out to lunch," I said and retrieved my handbag.

"He's not in his office."

"I'm sorry. I don't know where he is," I said amiably. Other writers, Bill included, treated Mickels with disdain to his face. I didn't see the point in that. I'd never met anyone who changed for the better by being badly treated. "I can give you some paper, if you'd like to write him a message."

He snatched a pencil from the cup and tossed off a note. He folded the page and creased the fold sharply between the nails of his index finger and thumb. He did it again and again, his features moving around while he did it. I imagined he was trying to recall what ordinary people said in social exchanges like this. He finally remembered. "Thanks."

"Glad to help."

He charged out.

I refreshed my makeup in the small mirror by the coat rack while he thumped down to Bill's office. He must have slid the note under the door. I didn't hear it open. He charged back to the elevator. It wheezed and groaned its way up, and the elevator gate rattled and squeaked when the operator opened it. The gate closed, and Mickels was gone, back to his office.

If Mickels hadn't come calling, I wouldn't have been leaving my office and standing in the hall at the precise moment a shadow moved across the pebbled glass in Bill's door.

I went along down the hall and knocked. Silence.

"It's Lauren."

I didn't have time to consider the possibility he might still pretend to be gone.

"Good God, woman," he called out, "get in here."

Bill Linden was lying on the sofa, one leg up on its back, a pad of paper on his knee, the way he usually wrote his rough drafts, throwing down ideas in his slurred handwriting.

The filled pages had been ripped off and tossed aside, floating over the floor. Somehow this disorganization suited him. Having to search reams of scattered notes inspired him. Among the pages was a ripped-through sheet of typing paper, almost certainly Mickels's note.

"Close the door," he said, waving his pen. "You never know if he's lurking."

I did as I was told and moved away from the door so I

wouldn't cast a shadow on the glass. "Where were you hiding that he didn't see you?"

"I ducked under the desk when I heard him coming. He's so sure we're all napping, he never looks beyond the couch. How the hell are you?"

"Fine. How about you?"

"Good, good. I haven't picked a fight with anyone in at least a month, even Mickels. I heard about the loan-out. I'm sorry."

"It turns out, I might get to write a decent script. They're looking for something to break Mary Ann McDowell into adult roles."

"You don't say."

There was a silence. Maybe three seconds. It never would have happened to us before, so tuned were we to each other's rhythms. We had been so practically from the moment we met, when he'd decided I had talent and might be a cut above writing evaluations of books the studio was considering buying. He took me under his wing and to parties, introduced me to people. He was bright, witty, handsome, gifted. A man who took me seriously. It was meant to be, I'd decided. We'd be the perfect Hollywood marriage, I thought, when I still thought in such terms. But he fell in love with someone else, who happened to be my Uncle Bennett. And had loved Uncle Bennett till the day he died, riddled with cancer, the pain eased only because Bill was willing to go anywhere, do anything to get him enough morphine. He had died peacefully in his own bed, Bill holding one hand and I, the other.

"What are you working on?" I asked.

"They want me to do a prestige picture. A noble piece righting social injustice."

"Will they let you offend anyone while you're doing it?"

"Not a chance," he said. "With Congress calling us all commies? Surefire way to get their attention would be to say there's something wrong in America that can't be fixed with melodramatic dialogue and a good musical score." He sat up, tossing the pad to the floor. The gust of air it created scattered the loose pages further. "I'd offer you a drink, but I know it's too early for you. Grab a chair. What's up?"

I turned one of the hard chairs by his desk to face him. "I was wondering if you could help me."

"If you're looking for an idea, sadly, I can't recall the last time I had one."

"I just want to ask you about somebody," I said. "You know a lot of people."

"Indeed. If I ever have to work for a living, I can sell maps to the sins of the stars."

I laughed, like old times. "Do you know Roland Neale?"

"A bit. Not to be chummy with. Don't let him get too chummy with you, and he *will* try. I don't think Epic would appreciate it if Mr. Winslow punched him in his profile. He hasn't, has he—Rolly, I mean—tried to get chummy?"

"No, nothing like that," I assured him.

"Good," he said. "I saw Savannah's column today."

"What?"

"Haven't you seen it? It's around here somewhere."

I found his copy of the *Eagle* in the trash can, the only thing inside it. Any crumpled notes Bill had discarded lay like balls of yarn around his desk chair.

The column was pretty much what Savannah had quoted to me last night at the Brackers' party. Except for the other woman. And Roland Neale.

" 'My spies report Marathon star Frank Atwill is enjoying both the warm Caribbean sun down in Cuba and the company of young society lovely Judy Pritchard, daughter of Calvin Pritchard, as in Pritchard Steel. Frank's divorce from screenwriter Lauren Atwill is signed and sealed. But his soon-to-be-ex is still in his corner. Looking spectacular at a chic soiree tossed by Epic chief Ben Bracker last night, Lauren told me she and Frank are still great friends, and she wishes him all the best. Don't worry about that gal. She and Roland Neale—a catch with a capital *C*—were casting eyes at each other last night.' "

" 'Casting eyes'?" I said.

"She's not a grammarian. No truth there, about Rolly?" Bill asked.

"No, but I might be writing the script for him and Mary Ann."

"Rolly and Mary Ann McDowell? I'd like to see him try to get chummy with *her*. He'll have to figure out how to get past that battle-ax of a mother. She never lets that child go anywhere without a chaperone."

"Except to date Len Manning."

"Well, we both know she's in no danger there."

"I met the mother, and she's pushing for a marriage. She wants to get Mary Ann settled, she says. But I think it's because Len's a star."

"It would be a good thing for Len. He'd get a nice shot of publicity, then after the divorce he could claim a broken heart is keeping him from ever marrying again. Not so good for a good little girl, though. Her fans might not take to a divorce. She'd have to stay with him. What's this got to do with the script?" After a second, he hauled a heavy breath, a twist of pain in his eyes. "Lauren, I'm not ready for another adventure."

I'd never meant to hurt him, but back in December I had, because I stuck my nose into a murder uninvited, and things had not ended well for some people he knew. Since then, I'd rarely seen him. He'd graciously declined a couple of invitations to dinner.

"It is, isn't it?" he said. "You could have lied, made up a reason it was important to the script."

"I did, standing out in the hall, but then I just couldn't do it."

"What's Rolly Neale done to sic you on him?" he asked. "Something you can't tell me?"

"I shouldn't have come. I'm sorry."

"I'm going to get over it, you know. So what the hell did you want to ask me?"

"Do you have any idea how I could find out who his closest family and friends are, without making anybody curious?" I said.

"What do you mean by closest? By blood? Or people he really likes?"

"People he would go stay with if he wanted to be unavailable for a while."

"We can eliminate his two ex-wives. For family, he did have an aunt who adored him, Penelope Grantlin, widow of Pembroke Grantlin, you know, the Gypsum King. She died in January. She left our Rolly a bundle, from what I hear."

"Wait. Grantlin? As in Kentwood Grantlin?"

"I do not know how you've survived all this time in Hollywood without any instinct for gossip. And you can't gossip if you don't know the scandal. Yes, as in Kentwood Grantlin."

"Who is Savannah Masters's husband."

"Very good," Bill said. "You can take off the dunce cap. You know him?"

"I met him last night at the party."

"If Savannah had to choose between them—and as far as I know, no one has ever asked her to—I'd put my money on Rolly."

"That's interesting."

"She was once heart and soul for him, back ten years ago when she was still an actress. You *do* recall she used to be an actress, don't you? She's not that keen on the husband."

"I had that impression."

"But his family had money, and I'm sure she thought she was marrying into it, but Kentwood couldn't hold onto any, between the ponies and cards. Of course, she's been known to lose a bundle on the dice. If you want the really hard gossip, his practice is rumored to be mostly in the syringe."

There were more than a few doctors who kept themselves afloat in Hollywood by making house calls with a doctor's bag full of whatever it took to get the actor to work, to sleep, or through the heebie-jeebies when he tried to dry out.

"Jean Bracker had a nervous collapse at the cocktail party," I said, "and they asked me to go get him."

"I'm sure the doctor's bag was handy."

"Please don't pass that on, about Jean. I shouldn't have said that."

Bill said, "That's old news, sweetie, Jean Bracker needing a little pick-me-up from time to time. God, you're beautiful when you're naïve. Well, where were we? Ah, the filthy lucre. Rolly's aunt dies and leaves him a bundle, including her mansion. Everything she left to the son, Kentwood, she left in trust. Guess who was executor?"

"Roland?"

"Very good. I hear that, if they want a nickel beyond the allowance, they have to get his approval. So I doubt Rolly's cuddling up on Kentwood's hearth right now."

I said, "Is Roland cuddling up to anybody? Somebody he might go stay with?"

"Rolly Neale is *always* cuddling where he shouldn't, but he gets himself in trouble because he *always* picks women who can't keep a secret. They fall in love and march right to their husbands and announce they want a divorce. Or march up to his other mistress and tell her hands off. There have been some entertaining episodes at parties, I can tell you, hair-pulling and torn dresses. But I haven't heard about anything—anybody—lately."

"Any other family, close friends?"

"I could make some calls," Bill said, "but I have the feeling you don't want me to do that."

"No, please don't."

"And I shouldn't tell anyone we had this talk."

"No."

"Does Mr. Winslow know what you're up to?"

"I'm not going to do anything foolish. Can I get you a sandwich? I'm going over to Madison's."

"No, thanks. I've got a lunch meeting about my prestige picture's progress. That's what Mickels came to remind me about. He doesn't realize what a bad impression a writer makes by being on time. Please be careful."

I promised. He didn't look entirely convinced.

CHAPTER 16

I decided to use the studio commissary instead. I'd promised Peter not to leave the lot. I bought a sandwich and returned to my office, shut the door, and settled down to work, eating the ham and cheese straight off the waxed paper.

I read three more chapters of *The Hard Fold,* continuing to make an outline of the plot, before I picked up the phone, asked the switchboard girl for an outside line, and called my friend Helen Ross's house. Helen wouldn't be there. She was in Hawaii on a second honeymoon with her husband, Sam.

I asked the housekeeper if she would go into Helen's address book for me, the big one. She hadn't taken that one with her, had she? I needed to send Roland Neale a story treatment, I told her, and he'd gone to his other home. I'd lost the address. I was such an idiot.

Patiently, she went to look. There was only one address in the book, she reported. She read it to me. It was the house in Holmby Hills. Gosh, I said, I *was* in a pickle. Oh, how about Savannah Masters? She was married to his cousin, Kentwood Grantlin. Maybe she'd know. Dutifully, the housekeeper flipped through the book. Why should she doubt my story? I was Helen's friend.

There were two phone numbers, she said. She gave them both to me, and I thanked her. I wasn't going to press my luck with any more requests. And I certainly had no plausible reason for asking her to give me the accompanying addresses.

One of these numbers was probably Savannah's office at the *Eagle.*

I hauled out the phone book from the bottom drawer and looked up the phone number for the newspaper for which Savannah worked. It was a Hollywood exchange, which meant you dialed HO (four-six), then five digits. For years, we'd been able to dial inside the county with only five digits. Now, the phone company was moving toward requiring the dialing of seven digits. There were just too many people now for the old five-digit system. The phone company didn't think most people could remember seven digits and so was using neighborhood names to represent the first two numbers, hoping that made it easier.

I asked the switchboard operator for another outside line and dialed the Hollywood exchange number.

"Savannah Masters's office," a woman's rather squeaky voice said. Savannah's *Eagle* office.

I apologized, wrong number, and hung up.

I flipped to the *G*'s in the phone book and looked up Grantlin. Kentwood Grantlin was a doctor. Many doctors also listed their home numbers for emergencies. Kentwood did not. The kind of emergencies he dealt with, maybe the people already had his home phone number. His office number, which was listed, would be of no use to me.

I went downstairs to the lobby and asked the switchboard girl for a reverse directory. She had one, but she wouldn't let me take it upstairs. Not on your life. Writers were always borrowing things from her, she said, and those things never came back.

A reverse directory was arranged by phone number. Through it, you could find the number's accompanying address. I looked. But the second number Helen's housekeeper had given me wasn't there. A private number. Or a new one, newly assigned.

I asked the girl to call it for me. She pulled a cord from the row in front of her and plugged it into a hole in the switchboard for an outside line. Then she called the number, using the dial set on her desk. She plugged another cord into the board, and I picked up the extension at the end of the counter. I listened to a dozen rings.

"The Grantlin residence," a woman said.

"I think I might have the wrong number." I read it to her.

"May I ask who you were trying to reach?" She was formal, but not quite all the way to impolite.

"I was looking for a Dr. Kentwood Grantlin."

"He's not here. Might I take a message?" she asked.

"Why don't I just call back later? What time might he be home?"

"You might try after six."

I thanked her and hung up.

I asked the switchboard girl if she knew anything about exchanges. Sure, she piped. The number I'd asked her to call started with "OL." What was that? Oleander, she said. Beverly Hills. All the exchange numbers were named for the area where the station was where they routed the calls through, she said with somewhat tortured grammar. I wasn't familiar with OLeander. Helen lived in Beverly Hills, but her exchange was CRestwood.

I handed back the reverse directory, promised never to borrow cigarettes, newspapers, or five bucks for the ponies off her, and went back upstairs.

Didn't I have work to do?

Work that wasn't likely to get me into trouble with Peter and, more importantly, didn't risk alerting whoever killed that woman that I might *be* trouble.

I read for another hour. Then I got a phone call. From my mother.

★ ★ ★ ★ ★

Martin and Cordelia Tanner, my parents, lived a few blocks from the university campus, in a house larger than the university president's. My mother had advised my father against that when they were considering buying the home—with a considerable contribution from Uncle Bennett, who was my mother's brother. But my father, in addition to being a well regarded professor, was a noted historian, a vibrant writer about the frontier American West. His books sold very well, especially among American men. He disdained campus politics, he said. I was sure he disdained the university president.

My uncle Bennett had given my friend Bill Linden a small fortune in art, property, and gifts of stock during his last illness. When his will was probated, my parents discovered there would be much less coming to them than they had expected. They were convinced Bill had taken advantage of my uncle, ill and vulnerable. They would sue. Bill's private life and my uncle's would be made public.

Uncle Bennett had left me plenty. I offered to give some to Bill, asked him to give back all the things my uncle had wanted him to have. He'd quite rightly thrown me out of his house, politely, of course. My father tried to get me to sign a deposition about Bill's undue influence. And I'd almost done it, to please my father. But in the end, I couldn't. It wasn't true. The lawyer said he'd call me as a witness anyway. Everything about my uncle's life would end up in court.

So I phoned the head of my uncle's oil company and told him what my father was planning. I didn't tell my father before I did it. Someone called my father and politely pointed out the disadvantages such action would create. The company had made generous contributions to the university and my father's department in the past, and these contributions might have to end because the company would almost certainly be financially damaged by my father's actions. Father dropped the suit. But he knew who'd told the company what he was up to. I gave them some of my money, through my lawyer. They took it. But they would not talk to me. Bill and I made up. Not me and my parents.

Would it have turned out the same had I first begged my father to reconsider? It was hard to recall now why I'd been so convinced there was no other way, that he would pay no heed to me. Because we were strangers? That answer was too simple. It was a movie answer, not real life.

The maid came to the door. I didn't know her. Moira had been the maid when I was last here. Moira and I still exchanged Christmas cards. My parents and I had hardly spoken in seven years.

My mother met me in the foyer, plumper now, but her good bones kept her handsome. I had regretted as a girl so much about my looks, and among the things I didn't like about myself was that I had her jaw. It seemed too strong. Of course, it wore beautifully and kept the aging of the neck at bay. At least in her. Her hair had gone almost completely gray and was smoothed back into a simple chignon. She wore a dress, not a more casual skirt and blouse. She was entertaining a virtual stranger.

The maid disappeared.

"Mother." I touched her on the shoulder and pressed my cheek to hers. "You look splendid."

"Oh goodness, I'm getting old." Her fingers on my upper arm tightened, then released. She stepped back and pressed her long, thin fingers together, as if in prayer. "It was good of you to come so quickly."

"Is he all right?" All I could figure was that she'd called me because Father was ill.

"A nasty cold over the winter he couldn't seem to shake, but much better now. Let's go in. We have some tea ready. I hope you still like tea. I forgot to ask."

"Tea's fine."

"Nora's made some cake. Oh, I don't think you know Nora."

"It was Moira in my time."

"Nora. Moira. I hadn't realized they almost rhymed. Let's go see your father."

My father's paneled study was lined with bookcases, the kind that ran to the ceiling and had ionic columns between them, fluted and scrolled. The desk and writing table were both piled with books and neat stacks of manuscripts. The furniture and carpets were old, expensive, and lived-on.

He sat by the fireplace, wearing a dark gray sweater. A lap rug had been folded and tucked away beside it, on the side away from me, but I could see a plaid edge and some of the woolen fringe. And the thick-knobbed handle of a walking stick.

His hair was more heavily streaked with white and had thinned a bit, though it was combed in exactly the way I remembered, with a razor part on the left, and a slight fold back where he had a cowlick. I set my handbag in a chair and went to him. His eyelids had crinkled folds now. And there were a few broken veins at the edges of his nostrils.

Arthritis had stiffened his neck, and he had to lean back to see me. I thought it was arthritis, and not that he was leaning away from the chance I might embrace him. I took a step back. I clasped my hands in front of me. "I'm glad to see you. How are you?"

"Picture of health," he said, in his slightly raspy voice, with still cultured diction. "If I were a hundred and ten."

I laughed.

"Sit down," he said and gestured to the sofa opposite.

I did. Nora came in with the tea tray and placed it on the low table in front of the sofa. Mother sat down at the other end of the sofa and removed the cozy from the tea pot.

"Is it just milk still?" she asked me.

"Yes," I said.

"Like your father. Here, hand this to him, would you?"

I did. The cup rattled on the saucer when he took it but then was silent, though I could see the small ripples in the cloudy liquid.

There were pictures on the mantel beside him. It seemed a lot of pictures for a mantel. Perhaps because they had added some of me to the memories of their life, Father's career, and of Marty, my dead brother.

"Doesn't she look well, Martin?" Mother asked. She saw me examining the pictures. She said, quickly, "Would you like some cake?"

"I would, thank you," I said.

I sat back down and accepted my tea. Mother set a small plate in front of me, with an exquisitely cut slice of dense cake, softly frosted like a swirl of snow.

"I'll get to the point," my father said.

"Martin. Dear," she said to me, "we'd like to ask a favor."

"Of course," I said.

"They're pushing me out," my father said. "Trying to push me out and take away the department chair." Years ago, there had been talk of his eventually becoming university president, but he had been passed over. "Stockard, with his usual mulish moggelry, has no respect for what I've brought to that school. He offered me a title of professor emeritus and would invite me to teach seminars. Seminars. Twice a year.

"He has half the regents on his side. They apparently think seminars should be enough to satisfy me. But they can't shove me out without a majority. And there are still a few souls there with the honor to recall the stature I've brought to the university. They want to create a chair, a new chair for me."

"That's wonderful," I said.

"In what way?"

"I'm sorry?"

"In what way is my going cap in hand to the regents to beg for the chair wonderful?"

"Why would you have to beg, if they want to give it to you?" I asked.

"Martin," my mother whispered, but she said it only loud enough for me to hear.

"Because they care about the reputation of the school, and they do not appreciate gossip. What do they say to Stockard, how do my supporters fight him when my daughter is in the papers again, and this time reminding people she's getting a divorce and having—what do they call it?—a fling with a man who's been married two times already."

"I'm not having a fling with Roland Neale," I said. "I'm not having anything with him. Savannah Masters was trying to be nice."

"Nice?" he asked.

"Telling people that handsome men thought I was attractive. Yes, nice."

"Nice would have been to keep you out of a gossip column. She said you talked to her. Did she lie about that?"

"No, sir."

"So you made divorce sound like changing your hairdo."

"I couldn't very well say divorce was a terrible thing and I was destroyed."

"Why not?" he asked.

"And make myself the object of pity? I'm not destroyed. It's done. I'm getting a divorce; my husband's not coming back. I don't want him to come back."

"You could have refused to speak to her."

"She walked up to me at a party. I can't stop her from writing, even if what she says isn't true."

"Who were you there with, then?"

"No one. The head of the studio invited me. He and his wife. I have a job at Epic, writing a script for Mary Ann McDowell. The head of the studio was kind enough to invite me to his party."

"A Hollywood party where men make eyes at married women."

"Roland Neale told me he liked my work; that was all he said. There's nothing between us. I'm sorry that got in the papers. How long will it be until the regents make a decision?"

"A month, perhaps. Why?"

"I'll promise to stay away from parties. I won't talk to reporters. I'll talk to Morty Engler at Marathon, their publicity director, ask him to keep me out of the papers for the next month or so. Would that be all right?"

He pressed his lips together and lifted his chin, drawing in a long breath.

"And at the end of the month?" he asked.

"I can't stop people writing. But I'm really not very important. They don't usually care whether I'm alive or dead. I can't guarantee there won't ever be another word about me in the paper. But I don't live that kind of life. I don't do anything I'm ashamed of."

I set my cup down and stood up. "I'm sorry to have hurt you and caused trouble with the regents. I'll phone Morty Engler." I laid a hand on my mother's shoulder, collected my handbag, and went out.

She followed me into the hall.

"It's a great blow to him, this change of heart by the regents. He and Mr. Stockard have never been friends. Mr. Stockard is jealous of your father's fame. And the money, I think. But the regents—They always adored him. But it's changed, as he's gotten older. They just want someone new, someone else. It's nearly broken his heart."

"I'll do whatever I can. I promise."

"I'm sure you will. Do you—? *Is* there anyone? If it's not Mr. Neale. Are you really all right?"

"I am. There is someone. He's very good to me."

"The detective?"

"Mr. Winslow. Yes." I bent forward and kissed her cheek, soft and fragrant with jasmine. She pressed her cheek to me. Then she was back under control.

"Maybe we could have lunch sometime," I said.

"I'd like that. I'll try. But you know, your father isn't well."

I kissed her again and left. I didn't cry. Not till I'd pulled out of the drive.

CHAPTER 17

I went to see Myrna Pearl. Looking back, it was because I was angry, and when I'm angry, I have to *do* something. And maybe because what I *didn't* want to do was go back to my office and be alone with myself.

Myrna was once a contract player at Marathon and had appeared in several of the B-movie comedies that I'd been called upon early in my career to cheer up with some snappier dialogue. Then she'd gone to work at Central Casting. I had her number in the small address book in my handbag and called her from a drugstore booth. She was in and had time to see me, but she could only give me ten minutes.

I plunged the nose of my Lincoln into the thick after-work traffic and headed over to the Producers Association Building at Hollywood and Western. The association supported Central Casting, to help provide extras—or background—when the studios needed more people than they had easily on hand. Beyond the filigree-iron entry arch, the cool, dim lobby was empty. It was too late in the day for the hopefuls who sometimes gathered there, wearing costumes and speaking their names to the people on the way to the elevators, hoping one would be a casting director who'd either let them register on Central Casting's rolls or, if they were already on the rolls, remember their name the next time there was a job.

Myrna came out to greet me at the office's front desk, an inch of cigarette in her hand. Myrna had always been buxom and had usually been cast as the girl tempting the hero. She'd grown even more voluptuous in the last years and wore blouses that wouldn't even think about hiding that fact.

"Come on back. Want some coffee?"

"No, thanks," I said.

She crushed the stub in a metal ashcan by the swinging doors as we went through.

The heart of Central Casting was a large room with tall library card-catalog-style cabinets at one end that held the names of everyone currently registered. A small photograph was pasted on each card, along with the vital statistics and special talents the actor or actress had: Could they ride a horse, dance, sing, play a violin while walking a tightrope? In the middle of the room under big scoop lights sat two rows of tables with a half dozen phones on each one, each a place for a casting director to field calls from extras, who would call the switchboard through the day. The switchboard operator would call out the name over the loudspeaker, and if the director needed that person, he'd push one of the row of buttons on his tabletop and take the call. Casting directors had hundreds of names, faces, talents memorized. Right now, all the seats were empty.

Lining both sides were other rooms, their walls half glass. On one side, the switchboard operators; on the far side, a meeting room and tiny offices, Myrna's among them.

"Half of us have gone home now," she said. "The rest are taking a break. The phones are off." I squeezed into her visitor's chair. She took the saucer off the top of her coffee cup and took a quick sip. "Somebody needs to clean that pot," she said and shuddered, but took another sip. "We've got a long evening ahead of us, have to make some calls. We've got some late lists coming over the teletype from Paramount and Columbia, have to find three dozen dancers by daybreak to go over for auditions, and—Let me see—" She slid a teletype list toward her.

"And a few dozen soldiers, so they can pick twenty to fill out a barracks. Note here, 'No chorus boys.' And that's coming from Jackie Key, the casting director over there, who is the personification of chorus boy." She pulled a cigarette from the nearly empty pack on her desk. "Maybe the coffee would taste better if I gave up smoking."

"Or worse," I said.

She lit the cigarette, tossing the match toward the ashtray, which was so piled with stubs, the match bounced off. "Come to see where the money went?" she asked and laughed.

Myrna had helped me before, and she'd kept a secret that needed keeping. I'd thanked her for that by insisting she let me give her something, something significant. She demurred, but I wouldn't take no for an answer. She finally picked dental work.

She smiled at me now, opening her teeth a bit and turning her head from side to side, so I could see a few of the new ones, toward the back. Other than the silver hooking of the partial plates, the teeth looked exactly the same as her real ones.

"They fit like a dream," she said. "My youngest, he's in his wisecracking stage. He now likes to tell me that I'm 'partially pretty.' He better study. He's got no future in vaudeville. So what can I do for you?"

It was a long, long shot. But what else did we have except that the dead woman turned up near a party, Roland Neale knew her, and she was unlikely to be anyone whose disappearance would make the papers? Costello—and the killer who sent him—didn't seem to think anyone would miss her, and if they did, I'd never hear about it.

Maybe our dead woman was a bit actress who paid her bills by prostitution. Maybe Roland Neale was a customer. Perhaps she'd run afoul of one of the men who controlled that racket, some brutal hothead who'd followed her there and shot her in an argument. Then found he had a body to get rid of.

While I was drying my eyes outside my parents' house, I'd recalled Jean Bracker's telling me Epic had invited a group of young dancers over to the party, to entertain and dance with the guests.

"I need to find somebody. She might have been among the girls who were invited from Epic to go to Ben Bracker's party last night. Would you be able to get me a list of their names, addresses, and phone numbers from Epic? Without letting anyone know I was asking."

"If this is a job for your friend Peter, tell him he can drop by himself. I'll be glad to help him out personally."

I laughed. "I'll let him know."

"I can call Casting over there. But what do you want me to say, if I'm keeping you out of it?"

"Tell them one of the girls got spotted at the party, and somebody wants to give her an audition, but the guy got too drunk to recall her name. You'd rather not say who."

"You know they might have thrown out whatever list they had."

"I know. I'd appreciate anything you can do." I gave her three phone numbers: home, Marathon, and Epic, since I'd probably have to go back there soon. "If you leave a message, just say, 'Call Myrna'."

It wasn't yet six o'clock when I returned to Marathon. I took a chance Morty Engler, the studio's publicity chief, might still be in his office in the Ice House, Marathon's executive building. His secretary had gone, and so I stuck my head in. He was still there, bent over the metal typewriter table beside his desk, pecking away as fast as I'd ever seen a man type with two fingers. A cigarette had been abandoned long ago in his ashtray. A long cylinder of ash led to the rim.

He paused long enough to reach for a short tumbler beside the ashtray and saw me.

"Hey," he said.

"Sorry to bother you," I said. "Could you give me a few minutes before you go home tonight?"

"Better take it now; we might not be going home tonight."

Through an open door on the left, I saw two assistants doing pretty much what he was, except they typed with all their fingers and didn't have a glass of gin beside them.

Morty Engler had the skin of a baby—smooth, poreless, slightly pink. The only sign of his occupation was in his posture. He was perpetually bent forward, from years of being ready for the next crisis. His body hummed with coiled energy. "Give me two seconds. Sit down." He went back to the furious typing. As he reached the end of the page, he called out, "Randall!"

One of the assistants jumped up from his desk and scurried in. Just as he hit Morty's door, Morty ripped the sheet from the typewriter and slung it behind him over his head. Randall caught it in the air and dashed back out.

"Sit, sit," Morty said to me and rolled in fresh paper. "Gin in the lower drawer, clean glass. Bit of bourbon in there, too, I think; you could check."

"No, thanks."

"Well, something else might interest you then, while you wait." He tapped a stack of letters twice without looking at them and went back to his typing.

I slipped the top letter from underneath his carved silver paperweight. In movies and books, people were always getting bumped off with paperweights like this one, domes that fit into the palm. I could never understand that. In order to get a good enough grip on most paperweights, your fingertips have to be underneath it. You'd be bludgeoning someone's head with your fingertips in the way. I often wondered how many people had actually been murdered with a paperweight. Not that many, I was pretty sure, although I was also pretty sure Morty'd been sorely tempted during his career.

I replaced the paperweight, sat back, crossed my legs, and read the letter. It was from Birdie Hitts, the scandal photographer who'd accosted me and Hawkins in Madison's last evening. God, was it just last night?

"What do you think? Should I say yes?" Morty said to me, still not looking up.

"This is disgusting."

"Yeah," Morty said and chortled, his slumped shoulders vibrating as he typed.

Birdie was pitching Marathon his idea about a classy layout of the legs of lesser-known Marathon actresses, girls who might need a push of publicity. He named a few. Then he suggested maybe some gals truly unknown to the public, maybe a writer, like Lauren Atwill. She had a nice set of stems.

Even in his letters, he talked like a B movie.

Morty ripped the next page out. "Randall!"

The assistant scrambled in, caught the next page on the fly. Morty said to him, "That's it. Clean it up. Bring it back. Close the door."

Randall bustled back out, pulling the door shut after him.

"When did you get this?" I said.

"This morning. He dropped it off at the front desk."

Morty refreshed his glass from the bottom drawer, raised his brows and the bottle to me. I shook my head. The bottle disappeared, and Morty sat back in his chair, heaved a sigh, rotated his neck, and took a slug of gin. "He's trying to squeeze his way into studio work. He'd like to start taking pictures of women who are still alive and have all their clothes on. It's not a bad idea, though. You know, when I saw your name . . ." He leaned forward and looked at my crossed legs.

"Okay, Morty, I need a favor." I stood up and slipped my skirt halfway up my thighs. He took a good look. I put my skirt back down. "And no, Birdie Hitts has never had that good a look."

"He'd have put you on top of the list if he had."

"Thank you."

"Sure you don't want a bourbon?" He wiggled his brows.

I laughed, and so did he. I sat down, he sat back. "So what kind of favor you need?" he asked.

"Would it be possible to keep my divorce out of the papers for a month or so? My parents saw Savannah Masters's column today. His university's not used to seeing the daughter of a department head in gossip columns about her divorce."

"I saw that, was going to have a word with you. If you talk to a columnist, you should let me know."

"I'm sorry. She just walked up to me at the party, told me what she was going to say, except she didn't mention the part about Franklin or Roland Neale."

"Were you and Rolly Neale really 'casting eyes' at each other? Whose eyes were they? Kind of gruesome."

"You don't have to be able to write to be a gossip columnist," I said. "Publicity chief? That's different."

"Yeah, yeah, butter me up."

"I need to stay out of the papers for a month or so. Can you help?" I told him about my father's battle with the university president and the regents.

"I'll call Frank. The accountants will scream bloody murder about the cost of a call all the way to Cuba, but Frank's got to behave himself till the divorce is final. Savannah could have made it sound worse, made him sound like a cad. She'll expect something because she didn't. I'll get Frank cooled down, throw something to her."

"I'd appreciate it."

"Studio owes you," he said. Though Morty didn't know all the details of the murder cases I'd been involved in, he knew that things could have turned out much worse for Marathon. "If anyone else tries to talk to you, just smile and send them to me. Uh, look, you probably don't need to be warned about Rolly Neale."

"No. And I'm not looking for company."

"Nothing wrong with him," Morty said, "if you just want a little diversion, but I don't think you're that kind of girl."

"Do you know him? Or only by reputation?"

"I worked five years at Paramount when he was there. He's always been an active man, shall we say."

"Is Savannah in love with him? I heard something about how she used to carry a torch."

"Tall and hot, that flame, about ten years ago. But she settled for his cousin."

"Kentwood Grantlin."

"Yeah. There was some money. He's a doctor, and she was thirty, unmarried, and at the tail end of what acting career she had. This was before she 'cast her eyes' on writing gossip. Of course, Rolly ended up with a lot of the money."

"That's what I heard. He was left it by his aunt."

"Why is it these rich old dames get so fond of Romeos when they get old? Why don't they ever fall for publicity hacks?"

"Do you know where Savannah lives?"

"Yeah. I got it right here. We have to know where to send the flowers and the invitations." He flipped into a large address book. "This is new," he said. "The old one's marked out. Randall!"

The assistant stuck his head back in.

Morty said, "Savannah Masters. Her address, phone number. Are these right?"

"The new one? Yeah. We got an announcement from her a couple of weeks ago, you remember?"

"Would I have asked if I had?"

"Sorry, no, sorry," Randall said. "New one. Beverly Hills. That's it."

"Okay, okay," Morty said, and the assistant disappeared.

Morty read me out the new address and the phone number. It was the Oleander number I'd gotten from Helen's address book.

I thanked him and stood up.

He said, "You got a 'nice set of stems.' Bring 'em by anytime."

CHAPTER 18

I went back to my office in the Tate Building and gathered up what I'd need to return to my Epic bungalow the next day. I'd probably have to go back there. I had to act like I believed the story that Roland Neale had just been the victim of a nasty, vicious prank. That no one was hurt.

There was a note waiting in my message box at the Tate's front desk from Peter, reminding me about the appointment with the sketch artist, although all the message said was that he'd pick me up at six thirty. He wasn't going to be happy if he found out I'd been off the studio lot without someone watching over me. He'd be even more unhappy if he knew I'd been to Central Casting looking for a lead on the dead woman.

I asked the switchboard girl what she'd told him, and she said only that I wasn't answering my phone. She didn't tell him she'd seen me go out, with hat and handbag. That wasn't her job, she said, to tell men what women were doing on their own time when it wasn't any of their business.

When Peter arrived, I told him part of the truth, that I'd gone to see my parents. That distracted him, and he didn't chastise me for going out without an escort. He knew that my parents and I didn't get along, and why. He didn't get along with his father, either. He'd lost his mother when he was twelve, and his father fell into the bottle, even harder after the crash took away his livelihood. His father had taken to smacking around Peter's stepmother and his brother and sisters. One night, when he was seventeen, Peter had tossed his father out the front door and told him never to come back. Peter had gone to the people who were still making money as the Depression set in: bootleggers. That's how he'd ended up running rum for Ramon Elizondo till Prohibition was repealed. Peter once told me that any polish he had was courtesy of Ray Elizondo. They remained friends.

We drove downtown to his office, at Fourth and Hill, on the third floor of one of those buildings that had an impressive lobby of green and black marble, with elevator doors and mezzanine balustrades of silver-metal bas-reliefs of California history. Above the lobby, however, the decor looked just like any other office building.

The sketch artist was waiting. Her name was Mrs. Hamby, no first name. She wore a thick tweed suit, buttoned to the breastbone, with a stiff-collared blouse beneath, and low-heeled, laced walking shoes. She flipped open her tall sketch pad, slid open her pencil case, and asked me to start talking.

I described Costello. She listened. Again, please, she said and set to work, with staccato questions. Ears? Width of the mouth? Eyebrows, how thick? Close your eyes, picture it. You don't have to watch me—better if you don't.

She kept working. She showed it to me, made adjustments. She had wide, puffy hands and short fingers, truly the most un-artistic hands I'd ever seen. And they produced a sketch of Costello that might have been drawn from life. I said so.

"It's what I do, dearie," she said, matter of factly. "He's not bad looking. Nice eyes."

"Yes, the kind that could fool a girl." I gave her ten dollars, which made a momentary impression. Then she folded the bill into a small, scuffed change purse, tucked it and her pencil box into her capacious handbag, looped the strap over her arm, picked up her sketch pad, and departed.

Peter examined the sketch. He'd keep it in the office safe, have copies made, and make sure any man assigned to be my bodyguard had one.

He took me back to Rocco's for dinner, where Rocco himself—delighted we'd returned—prepared the fresh sausages and peppers he'd bragged about that afternoon. Peter used his napkin. I wiped my lips with my fingers so I could more easily lick the sauce into my mouth. "I don't know how you keep your boyish figure, eating here," I said.

"Extra nights in the gym," Peter said.

Although he never got into the ring—he'd never been a boxer—he worked out at a boxing gym a couple of nights a week when he had time: the jump rope, medicine ball, punching bag, speed bag. I'd never seen him do it. Among the last places a woman would be welcome was a boxing gym. Not that I wanted to go to one anyway.

Perhaps it was time I thought about doing more exercise than occasional laps in my pool and playing a couple of sets of tennis with Helen on weekends. There were gyms and reducing parlors for women, where actresses went when the girdle was no longer enough. I'd been naturally slender all my life, but it couldn't last much longer. Some of my older dresses had gone a bit snug around the middle. If I didn't do something, I'd move from a very Hollywood-acceptable size twelve to a fourteen. I had a brief image of myself in what the stores called "half-sizes." A twenty-two and a half was not what I wanted to be buried in.

"What did your father have to say?" Peter asked finally as I was barely resisting sopping up the rest of the sauce with a piece of bread.

I told him everything that had happened, even the detail about the pictures of me placed on the mantel.

He said, "There's the chance they've been there all along."

"My father's only interested in how my divorce will affect his career."

He left it alone. He moved on to figuring out the best way to keep an eye on my safety for another few days. I wasn't inclined to have one of his men as a bodyguard, following me around. I had to go back to Epic, to work in my tiny bungalow. I couldn't have a man hanging around in that room, and if he just sat in a car outside the gate all day, it would hardly make me safer. Either move would announce to Bracker and Gettleman that I didn't believe their story.

So Peter made up his mind. Someone would tail me to Epic, to see if I was being followed. I'd have to get up early because he could get Johnny, his brother, to do it before he went to work each day. Then someone else would follow me home.

We picked up my car at Marathon, and I drove back home to Pasadena with him close behind. Juanita made coffee for us, and rather a lot of noise putting away pots and pans she hadn't been able to use.

There had been nothing on the car radio. Over coffee and brandy in the study, we searched the evening editions for any mention of the discovery of an unidentified murdered woman. If a woman had been found killed by a gunshot, she'd be a police case. She'd be likely to show up in at least one of the papers. She didn't. Wherever Costello had taken the body, nobody was going to find it.

Peter knocked on my bedroom door before seven, far earlier than I was used to getting up. Screenwriters are rarely vertical before eight, and certainly not ambulatory beyond their doorsteps. Juanita was already up, however, preparing plates of omelets, ham, and corn muffins. I thought that if Peter and I lived together, I'd gain ten pounds just from the breakfasts.

Peter asked if she'd wrap him up an extra ham sandwich. She

did and tucked in two buttered corn muffins. He presented it all to Johnny, who was waiting behind the wheel of his car at the top of the driveway. Johnny was ten years younger than Peter, with some of the same features: the jawline, the shape of the nose, but the eyes were paler and gentler.

"Thanks for doing this," I said.

"It's all right. I need the practice. And no better way to get it than knowing you." He tucked the sandwich and muffins into the glove compartment. He drove a new Olds, which Peter had probably helped pay for, as they weren't cheap. But he needed it. Just before the war ended in Europe, the jeep in which he was riding as part of a convoy had hit a land mine. He was lucky. The blast only crippled his left leg. The other occupants were killed. The Olds had a hydra-matic drive, so he no longer needed to figure out how to use a clutch.

"I circled around," Johnny told his brother. "There's nobody watching."

I left in my Lincoln, and Peter followed. Johnny hung back, watching for someone slipping in to tail us. I parked in the Epic lot down from the studio, and Peter waited for me to get inside the gate. I didn't see Johnny. But then that was the point.

My bungalow windows were still open, as I'd left them, hoping to remove the rest of the cigar smell; the cleaning crew hadn't closed them, so the room was chilled. I laid my handbag on the desk, along with the canvas bag in which I'd brought back everything I'd taken away from the bungalow just yesterday.

There was a wall heater beside the sink in the corner. I flipped the switch, and the motor whirred. After a full minute, a soft glow began to form at the base of the first coil.

Someone rapped lightly on the door.

"Come in."

It was Arky Kulpa, the messenger who'd assigned himself to me. He wore smart brown flannels and two-toned shoes. "You

159

could freeze waiting for that to heat up," he said.

"So I was noticing."

"I could borrow a sweater, off costuming. I know some girls over there."

"Thanks, I'll manage."

"Coffee? I can get you a thermos."

"I'll take you up on that. And some milk in it, please."

I set to work. He was gone only ten minutes. He also brought me back a mug from the commissary, which he'd heated up. I paid him and tipped him a quarter.

"I'll drop by later, pick up the thermos," he said. "Anything else you need?"

"As a matter of fact . . . Are you any good with a knife?"

He raised a brow. "Who you got in mind?"

I laughed. "I meant an art knife." I stood up, and, out of my canvas bag, I took the art knife, the ring-binder notebook, the glue, and the dog-eared second copy of *The Hard Fold*. "I need you to take this book, cut the pages out with as much margin on the spine as you can get. Then cut a rectangle out of the center of sheets of typing paper, a hole just big enough to expose the text. Glue the margins to the paper. Do you understand?"

"Sure. You want to be able to see both sides of the page through the hole and have room to write notes on the typing paper. Did Herbie tell you I wasn't too bright?"

"What? No."

"What *did* he tell you?" Arky asked.

"If he said anything at all, I don't think it would a good idea for me to pass it along, do you?"

He grinned. "Guess not. Mostly, he thinks I'm getting above my station in life. See, I know exactly what you need, and he doesn't like that, because he's got to be told what to do. When do you want this? Tell you what," he said and took a short step toward me. "I could work on it this evening."

"You don't have to do that."

"I got a little appointment, but it's not till nine. I'll leave it here if I finish it . . . outside in the basket."

"I appreciate it, but tomorrow or the next day would be fine. I'm still reading the book."

"All right. You got it, doll. Sorry. Miss Atwill. Okay, sometimes I do get a little above myself." The slow smile and steady gaze said he'd be willing to have me contradict him.

"Thanks for your help." I sat down.

He slipped the corked knife into his pocket and tapped the copy of the book. "You're writing a script about this?"

"I'm writing a story treatment."

"I've read it. It's . . . well, it's . . . I mean, for a lady."

"I'm tougher than I look."

"I never doubted it."

I leaned back in my chair. "Do you know any gambling slang?" I remembered Herb said Arky was the guy at Epic who'd be glad to take your bets. I didn't want him to know I'd got the word from Herb, though, so I said, "A young man must hear a lot around here, the way studio guys like to bet. The book has a lot of prostitutes in it. I have to get rid of them. I was thinking about giving the hero a gambling habit instead, but I'd like the slang to sound real."

"I know a little. I could help you there. You think the Code Office would go for it, the real stuff?"

"I don't think they'd know the real stuff."

"Our secret, then." He winked, gathered up the binder and the book, and strolled out, whistling.

I spent the morning drinking Arky's coffee, which was piping hot and had just the right amount of milk, and finishing up my re-reading of *The Hard Fold.* I made more notes on the elements that would have to come out, not just the ones that would create a furor at the Code Office but also the subplots that were too much for a picture that wouldn't run two hours.

And there was the ending. I had to change the killer's motive. In the book, it was the dead woman's brother, who turned out to have had some unsavory feelings about her. The movie couldn't have unsavory feelings. And making the prurience oblique would just cause the audience to scratch its head, an unsatisfying conclusion. Of course, people had frankly baffling motives in movies all the time, and the screenwriters tried to save it by having the other characters behave like they made perfect sense.

I didn't feel like writing one of those movies.

I kept thinking and tried to stop thinking about why someone would kill a woman and remove the body instead of just letting Roland Neale get arrested for it.

Roland Neale didn't show up at my bungalow to explain it. Or tell me who the woman was.

Herb, the messenger from Bracker's office, appeared, though, after lunch, with a request from his boss. Would I please go on over to one of the rehearsal rooms? Miss McDowell and Mr. Manning were shooting a short subject, and Mr. Bracker thought I'd like to observe.

Oh, and could I call *Mrs.* Bracker? Herb handed me a sheet of vellum notepaper, folded carefully in half with her phone number inside.

Sure, I said. He said he'd wait outside to escort me to the rehearsal room.

I called Jean Bracker.

"How are you?" she asked. "Ben told me what happened the other night, after the party. Such an awful thing. Who would play a dreadful prank like that?"

"I wish I knew. I'm fine, thank you. Recovering, anyway."

"Could I induce you to come over for dinner tonight? Just me and Ben. Drinks, dinner, very casual, no need to change.

162

We'd like to make it up to you, even if just a bit."

"That would be lovely."

"Great. Say, seven. Please bring a friend. Ben said there was a man who was looking after you. He'll probably want to come along. Would he be free?"

I said I thought he might be. We thanked each other, and I hung up.

Immediately, I called Peter.

For once, he was in his office. I told him about the invitation. Neither of us thought for one minute that Ben Bracker just wanted to see how I was doing and maybe talk about the script. He wanted to make sure I wasn't causing trouble and wasn't going to.

CHAPTER 19

The room was for dance rehearsals. Three walls of mirrors and, for more light, a fourth of windows. There were folding chairs scattered around and a couple of small tables shoved into the corner for coats, hats, and handbags. The air in a dance rehearsal room, no matter the ventilation, always hinted of the hard work that went on.

The choreographer stood against the far wall of mirrors, his hips against the barre, short, lithe, in black slacks and a black turtleneck.

"Who are you?" he asked me abruptly, standing upright and waving his hand sharply to stop Mary Ann and Len, who'd been practicing a lateral tap move.

I told him, and Herb avowed that I'd been invited by Mr. Bracker to sit in.

"*More* company, wonderful. Yes, please, please, take a chair. Do join us." He gestured exaggeratedly toward the windows, where Vera McDowell sat, in a bright blue suit, sporting a hat with a high pleated fan across the crown.

Herb ducked out. Vera and I nodded as I sat. She whispered, "I need to speak to you." Oh, God.

The choreographer said, "If you would kindly *not* talk." He turned to Mary Ann and Len. "I apologize for the interruption, my darlings. Shall we begin again?" They resumed their starting position, in the center of the room. Len wore a pair of lightweight tan trousers, belted high, and a simple white shirt with the sleeves rolled up. He looked strong, lithe, virile. Mary Ann was in a leotard and a knee-length bias-cut skirt made of some fabric that would twirl nicely. Her thick hair was caught back in a snood.

"Now, my dear," the choreographer said to Mary Ann. "Please be kind to the floor. It has done nothing to you, so do not kick it. Your energy, your enthusiasm, comes from above the waist." He placed his upturned palms at his hips and lifted them, his chest expanding, his shoulders opening, his face lighting as they rose. "If you have it here, the legs will follow, and the feet will be light. Once more, if you will. Your count, Len."

Len grinned reassurance at Mary Ann, took her hand. "Five, six, seven, *eight.*"

Mary Ann was an adequate, but not gifted, dancer. Len, however, had enough talent to make them both look good. The choreography had been designed as the story of a young man teaching a girl new dance moves, encouraging her to spend time with him. The choreographer framed Mary Ann's lack of first-rate skill as reluctance, caution and gave Len the lion's share of difficulty. At the end of the number, when she had accepted him, the steps were actually less challenging, although there were some showy spins to cover that up. Editing could take care of the rest.

A few more run-throughs, and the choreographer called for a break.

"All right." He clapped his hands twice in satisfaction. "Much better than last time, darling," he said to Mary Ann. "I could hardly tell you were counting. Take an hour. We'll pick this up again at four. With the accompanist." He snatched up a jacket and sailed out.

Mary Ann grabbed a towel from the back of a chair beside me. "See," she said, "I told you I wasn't that good a dancer."

"That's only compared to Len," Vera said, beaming at him.

"He makes me look like I can tap," Mary Ann said and bumped him lightly with her shoulder.

He put his arm around her, gave her a short hug. But it was a partner's embrace, nothing more. His affection had been much more believable when he was dancing.

Vera said to me, "Is it true about the movie, it's about that book?"

I said, "Mr. Bracker wants to see what can be done with it, yes."

"It's a nasty book," Vera declared. "The women are prostitutes."

"Those will have to go, of course," I said. "Mary Ann would have to be a new character."

Mary Ann said, "Mama's still cranky because I ran off from the party the other night. Len has forgiven me." She nudged him again. "He says Roland Neale came up and said some very nice things about you after I left."

"We've heard he might play the lead," Vera said. "It won't be my girl's picture."

Mary Ann said, "Mama, Mr. Bracker knows I can't carry an adult picture on my own. Let's get you some cake. You'll feel better."

Len said, "I'll stick around here, work on some steps."

"Lauren?" Mary Ann asked.

"Thanks, but I have work to do."

She bundled her mother off.

"What's this for, what you're shooting?" I asked Len.

"Just to keep her in front of the audience till her next project's finished. Looks like it's going to be this book you're working on."

"I hear there'd been talk about you two doing a picture."

"I don't have anything to say about that. I danced my rear end off at MGM and never got off the front row of the chorus.

I came here, and they're making me a star. I do what they tell me. If they say 'jump,' I ask 'how high?'."

"For the record, I told her not to run off and leave you with Vera the other night."

He laughed. "Vera's not that bad. Really. She wants to take care of her daughter. Mary Ann's had a lot handed to her, because she's beautiful, and the camera loves her, and girls love her movies. But she thinks it's all smooth, and she can go on getting what she wants. Whatever she wants. People think Vera spoils her, but she tries to shake a little sense into her sometimes. I shouldn't have said anything. I still think she and I could make a great team. Maybe she'll change her mind. Excuse me, now. I need to work."

I went back to my bungalow. There was a folded message slip pinned to the corkboard outside my door. I opened it. *Call Myrna.*

From a pay phone outside the Epic commissary, I phoned Myrna Pearl, over at Central Casting. She'd talked to the casting department at Epic, without bringing up my name. She had a list of the dancers who'd been invited to the Brackers' party. Good news: most of them were listed with Central Casting, so in addition to names, phone numbers, addresses, she could show me pictures. I could drop by and take a look at them, pick up the list.

Central Casting was bustling. The casting directors sat at their places at the tables in the center of the room, casting requests piled in front of them. Over the loudspeaker, the operators called out name after name of extras phoning in to see if there was work.

Myrna was in her office, a cigarette bouncing in the corner of her mouth as she spoke. "Hey, sit. Here's the list, and here are the cards on each of them. See if you see your girl." Myrna went back to reading over a casting request that had come over the teletype.

I flipped through the cards. They had small photographs of the girls' faces on one side, with their names and vital statistics. On the flip side, a list of special talents they might have.

I recalled seeing a couple of the girls on the tennis courts. But only a couple.

"They're dancers," Myrna said. "The casting guy over at Epic said he was busy when he got the call and just pulled up a sheet from one of the musicals they're shooting over there. Picked a dozen girls from the chorus and called them. Told them to dress nice, behave themselves, don't have more than two drinks, and don't go home with the first guy that asks you. I can't let you keep the cards, but the list is yours."

I had to find a phone. I didn't want to make calls from Epic, where anyone might listen in from the main switchboard, so I got a dollar's worth of nickels at a drugstore and settled into their booth. If I was lucky, I could finish my calls before an irate customer complained about my hogging the booth.

There was a problem calling in the middle of the day. Some of the girls were out working. But I was able to eliminate half of them: the first six came to the phone. I told them I was from Central Casting and was verifying phone numbers for the rolls. Sorry to bother them. Of the remaining six, four calls went to answering services. I didn't leave messages. I'd try later. One number didn't answer. The last name was Colleen Riley. I put another nickel in and dialed.

A sharp voice said hello.

"Is Colleen there?" I asked.

"She's not around. I don't know where she is," the woman snapped, a voice like nails on a blackboard. "You got a job to offer?"

"No, I—"

"Then you remind Colleen if you ever see her again, this

number is for business before six o'clock, not chats."

"When did you last see her?"

"Dangle, lady." She hung up.

Dangle? She'd been reading too many cheap novels or seeing too many B movies.

All I had to do was find out if this Colleen had been seen since the party. That was it. Simple. But I couldn't go there looking like myself, calling myself Lauren Atwill. I'd turn myself into a freelance writer, doing a story on extra girls.

I drove down to the May Department store, on Wilshire, where I knew they had a good millinery department. I needed a hat that looked nice—but not too expensive for a freelance magazine writer—and would conceal my hair color.

I found it. It was one of those a woman liked to wear at the end of the week before she got to the beauty parlor, a dark green felt with a bow of netting across the crown. Tucked underneath the brim in the back was more netting that could be slipped down over the uncooperative hair you'd pinned up. Presto, no one has to know what your hair looks like.

Then I darted down to a five-and-dime and roamed the aisles of ladies' products, examining the contents of the counters' shallow bins. Packets of hairpins and envelopes of permanent wave papers, long hair clips to create finger waves, the sort Mack Pace's secretary, Edna, wore. I found a card of bobby pins, some inexpensive button earrings, a compact of eyebrow color and one of rouge, an unflattering shade of lipstick, a pair of reading glasses, and was satisfied.

Nobody needed to see what I was doing, so I went over to Peter's house, picked his lock, pinned up my hair, put on the hat, and slipped the netting down. I smoothed on a flat mask of my own face powder over too-bold dots of rouge. I darkened my brows. I added the new lipstick and the fake eyeglasses. I looked fully ten years older. I hoped this wasn't what I'd look like in ten years.

I cleaned up every trace of what I'd done.

Colleen Riley's address was in Los Angeles, but not by much. It was just north of that jigsaw bit of unincorporated land known as West Hollywood, at the top of a street beginning its slope to the hills. It was a large Victorian-era home, painted in faded green, with long, narrow sash windows topped by ornamental pediments. There were gables in its mansard-style roof and, running up the center, a tall, square tower crowned by a cupola. It had most certainly belonged to a well-set family decades ago, maybe from the early railroad days, when land out here was cheap and labor cheaper. It was now a street of what dreams turned into when they'd been too big to begin with.

There were a couple of smaller, exhausted homes across the street, and down the slope, where I'd parked the car, squat resident hotels of stucco and rust. The war had made paint hard to come by, and the housing shortage made tenants plentiful. A lot of landlords had gotten used to that. If there were high rents to be made, places got fixed up. For ordinary workers, Los Angeles didn't seem to be making much of an effort.

I climbed the cracked wooden steps to the porch. At one end hung a weathered swing. Nearby a trio of fan-backed metal lawn chairs sat around a spindle-legged table, its top decorated in water rings. At the other end of the porch, against the rails, were two ladder-backed chairs with an ashcan between them, a field of stubs in the sand. A wooden sign hung from a chain by the door: NO VACANCIES. NO SALESMEN.

The front door had been kept polished, and its glass panel glistened. It was half open into a dark entry foyer with a flight of stairs to the left. The warped screen door was unhooked. I knocked on the edge of it. It rattled against the frame.

A woman appeared out of the gloom beyond, slight, thin, graceful, delicate, like a ballerina, with soft waves of gray hair about her face like a halo. The rest of her hair was caught at her neck in a ribbon and flowed down her back. She wore a cotton housedress in a cinnamon print and a black-and-red Spanish shawl with long black fringe.

"May I help you?" she said, in a soft, cultured voice, the diction a bit too precise. Was she an elocution teacher? Or was she drunk at four in the afternoon? Or both?

"I was looking for Colleen Riley," I said. "Does she still live here?"

"Oh, Collie. I haven't seen Collie in a while. Please come in, please. It's much cooler inside." It couldn't have been more than seventy degrees in the sun.

She laid fingertips on the knob and swept open the front door as if she were preparing a curtsy. I opened the screen and stepped inside. There was a large parlor to the right, a fireplace against the far wall. A slipcovered sofa under the front windows, and several armchairs, most in slipcovers as well. All different patterns. A floor-model radio. Small side tables. A couple of bookcases. A card table. A well-worn carpet. There were magazines and Sears and Montgomery Ward's catalogs on the sofa's coffee table. Across the front hall, on my left, was a large dining room, with a long table, all its leaves in place, surrounded by a dozen chairs.

"Is this a boarding house?" I asked.

"For young ladies, yes. I'm afraid we don't have any vacancies."

"What is it, Dorothea?" Another woman appeared through the swinging door at the end of the short hallway that ran along the stair riser, wiping her hands on a dishtowel. She wore slacks and a long-sleeved blouse with its sleeves folded and pushed up past her elbows. "No salesmen, I'm sorry," she said to me, "even when they're ladies."

"Oh, please, Harry. Harry," Dorothea said, "she's not a

tradeswoman. She has no sample case."

"I'm not selling anything," I said. "I'm writing an article about extra performers."

"Sure you are," Harry said. "Then you tell the girls about an acting school, and how the school's got connections at the studios and can get them contracts if they'll just sign yours. Move along."

"I was looking for Colleen Riley. Myrna Pearl from Central Casting gave me her name."

"I got work to do, but I'll give you five minutes to convince me. Dorothea, hook the door, please." She turned and stalked back past the stairs into the kitchen.

"It is cooler in here, isn't it? So hot outdoors." Dorothea retreated to the parlor. I hooked the screen door and followed Harry.

The kitchen had white metal cabinets, trimmed in small red flowers. They'd seen hard use, as had everything else in the room, but it was all spotless except for the wooden table in the center of the room. There was a blue bowl on the table, a scattering of flour beside it, a jug, a sifter, and a block of lard in its waxed wrapping beside a metal flour canister.

Harry spun a dishrag around inside a pot in the deep enamel sink, then rinsed the pot and set it in the dish rack to drain. She dried her hands on her towel, tucked it into her apron, and returned to the table.

Her short brown hair was well shot with gray. She wore a folded cotton scarf tied around her head to keep the hair out of her eyes, and out of the food. She wore no makeup, and I could see a bit of age freckling on her cheeks and strong lines around her eyes. I guessed her to be about forty-five. Her hands were clean and square, the short, serviceable nails without polish. She flexed her fingers, picked up a pastry cutter, and began cutting small cubes of lard into the bowl of flour. "You make biscuits?" she asked.

"Fluffy as clay pigeons."

She stopped for a second, uncertain what to make of the remark. Then she smiled, just a flash, a curve at the corner of her mouth.

"Good way to stretch the leftover Sunday chicken," she said and went back to cutting in the lard. "Make a stew and serve it over biscuits. Maybe fried apples with it tonight. I still have some I canned last fall out in the pantry."

"So the girls get breakfast and dinner?"

"It keeps them from trying to cook in their rooms. It's not fancy, but it's better than the drugstore every morning and night."

"What would you serve the other nights, just as an example? Do you mind if I take notes?"

"I haven't made up my mind yet," Harry said. "Not about the food, about you. So put the notebook away. If I decide to let you do this, you don't use my name, and you don't put my address in the article. You can say a boarding house for young ladies in Hollywood. I don't want a stream of girls coming to my door begging for rooms, and I won't have a flock of men come chasing. You should see the riffraff who come sniffing around here from those hotels down the street, soon as they find out there are girls up here. I have to keep my doors locked, the bunch of lowlifes."

"You want to know about the food?" she asked. "Eggs and toast in the morning, or oatmeal if they want, bacon, sliced oranges. Chicken for Sunday dinner, or maybe a pot roast, mostly carrots and potatoes of course, what beef costs. I serve stews mostly for dinner on weekdays, sometimes a thick soup, or fish cakes, or stuffed cabbage, though the girls complain about how it stinks up the house. In the summer, we eat vegetables out of the garden. We've still got a patch of our Victory Garden out back, might as well feed ourselves with it. A mess of green beans, cucumbers, cornbread make a fine meal. Good thing about a house full of women, they don't eat all that much."

"How many girls live here?" I asked.

"Ten, not counting me and Dorothea. How'd you say you found out about us?"

"Myrna Pearl, over at Central Casting. She remembered Colleen."

"Maybe I'll call this Myrna," she said.

"Please do."

"What magazine?"

"Maybe *Redbook,*" I said, "but I haven't sold the idea yet."

She poured milk into the bowl from the jug and with a wooden spoon folded it into the tiny crumbs she'd made of the flour and lard. When the batter was barely moistened through, she floured the table and poured out the dough, pressing it down into a circle and floured it a bit before she began to use the rolling pin. Then she deftly cut the biscuits, reformed the dough, and cut again. She dumped the small amount of remaining dough back into the bowl. "Ruins it to roll it out too much. I'll roll that into balls and freeze it. I can use it for dumplings or mix in some sugar and fry it to go with Easter Sunday ice cream. We don't waste here."

"This takes a lot of planning."

"I've been at it awhile." She wet a large dish towel under the faucet, wrung it out well, and laid it gently over the baking sheets of biscuits. "Harriet Virdon, by the way. Harry."

"Mabel Tanner," I said, using my maiden name. I'd been born Mabel Lauren Tanner. "Good to meet you."

"We'd have to have an agreement," Harry said, "besides you not telling anybody where the house is. Before you write a word, I check your references. Okay, I don't have much time, let's go find Colleen."

"She's here?"

"Sure, upstairs. She works nights, but she'll be awake by now."

She walked out briskly, so she didn't see the expression on my face.

CHAPTER 20

I wasn't sure why I was surprised. It *had* been a long shot, after all, a very long shot. I ought to be glad the girl was alive.

I followed Harry. I had to play this out. I might have to visit other boarding houses for young women to check the remaining names on my list. If I just walked away, word might get around to the landladies about a woman pretending to be a magazine writer. Harry seemed like the sort of person who'd make sure it did.

Colleen Riley opened the door of her third-floor room, wearing a Japanese kimono–style robe in vivid blue and gold. She didn't appear to have anything on under it. Her eyes were still puffy from daytime sleep. Her auburn hair was tied in pin curls along her hair line with thin strips of pink cloth so she could sleep on them.

Harry introduced us and told Colleen what I was up to. That is, what I'd told her I was up to.

"I have to go see to the vegetables," she said then. "She wants to talk to you, but you don't have to do it. If you don't like her questions or she tries to sell you anything, bump her out on her rear, or call me, and I'll do it." She disappeared down the stairs.

"Come in," Colleen said. "Mabel? Is that what she said your name was? I'm still half asleep. I start work at seven. So Myrna sent you to me?"

"She gave me your name."

"Sit down. Sorry, I didn't have time to wash those yesterday."

She cleared some lacy underwear from the small green horsehair armchair, the only chair in the room, which had lost some space to the slope of the roof, but not as much as I would have supposed. It was about twelve by ten, the floor mostly covered by a braided rug. She sat down on the iron bed, which was shoved into the corner, and scooted back till she could lean against the headboard. She snatched her pillow up behind her.

Her night table half covered a narrow closet door. There couldn't have been much room for clothes in it. At the foot of the bed was a wide square arch, covered with draperies of flowered flannel, maybe where she'd captured some oddball space these old houses had and turned it into a dressing room. I doubted it was a bathroom. A chest of drawers stood across from that, with a large mirror above it. She had a window seat in the gable, and because the window was on the side of the house that looked down the slope, she had something of a view, if you kept your eyes focused in the distance.

"You paying for this story?" Colleen asked.

"No more than five dollars, I'm afraid, if I sell it, and I haven't sold it yet."

"What kind of story is it?"

"The lives of extra girls," I said.

"One of those stories about how all the girls share their clothes and cheer each other on. How we're all bright and pretty and work hard to look stylish on a budget. Maybe including some pictures of us sharing a mirror, all smiles, in our perky hats, headed for an audition. Or the one about where we have to show our tits to the casting director if we want him to give us that speaking part?"

"I don't think *Redbook* would print that one," I said.

"You know much about Hollywood?" Colleen asked. "Or are you trying to start a magazine career now your kids are grown? I don't know why Myrna gave you my name."

"Maybe she thought you'd be honest. I'm not looking for a phony fashion item."

"I need a smoke. Come on upstairs with me, if you still want to talk. Harry makes us smoke outside."

She slid off the bed and grabbed a tin cigarette case from among a collection of small framed photos on her chest of drawers. She flinched at the mirror. "I'll have to soak my eyes in ice."

She led me down the hall into the tower and up a flight of steep, narrow steps not much more than a ladder, through an open trapdoor to the cupola, and out into the gathering dusk. Through the cupola's wall of opened windows, the low sun was a glow of orange behind a film of gray.

Colleen said, "We keep this trapdoor open as much as we can. It helps pull the heat out. Third floor's an oven otherwise, in the summer. Worse for my roommate."

"You have a roommate?"

"The glamour of Hollywood. Behind that curtain in my room, there's an alcove with no window. God knows what it used to be. She comes up here to sleep some nights, a pillow and a couple of folded blankets. Better than down there for her, even with a fan. We like to come up here, have a smoke, look around. Sip a little whiskey when we have some. She's got a good set of binoculars. You'd be surprised what people do with their shades up."

Colleen lit the cigarette and offered me one.

"No, thanks," I said.

She put the lighter back into the pocket of her robe. She smoked for a while, and we looked out over Hollywood, a light breeze stirring the pink pin-curl strips in her hair. She was pretty in a small-featured way, but her eyes looked exhausted, and there was a line already forming between her nose and the edge of her mouth.

I said, "You're a dancer."

"I dance at the Parisian Gardens five nights a week, three shows a night. Get home about four. Do some chorus work at the studios. Those are the days I don't sleep at all, though my boss lets me come in late, because he can tell the customers his girls are in the movies. I don't do extra work. First thing you should know, an extra girl doesn't make much money. Even if you work more than most, you're not likely to keep more than twenty bucks a week. You can't live on that, unless you're living with your folks."

"Where are you from?" I asked.

"Inglewood," Colleen said. "The folks still live there. Look, I don't want to be in your story. I don't want anybody feeling sorry for me. You want to know some things, I'll tell you, glad to. I'll introduce you to the girls here who do extra work."

"I wouldn't make anyone sound pathetic," I said. "Just hard-working."

"What did Myrna say about me?"

"Nothing. She's not a gossip."

"She's all right. I had a contract once. Seven years at Epic. You look down there, you can see the studio."

It wasn't hard to spot. There were no tall buildings in between, and we held the high ground. I could see roofs of soundstages, the upper floors of the office buildings. I wondered if, with her roommate's binoculars, I could see what Ben Bracker and Joe Gettleman were up to.

Colleen said, "From the time I was ten till I was seventeen, I worked over there. Epic used to take popular pictures from other studios, change the stories just enough not to get sued, film them fast, and distribute their versions to theaters in smaller towns. It's one of the ways Ben Bracker got the studio back on its feet. I was in a lot of them, even a few leads in some bobby-soxer pictures. But there was only room for one girl to come out a star from those, and that was Mary Ann McDowell. I don't begrudge her that. Truth was, I didn't like making pictures all that much by the end. Hard work, no friends, getting hopped up on that stuff they gave me when I didn't want to get out of bed at six in the morning, no education to speak of. I thought I might study nursing—the war and all—do my part." She took another long draw on the cigarette and blew the smoke out over Hollywood. "But it turned out my parents spent all my money. I ended up with no contract and two hundred and eighty-seven dollars in the bank."

She took the tin cigarette case from her pocket, leaned out one of the windows, and crushed her stub against the case, the ash blowing away. She put the stub into the case. "Harry ever finds a burn mark up here, or stubs on the roof, she'll lock that door on us."

"How is she as a landlady? She was adamant that I never reveal the address of this place."

"She doesn't gouge you, and she could have during the war. But she's got her rules, and I wouldn't cross her. She'll put you out on your ass if you break them."

"Who's Dorothea?"

"She was an actress once, long time ago. So was Harry, back in the twenties. She and Dorothea own this place, but Dot doesn't do much anymore except stay out of the sun. She likes to talk about the past, sometimes Harry's past, which doesn't make Harry too happy. Apparently, Harry was one of those flappers. Hard to imagine now. Dot likes to give us acting tips, and we listen, because she's Harry's friend, and there's no harm in her. But she once told me not to move my hands too fast. The camera would make them look like flapping wings. She probably hasn't been on a set since they were cranking the cameras."

"Hey, Collie! You up there?" a voice screeched up the steps, a voice like a grease-starved hinge.

"No, I'm in Kokomo."

"Dorothea says there's a writer here, wants to do a story on us. You seen her?"

Colleen whispered to me, "I got to get ready for work. Let's go down. You don't want to be up here alone with Gertie. Two minutes, and you'll want to jump."

We climbed down, and I introduced myself to Gertie. The girl had a sharp, eager face, with too much narrow nose, but I thought she'd be a good character type. She gave me her sales pitch to be in the article. I recognized her squawk as the voice on the phone when I'd called earlier, the girl who'd told me to dangle.

I asked Gertie for her calling card, told her I was writing a proposal for the article, and I'd let her know. Colleen grabbed my elbow then and hauled me down to her room and shut the door. "Dorothea's offered to give her voice lessons, but Gertie thinks she sounds just like Stanwyck. She lives on the second floor, thank God, and the walls are thick. You can hang out in here till the coast is clear, but I got to go grab the bathroom. Oh, here's what I was telling you about." She pulled the flannel curtains aside to reveal an alcove, maybe ten by ten. It had a bed, a trunk, a wooden chair, and a small chest of drawers in it. A door that presumably led to a closet. It had a full-length mirror on it, with photos stuck in around its frame. A large photo of a young man in uniform by the bed. Binoculars hung from the bedpost.

Colleen said, "You should talk to my roommate. She's got a lot of personality and the looks. She had a tough break. Her fellow got killed in the war. He was swell, but he died on D-Day. And his family wouldn't have anything to do with her. Their only son, and they didn't even answer her letters; they thought she was just some bit of skirt out for a touch, I guess. She was in bad shape. If you promise not to make her sound pitiful, I'll introduce you." She pulled the curtains closed again.

"Thanks for your help," I said. "I think I can safely slip out now."

"Let me check. Gertie might be prowling the hall." She stuck her head out the door and looked both ways. "One good thing about that voice," she said over her shoulder. "You can hear her coming your way. What? What is it?"

"That girl." I pointed to one of the framed pictures on her chest of drawers. Two girls at the beach, their arms around each others' waists, laughing, performing a barefoot can-can kick.

"That's me and Ida."

"That's your roommate? Is she around?"

"She's up in Yosemite for a few days."

It was the blonde in the slip, the one Savannah Masters rescued before her husband, Kentwood, could get his hand past her knee. The girl who called herself Mimi Delacourt. What had she said her real name was? Smoody. Ida Smoody. She hadn't been on Epic's list under either name. "I think I saw her at a party. At Ben Bracker's house. Were you there, too?"

"Don't tell anybody, please. I got invited, but I had to work. I gave the invitation to Ida. She can dance, and she's worked at Epic. That's all they were looking for, pretty girls to dress up the dance floor."

"Was she wearing a pair of evening slippers with a diamante strap?"

"Yeah." she said. "That might have been her."

"Did she enjoy the party?" I asked. "Have you seen her since then?"

"She had a late train to Sacramento. I was at work."

"Well, give her my regards, if you would, and I'd like to get in touch with her." I took a pencil and notebook from my handbag and wrote my home phone number on a page. I tore the page out and handed it to her. "As soon as she gets back. Thanks."

I slipped out and walked very carefully down the stairs, holding the railing all the way to the second floor. It was definitely the girl I'd seen at the party. And she'd had evening slippers with diamante straps.

Gertie was waiting by the front door to give me a final reminder of how I could reach her. I thanked her with a stiff smile. I left.

I didn't go back to Peter's house to change. It was getting late, and I risked his showing up. I pulled into a gas station, asked for a fill-up, and dashed into the ladies' room. I took off my hat, scrubbed the darkening from my brows, removed the lipstick and applied fresh, unpinned my hair, and combed it out. The time under the netting had given it some nice waves.

The gas station attendant had been checking my oil. He paused, his cloth halfway up the dipstick. I climbed in, asked what I owed.

"It's free," he said, "if you teach my sister that trick. Lady, I got to get her married off."

Any other time, I would have laughed. I paid him and drove off. I made it back to Epic and my bungalow before six. I double-checked the makeup and hair before Peter arrived. He'd put on his best suit.

I closed the bungalow door after him. "I think I know who the dead girl is."

There was no yelling. He was furious, of course, but we couldn't waste time fighting. We had a seven o'clock invitation to the Brackers' for dinner, and we still had plans to make: we had to find out if Ben Bracker knew more than he was telling about the incident he claimed to believe was a nasty prank, all the while convincing him we weren't planning on going to the police.

I sat down at my desk. Peter remained standing, his temper

needing to pace. I told him everything I'd learned at the boarding house, and then what I'd learned about where Roland might be hiding.

CHAPTER 21

Unlike the night of the party, the Brackers' house was modestly lit, and the driveway had only one car in it, a gleaming maroon Cadillac. Peter had his gun with him, but it was in his shoulder holster tucked under the front seat.

Lionel, the butler, took Peter's hat and set it on the table, then led us down the gloomy hallway to Ben Bracker's study.

He knocked twice, then opened the door. We went in, and Lionel withdrew, closing the door after us.

Jean Bracker sat on the sofa, in a version of the hostess gown she'd had on Wednesday night, this one in celery green. Her jewelry was casual. She had, after all, told me not to dress.

"Come in." She stood up to greet her guests.

Peter introduced himself, thanking her for her invitation. Then he shook hands with Ben Bracker, who was standing on the hearth, a large Scotch in his hand, and with the lawyer Joe Gettleman, who had one of the armchairs opposite Jean.

"What can I get you to drink?" Bracker said, jovially.

"Gin and tonic would be nice, thank you," I said. Peter asked for a bourbon.

"Sit down, please," Jean said to me and patted the sofa cushion. Peter took the other armchair. Bracker handed over the drinks and sat in the wing chair that had been pulled up at Jean's end of the sofa.

"Are you in pictures, Mr. Winslow?" Jean asked. "I apologize if I don't recognize you. I'm afraid I'm partial to Epic pictures."

"I'm a private detective."

Her eyes got wide. "My goodness, a real one? I've never seen a private detective offscreen."

"We're not very exciting in real life," Peter said. "Deed searches, alibi checks."

"Divorces," Gettleman said.

"Joe," Jean admonished.

"That's okay," Peter said. "He's right. We do as many rotten things as lawyers."

Bracker laughed loudly, then said, "Lauren, maybe we should put a private eye in our picture. What do you think? He and the lawyer can duke it out."

Peter took a sip of his bourbon, then rested his hand back on the chair arm. He said to Gettleman, "Have you found out who played that prank on Mr. Neale?"

"What happened was unfortunate," Gettleman said, "but it's Mr. Neale's private affair, and he's asked us to leave the matter to him."

"Mrs. Atwill was terrified," Peter said, "and I have only Mr. Neale's word, secondhand, that there's nothing for her to worry about."

"What is there for her to worry about?" Gettleman said. "It was a nasty thing for someone to do, but there are some unpleasant people in Hollywood. She's in no danger, except of course the danger of bad publicity. Anything that becomes public about this will necessarily involve her."

"We don't have any intention of going to the police," Peter said. "Or of telling anyone else. But having a woman pretend to be dead and men pretending to be police sounds more like the work of a person with a serious grudge against Mr. Neale. And now this person knows who Mrs. Atwill is. I don't want him to think he has a grudge against her, too, just because she knows Mr. Neale. We have an obligation to try to protect the ladies."

Bracker said, "Of course we do. But the papers are gunning for us these days, and we'd make a nice, easy target for a scandal."

"I understand," Peter said. "Publicity wouldn't be good for anybody."

Jean said, "Why don't the ladies go freshen up, and we'll come get you all in about a half hour, how's that? Talk fast—there's roast beef that doesn't want to be eaten dried out."

She stood up. My first instinct was to tell her to sit herself right back down, that I wasn't going anywhere. Working in concert with Peter to get information out of people excited me. I wanted to stay and help find out how much these men knew.

Nevertheless, I had to go with her. Although Jean issued the invitation, Bracker was sending me out. If he wanted me here, he would have told his wife to stay. I had to play along.

"Men," I said to Jean with a sigh as I stood up. "They ignore you while they're fighting over what's good for you."

The men laughed. Well, Peter and Bracker did. Gettleman gave me a tight, sour smile.

Jean and I went upstairs to her morning room. We sat down and kicked off our shoes.

She said, "I'm so sorry about this awful thing. I don't know how the men can keep calling it a prank. Some people have a very disturbing sense of humor. You didn't bring your drink up. How about a martini? Lionel always sends up a pitcher in case the women get sent out before dinner. Sometimes those male chats can go on forever, depending on what they're talking about. I've sat down there in that living room with wives for two hours, trying to find things to talk about, while the husbands talked business in the study. Then they come out like nothing happened, while we're passed out from hunger. Ben once said to me, why didn't you just get some sandwiches? I wanted to say, well, *you* invited them for *dinner, both* of them. Of course, men really only invite the men. You can bet that if we don't hear from the men in an hour, there'll be plenty of food and drink coming up the back stairs."

On her desk was a tray with glasses and a silver pitcher set in a bowl of fresh ice. She stirred the pitcher with a long glass spoon and poured us each a drink.

I said, "I envy you, knowing how to entertain strangers. I always found it so hard when the women weren't friends of mine, only married to the men my husband invited over. I never quite got the hang of it."

She handed me my drink and sat back down. "The best actresses in Hollywood are the studio wives. If I have a secret, it's that I try to find out what they're interested in, ask them questions, then just listen. Of course, we can always fall back on complaining about the children, can't we?"

There was no point in saying I didn't have children. It always embarrassed the person who'd brought it up.

I glanced around the room at the photos. "How many do you have?"

"Five, and what a handful when they were young. Three of them in six years, if you can believe it. I don't know how I did it, really. Not much time for anything else except home, kids, and husband. You know how it is."

"Five children, and all the temptations for them out there, growing up in Hollywood. You've done very well."

"I hope so. The youngest is off to college now. You wonder where the years went, don't you? So, a private detective. I'm sorry, but it does seem rather exciting."

"His job's not like it is in the movies," I said.

"Ben must think a lot of your work, to bring you over on loan."

"I was very surprised."

"He speaks highly of you." Her clear blue eyes regarded me

levelly, with the warm interest of the perfect hostess. Did she think I was having an affair with her husband, that he'd hired me in order to spend more time with me? That Peter was a private eye I hired to be my beard? Was the invitation to martinis in her private room surrounded by pictures of their children and the gracious chat about all she'd done for him a warning?

Or was I just a bit too suspicious these days?

I said, "I had no idea he even knew who I was. Have you been able to talk to Roland personally? I hope he's all right."

"Ben's taking care of it. And Joe. Joe's a bit of a bull in a china shop sometimes, but he's dedicated to the studio. And so loyal to Ben. People get the wrong impression about him sometimes. I'm sorry—what he said about Mr. Winslow."

"Don't worry about Peter. He can take care of himself."

"He seems fond of you, or am I being nosy."

"Not at all," I said. "I'm fond of him, too. I only went over to Roland's house to talk about the script."

"Oh goodness, that wasn't what I meant."

I said, "If I were you, I'd be thinking, what the heck was she doing visiting Roland Neale if she had a boyfriend? Roland was nervous about playing opposite Mary Ann."

"Why?"

"She's so much younger than he is. He's as vain as any man."

"Men get to chase women half their age, and people think they're virile," Jean said. "A woman looks ridiculous if the man is an hour younger than she is."

"I think Peter's at least two years younger than me."

"Is he? Oh, my God," she said. "Good for you!" She raised her glass to me, and we drank again.

There were two short raps on the door, and Lionel appeared. "Excuse me, ma'am. Mr. Bracker and the gentlemen have finished."

Jean said, "Your Mr. Winslow must be a pretty straight talker.

Let's see how they behave once they get some red meat in them."

There would be no table fight. Gettleman didn't stay for dinner. He had a previous engagement, we were told.

The roast beef was butter tender, and the wine was French.

Bracker and I talked about the script, particularly my ideas for convincing the censors that the romance could be the moral lesson to offset a few less savory elements of the book.

Peter and Jean talked about raising children, since he'd raised his brother and four sisters. Of course, he didn't tell her he'd thrown his drunken father out the door when he was seventeen and had to go work for a gangster. He just said he'd lost his parents and had worked driving a truck.

We left just after ten. We drove around the block to Roland Neale's house. There were no lights on. Roland had not come home.

So we drove to Beverly Hills.

The night had a coal-black sky, a hard moon, and vivid stars. It was one of those nights there was nothing between you and what you had to do.

CHAPTER 22

The iron gate was locked. I pulled my lock picks out of my handbag and made short work of that while Peter stood watch. We left his car parked at the curb and slipped in. There was no more than a handful of lights on inside the house. No one was expecting visitors.

We didn't ring the bell. We went straight around to the back. There were two terraces, one from the house to the upper lawn and a second whose stairs led down to a long, ornamental reflecting pool that stretched away, softly lit by tall carriage lamps.

Roland Neale had told me he liked to sit out in the evenings and listen to the solitude. We took a chance that, one: he was hiding out at his late aunt's house, which he now owned, and, two: that hiding out there hadn't changed his habits.

He was. And it hadn't.

He sat on one of two white Adirondack chairs on the wide alabaster-gravel walk that ran around the pool, his back to the house, a whiskey glass, half full, held loosely in his right hand.

The lawn had been watered recently; diamond drops still glistened in the moonlight. I took off my shoes and walked down to him silently on the chilled, wet grass. Peter followed at a short distance. I came up a few feet to Roland's right and stepped onto the smooth, cool stones of the path.

"Hello, Roland," I said.

He snapped around, with a sharp breath, squinting up at me,

a sudden shape rising upon him from the dark. I walked in a slow arc till I stood in front of him in the lamplight, the rippled glimmer of the long pool behind me.

"How are you?" I said. "I was worried."

"What are you doing here?" he demanded, his voice coming in sharp breaths.

"It's your aunt's house. You inherited it. Not a difficult deduction, really. If you wanted to hide out but stay close enough to easily find out what was happening, this seemed the perfect place. It was a place to start anyway."

"I don't understand. Why—?"

"Everyone else says it was a nasty joke," I said.

"I won't talk about this."

"Let me introduce Mr. Winslow."

Peter came down to the other side of Roland's chair. He didn't look at Roland. Instead, he stared calmly down the length of the pool. He said, "If Mrs. Atwill is going to have to pretend for the rest of her life that she didn't see a murder, she has a right to know why."

"Who are you?"

"Peter Winslow. I'm a friend of hers. I need to know that whoever pulled that trigger isn't going to come after her one day."

"I'm sorry, but you both have to leave. I have nothing to say." Roland struggled to his feet.

Peter turned to him. "If you want to throw me out, you can try. Or you can call the cops. Unless you plan to call Costello again to clean up your mess."

"I didn't call him. I don't know who he was. I swear. Who are you? You're not from the police."

Peter said, "And that's lucky for you. Why don't you sit down?"

I sat in the other chair and took a handkerchief from my

handbag. I blotted the water from my stockings. Then I put on my shoes, slowly, running my index finger carefully around the heel to slip them on. I gave Roland some time.

Finally, he sat.

We had to play this carefully. We couldn't tell him we were pretty sure we already knew who the dead girl was. We weren't supposed to be investigating.

So I asked him, "Who was she?"

"She said she was my daughter," he said. The whiskey glass was still in his hand. He looked at it with disgust, then placed it carefully on the gravel beside his chair. "I was foolish enough to want to believe her. When I was a young man, I—You know what Hollywood was like back then. No, of course you don't. Neither one of you. Whatever goes on today, it was nothing to how we behaved then. We had the whole world in our thrall. Movie stars were gods. We were the most famous people in the world. All the temptations money can enjoy, we enjoyed. It was only when a scandal ruined somebody else that we gave a thought to how we behaved, and then it was only to figure out how to make sure whatever we did stayed behind closed doors.

"There was a young woman. I was fond of her, but I was fond of a lot of women. When she told me she was going to have a child, I didn't think about marrying her. I didn't see why I should. Women just took care of that sort of thing. I'd give her the money, and she'd go somewhere and take care of it. But she didn't want to do that. My lawyer was a very clever gentleman, and he convinced me the child probably wasn't mine anyway. I let him convince me. I let him buy her off. It was quite easy, actually. She didn't want to charge me with paternity in court; she had a career, too. And a woman can never prove that sort of thing. So she'd go off for a while, give the baby away for adoption, and I would give her money. I never even bothered to find out if she was all right. I never saw her again. I was told by the clever man that she'd decided to raise the child abroad. So easy; all taken care of.

"Four months ago—it was early November—I was at Epic. We were shooting my first movie there, and a girl walked up to me outside the soundstage. She said her name was Mimi. Mimi Delacourt. So obviously a stage name. I was expecting her to ask for help in getting parts. I thought I even might do it, she had such a sweet face.

"Then she said she was my daughter. She dropped her head and whispered it. She was my daughter. Just like that. She said she didn't want to cause any trouble. Her mother was dead, she said, and she didn't have any relatives left. She could prove who she was, if I had doubts, and she had no intention of going to the newspapers or magazines. Nobody at the studio knew. She didn't want to cause trouble.

"She gave me a slip of paper with a phone number and said that, if I wanted to talk to her, I could call. I didn't tell anyone. I knew they'd all tell me to stay away from her. For two weeks, I did. But finally I called. It was an answering service. I left a message for her, just that Roland called.

"She had copies of letters; they were what had led her to me. There was more than I should have said in them, I suppose. Certainly it was clear her mother and I had been lovers. Mimi said they were copies because she'd been worried I'd bring a lawyer with me, and he'd take all her things away from her. Among the copies, there was a letter my very clever lawyer had made the mother sign all those years ago when he gave her the money to go away. A letter that declared I was not responsible for her condition. After all the secrecy, we left a written record of my involvement. Sometimes lawyers are too smart for their own good. She knew things, the sort of things a mother might tell her daughter, not about me, but about her life in Hollywood. Her mother was dead, she said. She'd lost her boyfriend, too, her fiancé, during the war. She showed me his picture.

"I invited her to come for dinner, and then every week. After such a terrible thing had happened to her, losing her lover, she was still full of enthusiasm for the world. I imagined this was how fathers stayed young: seeing the world through the eyes of their children, making them feel they'd done something worthy before they died, helping their children make their way in the world. None of which I'd done."

"Did she ask for money?" Peter asked.

"No. But I wanted to help her. I didn't want her to have to work. She needed to be able to go to auditions, pay for acting lessons, dancing, singing. I gave her some, a few thousand. Maybe five, six, just to make sure she had money in the bank if she was going to quit her regular job. I arranged to get her a small speaking role in my movie. She was so excited. She was quite good, too, unpolished perhaps, but natural. I thought she could get a contract. I told her I was proud of her. I gave her a ring on her birthday last month, one I'd given to my aunt years ago that she had left back to me in her will, not really expensive. She cried a little and told me she didn't deserve it."

"How did she end up with a trip to Yosemite?" Peter asked.

"I'd told her about it once. I'm not even sure how it came up. It's so beautiful this time of year. Quiet, peaceful. She'd never seen Yosemite. She'd never seen much of anything, really."

"I met a woman who called herself Mimi Delacourt at the Brackers' party," I said. "Was that her?"

"I had no idea she'd be there. And she didn't expect to see me."

"I met her down by the tennis courts."

"Ah, yes. I came down to see what the crowd was cheering about. And I saw her out there with those other girls, playing tennis in her slip. I almost went out there and pulled her off the court, just like a father. I stalked back into the party. Later, an hour or so, I saw her come downstairs, and I marched right up to her and asked her what she thought she was doing. She started to cry. There were people milling around, looking at us. I wasn't prepared to see her in public, to expect things of her in public. There was no place to talk. She begged me to let her explain. I said no; I was too angry. I was so angry with her.

"I walked around in the garden to cool off. I didn't want to see anyone. I knew I'd behaved badly. Finally, I calmed down. I looked for her, but I couldn't find her. She had a ticket on a late train to Sacramento, where she'd catch one into Yosemite. I figured she'd left. Then I saw you, we spoke on the terrace, and I decided to just go on home. My house was empty. I don't have live-in servants. I like my solitude. I changed clothes. I went down to the cabana, to see if the bar needed anything. At first, I couldn't figure out what I was seeing. I couldn't believe it could be someone lying there. When I got closer, I saw it was Mimi. It was dark, but I knew her face. Even though—I could still tell it was her. I kept trying to think of a reason she'd be lying there. A reason that she might still be alive. But she wasn't.

"I don't even remember going into the cabana. I was suddenly in there, with the phone in my hand, talking to Joe Gettleman. I knew what would happen. I'd be accused of killing her. Joe said he'd send Mack Pace over and not to do anything till Pace arrived. I don't know how much time passed, but then there you were, and then Pace came. And then the police. I thought they were the police. I really thought they were police."

"What did Costello say to you after Mrs. Atwill left?" Peter asked.

"He acted like a policeman. I told him I didn't do it. He took me up to the house and gave me a drink. He said he believed me, but it wouldn't look good for me. He asked if I knew any of her friends. I told him the truth. I didn't know anything. She told me she lived with some other actresses on the west side of

Hollywood, but she never told me where. I never asked. He said he hoped he could keep the scandal away from me. I said I didn't see how. There were ways, he said. I thought he was asking for a bribe, and I would have paid it. Then I started feeling light-headed. The next thing I recall, Mack Pace was putting cold water on my face, trying to wake me. My shoes were gone. We went down to the cabana. Everything was gone.

"Pace called Joe. I could hear Joe screaming at him on the other end of the line. When Pace hung up, he told me it was all a horrible prank. He said whoever the girl was, she wasn't really dead. And I pretended I believed it. I don't know who could have killed her. Or why they'd want to protect me."

Peter said, "They didn't move the body to protect you. They were protecting the killer."

"But they could have blamed me. If I paid you, hired you, could you find out who killed her?"

"Even if the police had to get into it?" Peter asked.

"There's nothing left at my house. No evidence. If you tell the police, what good would it do?"

"I didn't say 'tell the police,' " Peter pointed out. "But you never know when they might show up. And if I find the killer, what would you want me to do? Shoot him?"

"No. I don't know. Of course not."

"You need to think about this, Mr. Neale. We all do. Whoever killed her can summon a guy to clean it all up."

"Gangsters?"

"Rolly, who is that?" a woman's voice called from the upper terrace. It was Savannah Masters. "Rolly?" she called again.

Peter shot a whisper to Roland. "How much does she know?"

"Nothing. Nothing."

"How can that be?" I said. "Why did you tell her you wanted to hide out here?"

"I told her about it, yes. I told her and Kentwood, but I said it was a horrible joke. Somebody's played a joke. I said I was shaken up. I didn't tell them the truth."

Peter said to me, "Kill some time."

"Savannah, it's Lauren," I called out. "Lauren Atwill." I waved and strolled up to the foot of the terrace steps. "Sorry if we disturbed you. I know it's late."

She wore a long peignoir, one of those floating, diaphanous affairs, with billowing sleeves that caught at the wrist, and then extended down the hand in a cascade of lace. The kind of thing one often saw in movies because actresses were forbidden to wear lingerie, so costumers put them in satin nightgowns and covered the nightgown with a transparent robe. But it was the sort of thing that seemed rather impractical in real life, at least to me. Didn't the lace drag through the egg yolk?

Under the peignoir was a nightgown that would have been banned from the screen. No cleavage allowed.

"Who's that with you?" She craned her neck to see down to where Peter and Roland sat, talking. Then she glanced at her feet. She was caught between going down to see what they were doing and concern about what the damp grass might do to her satin mules.

"My date," I said. "We've been over at the Brackers', having dinner. I didn't know you lived here."

"Yes, for the last month or so. It belonged to Kentwood's mother. I thought the gate was locked."

I didn't know what story Peter and Roland were concocting about why we were here. But I knew not to say anything they might contradict.

"I'm afraid I wasn't paying attention." I laughed lightly, as if I might be slightly intoxicated.

"What the hell is going on? I told you not to go outside." Kentwood Grantlin charged out onto the terrace. He had a revolver in his hand.

"I was just apologizing to your wife," I said. "I'm sorry if we scared you. We didn't know anyone else was here."

Savannah tossed out my name.

Kentwood put the gun away in the deep pocket of his robe. I hoped he knew what he was doing and didn't yank it out carelessly later, catch it in the fabric, and blow off his foot. I had a healthy respect for guns, even before I got shot with one last year.

"I called the police," he said. "Rolly didn't tell us he was having friends over."

Peter and Roland strolled up the lawn. Roland introduced Peter and apologized for not mentioning he'd asked us over.

"Kentwood's called the police," Savannah said. "I thought I saw someone walking down the driveway. I guess I *did* see someone."

"Wasn't the gate locked?" Kentwood asked.

"Must not have caught," Peter said, amiably.

Roland said, "Lauren might write the next script for me."

Peter moved his arm, quite casually, but the elbow touched Roland's arm. A warning. Careful about making excuses. Less said, the better.

"Isn't it a bit late for a script conference?" Kentwood asked.

Inside the house, a doorbell rang, a solemn chiming.

"That must be them, the police." Kentwood went back into the house. He still had the gun in his pocket. Of course, the police weren't likely to care, the master of the house with a gun when his wife thought she'd seen a prowler.

"I got a call from Morty Engler today," Savannah said. She said it to me, but she was looking at Peter, giving him a good look now that she could see all six foot two of him. "We're going to have a chat in a month or so, he's going to set it up. You and me." The deal Morty made: I'd give her some quotes about my divorce, and she'd keep me out of her column till my father's situation with the regents was settled.

"That'll be nice," I said.

Kentwood appeared in the doorway, an officer behind him. "He wants to see everything's fine."

The officer stuck his head onto the terrace. I raised my hand. Peter nodded.

"Okay, sorry to disturb you, sir, ma'am," he said.

"Not at all," Kentwood said. "Thank you for coming so quickly." He escorted the man back through the house. Peter put his hand under my arm. "We'll be on our way. Nice to meet you, Miss Masters." He gave her the full-charm smile. The one with just a hint of appreciation of the figure she had on display.

She touched her chest, right at the best point of the display. "Nice to meet you, too."

"We'll make sure that gate's locked," I said.

CHAPTER 23

Peter put me in the car, then slid behind the wheel. I said, "Don't take this job. You were right. It's too dangerous."

"You're not worried about getting yourself killed, but you're worried about me. Neale's drunk and full of regret, maybe part of it for your benefit. He can't hire me to find out who killed her, anyway. I could lose my license like that. He can hire me to find out who played a prank on him. You're sure about the time he left the party?"

"I'm sure he couldn't have been gone more than twenty minutes before I found the body. That's not enough time to kill that girl and get Costello over there. And if he shot her earlier and came back to the party to establish some sort of alibi, he wouldn't have let me come to his house."

"How many people were there?"

"It was a mob. A few hundred."

"I wonder if any of them were his girlfriends. One of them spots him with another girl, a young girl, thinks something else is going on between them, and follows Mimi-Ida for a show-down. Too much booze. The girlfriend has a little twenty-two in her purse. Waves it around. Something bad happens."

I recalled Bill Linden had told me he'd witnessed fights over Roland at parties in the past.

I said, "And this girlfriend just happens to also have Costello's number in her purse next to the gun?"

"There are plenty of Hollywood women who know men just

like Costello. It makes as much sense as a gangster showing up and deciding to shoot the girl down with a party of a few hundred people not far away."

"Neither one makes much sense."

He didn't argue with me.

The street in front of Epic's parking lot was full of patrol cars, some turned to shoot their headlights into it, to provide more light. We pulled slowly down the block, waved impatiently by an officer to keep coming and keep to the far side. Peter stopped and rolled down the window.

"Move along," the officer said.

"What's happened?" Peter asked. We could see hardly anything beyond the patrol cars except that there were men in suits standing around. Several of them. That meant more than a stolen car.

"Keep moving, sir."

The police department must train officers to fight the instinct to give the public any sort of information whatsoever.

"The lady left her car in there," Peter said. "She works at Epic."

I'd pulled my laminated badge out of my handbag. Peter showed it to the officer. It didn't impress him. "She'll have to wait till tomorrow. Move along."

Another officer strolled toward us, laconic, square-shouldered. The department trained officers to stand behind their colleagues while they said "move along" if the citizen seemed reluctant.

But I recognized this one. So did Peter.

"Officer DiSalvo," Peter said. DiSalvo had watched over us once for a few hours after I'd turned up a body.

Peter explained about my car. DiSalvo said he'd go see if there was anything he could do. Slowly, he weaved his way between the patrol cars and disappeared.

When he returned, he said to me, "The sergeant wants to see

202

you." Peter started to open his door. "Not you. Just her. You can wait here."

DiSalvo came around and opened my door for me, and I followed him. Sergeant Phil Barty stood beside a dark green Mercury coupe, parked in a spot about a hundred feet in, facing the brick side of a building. Both its doors were open. There were stains on the seat, splatters on the windshield. Something bad had happened inside that car.

"Sergeant," I said.

"I thought I recognized your car," he said. My Lincoln was parked about halfway back, on the other side. There were only six cars left in the lot.

"Peter and I had dinner at Mr. Bracker's house. What happened?" I asked, looking carefully at him, not at the car's front seat.

He glanced briefly at it over his shoulder and guided me away. "Why don't we step over here? A guy got shot," he said. "Looks like the killer walked right up to the open driver's window. We're not sure when. At least a couple of hours ago. There's no attendant after seven. Some guy with a car parked near him found the body. You know a guy named Arky Kulpa?"

"Arky? Oh, my God! Yes. I've met him. He's a messenger, he runs errands. He was doing an errand for me."

"What sort?"

"I asked him to put together a notebook for me. For a script I'm working on."

"*The Hard Fold?*" he asked.

"How did you know that?"

"We found it in the back seat, along with a copy of the book with all the pages missing."

"Yes, he said he was going to work on it tonight. He told me he had an appointment at nine."

"You didn't get him killed," Barty said. "This wasn't some

guy after a wallet. What else did he say about tonight?"

"Nothing, except he did say he had a 'little appointment,' in the way somebody does when it's really not little. I thought he meant he had a date. I heard Arky was the man to see if you wanted to lose your paycheck on the ponies."

"Yeah, that would have been Arky's job around here. He was a bookie for Julie Scarza."

I told him everything I'd ever said to Arky and heard about him, which wasn't much.

"If you think of anything else, or hear anything around the studio, let me know," he said. I promised I would. He said he had to log the notebook. I told him that was fine, I'd make another.

Barty let me have my car. Peter followed me home. Two deaths associated with Epic in less than a week. But there was absolutely nothing to connect them.

Peter was gone when the phone woke me up the next morning just before ten. Juanita answered it downstairs before my extension jangled again, but I was awake, and that was just as well, I thought. I had to get to work on my recommendations for turning *The Hard Fold* into a script that could get past the censors. Peter would have to deal with Roland and the search for Ida's killer.

Of course, it didn't turn out that way.

I shuffled to the kitchen, and Juanita handed me my coffee in a mug, rather than a cup and saucer, knowing how clumsy I tended to be after heavy sleep. She waited until I'd managed to get both hands on the mug and both swollen eyes focused on the liquid before she spoke.

"You had a call for Mabel Tanner," she said then. Suddenly my eyes were sharply focused. "I put the message on your desk."

Juanita never answered the phone with my name, as she once

did, and as most other people's household staff would: "Mrs. Atwill's residence." She now simply said, "Hello." It allowed me to give people my real phone number but a phony name if I needed to.

She gave me the look I'd become familiar with in the last several months. What was I up to now? But she could hardly complain. Since I'd met Peter and started getting myself into fixes, she hadn't once found me in my bedroom dissolved in tears over the loss of my marriage.

I'd only given my phone number to one person while claiming to be Mabel Tanner: Colleen Riley at the boarding house.

In my study, I found a number and a message. Call Harriet Virdon.

Harry?

Yes, Harry, Ida's landlady. And she was not happy.

"I had a piece of trash in my house this morning," she said, "calling himself a photographer, leering at my girls, telling them he could get them into pictures. He wanted to know if a woman had come by here, asking questions, what did she want? He described *you*. What the hell is going on?"

"Was he a little weasel, glasses, tongue darting around?"

"Yes."

"His name is Birdie Hitts. He mostly shoots crime scenes, the more sordid the better. He can't get your girls into any pictures fit for decent people to see. He must have followed me to your house. I have no idea why. Let me come over. Please. I'll explain."

"He didn't call you Mabel Tanner," Harry said.

"Lauren. Lauren Atwill. It's my real name."

"You better be able to prove that." She hung up.

I called Peter's office. It was Saturday, but someone was always there till noon. The receptionist said he hadn't come in yet. He must still be at his boss's house, filling him in on Roland Neale, to see if there was any way for them to take him on as a client, or if whoever killed Ida and called in Costello was too dangerous to play with.

I had to go talk to Harry. And now I'd have to do it alone. I left a message with his office about where I was going, and the phone number there if he needed to call me.

"She's upset with me," Dorothea said when she unlatched the screen. "I let that man in."

"It's my fault," I said. "He must have followed me here, somehow."

"Harry's in the kitchen. You have lovely hair, you shouldn't cover it up with that hat you had on."

"Thank you. You, too."

Her small hands flitted around the clouds of waves that framed her face. "It was always my best feature."

"I promise not to wear that hat again."

"And those glasses you had, if you don't really need them."

She floated back to the drawing room. I re-latched the screen and went through to the kitchen.

Harry was punching down dough. I sat down on a chair against the wall, well away from the risk of flying flour. She dumped the dough into a large bowl and snapped a damp towel over it. Then she washed her hands and scrubbed down the table top. She dust-mopped the floor and put the mop and the bowl of bread away into the pantry.

She came back and stood glaring at me from the end of the table.

I said, "I don't know why that man came here. Did he ask about anyone but me?"

"You talk first. Who the hell *are* you?"

I opened my wallet and showed her my driver's license. "I'm

a screenwriter. I work at Marathon. Right now, I'm on loan to Epic."

"That doesn't explain anything," Harry said.

"I'm looking for Ida Smoody. Do you know where she is?"

"She went on a trip."

"Did you see her leave?"

Harry yanked a chair from the end of the table. For a second, I thought she was going to break it over my head. She slammed it down and sat on it. "What the hell is going on?"

"I saw something three nights ago, after a party, but there's no evidence left that it actually happened, no witnesses. Except me. I couldn't go to the police. They'd never believe me. I've been trying to find the girl, the one I saw. Ida might not be the girl. But if she is, I'm afraid something terrible might have happened to her."

"What do you mean 'terrible'? Spit it out. Is she dead? Is that what you're trying to say?" She jumped up and stiff-armed the swinging door. I followed her, three flights. She rapped sharply on Colleen's door. "I need to talk to you," she announced when a groggy Colleen had opened the door. Harry strode into the room. I went in after.

"I'm asleep," Colleen said. "Can't this wait?"

"Have you seen Ida since she went to that party?" Harry asked.

"What? No, I was at work."

Harry snapped aside the flannel curtains that covered Ida's alcove bedroom. She opened the closet door. On the top shelf was an overnight case, the sort with a makeup tray and, beneath, enough room for lingerie and a change of underwear. She took it down.

"That's new," I said to Colleen. "Did Ida buy it for her trip?"

Colleen stepped back, pulling her kimono robe across her chest, putting two layers between us. Harry put it on Ida's bed and opened it. It wasn't locked. The makeup drawer was full, neatly arranged with what Ida would have needed. Beneath the tray, a nightgown, underwear, handkerchiefs.

"She might have decided not to take it," Colleen said. "She bought a nice little suitcase too."

I went back to the closet and pushed the clothes aside. There it was, on the floor, in the corner.

"I thought she was on the train," Colleen said. "What's happened to her? Who are you?"

"Why don't you sit down?" I said gently. "Come on." I guided her back to her room and to the armchair in the corner. I brought the wooden chair in from Ida's room and sat on that. I told her and Harry as much as was wise about my short career as a sleuth.

Colleen said. "I remember that story. It was in the papers last summer. That was you?"

"Yes," I said. "I've been looking for a woman. After that party the other night, I found a body not far away. Some men came; they said they were police. They sent me away. But they weren't. And everything disappeared. I started looking with the list of dancers Epic had sent over to the party. That's how I ended up here. I'm afraid the girl I saw was wearing shoes with diamante straps."

"No," Colleen said. "This is a mistake. See, she wasn't even supposed to be there. I told her she could go. I mean, lots of girls have shoes like that. It's a mistake. She can't—" She began to cry. She tried to find the pocket of her robe, but her hands just slid around her shaking body. Harry pulled a handkerchief from her slacks and held it out to Colleen. The girl stared at it, her hands still working around her body. I laid my hand on her arm, and she quieted. With the other, I took the handkerchief and pressed it into her palm.

"It's that guy," Colleen said. "It's that guy, isn't it?"

"I don't know who did it," I said.

"She met this guy over at Epic, when she was doing some extra work. He was older than her. He bought her stuff, gave her money."

"But she never told you his name," I said.

"Of course she did," Colleen said. "Why wouldn't she?"

I said, "It's possible he had nothing to do with what happened."

"Let him tell that to the cops. I'll tell them they better go have a talk with him. Arky. What kind of name is that? Arky."

"I'm sorry, what? She was dating Arky Kulpa?"

Colleen said, "You know him?"

"I met him at Epic. I'm writing a script over there. Ida was dating Arky?"

"The cops can go talk to *him.*"

"He's dead," I said. "He was shot dead last night."

"Dear God," Harry said. "What the hell is going on?"

I said to Colleen, "Tell me what you know about them. When did they start seeing each other?"

"Back in October maybe . . . yeah, October. He didn't hang around here. Harry didn't like him."

"He was a slick one," Harry said. "Full of big deals and schemes."

"He used to bring her to the Parisian," Colleen said, "down on Sunset, where I'm dancing. He liked to brag, act like a big guy, with big deals cooking. We see those a lot around the club. Most of them are so smart, they spend half their time in jail. But she was lonely, and a guy like that sounds like he could take care of you. And Ida was the kind of girl who needed a guy. But then she met someone else. Maybe it was him, and he killed them both."

"Who was it?"

"She never said who, but he had money." Colleen wiped her

face, and then stared at the handkerchief clutched in her lap. "Arky wanted her to put a touch on him. I think maybe she did for a while. She gave me some money for nursing school. Five hundred dollars. But she liked the guy. And he helped her get a part, a speaking part. That's when she started seeing Arky was trash."

"Did she ever seem afraid? Of Arky or this other man, or of anyone else?"

"No," Colleen said. "I asked her once about Arky, how he'd taken it, her calling it quits. She said she hadn't heard from him, didn't want to. She wasn't scared, nothing like that."

I said, "I have no idea if Arky's killing has anything to do with Ida. It could be something else entirely. He knew some rough people, gangsters."

"Could they have hurt her?" Colleen said.

"I don't know. When did she break it off with him?"

"More than a month. Valentine's. I remember because it was at the Parisian. He brought her there for dinner. I was going to join them for a drink in the bar between shows, and she comes into the dressing room, says she's through with him. I take her to go get a cab. I saw him in there on my way back, still in the bar. Jerry, the bartender, and some guy with a camera were calming him down."

"With a camera?"

"Not like a tourist. A guy who hangs out there."

"You know his name?" I asked.

"Wait a minute. Yeah. No, but I should know it. Odd little guy."

"Birdie Hitts?"

"Yeah, that's it. He hangs out there, in the bar. We have to call the cops."

"There's no evidence left where I found the body. I want to find out what happened, but we have to be careful. Very careful.

There are men involved in this who could make a body disappear. Arky worked for gangsters."

Harry said, "Stop it. That's enough. What do you mean gangsters?"

"He was a bookie for one, a pretty bad man. I have a friend who's a private detective. Please don't say anything till you've both talked to him."

"She's had enough questions. You and I need to talk. Right now." She put her hand out to Colleen. "Come on, you lay down. I'll send you up something. You stay in bed. Rest."

"I have to go to work."

"We'll see about that. If you're not feeling well, you call and tell them you're sick. I'll pay you what you'd get for the night. We'll talk about it later. I'll take care of it."

Harry tucked her in. Colleen lay on her side, crying softly. Harry touched her head gently and led me back into the hallway.

"Want a drink?" she asked.

"I sure do."

We went downstairs. There were a couple of girls in the front parlor now, reading magazines. The radio was turned on, its volume low. It was Saturday. The rest of the girls were probably out with friends or at work, either in a store or working their Saturday half-days in an office.

Dorothea was cleaning up the dining room of the remains of breakfast, folding the table cloth with great care.

"Dorothea," Harry said, "would you take something up to Colleen? She's not feeling well."

"Of course. The poor child." Dorothea followed us to the kitchen where Harry unlocked a cabinet and pulled out a bottle of good brandy. She poured a couple of fingers into a glass and handed it to Dorothea. "She's lying down. Just give this to her, and leave her alone."

"I understand. Quiet as a mouse. In and out." Dorothea

glided away through the swinging door.

Harry poured two more glasses and handed me one. "Come on."

She led me down a short hallway, more like a linen cabinet, with stacks of drawers and shelves on either side, into a bed-sitting room, converted from what would have been the rear parlor in the days when a family lived here. The double sliding doors that would have opened into the front parlor were closed, a long dresser in front of them. I could hear the radio in the front room, a band playing some lush tune.

Harry sat down in one of the generous armchairs by her fireplace, and I took the other. She said, "I don't want to scare Colleen, but I want to know if we're in danger, and what the hell you're up to."

"I was trying to find out who the girl was. Trying to see if there was some way to go to the police. Some proof to be found that would lead to the real killer and not get innocent people hurt."

"That man, the photographer who came here this morning. It was the same guy Colleen saw with Arky? Birdie Hitts?"

"Yes. But I have no idea why he'd come here asking about me. Did he ask about Ida, too? Or just about me?"

"I didn't hear most of what he said. A couple of the girls came into the kitchen, told me there was a guy giving them the leer out in the parlor, talking to Gertie and Dorothea. I marched in there and told him to get the hell out. I heard Ida's name mentioned, but I can't say if he knew her name *before* he arrived."

"How long has she lived here, I mean, in Los Angeles. Do you know?"

"Since she came out from Tennessee, four years ago. And that room's the only place she's ever lived since she got to town. She couldn't have been more than sixteen when she showed up on the porch. She was a bit of a hick then, and I tried to keep an eye on her."

"Has she ever talked about her parents?"

"Sure. They owned a farm in a small town out there. Can't recall the name of the town right now. They're gone, though. She still has an aunt she writes to, back there."

"They were her real parents? Not adopted?"

"What do you mean?"

"Ida was involved in something. She was pretending—at least, I'm pretty sure she was pretending—to be the illegitimate daughter of a rich man, that other man Colleen mentioned. He became fond of her, and I think she began to like him, and maybe had second thoughts about what she was doing."

"It was that Arky put her up to it. She wouldn't do something like that on her own."

"She had letters, copies of them anyway. If they weren't actually hers, somebody gave them to her."

Harry was quiet for a moment, staring down into the glass she held in both hands. "Dorothea talks too much. It's not her fault. She can't remember what she's supposed to do. And not do. I guess she talked too much to Ida. Ida's always been nice to her." She sat back. "Did that bastard Roland Neale kill her?"

CHAPTER 24

I took a long, slow breath before I said, "I don't know. There's no evidence he did. He wanted to believe she was his daughter."

"*Now* he wants a daughter. You a friend of his?"

"No. I was hired to write a picture for Mary Ann McDowell. The studio's thinking about casting him, too. I was going over to his house that night, to talk to him about the script. I found the body nearby. If the body was Ida's, she might have been on her way to see him, maybe even to tell him the truth."

"Sounds like a reason to kill her."

"However, he can't have called those men who moved the body. There wasn't enough time between his leaving the party and my seeing the body for anyone to have put that whole charade together."

"You like him?" Harry asked.

"I liked him better before I met him."

She laughed, one sharp jolt. "I used to be in pictures, back twenty years ago. But I had the great misfortune to fall in love with Roland Neale. When I found out I was pregnant, I told him. I knew it was his. So did he. He knew I didn't play around like that. Hell, I was wild about him. I wanted him to marry me, but I could see—finally—that it wasn't going to happen. His lawyer offered me ten thousand, but I had to sign a paper saying Roland Neale and I had never been lovers, even though I had letters that showed otherwise. I came back after having my baby to find I couldn't get a job, not at a major studio.

Somebody had put the word out, and I'd ended up on a list of people not to hire for moral reasons."

"Was Roland's lawyer named Joe Gettleman, by any chance?" I asked.

"Yeah. What's he doing these days? Dying painfully, I hope."

"He's a lawyer at Epic. Counsel to Mr. Bracker, I think."

"Well, then," Harry said, "whatever this is, you better keep a close eye on him."

She took a small framed photo from a table under the window and handed it to me. A little girl, maybe two years old, lying against a pillow, a ribbon in her silken hair. Her feet showed from under her nightgown, in booties, small and precious.

"Alice died six months after that picture was taken. Influenza. Just like that. Gone in a week." She sat back down. "I never would have thought Ida could do something like this."

"She lost the man she loved. It changes people, at least for a time. Maybe she thought if she got tough, she'd never get her heart broken again. Colleen told me his family rebuffed her."

"I didn't think straight for a year after Alice died. If it hadn't been for Dorothea, I would have killed myself. I did some work on Poverty Row, just trash. Then we moved to New York. We did some plays, toured in third-rate companies, neither one of us getting any younger. And we missed California. I still had most of the money I'd got in the deal from Gettleman. Dorothea and I bought this place cheap during the Depression. Neither one of us knew much about how to earn a living outside of acting, but I could cook. She kept the place clean. She still tries. She really tries to help. It's not her fault. I'd forgotten about those letters. They're up in the attic, in a trunk. Dorothea must have let it all slip."

"I'm guessing Ida then told Arky, and he decided they could make some money out of it."

"Could this Arky have killed her?"

"I don't know. We don't even know if he was part of the scheme."

"What are you going to do now?" Harry asked.

"Talk to Mr. Winslow. He's the private detective I mentioned."

"Can he find Ida's killer?"

"We have no idea what's going on, except that two people are dead, and there's somebody in this who can make a body disappear. I'm not sure how far we can go against people like that."

"And yet, here you sit. You didn't have to come over here. You're not about to let this go."

When I left the house, I was thinking about Ida and Harry, and a long-dead child named Alice, so I didn't pay any attention to the wine-colored sedan parked ahead of my Lincoln. As I reached for my door handle, the sedan's passenger door opened.

"Mrs. Atwill."

His name was Eddie. He was a short square of concrete with a nose and cheeks mottled red with rosacea. He worked for Julie Scarza, who was maybe the second most dangerous gangster in Los Angeles, after Jack Dragna. Right now, it didn't really matter whether he was second or third. His henchman was staring at me across the roof of his car.

Then the driver's door opened, and another man got out. I didn't know him. That didn't matter either. They weren't going to let me go anywhere their boss didn't want me to go. That was what mattered.

Eddie laid his hands on the roof of his car so I could see them. They weren't holding a gun.

"Mr. Scarza would like to talk to you," he said.

There was nothing to say, nothing to do really, except to go with them.

Eddie came over, opened my passenger door and got in. The

other man just stood there, his right hand flat across his stomach, in front of his open jacket.

I climbed in, started the Lincoln's engine, pulled away from the curb. The other car fell in behind. Eddie said nothing except to grunt the turns I should make. We headed downtown. I rehearsed ways I could tell Scarza I'd butt out of anything he didn't want me doing. I rehearsed ways to remind him he owed me a favor, although I didn't think it would count for much if he was really unhappy, for example, if I'd accidentally stumbled into a killing he wanted cleaned up forever.

South of downtown, just west of Central, Eddie pointed me to a curb in front of a narrow diner. The cracked neon sign in the window had seen better days. The diner had never seen any better days.

Eddie and I went in through the puckered screen door, past the line of tables shoved against the left-hand wall and the battered stools at the greasy counter on the right, through the smell of decades of frying oil and wasted dreams. We passed a broom closet that smelled of mildewed mops and a men's room that smelled worse. Eddie knocked on a thick steel door at the back. It was opened by another thug.

Inside, the room was scented with the smoke of the Cuban cigar Julie Scarza was enjoying at a poker table, his back to the rear wall. There was nothing else in the room except piles of liquor boxes.

Eddie shut the door.

Julie Scarza was not a handsome man. He'd made his way in the world with other talents. He had a large head he kept nearly immobile; the skin was coarse and the lips thin. He had thick glasses and behind them a set of vicious eyes. His black hair was precisely groomed and his shave close. His hands were manicured, though the flesh was mottled.

"Please sit down," he said. I did, in a chair to his right. I didn't want my back to the door. As if that would make a difference.

He raised a finger, the index finger of the hand resting on the immaculate green felt top. Eddie went to a table I hadn't seen that was squeezed between two columns of boxes. He mixed a drink from the skyline of bottles, scooped in ice from the bucket with a silver scoop, stirred, and set the glass and a napkin in front of me. A gin and tonic, with a perfect slice of lime hooked on its rim. I had no idea how he knew it was my drink of choice, and it scared me even more that he was giving me my favorite.

I tried it. The drink was excellent. Eddie apparently had skills beyond hurting people.

"It's very nice," I said. "Thank you."

Eddie said, "We found her at the boarding house. She was in there over an hour."

Scarza nodded an inch, tilted his head an inch, and the other thug went out another door, straight across from me. When he came back, he was half leading, half dragging the photographer Birdie Hitts.

Birdie's shoulders were hunched, and he'd pulled himself in on himself as if he were trying to hide inside his suit. The sweat hung in beads on his forehead and sparkled in his eyebrows. His shirt collar was gray with it. The thug sat Birdie down in a chair a few feet from the table.

There's a law of physics that no two objects can occupy the same space at the same time. It wasn't possible to be more frightened than he was, and somehow that made me braver. I squeezed the lime and dropped it into my glass, then used the napkin to delicately wipe the pulp from my fingers and the sweat from my palms. I took another sip. My hand wasn't shaking. Not too much.

"You know Mr. Hitts," Scarza said.

"I do, yes, slightly."

"Did you know he's been following you?"

Peter had taught me that, when you have to answer questions, you try not to give away more information than you're asked for. You could get yourself into worse trouble. Try to get the other guy to tell you something first.

"I just found out this morning. Why would he do that?" I asked.

Scarza set his cigar straight across the ashtray beside him. He put his fingertips together on the perfect felt. "Tell her," he said to Birdie

"It was just because she came to Epic," he said, his head down, the breath hard between his teeth. "I didn't mean she did anything."

"I appreciate that, Mr. Hitts," I said. "But as you see, Mr. Scarza would like to know more, and from me. But I have no idea why you'd think my being at Epic would interest him."

"I didn't think you were there just to write. When you turn up, things happen, so I thought something else must be going on. I had nothing better to do, so I followed you around, last couple of days. Last night, I'm over at the Hollywood substation, and I heard about a guy shot dead in the Epic parking lot. I went over there, with my camera, and it's Arky Kulpa. And there in the lot, I see your car. I give one of the uniforms a sawbuck to keep his eyes and ears open. I go down to the morgue with the body, get some pictures, then when I come back, the uniform tells me you've been there, talking to one of the detectives. That's all I said."

Scarza said, "Mr. Hitts doesn't want to look like the sort of man who'd rat out a lady."

"I have no idea who killed Mr. Kulpa," I said.

"But you were talking to the detectives," Scarza said.

"To one of them, yes. I had dinner last night at Ben Bracker's home. He's the head of Epic. My escort drove me, so I'd left my car in the lot after work. The detective found something of mine in the back seat of Mr. Kulpa's car." I explained about the binder and how Arky had ended up with it.

"Who was this detective?" Scarza asked.

"Barty, Sergeant Phil Barty. He thought the killer walked up to Mr. Kulpa's open window, that he'd been waiting for him."

"Arky was waiting for the killer? Or the killer was waiting for Arky?" Scarza asked.

"The killer was waiting for Arky. I'm sure you don't need me to find out what the police think. At any rate, that's all the sergeant told me."

Scarza repositioned his cigar. "It came to my attention that last night Mr. Hitts told some people in the bar at the Parisian Gardens club that he might have an idea about why Arky was shot. Once he announced this publicly, I could not ignore it, nor that he chose not to tell me. Birdie, why don't you tell Mrs. Atwill what you have now told me?"

Birdie's tongue darted over his lips, trying to find some moisture.

Eddie slapped him hard on the back of the head.

"Go on, Birdie," Scarza said.

"We were talking, a few nights ago, four nights, over at the Parisian, in the bar," Birdie said. "Arky told me he had his hooks in something good. He was drunk, you know, bragging. I told you, I don't know what he was into."

Eddie smacked him again.

Scarza raised his finger, and Eddie lowered his hand. Scarza said, "Let me decide when I've been told a sufficient number of times what Arky said to you."

"He said he'd found something I'd be interested in, just my kind of thing, if only he could tell me about it. A nice bit of dirt, going to pay off like gold. Like gold. He was talking kind of loud, and I guess he realized there were ears around, because he hauled himself out of the bar. I never saw him again, not alive."

Scarza turned to me, his head moving two inches. "What were you doing at that boarding house? Birdie says he followed you there yesterday. Today, he tried to find out. He's a skilled photographer, but clumsy, it would seem, in questioning ladies. The landlady threw him out. But he discovered you hadn't used your real name. If you're writing screenplays and minding your own business, why are you using a fake name? And you went back there the morning after Arky died. What should I make of this?"

"Not in front of Mr. Hitts," I said.

"Of course. We're finished," he said to Eddie, with only a slight jerk of his chin. Eddie and the other man hauled Birdie from the chair. Birdie tried to dig his heels into the linoleum.

Scarza picked up his cigar and re-lit it, puffing once, twice, in satisfaction underneath Birdie's strained breathing, as the other man wrestled him out. Eddie remained, closed the door.

I said, "I found a body, a girl. She'd been shot in the face. A man showed up pretending to be the police, and I believed him. The body disappeared and all traces of the killing. I started trying to find out who she was. If you want me to stop, I will."

"Where did you find this body?"

"In Holmby Hills. There's a lane behind the backyards of some of the houses, a path for golf carts. I was walking there after the Brackers' cocktail party a few days ago. I discovered she had come to the party with a group of Epic dancers, invited at random just to be pretty and dance with the guests. I managed to trace her to that boarding house. I went there today to apologize to the owner, to explain that I had nothing to do with Mr. Hitts showing up, at least not on purpose."

"What was her name, the dead girl?" Scarza asked.

"Ida Smoody. She was an extra player. She did some work at

Epic. I found out today she dated Arky Kulpa for a while but had broken off with him a little over a month ago, in mid-February. She'd been getting some money out of a man, maybe in a scheme with Arky. Now she and Arky are both dead. Mr. Scarza, please don't play with me. I did you a favor last year. You know I didn't do it for you, but it ended up being what you wanted. If you want me to butt out, I will. Just tell me."

He took a pull on the cigar, then held it just outside his mouth between the tips of his blotched fingers. "I have no objection to you trying to find this girl's killer. But if you find the name of Arky's killer, I would want to know."

"I'm not sure I want to go any further with it."

"I wouldn't rely on the police overmuch."

"I don't, as you know."

"I will give you a number where you can reach me, if you should decide to continue."

Eddie stepped forward and handed me a card. A business card with only a phone number on it. If I put something like that in a movie, the audience would laugh.

"Thank you," I said to Scarza. "If you're finished with Mr. Hitts, I'll see he gets home."

"Why would you do that?" Scarza said.

"I don't think his heart would survive another trip with Eddie."

Scarza laughed. He pulled his lips back flat on his teeth and made short coughing noises that I took for laughter.

I said, "And if there is anything he's too scared to recall right now, maybe he'll recall it talking to me."

He nodded to Eddie, who opened the door and jerked his head. "Put him in the car, the Lincoln."

"Good-bye, Mrs. Atwill," Scarza said. "Give my regards to Mr. Winslow."

"I will."

"I assume he is involved in this pursuit of yours?"

"Yes."

"A valuable man."

CHAPTER 25

I followed Eddie back through the diner, the way we came. The other thug was waiting by the passenger door of my car. Birdie was inside. Eddie held my door for me, touched his hat, and stepped back from the car. I pulled away. When I hit Central, I stomped the accelerator.

"For God's sake," I snapped at Birdie, "roll the window down. You need some air." And I needed not to smell the sweat on him.

"Where are we going?" he asked.

"Away from here. Where's your car?"

"I know how this works," he said. "They play with you, let you go, then come up behind you one night and shoot you in the head." He whipped around and watched out my rear window, his tongue darting madly.

I wasn't going to argue with him. He wasn't thinking straight. And I wasn't sure I was. I cut through some alleys, ran some yellow lights.

Finally, I asked him again, "Where's your car?"

"In front of my place. They lifted me right off my porch."

"Tell me how to get there. Tell me! They're not going to let you go, then go right over to your house."

He lived in a horseshoe of semi-detached bungalows with dark green siding and narrow windows that had no glass, no screens, just the kind of permanent blinds you crank open and shut. A much-patched sidewalk ran through the court. The grounds were mostly sand and reminders that some of the neighbors had dogs.

He had two rooms; the living room had a sort of kitchen along one wall—a small refrigerator with a whirring motor on top, a two-burner stove, sink, two feet of counter space, a couple of pine cabinets. A table, chairs. A rutted sofa and an armchair.

"I save my money," he said.

"I didn't say anything." But I thought he must be saving plenty of it.

I opened the cabinets. I found a bottle of bourbon and a clean glass. I poured him a couple of shots and handed it over.

He sat down. "I know these people," he said. "I know how they work."

"You know a lot of gangsters?" I asked.

"More than you."

"But I know the important ones."

"That's real funny." He tossed back some bourbon.

I went into the bathroom and ran cold water onto a washcloth I got from the shelf above the bathtub. I rung it out and brought it back to him.

He took it and threw it across the room.

"I'm sorry," I said. What it must have cost him to be rescued by a woman he'd ratted out to Julie Scarza.

I poured myself a drink and sat down at the cheap plywood table.

He pulled out a handkerchief and wiped his face. "How the hell do you know Scarza?" he said finally.

"I did him a favor once. And I don't mean I slept with him."

"Christ, I hope you got better taste than that. I *knew* you were working on something at Epic, I *knew* it."

"I wasn't, not the night I saw you at Madison's. I didn't lie to you. I'm not working on the Arky Kulpa killing."

"The morning after Arky's shot dead, you're back at that

boarding house, and that's where his chippie lives. So that means you're working on it. Well, you *were*, anyway. I think we both ought to get out of town for a while."

"Scarza didn't warn me off."

"What the hell do you think just happened?" he shouted. He snatched at his hair with his free hand. "For the love of God, if he asks you what you're doing, he means stop doing it!"

"He said I could keep going, as long as if I find out who killed Arky Kulpa, I tell him."

"You're crazy, lady."

"I want you to tell me everything you told Scarza," I said.

"You're crazy."

"If he wanted to kill you," I said, "you'd be dead. He wouldn't have shown you to me, and if he wanted us both dead, he wouldn't have let us go."

"What the hell did you do for him?"

I'd found the killer of a young man he thought of as a son, but it was none of Birdie's business.

"What did Arky Kulpa tell you?" I asked. "And how much do you know about Ida Smoody?"

"I didn't even know she lived there, in that boarding house, till today. I met her a few times, with Arky, starting back last year, over at the Parisian. He called her Mimi Delacourt."

"That was her professional name," I said.

"He said he'd made her change the name. He said it used to be Ida Smoody, but Mimi Delacourt had more sex appeal. I thought Mimi made her sound like a chippie, but I didn't say anything. I hadn't seen her in months, around Christmas. This morning, I went up to that house, the boarding house. I asked the batty dame who answered the door—"

"Dorothea. Her name's Dorothea."

"What? Yeah, well, I wanted to see what you were up to. So I tell her I'm a friend of the lady who came by yesterday, Miss

Atwill, and I start to describe you. Suddenly, she's opening up like a ripe watermelon. Oh, she says, you mean Miss *Tanner.* So I say yeah, sure, sure, Tanner. And she tells me all about how you're a magazine writer and going to do a story on some of the girls, some of her actresses. I knew you're up to something, not using your real name. And I knew Arky's chippie was an actress, so I—"

"Stop calling her that. Call her by her name."

"You're awfully particular for a dame who gets on so nice with Julie Scarza. Arky's dead. You're sniffing around a boarding-house with actresses, his girlfriend was an actress, so I asked if there's a Mimi lives there. Or a girl called Ida, because I remembered her real name. The dame says, yes, but she can't remember where Ida is right now. Then some other girls come in. I tell them I'm a photographer, know some people at studios, try to get some information out of them. One of them likes to talk; her name's Gertie. A voice that'll crack your teeth. The others go off and bring back the gorgon."

"Harry, the landlady."

"She's plenty steamed when she finds out I was looking for you. *This,* the batty dame remembers and tells her all about. *And* she remembers I said *Atwill.* The gorgon throws me out on my ass."

"What do you know about Arky, about what might have got him killed? Look, Scarza didn't kill him, didn't have him killed. He wants to know what happened."

"And you trust him."

"No. But I believe him about this."

"Arky had a deal going," Birdie said, "one he didn't tell Scarza about. Did you think about how there might be some other guys working for Scarza involved and also not telling their boss? Guys who wouldn't like you stirring things up?"

"Of course."

He stood up. "Good luck. And good-bye. I'm getting the hell out of town."

It wasn't going to be that easy for Birdie. I said good-bye, then found the nearest pay phone, which turned out to be right outside the manager's office. I gave him a dollar to stop leaning on the screen door leering at me and go back to minding his own business.

I called Peter's house. He was there. I gave him a very short version of why I was at Birdie's. He was there in ten minutes.

I knocked on Birdie's door, while Peter positioned himself where he couldn't be seen. Then I went to one of the windows and called in to Birdie through the open blinds that my car had died, could I use his phone. Nobody came to the door. I used my lock picks, and we went in.

I could hear the water running. Birdie was taking a shower. We went into the bedroom. He'd hauled out a suitcase and laid it on the bed. His closet door was open. He was getting ready to go. His drink and the bottle of bourbon sat on the chest of drawers. Quickly, Peter searched the chest, the pockets of the suitcase, and the drawer in the night table. There was nothing there to interest us. Especially not a gun for Birdie to grab if he didn't like the intrusion.

We waited. I had a little time to fill Peter in on what I'd found out at the boarding house, but not enough time for him to express his consternation that I'd been asking questions without telling him. Or to express whatever he felt about my having been picked up by Scarza's thugs.

The water stopped.

"Birdie?" I called out. "Put a robe on. We have to talk some more."

"What the hell?" He charged out, tying a bathrobe, a towel around his neck, his hair wet. I was sitting on the chair in the corner. Peter stood in the doorway to the living room.

228

"This is Mr. Winslow," I said.

"I know who the hell he is," Birdie said. "How'd you get in here?"

"You might want to get a better lock," Peter said.

"Look, I didn't mean for any of this to happen," Birdie said to him.

"Which," Peter said, "is why you don't have to apologize to her for getting her picked up by Scarza's goons. Mrs. Atwill's capable of finding trouble all by herself. Why don't you sit down?"

"You're both crazy," Birdie said. "You can get the hell out."

Peter just stood there. There was no sense in pointing out the obvious: He wasn't leaving till he was ready to. Finally, Peter said, "Mrs. Atwill doesn't scare easy, and even when she's scared, she doesn't stop thinking. She wants me to have a talk with you because you're holding out. Tell us what it is, and you can be on your way."

"I told her what I know."

I said, "You told me you hadn't seen Ida since around Christmas. You made it very clear that you hadn't seen her in months. You lied, Birdie. One of the dancers at the Parisian saw you and your camera in the bar there the night Ida broke up with Arky. Valentine's Day."

Peter said, "Don't waste our time saying you don't remember. You know more about what this Arky Kulpa was up to than just two minutes of him bragging a few days ago when he was drunk. If that's all you knew, you wouldn't have been that scared of Scarza. You had more. I'd say plenty more, and you were scared he'd think you knew too much about whatever it was."

"Why do you care what happened to Arky?" Birdie said.

"I care what happened to Ida," I said, "and she's missing."

"I had no idea about that. What's she to you?"

Peter said, "You'll be on your way out of town a lot faster if you just answer her questions."

"She hasn't asked me any yet," Birdie pointed out.

I said, "We want everything Arky Kulpa told you about the blackmail and everything you talked about when he was *with* Ida or everything he said *about* Ida."

"I don't have a photographic memory."

"Start at the first time you met her," Peter said.

"If it'll get you out of here." Birdie shoved his suitcase roughly toward the headboard and sat down on the bed. "I saw her three times in my life. All three times at the Parisian. It's the kind of club guys like Arky take their dames. Or go to try to meet some dames. I knew Arky off and on for years. Look, I know a lot of guys like him. It's the business I'm in."

"Did Scarza ask you about Ida Smoody?" Peter said.

"No, but her name came up, because I told him all I knew about Arky. Everything."

Peter said, "But you didn't tell the cops any of it."

"First, lots of things could have got Arky killed. Second, he liked to brag. Yeah, okay, I was thinking maybe I could find out who he'd been blackmailing *before* I told the cops anything. Sell the story. A guy's got to make a living."

"Tell us about Ida Smoody," Peter said.

"The first time I saw her was back in November, some time before Thanksgiving. I don't know the exact date. I wasn't Arky's secretary. Arky was showing her off in the bar. She was a little looker. Not from class, but she had the makings. And she didn't seem to care for him showing her off and telling everybody he bought her the dress and the jewelry. Later, she goes to the ladies', and he leans over, tells me she's got her hooks in a sugar daddy. They got an angle to play, make them both some money off the guy. Maybe the guy might even set her up in a place of her own. She came back, and they took off, so that was all I got.

"I see them a few weeks later, some time around Christmas, and I remember this because the Parisian had the decorations up in the bar, and I was thinking how they make the place look cheap, that green junk draped all over the mirror. They're in the bar, too, waiting for a table for dinner. So we start making small talk. I start thinking maybe she's getting tired of him, the way she looks when he's showing her off. She points out she paid for the dress herself with the money she got from the picture she did.

"Then Arky puts his arm around her, tells her to go freshen up her face before the other couple gets there. He wants her looking extra nice. Me, I think she looks just fine. When she's gone, I offer the opinion that he might not want to imply she could look better if he wants to keep her impressed. He tells me I don't know nothing about women. They like being told what to do. Too bad he never got to know *you*," Birdie said to me. "I asked him how the sugar daddy was coming through. He said not bad, but he's got more on the line. I said more sugar daddies? She must be a busy girl. He laughed, said she wouldn't go for that. But he had an ace in the hole. Could be plenty more. Plenty more. It could be a very nice New Year. But I don't know what he meant."

He got up and retrieved his glass of bourbon from the chest of drawers. "I guess you searched the place," he said to Peter.

"Just to make sure you didn't have a gun you could get to," Peter said. "I figure anything important, you're not going to keep it where a three-minute toss would turn it up."

Birdie grunted. "Well, if you need any more pictures, the shop's closed. Uniforms wouldn't let me near a killing for three months after you."

I glanced between them.

"What?" Birdie said. "She doesn't know?"

231

"She knows part of it." Then he said to me, "Birdie holds a grudge."

Birdie said, "Let's say I'm careful now if a guy comes by looking for pictures." He turned to me. "It was over a year ago, New Year's Eve a year ago. I was down at the local substation, thinking I might be able to get something. When people are drinking, trouble's going to start. At least there'd be a car crash worth shooting. Then the call comes in about a doctor getting shot. I got shots of the kid who did it, just when they were clapping the cuffs on him. The detectives staged it real nice for me. A couple of days later," he said and gestured to Peter, "*he* shows up. Wants to see all the shots I got. Everything, all the negatives. I don't know what he's up to, but the money's good."

Peter said to me, "You remember Rocco. It's his kid, Pauly. He's still got the jacket on, before the cops took it off of him for evidence—the jacket that disappeared when Pauly's lawyer asked for a test to see if the kid had fired a gun."

"Cops wouldn't let me near a killing for months after that," Birdie said.

"You saved the kid's life," Peter said.

"Christ, okay, so what else you want to know so I can get the hell out of here?"

"What else did Arky say?"

"I don't remember he said anything else, not that night. Next time I saw him to talk to was Valentine's Day. And it's the only other time I ever saw her. I can see they're almost history, at least on her part. He's drunk, gives the cigarette girl's behind a squeeze right there in front of her. She packs herself up. Pours her drink right in his lap. Jerry gives him a bar towel fast and gives me the nod to go sit next to him, calm him down. But Arky doesn't follow her; he just dries himself off. He says she'll get over it, and if she doesn't, well, there's more on the way. Plenty more. That was the last time I saw them together. The last time I saw *him* was Wednesday night, maybe nine or so. After I saw you over at Madison's," he said to me, "I checked in with the sherriff's boys, and I find out they got a vice raid coming later, over in West Hollywood, so I figure I'll kill some time at the Parisian, which isn't too far. Arky was sitting at the bar by himself. I said hello, how's the girl, did they make it up? He said she'd given him the heave-ho. I asked if she ran off with the sugar daddy. He said, hell, that didn't net him more than three grand. She got to *liking* the guy, and she started thinking maybe she was better off playing it straight with him. Arky said if he wanted to cause her trouble, he could, but she was an okay kid; maybe he should have treated her better."

"Are you sure it was Wednesday?" I asked.

"Yeah. Why?"

"Go on."

Wednesday was the night of the party. It was unlikely Arky had killed Ida if he was sitting, drunk, at the Parisian about nine o'clock.

Birdie threw back the last of the bourbon from his glass. "That's when he says his new deal would be my kind of story, if he only could tell me about it. He was laughing and punching me on the shoulder, almost knocked me off the stool. Dirt that turned into a gold mine. That's what he said. A gold mine." He yanked the suitcase to the edge of the bed and threw it open. "I told you what I know. Now I'm leaving."

Peter said, "Look, Mrs. Atwill feels bad about what happened; this was partly her fault. If you're nervous about staying here, why don't you let her pay for you to stay somewhere else?"

"What kind of place?"

Peter said he knew a nice hotel, out in Manhattan Beach, not that far, but far enough. A room with a view of the ocean. He'd hidden some people out there before. He'd make the reservation. The hotel would bill the agency, and I'd pay the bill.

233

Peter made the call from Birdie's phone, gave him the address and directions, told him he'd wait outside till Birdie was safely away.

They shook hands, and Peter and I left.

Rapidly, Peter wrote down two numbers on a page from his notebook, tore it out, handed it to me. "Get to a phone. The first one's Johnny, then his girlfriend's. Tell him I got a tail job for him and to get here fast. I want somebody making sure Hitts goes where he's told and stays there."

I jumped into my Lincoln. We didn't want to make the call from outside the manager's office, with him lurking. I found a drugstore a block away. Johnny was home. He made it to the bungalow court before Birdie came out with his suitcase. Peter helped Birdie get it into the trunk of his car, and they shook hands again. Birdie drove off, and Johnny waited, then eased his car into traffic after him.

We sat in my car, and Peter told me about his meeting that morning with his boss and the agency lawyer. The lawyer was satisfied the agency could accept Roland Neale as a client—as long as it was clear the agency was being hired to discover who might have perpetrated a vicious prank on Mr. Neale, *not* to investigate a killing.

They hadn't said much about the danger. They seemed to think the fact that Costello hadn't got rid of witnesses meant something. I was sure the opinion had been influenced by the size of the expected fee.

The contract had been signed.

Peter's first step would be to arrange to search Ida's room.

He followed me home, ate two beef sandwiches Juanita made him, called Harry, and went back to work.

CHAPTER 26

I returned to Epic late the next morning, locked myself in my bathroom-turned-bungalow, and tackled a problem I could handle: how to get more women into the script. First, I decided to keep Ruby, the young mistress from the novel. Fans of the book would expect it, and she'd be my way to show the degradation in the hero's character. She'd remain a mistress, which in the movies meant a young woman who had a nice apartment, no apparent job, and a rich older man who dropped by regularly but who was never seen laying so much as a finger on her.

In the novel, the reporter visited Ruby from time to time but never got caught. In my script, Ruby's keeper would find the hero at the apartment. I needed a way to suggest he and Ruby might have just had sex. Maybe she could be in a gown made of a fabric that suggested lingerie and handing him a drink while he's reclined on the sofa.

Maybe when the rich guy discovers them, he tells Ruby to "go freshen up." That could mean "You smell like another man." Maybe he offers the hero a handkerchief to wipe the lipstick off.

Then the rich guy calmly points out that whatever the hero means to Ruby, whatever she means to the hero, he is going to win. The hero isn't the man to take care of a woman the way she needs to be cared for. The rich guy points out that neither Ruby nor the hero has enough character to change. "I like that about both of you," he says.

And I liked that idea.

I began clattering away on the typewriter and didn't even stop for lunch. By the time I came up for air, the sun was beginning to set. I was very pleased with myself.

Real life is not so easily fixed.

There was a knock on my door. "Yes?" I called out. The knob turned. Nothing. I remembered I'd locked it. It turned again.

I got up. "Who is it?"

"It's Sergeant Barty, Mrs. Atwill. Open the door, please."

I did.

Sergeant Barty stood on the porch. Behind him, a man about a half-foot taller, with a natural curl of disdain to his upper lip. He was sure you were lying before you opened your mouth. Probably before you opened the door.

"This is Sergeant Loomis," Barty said.

I nodded to the man. He looked like he thought that was a lie, too. I remembered him then: he'd been with Sergeant Barty outside Bracker's office my first day on the lot.

"We should step inside," Barty said.

"Of course," I said. I stood back. I really didn't have much choice. Loomis had already put a hand on the door and now pushed it open.

They didn't remove their hats. "Get your things," Loomis snarled. "We're going downtown for a while."

"What's this about?" I asked Barty, feigning ignorance.

"I think you know," Loomis said.

Barty stood there, silent, working a matchstick between his teeth. His sharp blue eyes scanned the room. He didn't look at me.

"I don't know why you're here," I said to Loomis, in complete honesty. I went back behind my desk and started to sit, but Loomis would tower over me, so I remained standing, the desk between us. "You're welcome to sit down, gentlemen. I'm glad to talk to you. But here. Otherwise, you'll need a warrant."

"Or we can arrest you as a material witness," Loomis said.

"To what?" I wasn't sure I wanted to play too cute with him. He could be bluffing. Or I could be in very big trouble. I picked up the phone.

"If you're calling Winslow," he said, "he already knows where you'll be."

They had Peter?

"I'm calling my lawyer," I said.

"You can do that later," Loomis said. He took a step around the desk.

I sat down. "I'm going to do it here. I'm going to do it now."

"Or you'll what? Lay down on the floor? You can come downtown now, or I can put you in cuffs and take you out. That what you want?"

Barty still said nothing. He knew from experience the best chance of getting cooperation from me was for him to do the talking. He knew me. I trusted him. He probably even suspected I liked him. But Loomis apparently didn't think he needed advice from an older, more experienced cop.

"One call," I said. "To my housekeeper. Then I'll come with you." I picked up the phone. Loomis didn't snatch it out of my hand.

I dialed my house. I didn't have time to find the phone number of Harned Chalmers, my lawyer.

When Juanita answered, I quickly told her to call Harned and tell him I needed him downtown, at the detective bureau in City Hall. I told her the names of both the detectives that he should ask for.

"That's it, let's go," Loomis barked.

I said good-bye and hung up. He reached for my elbow.

"No," I said. "I've agreed to come along. I can walk on my own." I stood up on the other side of the chair.

"Why don't I cut you a path? I'll hold up my badge for

everybody to see." Loomis reached for me.

"I'll take her," Barty said. "I've done it before. You're not going to cause any trouble, are you, Mrs. Atwill?"

"No," I said.

"Good," Barty said. "Then we can all just walk out to the car."

I picked up my handbag. "May I go to the ladies' room first?"

"Let me take a look at that." Barty held his hand out across the desk, and I put the handbag in it.

He looked inside, examined the contents. "Okay. You can take it."

Loomis opened the door to the bathroom and glanced around, making sure there was no window for me to crawl out of. Then he went back to my desk and began searching the drawers. I didn't point out he should have a warrant for that.

"Don't lock the door," Loomis snapped.

I went in, closed the door, didn't lock it.

I took out the lock picks, the chamois bag Barty had seen, squeezed, surely identified for what it was. I climbed up on the toilet seat and placed the bag carefully on the lid of the overhead tank, so no one could see it. At least I wouldn't get arrested for carrying burglary tools.

When I came out, Loomis looked through the handbag to make sure I hadn't added anything to its contents. Then I locked my door—with a real key—and walked off the Epic lot between them. The sunset was casting pink-gold ribbons along the edges of deep violet clouds.

As we passed the gate box, the guard picked up the phone. Barty put me into the back seat of the car, double-parked across the street.

Mack Pace, the head of security, appeared at a run, past the guardhouse, and came toward us.

"Gentlemen," he called out. Loomis folded himself under the

wheel and put the key in the ignition. Barty remained standing by the car, his bulk between me and Pace.

"What's going on?" Pace said. "She's an employee of Epic, and she was on private property."

"If you want to file a complaint, you can do that, sir," Barty said.

"Is she under arrest?" Pace asked.

"No."

"What's this about?"

Barty got in beside me and closed the door. He tapped Loomis on the shoulder, and we pulled away from the curb, leaving Pace standing in the street. He turned and dashed back onto the lot.

CHAPTER 27

By the time we reached City Hall, it was dark.

Even so, it was impressive—its broad shoulders gleaming white, and its towering spire stabbing the LA sky. Since it was completed, at the beginning of the last decade, some citizens had snickered at what the shape reminded them of. City fathers had passed ordinances limiting the height of structures around it, allowing the city to see its grandeur. And unintentionally allowing citizens to more easily appreciate what the snickering was about.

Barty and Loomis took me up to the homicide detective squad and one of the small rooms where the detectives who were assigned here questioned their witnesses and suspects. The room had no window. It was stuffy, harshly lit, and reeked of stale cigarette smoke.

I sat down at the table. Loomis sat opposite. Barty took the chair at the table's end, on my right, his chair pushed back. He took a fresh matchstick out of a box in his jacket pocket and stuck it between his teeth.

Loomis leaned forward and placed his elbows on the table.

"Why are you looking for Ida Smoody?" he asked.

I glanced at Barty. He looked back, impassive. It had not taken them long to get the name of Arky Kulpa's former girlfriend and find out where she lived.

Don't tell them anything they might not already know.

Loomis said, "You're going to tell me why you were asking

240

questions about her."

Asking questions. Did this mean they didn't know I'd told Harry and Colleen that Ida was dead? I could imagine Harry's disgust at Loomis's rough behavior. I could imagine his manner with Dorothea. He'd probably threatened to take her downtown, take her outside. I could imagine Harry and Colleen snapping shut like clams.

Who could have talked to them? Gertie? She'd talk. But she didn't know much.

"Detective," I said, "I'd like to wait for my lawyer."

"While we do, I can put you in a holding cell," Loomis said, "down in the basement. When your lawyer gets here, the desk sergeant just might have trouble finding you. Paperwork gets lost. You'll like the company, especially late at night. Maybe we can get reporters down here, take some pictures of you. Would you like to get your face in the papers? You won't look so pretty."

"You can humiliate me," I said. "I know that. I know you're willing to do that."

"You want to test me?"

"Why should I trust you to take care of the truth? All you've done so far is make me think you'd rather rough up women than solve a case. Why would I—?"

He jumped up, shoving his chair back violently. It crashed against the wall. I thought he was going to snatch me out of my chair, or punch me till I'd never be able to stand up any other way.

Barty was on his feet too, but slowly, while I stared at the table top. I didn't think Loomis needed any more provocation.

Methodically, Barty walked over to the fallen chair. Methodically, he picked it up. While he did it, he said to me, "You're in big trouble, and you smart-talking Loomis isn't going to get you out of it."

I kept staring at the table top. I said, "I'd never heard of the

241

girl the day I saw you at Mr. Bracker's office. I didn't lie to you.
I only went to Epic to write."

He set the chair back at the table. "What has Pete Winslow
got you into?"

"It's not Peter."

"We know he was at the boarding house yesterday afternoon,"
Barty said, "pretending to be checking the plumbing. A couple
of the girls noticed him, identified a picture. He searched the
girl's room, didn't he? That's the only reason he would have
been there. She's dead, isn't she?"

"Could I have some water, please? I'm not feeling well." I
pushed my fingers against my lips and took big pulls of air
through my nose, mimicking the way I feel when I'm about to
be sick. My performance might have been aided by the fact that
I was actually shaking.

I don't know what passed between them. I didn't dare look at
Loomis. But he left to fetch the water. And maybe to cool off.
Barty sat back down, in Loomis's chair.

I said, "Thank you. For now, for earlier, the handbag."

"What have you been breaking into with those picks?"

"My desk. I work in borrowed offices. They don't always have
keys for things. He scared me."

"Not that much," he said. "You're still not talking."

"I guess I knew you wouldn't let him hit me," I said.

"I might change my mind; the night's still young."

"I didn't lie to you."

"The other night, in that parking lot, I asked you about Arky
Kulpa, and you said you barely knew him. Then today, I find
out you've been hanging around the boarding house where his
girlfriend lives."

"I didn't know anything about him then, except what I told
you. I would have told you about *her,* if I could."

"Did Pete tell you to keep quiet?" Barty asked.

"No."

"Then what?"

"You're only one detective." I looked at him.

"What the hell does that mean?"

The door opened. Two men came in. One was Loomis. The other was my lawyer.

Harned Chalmers is my personal attorney, not a criminal lawyer, so he'd come from a day in his office. For Harned, that meant a $500 suit and gold links that pressed together immaculate shirt cuffs that had never rubbed up against anything as unhygienic as an interrogation room table top. Nevertheless, he knew enough about criminal law to assure Loomis and Barty there was no possibility of my speaking to them until we'd had a quiet conversation alone. And he knew enough about microphones and listening holes to tell them we wouldn't be talking to each other in any of the rooms in which they were likely to agree to leave us alone.

"As far as I can see, my client has broken no laws," he said in his starched precision. "She is not under arrest, and I don't see you have sufficient grounds to charge her."

"Withholding evidence, to start," Loomis said. Barty sat quietly, watching me.

"What evidence?" Harned asked. "You will need to tell me and demonstrate she had reason to believe it was evidence of a crime."

"We don't talk about the evidence with the people who get put in this room. We're investigating a murder."

"Whose?" Harned asked.

"Arky Kulpa. You might have read about it."

"And you believe Mrs. Atwill is complicit in this murder? Is that why you won't tell us one thing you think she might have done in violation of the law?"

The curl in Loomis's lip arched higher, but he said, "She's a material witness to a murder. She's as good as admitted she knows something. If she doesn't tell us what that is, we'll see she ends up in the papers, and she's not going to like that."

"That possibility will certainly encourage my client to give you all the help she can to stay *out* of the newspapers," Harned said. "I remind you, however, that once she appears there, the damage is done to her reputation, and the inducement of your threat is lost. I'll take my client home, I'll talk to her there, and if it is at all possible for her to speak to you, we will return tomorrow morning."

Loomis said, "Why wouldn't she want to talk, if she's innocent?"

"There could be several reasons, detective. One of which is she's afraid that if she tells you anything, either she or someone else could be in grave danger. At what number shall I call you, gentlemen?"

I looked at Barty then. After a second, he took the matchstick out of his mouth and gave Harned the number.

Then I said, "Where's Peter?"

By the time we reached the front desk, the criminal lawyer whom Harned had called before leaving his office had arrived. Larry Skiller had a round nose and face and wore about thirty extra pounds of success around his middle under a suit tailored to hide it. I'd never heard of him, but they appeared to know him at the front desk and agreed to let him see Peter, without argument. That probably meant they knew about generous contributions Skiller made to police funds, politicians, and power brokers. Before the officer led Skiller off to the holding cells, Harned said he'd drive me to his office and we'd wait there. He didn't want to risk my being seen by a reporter who'd recognize me.

It was too late.

Savannah Masters swept in through the swinging doors from

the hallway. Close behind her was her husband, Kentwood Grantlin, who appeared to be trying to stop her.

"Lauren!" she snapped out when she saw me. She stalked over, dropped her voice, and demanded, "What's going on? Have you been arrested?"

"Are you all right?" Kentwood asked. He glanced over my face as a doctor would, as if he expected to see bruises.

"Fine. I'm fine," I said. "I'm sorry, but what are you doing here?"

Savannah said, "The *Eagle*'s a newspaper, honey; it has reporters. You were recognized down here. I got a call from one of them for some background on you. I told him if he published a word before he heard from me, I'd make sure he never published another one." Before I could say thank you, she grabbed my elbow and dragged me out of others' earshot. "Has this got something to do with Roland?" she whispered.

Kentwood had followed. He said, "This is not the place to talk about it. Certainly not the place to mention his name."

Harned strolled over calmly, introduced himself, and suggested we step into the hall. It was a wide, waxed corridor lined with the pebbled glass doors of the offices belonging to the other people I might have to deal with soon—the prosecutors who charged people with contravening the law.

Savannah said crisply, "That man who was with you the other night. Mr. Winslow. I know who he is. He's that bodyguard you had last year. You didn't just drop by with a private detective to talk about a script."

"She's upset," Kentwood said to me, softly. "We both are. We're worried about our mutual friend. We know something happened, far more serious than what he told us."

Savannah said, "Any fool can see something is very wrong. What's going on?"

Harned said, "We appreciate your help in keeping Mrs. Atwill out of the papers. That is, of course, in everybody's best interest. If there is anything she can say to you, she will. But not tonight."

"Well, tomorrow might be a little late," Savannah said.

"Mrs. Atwill is not speaking to anyone except her attorney tonight. If I might offer an opinion, should the detectives see you here with Mrs. Atwill, they might think you're someone they should question. If this mutual friend is in trouble, those questions might prove awkward for you."

One side of the swinging doors opened, and a couple of uniformed officers came out, chatting, minding their own business. They went the other way, but one of them glanced over at us.

Kentwood said to Savannah, "He's right. Somebody's going to recognize you and wonder why you're here. Mrs. Atwill, we'd appreciate whatever you can tell us."

I said, "I think that's up to our mutual friend."

Savannah said, "I'm keeping you out of the papers."

"We realize the favor you've done her," Harned said.

"Well, good. Look, I'm sorry how that sounded."

"She usually only takes that tone with me," Kentwood said. "I'm sure you understand how worried we are about him."

"Of course."

"Let's go," he said softly to Savannah. He slipped his hand under her elbow. She let him lead her out. She even leaned on him. But she said, "Call me tomorrow," to me over her shoulder.

"I'll explain all that," I said to Harned when they were gone.

"You most certainly will."

He drove me to his office and settled me in one of the leather chairs by his desk. He gave me a short brandy and phoned a nearby restaurant to order sandwiches be sent over. I called Juanita and told her where I was, that I was fine, and not to wait up. I'd be late. I might not be home at all. She said there had been urgent messages for me from a Mr. Gettleman to phone him. Mack Pace would have told him I'd been taken off the Epic lot by the police.

Peter and Skiller, the defense attorney, arrived just after the sandwiches. Peter didn't look as if he'd been shoved around too much.

He said, "The guys who picked me up were just running an errand. They threw me in the holding cell. The cops figured they'd break you, then they could nail me."

For what amounted to protecting me.

"You'd think Phil Barty would know better," he said as he sat down.

"He's not in charge," I said. "It's Loomis."

Harned gave them drinks and offered to make coffee, although, since his secretary had gone home, he couldn't vouch for its quality. We all declined. I took a sandwich.

Skiller explained that he could represent both of us only if there was no conflict of interest. If we ended up being charged, it would be best if we both got new attorneys.

I began, telling him my whole story, from the Brackers' party to my encounter with Savannah Masters as we were leaving City Hall. Then Peter told his, up till the point where the officers grabbed him. They had waited till he came out of his office building, so no one could intervene or call a lawyer for him.

When Peter finished, Skiller said he thought we could probably avoid being charged with withholding evidence, even though Peter had carried off what might rightly be considered evidence from Ida's room when he'd searched it the day before. There were extenuating circumstances. I had reason to fear going to the authorities, because Costello had shown me a badge. I'd asked Peter for help. We'd been trying to discreetly find out if it was safe for me to come forward. That was what Skiller would tell the police.

However, the items Peter took during his search of Ida's room would have to be returned promptly, and we would need to satisfy the police we'd returned everything we found. Threats would be made, but the police were unlikely to follow through on them and risk publicity about the involvement of a man carrying a detective's badge.

"Everything I took from the room's in a safe place," Peter said. "And last night I got a few sets of Photostat copies made from some of it. I can get all of it here in an hour."

Skiller agreed it would be best if all of it was in his possession. Peter phoned his boss, filled him in, and arranged to get everything delivered to us. The hour it would take to deliver it would be mostly taken up with making sure to avoid any police who were keeping watch either on us or the agency staff.

I asked Skiller what would happen to Harry, Colleen, and Dorothea. I said, "Can we keep Harry's past quiet?"

Skiller said, "We can't prevent the police from telling the press as much as they want to." He held up a hand when I started to speak. "Let me finish, Mrs. Atwill. *However,* the police don't usually tell reporters anything they don't have to. They use reporters, but they don't particularly like them. I can't see any advantage in the police announcing what they've discovered. I'm sure Mr. Neale's attorney will point that out to the Chief, as will Epic's lawyers. I'll call Mr. Bracker tonight and Mr. Gettleman. Not to tell them anything you've told me, but as a courtesy. It's in the best interest of your career to keep them informed as much as we can."

"Yes," I said. It was going to take a miracle for Epic not to fire me.

I phoned Harry, told her what had happened and that we were out of custody now. I apologized for what I'd brought to her doorstep.

"You didn't bring anything here," she said. "If it hadn't been for you, they would have shown up, and I would have had no warning about what was going on."

I asked if we could come over. Peter wanted to show her copies of what the police would have about her past. She was pretty sure there were two men in a car down the hill, she said, watching the house. She'd used Ida's binoculars to spot them.

We'd have to come up the back way, she said. She told me how to find it.

"How's Dorothea?" I asked.

"Not well. I've put her to bed. One of those detectives scared her. I need to go see to her, get her to sleep."

In just over an hour, Peter's brother, Johnny, showed up with a small case, filled with what Peter had found in Ida's room, and the copies.

Peter took the originals and arranged everything in separate piles on a meeting room table. He wanted me to take a look before he packed it all up to give to the police.

I started with Ida's bank book and checkbook. Beginning in the first part of December, she had made steady extra contributions to her account. A total of about three thousand. She'd made some small withdrawals with checks, for the acting and singing lessons, and to pay her rent. But nothing noteworthy. There was a cash withdrawal of five hundred, the money she gave Colleen toward her nursing school tuition.

Roland had said he'd given her perhaps six thousand. It appeared Arky had split the money down the middle.

There was a photo album, relatively new, with a smooth white leather cover. Inside were pictures of Ida and Colleen, and some with other girls her own age; pictures of her on movie sets she'd worked on, most as an extra, but one of her working on the film in which Roland had got her a speaking part. She sat at a small dressing table. A makeup artist had indulgently frozen in place long enough for the picture to be made. Ida smiled radiantly. In silver ink, the caption said, MY FIRST PART! If there had ever been pictures of Arky, she'd removed them.

At the back were pictures of her and her dead fiancé. There weren't that many. Even during the war, you'd always think you'd have more time later for pictures, that you'd have the rest of your lives. There was a wooden box, with a lid decorated in seashells. She'd kept his letters there. And copies of the letters she wrote him. She'd used carbons when she wrote to him. She'd wanted to be able to happily show him every letter she sent, in case some of them never caught up with him in Europe. The originals had not been returned to her. They'd been sent with the rest of his possessions to his parents, who'd almost certainly thrown them away. They'd wanted nothing to do with this girl who loved their son. There were times I wanted to believe people were reunited in heaven.

There was a stack of clippings about Roland dating back several months, probably beginning at the time Ida (and Arky) decided to try to get money out of him. Articles about his first movie for Epic, the first of his two-picture contract. Articles with staged photos of him with the other stars of that movie and its director. An interview in the *Los Angeles Times* about his life as a "freelance." An "at-home-with" article from the *Saturday Evening Post*.

There was a list of details about Harry's past that Ida had made.

"YOUR MOTHER WAS BORN IN TULSA. SHE NEVER TALKED ABOUT HER FAMILY." "SHE HAD A FAVORITE DRESS, WHITE WITH CAMELLIAS. HE GAVE IT TO HER." "YOUR MOTHER LOVED TO DANCE AT PERRINO'S." "HER FAVORITE DANCING SHOES WERE RED." "HER FAVORITE COLOR WAS RED." There were more. The sheet was full, front and back.

An admonition at the end: "Don't give him too much at once."

It was Ida's handwriting. I compared it to the copies of the letters she'd written her fiancé. Nevertheless, she had probably made it in conjunction with Arky, culled from everything Ida had gotten from Dorothea. She'd gone back at some point and struck through the "Your" and substituted "My." "MY MOTHER LOVED TO DANCE . . ." The additions were in a different color ink.

There were some of Roland's long-ago letters to Harry, Photostat copies Ida had made of them, the copies she'd shown Roland to prove her identity. I read them. They weren't literature but obviously written by a man deeply infatuated with a woman. "I want to wake up with you forever," one said. Not a promise of marriage, but enough that Harry might have expected an offer when she told him she was pregnant.

There was another album, older, in black tooled leather scuffed at the edges with age. It was Harry's—memories of her short-lived Hollywood career. On the first page, a studio publicity picture from one of her silent movies. It was a dramatic full-length pose, her hands raised and delicately poised beside her face, which was full of rapturous wonder and considerable beauty. But her face was nothing compared to her body, and you could see that almost as well. She wore a long, pale, diaphanous dress, which had nothing under it. Two narrow strips of ruched satin at the breasts and hips were all that prevented her full exposure. In silent films, women often appeared like this, nearly naked, and not only in publicity stills. It was one of the reasons men liked movie houses. And one of the reasons we ended up with the Production Code.

I turned the picture around and showed it to Peter, who sat across the table. I raised my brows.

"Boy, I miss silent movies," he said.

The rest of the album was full of both studio photos and candid shots taken on sets, at parties, on vacations. In a few of

them was a woman with long, wavy hair, as graceful as a ballerina. Dorothea. Judging from the street clothing, and the cars
and movie cameras in the background, none of the pictures was
taken after the mid-20s. Harry's career was over when she was
no older than twenty-five, blackballed as a woman of easy virtue.

Here and there were empty holders, the small triangles that
were glued to the paper to hold the corners of photos. I guessed
they'd once held shots of Roland. Long ago.

"Do you have to give this to the police?" I said.

"Yes," Peter said. "And the letters. I'm sorry."

Skiller said, "It's time you two got some sleep. I need you
rested for tomorrow. I'd rather neither one of you went home
tonight, in case the police are tempted to pick you up again.
Find a hotel and stay there. Call me at nine o'clock tomorrow
morning." He handed over a business card to Peter. "By then,
I'll have arranged the appointments. One of you will go with me
downtown and the other remain at my office. I don't want either
of you downtown without me."

Peter had made several sets of Photostats of everything that
could be copied. Each set was in its own manila envelope. He
shoved a set into the waistband at the back of his trousers.
Skiller would keep everything else.

Harned drove us back to Peter's car, which was still in a lot
near his office.

As soon as we were inside the car, I said, "There's nothing
that can be done about Epic. Maybe Mr. Skiller can convince
them not to fire me, because there'd be too many questions
asked if they did, but I got myself into this, and you warned me
not to. I don't want to hear you trying to blame yourself for it. I
don't want to talk about it. Let's just drive, all right?"

He pulled out the envelope of copies and handed it to me. If
he spotted a tail, we might have to ditch them fast. He turned
the key and pulled into the near-empty street. It was almost

eleven. Before the war, downtown still had car and pedestrian traffic this late, from the restaurants, clubs, and bars. People going in and out of the small commercial-traveler hotels and the larger resident hotels. But the downtown streets all seemed emptier since the war ended.

It made watching for a police tail easier.

Peter drove several blocks past Harry's street, then cut up and over so we came down the street behind the boarding house from the north. If there were police watching, they wouldn't be expecting us to come that way. The parked cars all appeared to be empty. We didn't see any men suddenly hunch down, out of the headlights. There were no cars with tall radio antennae.

We circled again and parked. On our left was a short row of houses, cottages really, whose backyards were hardly more than the slope up to Harry's street. One was a yellow house Harry had told us to look for. At the end of its driveway, there were remnants of a flight of steps, a long-ago-built passage from one street up to the other without having to go around the block or hike through the tangle of branches and vines. The iron-pipe railing was missing in places, the wooden steps rotted or overgrown, but we found our way through the foliage and the smell of the rotted wood to Harry's backyard with the help of Peter's flashlight and his surer footing.

The backyard was half taken up by rows of clothesline, half by the remaining Victory Garden. There was a scattering of lawn chairs closer to the house. Harry's car was parked on a cracked concrete slab that must once have supported a garage. She'd turned on the light on the screened back porch. Harry opened the back door at our soft knock and led us silently through the pantry, which was lined with shelves for the stacks of dishes she needed and sacks of beans, flour, and meal. There were bins of potatoes and onions, and hooks for coats, brooms, and feather dusters.

She said, "That used to be the back stairs, the servants' stairs. I took them out to make more room. These big old houses and no place to store anything." She pointed to chairs for us on either side of the kitchen table.

"I can make you some tea, if you'd like," she said. "I got brandy, if you need it."

"No, thanks, we're fine," I said, and she sat down at the end of the table. There were puffy circles under her eyes.

Peter laid the manila envelope on the table. "Inside are copies of what I found in her room, in case you want to see some of what the cops have."

She opened it and thumbed through the pages till she reached the copies Ida had made of her letters. She stopped. "She took these out of a trunk in the attic. They'll read all this."

"Yes," I said, "but they're romantic. If there were more explicit letters anywhere, she didn't use those. They wouldn't have been appropriate for a daughter to show to the man she thought was her father."

Peter said, "If there are any letters you don't want the cops to see, get rid of them. She had an album of yours, too. A black leather one. She was using it to remind herself what your past looked like."

Harry pulled out the list of details. YOUR MOTHER LOVED TO DANCE AT PERRINO'S. SHE HAD A FAVORITE WHITE DRESS WITH CAMELLIAS. HE GAVE IT TO HER. HER FAVORITE COLOR WAS RED.

"They did a lot of research," I said.

"You don't have to lie to me. They got this from Dorothea. I know that."

"They used her, yes," I said. "I'm sorry."

"Why is it written like this? '*Your* mother loved to dance.' Dorothea wouldn't say it like that. She'd say 'Harry loved to dance.' The police won't think Dorothea was in on this, that she was coaching her, will they, because Ida wrote it down like this?"

"No," I said. "Ida got the information, gave it to Arky. He made a list of things for her to remember, to drop into conversation. Ida copied it down. The police won't bother Dorothea anymore."

"I can't let her ever see this." She tore it to pieces.

"You and Miss Riley didn't tell the cops much about us, did you?" Peter said.

"They didn't have to treat Dorothea that way. That tall one, he accused her of lying when she just couldn't remember. He told her she was a bad liar, and he was going to take her downtown and throw her in jail. Colleen and I didn't have to say a word between us. We just looked at each other and decided we weren't going to help them, not till we'd talked to you. That other one, the beefy guy, he had Gertie cornered in the dining room. That voice of hers . . . She didn't really know much, but that didn't stop her from talking. I think she was flirting with him, and he must be fifty if he's a day."

Peter said, "You should call him. His name's Phil Barty. Tell him you were angry at the way Loomis—the tall one's called Loomis—angry about how he treated your friend. Then answer his questions. It's all right."

"Should I tell him you told me to call? Would it help you?" Harry asked.

"Probably not," Peter said. "We really shouldn't be here."

When we got back into the car, Peter said he knew a small, comfortable hotel in Santa Monica, nothing fancy, but quiet and clean, and not overrun with traveling salesmen. We could stay there for the night.

Then he said, "She's right, you know, about the cops. They would have ended up at her place anyway. They would have found those letters, and she and Dorothea and Colleen wouldn't have you to try to help them."

"It doesn't make me feel much better."

"Hold on." He suddenly pulled the car across the left lane and took a sharp turn onto Wilshire, headed east. He glanced in the rearview mirror. "Nobody there." Nevertheless, he stomped on the accelerator and made the next light, just as it turned red. He made a quick sharp turn into the next side street, did a U-turn, and came back to the intersection. We waited. Then he headed west.

I said, "I'm losing my touch. I used to think I was pretty good at this, spotting tails. My big fat ego. I didn't see Birdie Hitts or Scarza's men."

"Scarza's men were following *him*, not you. They were waiting at the boarding house to see if you showed up again."

"I didn't spot Birdie, and he followed me for two days."

"It's his line of work. He'd be good at it."

"I hope so. Otherwise, I'm losing whatever—" I broke off, staring through the windshield at the corridor of streetlights narrowing in the distance. Then, slowly, I turned to Peter. As I did, the car slowed down, way down, almost to the speed limit.

"Damn it," he said, softly, but with hard realization. "Damn it, I should have seen that before now."

"*That's* what it was, what's been nagging at me, what Birdie was holding back."

Peter said, "I think it's time we paid Mr. Hitts another visit."

CHAPTER 28

Birdie had an ocean-facing room, so from his window, the waves would be brushed in liquid silver throughout the day, and in the evenings, the sun would paint the horizon in pulsing strokes of pink and orange. The tide would rush rhythmically under the caw of seagulls.

He was getting a good deal.

That was about to change.

Peter already knew the room number, so we went straight up in the elevator. Its operator didn't stop us. I'd taken off my gloves and held Peter's arm, my wedding band on display. A respectable-looking couple at a respectable hotel. Even at this hour, nobody gave us a second look.

Peter knocked on the door, a code knock.

"It's Winslow," he said then. "Something's happened. I have to talk to you."

There were scurrying footsteps, and the door flew open. Birdie wore his robe and a pair of battered house slippers. "What? Do I got to get out of here?" He scuttled to the closet to get his suitcase.

"No," Peter said. I went in, and Peter closed the door, relocked it.

Birdie stayed at the closet, one hand on the knob, unconvinced. Behind his thick, round glasses, his eyes moved back and forth between us. His tongue flicked.

The room was well-sized and airy: a steady chill of ocean

breeze flowed through the open door to a narrow balcony. There were a couple of single beds, "Hollywood" beds with no footboards. One of them was rumpled; the remains of a sandwich sat on waxed paper on the night table along with a bottle of good Scotch.

This sort of hotel provided a small desk radio and trusted its guests not to steal it. There was a band playing. Peter flipped it off.

He said, "The cops found out Ida Smoody and Arky Kulpa used to see each other. They traced Ida to the boarding house. They found out Mrs. Atwill had been there, asking questions."

"That didn't take them long," Birdie said.

"One of the cops knows what he's doing," Peter said. "They know you were there, too, and tomorrow we have to tell them what else we know, and that includes about you."

"So now they can arrest me for withholding evidence."

Peter said, "Phil Barty, you know him?"

"I've met him a few times," Birdie said. It didn't seem as if the experiences had been all that pleasant.

"Call him," Peter said. "Tell him you just remembered something Kulpa said the last time you saw him. Say he was drunk, and you didn't think much of it at the time, but you thought he should know."

"Ah, cripes."

"Call him. Set it straight," Peter said. "They're going to be looking for you anyway. They'll talk to the bartender at the Parisian."

"Okay, okay, I'll do it. You planning to sit on my chest all night to make sure?"

"Do I have to?"

"I figured that's why you came all the way out here, why you didn't just call me. This place's got phones, you know."

Peter glanced at me, and I said, "Well, there was something

else we needed to talk about."

"Oh," Birdie said. "So you saved the really bad news for last? What is it? *What?*"

I said, "How long were you following me before I led you to that boarding house?"

"Since I saw you at Madison's. A few days, off and on. Why?"

"I didn't see you, and I was watching for a tail."

"I'm good at what I do," Birdie said, and hefted his robe's lapels.

"Precisely. If you were looking for a story, a scandal, you'd know how to make sure nobody saw you."

"Yeah. Okay. So?"

"So why did Mary Ann McDowell know you were following her?"

The pause was a touch too long. "What the hell is she talking about?" he asked Peter.

I said, "Her mother spotted you at Madison's. She told us you'd been following her daughter. They both knew."

"So I screwed up. It happens."

"They knew your *face*. You let them see you. Somebody hired you to follow her *and* to let her know you were doing it."

"You two can get the hell out."

Peter flexed his hands, and Birdie saw him do it. Then Peter said, "Sit down. We're not going anywhere."

Huffily, Birdie stalked across the room and threw himself into the upholstered chair. In the robe, it didn't have quite the dramatic effect he was looking for. The part below his knees fell open, exposing his pale calves. He jerked the flaps across his legs like an insulted wallflower.

The breeze coming through the balcony door beside him was cold. I closed it.

"Hey," Birdie snapped. "Leave it. I don't get the ocean that often."

I reopened the door, not quite as far, and sat down on the end of the bed next to it.

Peter didn't sit. He stood very tall beside the desk. He said to Birdie, "I owe you for that picture. If you hadn't taken that shot of Pauly Spinelli still in his jacket, he'd be on death row right now."

"And don't think I didn't hear about that. It cost me most of what you paid me to get back on the cops' good side."

Peter took out his wallet and laid fifty dollars on the desk. "I'll owe you another fifty, how's that?"

"Look, what you're asking, it's got nothing to do with Arky."

"Fine," Peter said. "That'll be one thing we've cleared up, one thing we don't have to tell the cops about tomorrow."

"Ah, Christ. A guy's got to earn a living. Because of *him*," he said to me and jerked a sour look back at Peter, "I didn't get near a murder scene for three months after I gave him that picture."

"I'll throw in another fifty, to make up for that," I said. "Tell me who hired you, and maybe the police don't have to know."

"I got nothing against her. For cripes sake."

"Who?" I said. "Who hired you?"

"Ah, Christ."

"Who?"

"She did," Birdie said.

"Who?"

"Mary Ann."

I stared at him. Peter and I both stared at him.

"Yeah," Birdie said then, with some satisfaction. He yanked his robe up on his shoulders. "She'd heard about me, seen me around, knew what I did. She came to see me, said she wanted to hire me to follow her, and let her mother see me doing it. She'd pay me, and pretty good. After her mother saw me, all I had to do was show up at some nightclubs from time to time and get spotted when she was leaving."

"And she trusted you not to spill what she was up to?" I said.

"I make a deal, I play it. Is this how you get a guy to talk to you? Insult him? Besides, why should I try to get a few hundred for a story when I can get more than that to go loiter outside some club when I got nothing better to do that night? Before you ask, yeah, I guess she's slipping around, and I got no idea who it is."

Peter said, "How long has this been going on?"

"Since she started dating that Len Manning character. A couple of months, just under. At first, she wanted me to follow her when she went someplace with her mother, make myself just obvious enough for her to be able to point me out to the old dame. Then, after that, whenever she went out with Len, she'd tell me to show up outside whatever club they went to."

I asked, "But why would she want to convince her mother she was being followed if she wanted to slip around?"

"And I heard you were smart. The old dame *already* watches her like a hawk. So she wants her mother to think she wouldn't *dare* be up to anything, with me following her. Her mother thinks she's out with Manning—who's about the safest guy she could be with—dancing or maybe over at his place listening to Berlioz."

"Who?" I asked.

"Berlioz. Where did you go to school? So she's got the old dame covered."

Peter said, "Tell me how all this worked. When she'd leave a club with Manning, what did you do?"

"Make sure he could spot me. But he's smarter than the mother, so I'd be sitting way down the street in my car. Make him have to look for me. Then I'd follow, but hanging back, like I was trying to hide. I'd let him lose me."

"Did you ever *not* get lost?" Peter said. "Come on, you had to be curious."

"She or Manning spot me, I'm fired. I liked the tax-free cash."

"Come on, Birdie."

"Okay. Once. I cut over a few streets, took a chance they'd turn that way. They did. I followed them, but they're sure they've lost me, so they're not being careful. They go to his house, so I wait. In five minutes, a car comes out of the garage, down the drive. I got my binoculars. It's her, by her lonesome. She heads off the other way. I decided not to risk it. She'd fire me for sure, she sees me. I never did it again."

"Who else might have known what you were doing?" Peter asked. "Anyone who might have found out, even accidentally?"

"Why?"

"Answer the question," Peter said.

"You thinking this was Arky's new blackmail scheme? Come on, he said whatever he had was tied to his scheme with Roland Neale."

"He was drunk when he said it. We don't know what's going on," Peter said. "Could anyone have found out what you were up to, even by accident?"

"Ah, Christ," Birdie said.

I poured him a couple of fingers from the bottle on the night table. Birdie took a swig and regarded me through his thick, round lenses. "You've seen her, the McDowell dame. She's a doll, the kind a guy wants, yeah, but also wants to take care of. She's a kid, never been out on her own: the studio, her mother, telling her everything to do. She's in over her head. She hires a guy like me, for God's sake. I've seen what happens to these girls, these Hollywood girls. Hell, sometimes I help it happen. A girl falls for some big talker, some good-looker, some guy her mother sure wouldn't like. He'll protect her, marry her, and they'll live happily ever after, so he gets her to sneak around, then the story comes out in some rag that he's got a wife in

Cleveland or did five years in Quentin, and the girl's the one with the broken heart and no reputation left. So, sue me. I felt sorry for her."

"Who did you tell?" I asked him.

"A guy I know. A guy at Epic. I put a word in his ear that somebody maybe ought to have a talk with her. A little advice."

"Who was it?" Peter asked.

"Mack Pace, the head of security over there. You know him?"

"Yes," Peter said. "How much did you tell him?"

"All I said was that I'd heard she was meeting some guy on the quiet after her dates with Len Manning. That's all. I didn't tell him she hired me to follow her, none of that. Just that I'd heard a whisper and thought he ought to know. He said he'd look into it. And yeah, before you ask, he gave me five hundred to keep my mouth shut. I took it. I got to take care of myself."

"When was this?" Peter asked.

"That day at Madison's. I went over to pick up the cash at Epic, then dropped on over to Madison's. She'd asked me to show myself to the old dame again, just to remind her. I don't know if anybody at Epic said anything to her or not. Maybe they did, because she hasn't called me again. I might have put myself out of business there. Do I have to tell the cops about that? I don't want the cops knocking on her door, all right? Epic paid me to keep my mouth shut. She did, too."

"Let me think it over," Peter said. "I'll tell you in the morning."

"I guess you're going to be right next door," Birdie said sourly.

CHAPTER 29

Peter ended up next door. I was in the room beyond. It was, after all, a respectable hotel.

I was hanging up my rinsed-out stockings and panties over the towel bar, dressed only in my slip, when Peter rapped on my door. He had a flask and poured us each a drink.

He said, "Arky's new blackmail scheme might have gotten him and Ida killed."

"It can't have anything to do with Mary Ann unless she's playing around with Roland." I tilted my head deeply to one side to catch the attention of his eyes, which had wandered over the slip, under which there was nothing. "You men," I said. "No discipline."

"I can show you some concentration, if you'd like."

I pulled the blanket from the foot of the bed and wrapped it around me. He sat down where it had been, and I took the chair.

Peter got his mind and his eyes back on his work. "If she's playing around with him, why the midnight cloak-and-dagger? Actors, producers, studio bosses have affairs all the time. The town's full of hotels ready to help them out, with bungalows and grounds patrolled by security. They spot anybody who even looks like a private detective or a scandal rag reporter, and the guy'd be lucky not to end up in the hospital. She'd tell her mother she was going shopping and spend the afternoon with her boyfriend. There'd be no need to involve Birdie Hitts."

"That might be what that fight was, in the study at the party. Birdie had told Epic, and Vera found out. She slapped Mary Ann because she found out Mary Ann had a boyfriend. If Mary Ann needed to play around late at night, maybe it's somebody who can't get off work during the day. It couldn't have been Arky, could it?"

"And Vera shot him for it? Is that what you're thinking? She has two days to calm down and then decides to shoot him in a public place? Then who shot Ida? And why?"

"You're just upset because I'm wearing a blanket."

I wasn't for much longer.

Afterward, Peter went back to his room, and after that, I didn't sleep very well. Without the distraction, I got to spend hours thinking about how the police wanted to put me in jail, and I might well have made an enemy of the head of Epic Pictures.

My face looked like it had tossed around on a pillow all night.

As we'd expected, the police wanted to see me first. They figured it was more likely they could trip me up than Peter.

An assistant district attorney named Betts sat in with us. He was short, no more than five-four, with sharp eyes and soft hands. He wore a dark gray suit, with a lavender handkerchief pulled a full two inches from his breast pocket. He was a snappy dresser, especially for someone in the DA's office, where ruthless ambition was tempered only by the sure knowledge that if you got more attention than your boss, you'd end up prosecuting gin-heads and shoplifters.

I told my story, emphasizing that I'd been afraid to report the body I'd found because a man with an authentic-looking badge made the body disappear, and that Mr. Winslow was simply protecting me as best he could.

I gave them the sketch of Costello. "It looks just like him.

Does he look familiar?" I asked Barty.

Betts said, "I'll ask the questions. Mrs. Atwill, the point of this meeting is to encourage you to stay *out* of the investigation."

Skiller, my lawyer, handed over everything Peter had taken from Ida's room. He said nothing, of course, about the copies Peter had made.

We went over my story several times. They brought in ham sandwiches that hadn't been properly wrapped in the waxed paper. The crusts had dried out.

They brought in files of Los Angeles police photos—officers and detectives. No Costello. Then piles of mug books. I looked through them all. Costello wasn't there.

By the end, my eyes were burning from the cigarette smoke and lack of sleep. But at least Betts didn't seem inclined to put me in jail, especially when the accompanying publicity might well alert the killer to consider disappearing or, at the very least, making sure the gun that killed Arky did. I like to think it was also because he was reluctant to ruin Roland Neale when he might be innocent. And Harry Virdon, because she was.

I remain an optimist.

They might have more questions for me later that day, they said, after they'd talked to Mr. Winslow. I should go home and stay there.

But I didn't go home. I had things to do.

The first was a trip to Epic: I had to talk to Ben Bracker.

By the time I reached my studio bungalow, my phone was ringing. The guard had reported my arrival. It was Grace, Bracker's secretary. Would I come to Mr. Bracker's office, right away, please?

I delayed only long enough to retrieve my lock picks from the top of the toilet tank where I'd hidden them when the detectives picked me up, and to call Savannah Masters's office. Last night, I'd promised to tell her what I could after my interrogation.

"Rolly's already heard from the police," she said. "They want to talk to him. Today. He told us what really happened that night. Finally. You have to tell me what you know."

"This is a police case now. I can't tell you everything. I can tell you what I can, but not today. I'm tied up all day. Tomorrow, I'll be working at my Marathon office."

"Are you suggesting I pay you a *call* there?"

"No, I thought we'd meet for lunch. Would Madison's be all right? It's hard to overhear conversation there, and people don't pay as much attention."

There was a sniff of disdain. "Very well. Probably best not to talk about it at the Derby, where everybody's got their ear in your booth. One o'clock." She snipped a good-bye and was gone. I wrote myself a note in my small appointment book and dropped it back in my handbag. I called Anthony at Madison's and asked if he could hold me a quiet back booth for one o'clock tomorrow. He said sure.

Grace showed me into Bracker's office. She didn't offer to get me coffee before she went out.

Bracker sat behind his desk, watching me, tapping his gold retractable pencil relentlessly on his blotter. He didn't look happy, but he didn't look like he wanted to tear my head off. That was Gettleman's job.

"Sit down," Gettleman shot at me. I sat, tamely, and held my handbag in my lap. Then he said, "You *persisted* in this. You *had* to go to the police. You will explain why you'd want to ruin this studio, Mr. Neale, and your own career. Because if either of the first two occur, I promise you the third will follow."

"I did not go to the police, they came to me," I said quietly, and I said it to Bracker. He stopped tapping his pencil. His eyes were tired and red, the skin of his face sagging in fatigue. His shave was haphazard at best. "Sir, I have no reason to want to harm you. I didn't go to the police, nor did Mr. Winslow. I came here today as soon as I could and will do whatever I can to help you and Mr. Neale. I believe he's innocent."

"*Innocent?*" Gettleman grabbed the arms of his chair to hold himself in it. "It was a *prank.*"

"Mr. Bracker," I said, "the first thing you must do is stop whatever plans might have been made to prove it was a prank."

"You aren't here to give orders," Gettleman said. "You will call the police, and you will take back whatever you've told them. You were mistaken. *Mistaken.* If one word—*one word*—appears against this studio or Mr. Neale, I promise you'll regret it."

"Perhaps, instead," I said to Bracker, "the first thing you might do is ask Mr. Gettleman to hear me out. Just five minutes. Please."

Bracker considered me for a long, exhausted moment, then he tossed down his pencil and scrubbed his face with his weary hands. "All right, what do you have to say? Joe, give her five minutes. She's not going to be bullied."

"Thank you," I said. I repositioned myself in my chair. I'd been sitting sharply erect on the edge of it, my back muscles clutched tightly. "After what happened, the studio might have thought about finding a young woman who could be paid to say she was the girl pretending to be dead, to say some man she didn't know had hired her to play a nasty joke on Roland Neale. If anyone is even considering such a plan, you must stop it. It will only make this studio look as if it were trying to cover up a murder. Sir, do you really think this was a joke? Twenty minutes passed between Roland Neale's finding the body and the fake police arriving. If it had been a prank, the fake police would have arrived immediately.

"The detectives who picked me up yesterday are investigating the killing of Arky Kulpa, the man who was shot to death not a hundred yards from this office. They'd been to a boarding house, looking for a girl who used to date Mr. Kulpa, to ask her what she might know. They found out she was missing. And that I'd been there, too, asking about the same girl." I raised a hand before Gettleman could say anything. "Yes, I tried to figure out who the dead girl was. And I traced a girl who'd been a guest at the party to that boarding house."

"*My* party?" Bracker said, more a whisper.

"She hasn't been seen since. Please understand, even if I had left this alone, never asked a single question, the detectives would still have found out the girl they were looking for was missing, and they would have searched her room. They would have discovered things that would have led them to Mr. Neale. They would have questioned his staff. The girl had been to his house. The staff would have recognized her picture. I've told the detectives what I saw the night of the party, and I've told them there is no evidence to prove it. Nevertheless, there is *no* chance you can convince the police I'm mistaken. Or crazy."

"Because the police will just take your word for it," Gettleman carped.

"They have before," I shot at him.

"What does *that* mean?"

I went back to Bracker. "This is a company town, and the detectives investigating Arky Kulpa's killing will keep Mr. Neale's connection to the missing girl secret from reporters for as long as they can, but it probably can't be more than two days. Reporters have too many policemen paid to slip them stories. Once it's out, you might as well not bother to release Mr. Neale's new movie. It won't matter whether he's innocent, not one damn bit."

Bracker said brusquely, "You said you came to help. Warning

us about the obvious isn't the same as help."

I said, "The day we met, I told you about the wisecracks going around town that, when I sign on to a picture, a body turns up. That's not exactly what happens. If a body turns up, and I happen to be around, the killer gets caught." I told them something of what I'd been up to in the last year. Then I said, "We have to find the killer before the reporters get the story."

"She was dating this man, this Kulpa," Gettleman said, his eyes narrowed. I could see the gears turning. "He was a small-time hoodlum. The police have already told us that. If, *if* a girl was killed that night and *if* it was her, then it is likely he did it. Jealousy."

"Except," I said, "that Mr. Kulpa had an alibi for the night of the party."

"Provided by another hoodlum?"

"No, by a reliable person." Well, maybe Birdie Hitts didn't qualify as "reliable," but I had to steer Gettleman off this course.

Bracker's intercom buzzed, three short buzzes. Grace wouldn't have interrupted if it weren't important. He snapped the button down. "Yes?"

"There is a gentleman from the police wishing to speak with you."

They wanted to set up an appointment. Fortunately, when they talked to rich people, they called first. They would not have been pleased to find me talking to Ben Bracker the second they let me go.

I said as much to Bracker. He agreed it was to no one's advantage for the detectives to know I'd been there.

We didn't shake hands before I left.

CHAPTER 30

I drove to Marathon and rode the rattling elevator up to my office in the Tate Building. I deposited my handbag in the desk drawer and went down the hall. I knocked on Hawkins's door.

"It's Lauren," I said.

"Enter!" she called out. "And stop!"

I did, closing the door after me but then not advancing, not moving at all.

Hawkins sat behind her typewriter, her fingers poised above the keys, immobile, staring at the paper, her eyes narrowed in thought, her tongue caught between her lips.

"Ah!" she exclaimed then. Rapidly, she typed, punching the keys with enthusiasm. Then she cried, "Yes! Done!" She pushed herself back in her chair and saluted me. "Sit."

I did, on her sofa, and crossed my legs. "So, it's going well?" I asked and gestured at the typewriter.

"A blazing half hour. Rest of the day's been crap. How about you?"

"Some ideas," I said. "Not much follow-through."

"I once hired a wrestler to come drag me out of bed every day. The script wasn't any better, but it was faster. If you're close to a deadline, I still have his number. What can I do for you?"

"It's sort of personal."

"Indeed." She folded her hands piously at her chest. "Well, Sister Hawkins is always ready to hear your confession."

"You remember at Madison's, you told me I should act like Aunt Lauren to Mary Ann? Well, I heard—I have it on good authority—that she's been sneaking out, after her dates with Len, when she's supposed to still be with him. I don't know where she's going, but it sounds like an affair, and if she got caught, it could be a scandal, depending on who she's with. A rendezvous at midnight doesn't sound like just an ordinary slip-around. She could do that in the daytime. There wouldn't be any need for this kind of subterfuge."

"So you think it's an affair that would *have* to be conducted under the heavy velvet cover of darkness? I'll save you some gas, beating around the bush. It's not me."

"Hawkins—"

"Who whispered this to you?"

"I can't say, but I believed it. Maybe it's some bad boy she's seeing."

"Len knows a few of those, but they wouldn't be interested in her. I don't know her that well. She wouldn't confide in Sister Hawkins. But I will observe that most people who do things they shouldn't do secretly want to get caught. Maybe she wants to marry the guy and doesn't care if the studio finds out. She thinks they'll force him to do it."

"I wouldn't want to see her do anything stupid."

"I'm glad this is only about sex. For a moment there, I thought you were going to tell me you'd got yourself up to your ears in another killing. I read about that guy over at Epic who got himself shot."

"Arky Kulpa."

"Good Lord! . . . don't tell me you *knew* him."

"He ran some errands for me. That's what he did there."

"Are you sure Mary Ann's slipping around? At Madison's, didn't her mother say Birdie Hitts had been following her?"

"Yes."

"That *would* be taking a chance, with him on her heels. But young people," she sighed, "what can you do with them?"

I went back to my office, retrieved my handbag, and set off to make my last stop. I had to go see my parents.

There wasn't much rehearsing to do. There was no way to make it sound any better than it was. I might be in the papers again. SCREENWRITER QUESTIONED IN KILLING. It didn't really matter whether any of the stories pointed out that my father was the noted historian Martin Tanner. The university regents would see it. My father would be forced to retire, and on the university president's terms.

I hadn't phoned first. A week ago, the maid, Nora, had probably never heard of me. Now, I'd turned up twice.

She showed me into the living room, not my father's study, and went to tell my mother.

My mother came. She wore a simple long-sleeved day dress of rose-pink wool, with a seed-pearl pin at the angle of the collar. A soft-gray cardigan was pulled over her shoulders.

I kissed her cheek. "I need to talk to Father."

"He's resting at the moment, a nap before dinner." She wasn't a good liar, because it wasn't in her nature to lie. It was, however, in her nature to protect my father.

"Is he in his study? Please ask him to see me. It's important. I wouldn't have come otherwise. I mean, I wouldn't have come uninvited."

"I knew that's what you meant. Wait here. Let me see."

It took a couple of minutes. She returned and led me back across the hall to the study.

Father sat behind his desk, in a heavy tweed jacket. His pipe lay in a carved stone ashtray nestled among the neat piles of papers. The room was fragrant with its aroma.

I stood in the middle of the rug, like a truant called to the headmaster's office, my fists clenched. Then I reminded myself

I was the one at fault.

"May I sit down?" I asked.

"Of course," he said.

There was no chair on my side of the desk. It wasn't an office; it was his study. I sat down at the end of the sofa, where I'd sat only a few days ago. I glanced at the mantel. My pictures remained there. And they hadn't been retrieved quickly by my mother from some drawer. They were in the same places as before.

Mother sat down at the other end. She pulled her sweater gently forward on her shoulders, then fingered the placket with her right hand.

I turned toward my father. "I'm afraid something has happened, and the police are involved. Not because of anything I've done wrong, but that doesn't matter. It could end up in the papers. You know something about what I've been up to, that I've been involved in some police investigations. I tried to find a girl, a missing girl. But now it's become part of a murder investigation." There was a newspaper folded into the magazine rack beside the armchair across the hearth. I found a story about Arky's killing and handed it to my father. "She knew this man. The police found out I was trying to find her. I've hired a lawyer."

"I don't understand," my mother said. "Why don't you just tell them everything?"

My father said, "Because if she does, they could say she withheld evidence. Of course, there's more to it than just trying to find a missing girl."

"Yes."

"Who's your attorney?" he asked.

"Larry Skiller. He has experience. Harned Chalmers found him for me. I'm sorry, but I can't tell you more."

"How soon will I read about it?" He tossed down the paper.

"It depends on whether the police find the killer before the papers get wind of the whole story. If they can do that, my name might not come up at all."

"Is it a sordid case?"

"People could be ruined. Some of them did nothing wrong."

"Could you be arrested?" he asked.

"I don't think so. It would only warn the killer."

"And this man you've been involved with, the private detective. Is this his doing?"

"No, I started it. I got him into trouble, too. I couldn't let it alone. He told me to. I'm sorry."

"It would seem the apology is owed to Mr. Winslow. Isn't that his name?"

"Yes. But he knew what he was getting into. I took the coward's way when Uncle Bennett died. I should have come here and begged you not to sue. I should have tried to convince you instead of going straight to his company. I'm sorry for that. Not for defending Bill. But for being a coward. If the reporters find out about me, I'll make sure someone lets you know first."

I picked up my handbag from the table and walked out.

Finally, I went home.

Dusk was settling. My neighbors were going inside, mothers starting dinner, setting the table, gathering the children from play. There were a few protesting shouts from young boys down the street. But silence was falling with the dusk. A light mist was rising.

Juanita's car was gone. It was her day off, and she often went to visit her sister and a niece, who was just learning to walk. She'd left lights on inside. There would be food in the refrigerator, of course. At the very least soup and the makings for a sandwich.

I left the car at the top of the drive and went around to the kitchen door, the shorter way. Food sounded good. Food, a hot bath, a short gin, and a long sleep.

"Mrs. Atwill." He wore gardener's coveralls, but he was stocky for a gardener, and too tall. Around here, they were mostly Japanese or Mexican. I might have noticed that, been warned, but he'd been hiding behind the garage. I didn't see him until he was ten feet away.

"Mr. Costello." Behind him, my neighbor's yard was empty. No lights in the house.

"The neighbors are gone. So's your maid."

"Housekeeper. It's her day off. She knows nothing about any of this."

There was no way to outrun him. No amount of screaming that would help. Even if my neighbors on the other side were home, by the time anybody arrived, it would be too late to do any good.

"I knew you'd be trouble," he said, with a sort of resigned admiration. "You found a body and that character, that Pace character. You thought maybe he was there to kill you and what do you tell me? The blood's only on the bottom of the other guy's shoes. You were that scared, and you were still thinking."

I didn't tell him the police knew about him, that they had a sketch of him as good as a photograph. I didn't think it would do any good. But I decided if he pulled out a gun, or if he ordered me into the house or into the garage, or if he took another step toward me, I'd tell him then. And I'd bargain every way I could to save my life.

"You haven't been home for a while," he said.

"What do you want, Mr. Costello? I guess that's not your real name."

"You don't want to know any more about me."

"What do you want?"

"Nobody cares about that girl. She's gone. Leave it alone.

This is how easy it is for somebody to get to you, if you go to the police."

"Why would I do that? There's no evidence. You took very good care of that. I know what would happen, even if the police bothered to look. The studio would tell every reporter in Los Angeles I must have had a nervous breakdown. I'd be the crazy woman who tried to ruin Roland Neale. I'd be lucky to ever get another job."

"You should think long and hard about that. And about your boyfriend. It would be almost as easy to get to him."

"He's already told me to let it go. He says sometimes things can't be fixed."

"He'd be right. Take care of yourself." Costello touched the brim of his cap and stepped back toward the corner of the garage, the mist now thick around his ankles. "Maybe we'll never have to see each other again."

I managed to get the key in the lock and get into the house. I tossed my handbag on the kitchen table, grabbed one of its chairs, and shoved its back under the doorknob. I ran to my study, shut the door, turned the key, shoved aside the row of Shakespeare, and opened my safe. I yanked out the chamois bag, fumbled with the drawstring, pulled out my gun. It was loaded. I sat down in my desk chair and sat down hard. My legs were too weak to hold me up.

I laid the gun on the blotter. I clenched my hands into fists, unclenched them, again and again, hoping that would stop the trembling.

I had to get out of here. But go where? I snatched up the phone. I called the Homicide Bureau. I need Sergeant Barty, please. Tell him it's Lauren Atwill. Tell him I've seen Costello. And then Barty was on the phone. And Peter, too. He was still there being questioned. I'm on my way, he said. No, I can't stay here. Where would you feel safe? With you. Get in the car, drive to City Hall. Come here, he said. I'll be waiting.

It took me a second to remember where I'd left my handbag. Carrying the gun, I dashed to the kitchen, retrieved the bag, removed the chair from the back door. I pulled out my keys. I ran to the car, jumped in, laid the gun by my hip, locked the doors, shoved the key into the ignition, put the car in gear, backed to the curb. A car came slowly up the street. I watched it over my left shoulder, my hand on the gun, beneath the folds of my skirt. The car kept going, minding its own business.

Someone knocked on the passenger window. I jumped a foot, cried out. It was my neighbor from the house on the other side, bent down, his face enormous in the glass. I shoved the gun under my hip, leaned across the seat, and rolled down the window. We might have exchanged two dozen words in all the time I'd lived there.

"Sorry to scare you," he said cheerfully. "Thought you saw me nipping on over. I wanted to ask. Your gardener. The wife saw him out in your backyard today. He takes his time. Can I ask, what does he cost?"

CHAPTER 31

I was sitting in one of the interrogation rooms, with Peter and Sergeant Barty. Barty had a flask and poured me whiskey in a paper cup.

I said, "Do you get many hysterical witnesses?"

"You're not hysterical," he said, "just a little shaky. This guy didn't show you a gun?"

"He didn't have to. He knew Juanita was gone, the neighbors were gone."

"That's not too hard to do, neighborhood like yours."

I said, "Someone has to call Juanita. She's at her sister's. She should stay there till she hears from me."

"We'll do it," Peter said. "Give me the number. I'll call her. You sit here. I'll take care of it."

"Then what?" I said.

He grinned. "Costello's still in town. You didn't tell him you'd been to the cops. He might stay in town. We still have a chance to find him."

Barty said, "What did his clothes look like?"

"He was wearing coveralls," I said.

"His suit," Peter said. "On the night of the killing. Was it expensive?"

Barty jerked at his own suit coat. "Better than this?"

"I didn't see much of the suit, but the overcoat was. It was a good overcoat. And the shoes, now that I think about it."

Barty said to Peter, "Our boy's used to better."

279

"And he's smart," Peter said. "He found two people there that night with Neale. Two people he probably didn't know would be there, and he played it, without batting an eye."

"He won't call attention to himself," Barty said. "Nothing swank."

Peter said, "But no fleabag. The first place cops would look."

"Thanks," Barty said.

They had to move fast. We had no idea how soon Costello might find out I'd been to the police, that there was a sketch of him. If he left town, they'd probably never find him. It was hard enough to get cooperation from other police departments inside your own state. If he crossed a state border, he might as well be in Timbuktu.

Peter knew how to find witnesses. He supplied Barty with lists of the places he'd send his men to search for Costello. He gave him names of rental agents through whom Costello could have found a house. A man in his line of work might not like to live in a place where his comings and goings were more easily noticed. There was a list of resident hotels as well; these were comfortable and didn't cater to salesmen. Salesmen can't leave anybody alone who could be a customer. They'd pay too much attention to him.

Peter wanted to send his men out, too, to add to the searchers, but Barty put the kibosh on that in a hurry. It was a police investigation. He didn't have time to referee disputes between cops and a bunch of shamuses trying to act like cops.

And so we were relegated to the sidelines. Peter and Johnny took me back to my house, just long enough for me to pack a small bag. I slept, or tried to, at a hotel.

Marathon was the safest place for me to spend the day, unless I wanted to sit around at Peter's office. I went to my office in the Tate Building. I locked the door.

I worked for a couple of hours, my forehead gradually edging toward the typewriter. I decided to take a nap. I hadn't slept in two nights. I lay down, pulling an afghan from the back of the sofa over my legs. I fell asleep immediately.

Far away, a bell was ringing. A jarring clanking that kept getting closer.

My phone.

I hopped up, tangling my legs in the afghan and almost falling down while snatching for the receiver.

"Miss Atwill, it's Anthony, over at Madison's. Sorry to bother you, but— "

Savannah! I had completely forgotten about our lunch date.

"Miss Masters asked if I—"

"Tell her I'm so sorry. I'll be there in ten minutes."

I took time to dab cold water under my eyes, comb my hair, and apply some fresh lipstick, then I dashed for the elevator and sprinted for the studio gate. I made it to Madison's in eight minutes. It didn't improve Savannah's mood. She was not used to waiting for anyone except the biggest stars and, maybe, the head of a studio.

Before she could remind me of that, I slipped into the booth and began my apology, telling her frankly that I hadn't slept in two nights, being so worried, and had fallen asleep on my sofa.

She scowled. But perhaps her instinct to scold was mollified by the excellent gin and tonic Anthony had made for her, which was half gone. And maybe because, no matter her position in Hollywood, she needed to talk to me.

She'd brought her husband along. At the Brown Derby, Savannah Masters could wait alone at a table, and she'd receive supplicants till her lunch companion arrived. Not at a place like Madison's.

Kentwood said, "It looks more like a friendly lunch and less like an interrogation if I'm here."

Savannah said to me, "That Mr. Winslow didn't even talk to Roland yesterday."

"Well," Kentwood said, "it *will* look less like an interrogation if we can induce Savannah to smile."

She shot him a look but sat back in the booth, relaxed her features, and placed her fingers lightly on her gin glass. She couldn't get all the way to a smile.

I said, "Mr. Winslow was tied up with the police. I believe he's talking to Roland and his attorney this afternoon. He'll tell them what he can. But it's important Roland tell Mr. Winslow what he knows, too."

"He won't do that," Kentwood said. "Private detectives don't have the protection of confidentiality. He could be forced to reveal whatever Rolly told him or even what Rolly's lawyer told him. If he didn't, the authorities could take his license away."

I said, "Roland's already told us plenty. Is his lawyer out of his mind? If he thinks he can just get Peter to funnel police information to him, he's going to be very disappointed."

Anthony came over, asked if I'd like something from the bar. I declined.

Savannah waved him away.

Kentwood said, "We'll look over the menu and let you know about lunch."

Anthony allowed how that was just fine, take your time, and melted away.

Savannah said, "That girl was a chiseler. She told Roland she was his daughter. He was a fool to fall for that, without any proof."

"I believe she had some proof, some letters. She was convincing."

"Conniving is what she was. He was a fool not to hire someone to check her out first. He gave her money, for heaven's sake. How's that going to look? She was a tramp."

"When you talk to the police," I said, "you might want to keep your opinion of her to yourself. It's better for Roland if the police believe he still thought she was his daughter when she died."

"He did," Kentwood said. "He's devastated. But you're right, of course."

I said, "Maybe it would be better if I knew more about what Roland told you."

"Why?" Savannah said. "So you can go traipsing off to the cops if there's something they don't know?"

"Mr. Winslow and the police have a day, maybe two, to solve this before reporters get the story. Somebody downtown will talk. Anything you know about what happened could be helpful. You were one of the last people to see her alive. Were there any women Roland was seeing who were extremely jealous? Any women who might have been at the party?"

"Why the party?" Savannah asked.

"Ida was probably followed to Roland's house, or lured. Why else would she have been killed there? A jealous woman, who might have thought Ida was a romantic rival and confronted her, drunk, with a gun. A horrible accident. It's happened before."

"There's nobody I've heard of."

I turned to Kentwood. "Had you heard anything about trouble he was having with a woman? It might be something a man might confide in another man."

"I don't have that kind of friendship with Rolly," Kentwood said. "He has plenty of female admirers. Some of them might have been overly possessive. But I wouldn't have names to give you."

"Who else did you see talking to Ida?" I asked. "Did anyone else show interest, ask who she was that night?"

"Other than me?" Savannah said.

"For God's sake, Savannah," Kentwood said. "I'd had a hard day. I had a bit too much to drink. And she was wearing a slip."

"Which meant your hand had to go straight to her knee. If you hadn't been trying to get her in your lap, Lauren wouldn't be implying I was the last person to see her alive."

I leaned forward and put my elbows on the table, holding my hands up in what I hoped looked to the other customers like a perfectly natural gesture. Savannah and Kentwood fell silent.

"I said you were *one* of the last people," I pointed out.

Savannah said, "Rolly didn't tell us anything about her till yesterday."

Kentwood said, "He gave us no reason to believe he'd harmed her. He's quite distraught."

"Can I ask what you and Ida talked about at the party?" I asked him.

"As I said, I was a bit tight," Kentwood said. "I didn't even recall her name. When Rolly told us what had happened, Savannah realized it was the same girl. It was inconsequential, what we talked about . . . party talk. I pointed out some people she might want to know. I did say I'd introduce her to Savannah. That's it. I never saw her again."

"What about you," I asked Savannah, "after you two went off together?"

"Nothing important," she declared. "We retrieved her dress; she put it on. She said she was sorry for letting Kentwood touch her knee. I told her she had to remember that Hollywood was full of men who wanted their way and figured every girl should give it to them. It didn't mean they'd make her a star. We went up to the house, so she could get herself put back together. She talked about a fiancé she said she'd lost in the war. How she needed a good steady man like he was. I have to say I thought she was charming, natural. I was thinking about giving her a leg up, maybe calling some casting directors. The little liar."

"She was telling the truth about the fiancé," I said. "He was killed in the war. She met another man, but he wasn't very nice. He's probably the one who talked her into the charade."

A waiter approached and asked if we'd decided. Savannah announced she'd just recalled an appointment, and they wouldn't be able to stay for lunch.

I said to the waiter, "Could I have a roast beef sandwich, no gravy? I'll take it on back to the office." He said sure and departed. "Before you go, tell me about the last time you saw her that night."

"I took her up to Jean's morning room, so she could freshen up. I gave her a card, said to call my office. She thanked me and said good-bye like a little lady. I dabbed on some lipstick. Jean came in. I poured us a couple of martinis. Her nerves were shot. She's high-strung to begin with, and Ben expects so much from her—those big parties—and he's no help at all, of course. I told her she was taking too much out of herself, ought to go lie down and think about going away for a short vacation, by herself. Then Mary Ann McDowell stuck her head in, said good night, left. Wait a minute. You saw me. You were there."

"Mary Ann and I had been talking."

"About what?" she said. Her gossip column instincts had kicked in.

"About whether she ought to get married so young." If I gave her something, even a snippet, I could keep her talking.

"Doubts about Len?"

"Just whether she should think about marriage just now, with all the attention her career will need. She's not seeing anyone else, is she? Any rumors at all?"

"It would be news to me. Not that most every man she meets doesn't want to take her on home with him. But she's not the type to get her head turned easily. As far as I know, she's still saving herself."

"What time was it, do you recall, when we were all up there?"
I asked.

"Don't you know?"

"I'd like to see if our memories match."

"I have no idea. I took Jean to her room, then I ran into you
again on the back stairs. No idea."

"Where did you go afterwards?"

"Why?" she asked suspiciously. "I was circulating. Any of a
few dozen people could verify that, if they have to." She shoved
Kentwood on the shoulder, and he slid out. She said, "I wasn't
the last to see that little chiseler alive."

CHAPTER 32

I went back to my office, ate my sandwich at my desk, and washed it down with a coffee mug of tap water. My Hollywood lunch.

Some dialogue for my script began to float around in my head. I began to type it, roughly. A line here, line there. A scene between the jaded hero and the girl, the young reporter who wants to climb into a murder case. You got no instinct for this business, kid. You got to know when somebody's lying to you. He could list the suspects for her, a reminder to the audience, and ask her who's lying. She would have no idea.

I sure didn't.

At six, my phone rang. It was Peter.

There was no news about Costello, not that I'd expected they'd find him. How effective can a manhunt be when you can't ask the general public for help?

"So where do I spend the night?" I asked.

"I'm still thinking about that. I'll come pick you up, get you some dinner. You can tell me what you were doing at Madison's. Did you think I wouldn't have somebody outside the gate watching for Costello?" He hung up.

He took me to Rocco's. On the way, I explained about my meeting with Savannah and Kentwood. Then I said, "I had to go to Madison's. Savannah Masters wouldn't meet me at my office. There was a crowd. I was safe."

"There's not much chance you'll ever do what I tell you, is there?"

We were given a booth against the far wall. A couple of Peter's men settled into a table by the windows.

Rocco came out, greeted us, ordered for us. A small antipasto, he said, followed by scaloppini. The veal was fresh this very day from his cousin's farm.

When he'd gone, I said, "Did you learn anything from Roland or his attorney?"

"Yeah, that the lawyer still thinks his client's best shot is to keep his mouth shut. Mr. Neale's gone back home."

"I hope it's not to tell the maid to scrub the cabana."

"They have to know what a grand jury would think if he did that and claimed to be innocent. The cops should have their warrant to search his place by tomorrow."

The antipasto came. I made an effort not to talk with my mouth full, a difficulty when I wanted to keep my mouth full. Spicy slices of Italian sausage and paper-thin curls of Italian ham, bite-sized balls of soft cheese, tangy peppers, olives that didn't come out of a can, and slices of pickled eggs. This was what Rocco called a small antipasto.

"When I move back into town," I said, "I *have* to live somewhere near here."

"You're moving back?"

"Well, I've thought about it," I said. "It's a long drive from Pasadena. For me, for you. I'm not expecting to move in with you."

"You, me, and Juanita would be a tight fit in my house."

"It wouldn't do me any harm to be a little closer to Hollywood, assuming after this is over, I still have a career. It might mean going to more parties. How would you feel about that?"

"About you going to parties?"

"About you going with me?" I said. "Women don't get to go many places without an escort."

"Are you ready for what people would think?" he asked.

"Which is?"

"That I'm nuts about you, even when you've got egg yolk on your chin."

I wiped it off. "You could have told me that sooner."

"Which part?"

"You're not going to be serious about this, are you?"

"Not here. Two of my men are sitting right over there, and I need your attention on other things."

Before coming to get me, he'd met with Ben Bracker and Joe Gettleman, going over what they remembered about the party. Neither of them recalled seeing Ida Smoody. "They neither one have what you'd call alibis, but I can't figure out what their motive could be," Peter said.

Then the scaloppini arrived, with mushrooms and artichokes. I reminded myself to keep the wine sauce off my chin.

Peter said, "There's plenty that doesn't make sense yet. Ida Smoody and Arky Kulpa are extorting money from Roland Neale. They're making money, but when she gets cold feet, Arky just lets her walk away. It's too big a coincidence they both get killed within a couple of days of each other. It's got to be the same killer. Yet Ida's killer makes the body disappear, and the guy he sends to clean it up doesn't get rid of witnesses; in fact, he walks you out to safety. Arky Kulpa's ambushed in a public place, where the killer has to leave the body. Costello comes to warn you to stay away from the cops. *Warn* you. The killer wants you quiet, but not dead, unless you force his hand. It's like we have the last pieces of a jigsaw puzzle, and no matter how you arrange them, they don't fit."

"I've hardly thought about anything else."

"You thought about moving back to town."

"We weren't going to talk about that, remember? Your men might be able to read lips. I've thought about you, moving, my script, and this case. In reverse order."

He flinched but grinned.

When we finished the veal, while I was considering dessert, he borrowed Rocco's phone in the kitchen's office to call his office's answering service to check for messages.

"Let's go," he said when he returned. "They found Costello."

CHAPTER 33

Costello sat in an interrogation room, his cuffed hands on the table, being watched over by a young, thick-browed officer. I watched him through a two-foot square of one-way mirror, in his brown tweed sports coat and a crisp white shirt, open at the throat. His broad shoulders were straight, his heavy features relaxed, his cautious eyes alert but not nervous. He looked very much out of place.

"Is that him?" Barty asked me.

"Yes. I'm sure."

"Loomis is out at the guy's house, running the search. So far, no badge. They didn't find the clothes you described either."

Peter said, "And there won't be any clue to the killer. He's too careful. No notes, no phone numbers, no trail. You had to pick him up. You couldn't watch him, tail him, see where he went."

"Back up, right now," Barty said fiercely. "You only got this far because you came in with her."

"I'm here because my list helped you find him," Peter said.

"I don't give a damn. You don't tell me how to run my job. He spots a tail—he just *thinks* he spots a tail—and he's gone."

I said, "Could I sit down, do you think?"

Peter put a strong hand under my elbow and guided me into the squad room and put me in the nearest unoccupied chair. Barty fetched me some water in a paper cup. "We're going to do everything to nail this guy and find the killer," Barty said.

"I know. Thank you." I took a sip. The tepid water tasted like paper.

"He's not talking," Barty said. "He hasn't asked to call anybody yet."

"How long can you hold him?" Peter asked.

"At least a few days. We got a sketch that matches him and a witness who puts him near the body of a woman wearing shoes like Ida Smoody's. And she's missing. Tomorrow, we can turn Neale's place upside down. We got the warrant. We'll find something so we can charge this guy with more than impersonating a cop and moving a body. His name's Tallis. Mike Tallis, at least on his driver's license and some army discharge papers we found. He spent twenty years in. Master sergeant. No warrants out for him under that name, not in California so far."

"Those papers," Peter said. "He was honorably discharged?"

"Yeah. Probably riffed after the war. No use for a man his age anymore."

"Can I talk to him?" Peter asked.

"And say what?"

Peter told him.

Barty said, "Okay, hand over your gun."

Peter walked into the interrogation room behind Barty. I remained on the other side of the window, my water cup in hand.

"Mr. Costello," Peter said.

"My name's not Costello." He said it calmly, like a gentleman.

"I'm Winslow."

Costello said nothing.

Peter sat down on the other side, pulled out a folded copy of the sketch from his jacket, spread it on the table, and turned it toward Costello. "It's an exceptional likeness. You made quite an impression."

"I don't know what this is about. I'm not answering questions, detective."

"You know I'm not a detective," Peter said. "This picture, this is the only face the cops have. They're looking at two killings, and you're the only face. I don't make you for either one of them, but I'm not a cop. The girl's name was Ida, did you know that? Did you look inside her purse before you threw it away, wherever you put her? She was an orphan. She was twenty. She wanted to be an actress. She had a fiancé, who was a soldier. He was killed on D-day. She loved him, and without him, she took a wrong turn for a little while, but she was trying to make it right. That's what she was trying to do that night, and somebody shot her in the face. You got a call to clean it up. What you didn't expect to find was another woman there, terrified. It wasn't what you planned for, wasn't what you were being paid for. You could have turned around and disappeared. But you didn't. You walked her out of there. You didn't leave her with those men, and they both had good reason to want her to never open her mouth again. I appreciate that.

"The lady's told the sergeant everything she knows. It's all on record." Peter refolded the sketch. "I don't have to tell you what will happen if she gets hurt, and you're still the only face I know. But I wanted to thank you for not leaving her there."

Peter stood up.

Costello said, "I didn't kill anybody."

"I believe you. But that won't make any difference to the cops."

I went on down the hall and left Barty and Peter alone, just in case Peter wanted to apologize for questioning Barty's decision to pick up Costello. And Barty for yelling at Peter when he knew Peter was just worried as hell about me. Men like them didn't really apologize to each other. They'd just stand there and talk about the case, and let the tone of their voices and their gestures say it for them.

Then there'd be silence. Then they'd shake hands.

There was. And they did.

"I'd rather not try to sleep in a hotel again," I said when we were back in his car.

"We'll get you home. Barty's sending some uniforms with us; they'll stay. Tomorrow, we'll decide where to go from there."

The patrol car pulled up behind us. Peter got out, told the driver where we were going, which I thought was a good idea. The way he usually drove, he could lose them in two minutes. We swung out of the lot and headed toward the Pasadena Parkway.

I laid my head back on the seat. My mind was numb. How long had it been since I'd slept properly? My thoughts began to float, unrestricted, the sort of half-dreams you have as you begin to fall asleep, the ones that seem like real thoughts until you wake back up and realize they don't make any sense. There was a never-ending row of cars behind us, all following me. We'd turn, lose one. But the line never got any shorter. Hawkins remarked on it. She was reclined in the back seat. She had a typewriter on her knees. I thought it must be hard to type like that. She struck a key, and the type bar came up, a piece of a jigsaw puzzle on the end. Then another. The pieces were too big. They jammed. She flicked at them with her finger, trying to separate them. She said, "They secretly want to get caught."

Hawkins.

"What?" Peter said.

"Huh?"

"You said something."

"I was half asleep," I said.

"Who's Hawkins?"

"A writer. At Marathon. Something she said to me. She was

in the back seat."

"I think you're still asleep."

"No, I'm—I don't know why it seemed important. It was only a dream. It's nothing."

Juanita was still at her sister's. I'd made a note to myself to send her sister and brother-in-law a nice gift. And give Juanita a raise.

Johnny Winslow and Lou Brandesi would stay the night at the house. Lou had a stocky but solid body and a hound-dog's face. They checked the windows and doors and searched the house. The officers would spend the night watching the house from the outside and do occasional walks of the perimeter. Johnny would take the first watch inside. Lou would sleep on one of the beds upstairs and take the second watch. I made sandwiches and took some of them and a thermos of coffee out to the officers. I put the others in the refrigerator wrapped in waxed paper. I checked the supplies for breakfast. Juanita had plenty.

Peter would stay in the guest room down the hall.

I hauled myself upstairs and undressed. I stared at the bathtub but decided against it. I'd probably fall asleep and drown, I was so tired. I ran a sink of warm water and washed myself standing up. I slipped into a nightgown and into bed. I plumped the pillow and lay my head on it . . .

. . . I knew I'd been sleeping. I saw the moonlight's soft frame around the draperies, and I'd lain down facing the door. I rolled over and checked the bedside clock. Two fifteen. Two hours had passed in an instant.

I closed my eyes and tried to listen to the silent house and not my thoughts. It was a dream, a half-dream, for heaven's sake. Why did I think it meant anything? Want to get caught? The killer did not secretly want to get caught.

Against my will, I was back in the car, driving home. Peter

was watching the rearview mirror, making sure he didn't lose the patrol car behind us. Hawkins was in the back seat saying people secretly want to get caught.

This was stupid. I needed sleep.

Or maybe . . .

Maybe it wasn't so stupid if you took out the "secretly."

I sat up and pushed the pillows up behind me. I stared, frowning, at the footboard. When I looked at the clock again, a half hour had passed.

I got up, slipped on my housecoat, and crept down the hall and into Peter's room.

"Peter," I whispered as I closed the door after me.

He was already awake, alert, at the sound of the knob turning. He sat up. "What is it?"

"Nothing's wrong. I needed to see you." I sat down on the edge of the bed.

"You can't stay in here. Lou's just down the hall. I appreciate the offer, but you can't—"

I said, "What if we're not looking at the last pieces of a puzzle, but the last pieces of two puzzles?"

CHAPTER 34

Sergeant Barty led us down Roland's backyard to some lawn chairs, which had been examined already for traces of blood, at one end of the pool. The mid-morning light was sparkling on the water.

"Before you ask," he said, "no, we didn't find anything yet. Neale's not going to help us. He's come home. But he's still not talking."

"Here," I said, "maybe you should hold this." I offered him my handbag. "There's a gun in it, and right now, I'm too tempted to shoot somebody."

"I feel that way most days." He looked back and forth between us. "Is this going to be one of them?"

"Mrs. Atwill had an idea," Peter said. "We've spent a few hours working it out."

"Okay," he said cautiously. "Sit down."

We did, then I said, "Why is Costello still in LA?"

"When he decides to start talking," Barty said, "I'll be sure to ask him."

"I'm a witness. I've seen his face. He doesn't kill me. He just reminds me not to go to the police. Yes, he scared me, but I'm still alive. Because his boss thought he had me under control."

"And who's his boss?"

"Joe Gettleman."

"Wait a minute. You told me that was impossible, that Gettleman didn't have time to get Costello here."

"He didn't, *if* he didn't learn about the killing till Roland called him."

"But yesterday, Gettleman knew you'd been to see us."

"But Costello spent the entire day in my backyard, waiting for me. Gettleman wouldn't have been able to reach him after he found out I'd told you the truth. Before they could decide whether to get him out of town, you found him. What I believe and what I can prove are two completely different things, but I think we might have two unrelated crimes. The removal of the body, and the killings of Ida Smoody and Arky Kulpa."

I told Barty my theory.

"Are you telling me the girl's killing had nothing to do with the cleanup?" he said.

Peter said, "Yes. You need to start by having a long talk with a photographer named Birdie Hitts."

A young maid answered the door. She wore a starched apron over her uniform. Both were a bit too big for her, as if they'd recently belonged to someone else. I handed her my calling card and a small envelope with the recipient's name on it.

"I'm sorry to have to disturb her," I said, "but it's important."

"If you'll wait here, I'll see." There was no reproof in her voice about a woman calling at five o'clock in the afternoon, without the courtesy of a phone call first. At five o'clock, a household began preparing for the evening. The lady of the house was not expected to entertain uninvited guests. However, although the maid was young, she probably already knew that social protocols in upper-class Hollywood homes were sometimes different than those in other upper-class American homes.

I waited on the pillared, brick-lined porch in the settling dusk. Finally, the girl returned and invited me in. Peter and Sergeant Barty came quickly around the corner of the house and hurried up the steps. Barty flashed his badge and went right past her. The girl was so nonplussed she just escorted us all to the back of the house and a small glass-walled conservatory, where one of the ladies of the house had been having a casual afternoon tea before dressing for the evening.

I went in alone.

Mary Ann McDowell stood beside the tea table, in a full-length dressing gown of yellow polished cotton. Her thick hair was tied back on her neck. She held out the opened note.

THE POLICE WANT TO KNOW WHY YOU HIRED BIRDIE HITTS

"What does this mean?" she asked me sharply. Then Peter and Barty came in behind me. "Who are you?"

"I'm sorry, miss," the girl murmured. "But he's the police."

Peter guided the maid back out and shut the door. "My name's Winslow," he said to Mary Ann. "This is Detective Sergeant Barty. Where's your mother, Miss McDowell?"

"Having her afternoon nap. What do you want?"

"Good, I think it's better if we do this quietly, without her, don't you? I'm assuming she doesn't know you hired Birdie Hitts."

"I did not hire that man," she declared.

Peter said, "Why don't you sit down, Miss McDowell? Please." She remained standing. "Look," he said calmly, "right now, you're trying to figure out how to play this. You're trying to decide if throwing us out is a good idea because then you'll never know what that note means. But if you try to find out, you might look like you're admitting you hired him. It doesn't matter how you play it, we know you did. And we know why."

"You're making that up. What do you want?"

Barty pulled out his badge, showed it to her, then put it away. "This isn't an official visit, Miss McDowell. We don't want to make it one. But I'm investigating a killing over at Epic, a guy named Arky Kulpa."

"I read about it. I didn't know him," she said.

"Why don't you sit down, ma'am?" Barty said.

She did, elegantly, in the Edwardian armchair. I took one of the fan-backed wicker chairs. Peter turned another of them toward her, about five feet away, giving her some room. He sat down. Barty remained standing.

"So?" she said.

Peter said, "Birdie Hitts is downtown being questioned. He knew Kulpa. He knows some things about why Kulpa might have gotten killed. He knows other things. Things that don't necessarily have to make it into the case file. Reporters will never have to know. We asked Mrs. Atwill to come along so we could get inside the house to talk to you, and so you'd know we didn't come here for a bribe."

Mary Ann continued to regard him with self-possession. "How can you or Lauren or anyone else think I would associate with that man?"

"Not associate with," Peter said. "Hire. But why? There are two possibilities. You were naïve enough to hire a man like that, thinking he'd keep your secret. Or you wanted him to do what he does best, peddle scandal. You wanted him to try to get a fat payoff from Epic to tell them what he knew. Frankly, neither one made sense. At first. Why would you *want* Epic to find out what you were up to? You hired Hitts about the same time you started dating Len Manning, that is, about the same time the studio started *making* you date him. They were pushing for a marriage. It's easy to see the advantage for him, but not for you. Why would the studio want to force on you what amounts to an arranged marriage? A husband who doesn't mind what his wife gets up to has its advantages. An affair can be carried on, and if there are accidental children, there's no scandal. The reputation of a valuable young star wouldn't be ruined. If a powerful, but married, man wanted to have an affair with you, what better way than through Len Manning? But you didn't want a back-street romance and an arranged marriage. You wanted the man, a rich powerful man, you wanted a wedding ring."

Barty said, "Miss McDowell, I'm not interested in prying into your private life. But some things happened the night of the Brackers' party, and they're connected to Kulpa's killing. We'll leave you alone, if you convince us the deal you had with Hitts had nothing to do with the killing. Tell us what you asked him to do."

Peter said, "Did you have any other deal with Birdie Hitts than hiring him to follow you around, so you could make Ben Bracker realize how easily another lover could get to you before him if he didn't divorce his wife?"

"That's a rather ugly way to put it," Mary Ann said.

"Did you have any other deal?"

"No, absolutely not. He followed me, that's all. If that man is saying there was anything else, he's lying. And I went home the night of the party after I said good night to Lauren. I have no idea about any other things that might have happened."

Barty said, "Mr. Bracker was in the study during the fight with your mother, is that true?"

"Yes."

"Were you alone in the study with him afterward? Just answer the questions, and we'll go away," Barty said.

She snapped her head in irritation. "He sent my mother and Len out. We talked, for maybe fifteen minutes, twenty. I don't recall how long. It took a while. He was still angry."

"And talking loud?" Peter asked.

"For a while, of course. But I reminded him he had guests. And he calmed down. We got things settled."

"That he would marry you," Peter said.

"I hired that awful little man to follow me, that's all. I'm not going to answer any more of your questions. Does Ben know what you're up to?"

Barty said, "We're conducting an investigation, and we appreciate your cooperation, Miss McDowell. Did you see this girl at the party?" He showed her a picture of Ida.

"I don't think so."

"We'll keep this out of the record if we possibly can. And Mr. Hitts will keep his mouth shut. Mrs. Atwill has been very discreet."

"Is that what you call it, bringing them both here?" Mary Ann asked me.

I said, "Sergeant Barty gives me too much credit. I wasn't being discreet. You completely took me in. You were so careful to come find me that night and tell me your side of what happened in that study. That the fight was about Len and your mother pressuring you to marry, not that your mother was terrified you had so angered the head of the studio that it could endanger your career. You used Len. He had no idea how Bracker felt about you."

"Are we finished?" she asked Barty. "I need to dress."

"Yes, ma'am," Barty said. "Thank you for your time."

I stood up. "You drove a man to a jealous fury and a woman to desperation. You didn't think that could have consequences?"

"You're being a bit melodramatic, aren't you?" Mary Ann said.

"Let's go," Peter said. He stepped in front of me.

The door opened, and Vera McDowell charged in, wearing a long aqua-colored dressing gown. Her pin-curled hair was covered in a fluffy net.

"What is going on?" Vera said. "Who are you? The maid said you were police."

Peter looked at Mary Ann, and she looked back steadily. Then she crossed her legs, dangled her slipper. "They are. Lauren knows them and has kindly brought them over. I wanted to see if they could make that nasty little photographer leave me alone."

"Well, that's a waste of money," Vera declared. "Pay them to tell that man he's wasting his time?"

"I wouldn't have to pay them. Please forgive Mama, she's always a bit cranky after her nap. Thank you for your help, gentlemen. You've been very kind. The maid will show you out."

"Yes," Vera said, "my girl needs to dress. We have dinner guests at seven."

"We'll see that man leaves you alone, ma'am, happy to do what we can," Barty said.

Vera stepped out into the hall and signaled sharply for the maid to show us to the door.

"Good-bye, Lauren," Mary Ann said. "It was lovely to see you again. Thanks for your help."

In the hallway, I asked the maid if I could borrow the phone. She directed me to a small alcove by the stairs. I picked up the receiver. There was no dial tone. "It seems to be dead," I said.

"Really? I'm sorry, ma'am, it was working earlier."

"No matter. It happens all the time these days with all the new phones. I guess the lines just got overloaded. Thank you."

I went outside, where the men were waiting. "The line's dead. Mary Ann won't be able to call Bracker."

"Not in time, anyway," Peter said.

"Good work," I said to him.

"It's not that hard. You just have to cut one wire, right there around the side of the house."

"And I didn't see a thing he did," Barty said.

CHAPTER 35

Gettleman said, "We were told you had a break in the case. I'm not sure why it would take four people to announce it."

"I'll explain once we're settled," Assistant DA Betts said politely. "Please, if you'd all sit down?"

We were in the study. Jean and I took the armchairs opposite the sofa; Bracker, his wing chair. Loomis had a side chair near the door. Gettleman sat down on the sofa, and Peter took the other end.

"And," Gettleman said, "Mrs. Atwill and Mr. Winslow aren't even with the police."

Betts said, "I hope you'll agree, after what she's been through in the last week or so, Mrs. Atwill is an interested party. Mr. Winslow has provided information to this investigation." He pulled himself up to his full five-four. "Mrs. Bracker, gentlemen, let me be frank with you, as that seems to be what you want. I'm going to tell you some things, and you'll listen to them. Then you'll answer some questions, and at the end of this, I'll decide whether any of you ends up in jail."

Mouths opened. Betts held up a hand. "If any of you wish to leave before I'm finished, Sergeant Loomis here will escort you downtown for questioning as a material witness, and that's going to make the papers. We have two killings to solve, and people in this room destroyed evidence, lied to investigators, and threatened a witness. If I were Mrs. Atwill, I wouldn't feel too kindly toward any of you, but she seems to think there might

304

ating circumstances, and that's part of the

hav

re ind not downtown."

ward me. I looked at the wall above Peter's

p.

u all know the name Ida Smoody, even

ie h   tending otherwise. She came to the party

ity wo   s, invited at the last minute. She was

ut he was   ccident.

g the real

Neale once fathered an illegitimate

t the time, Arky Kulpa, helped her

with you.   the instigator of—a plan to extort

sider that   has said he believed her to be his

ing if she

tleman insisted.

."

t, but we have no proof of that. She

e, and her body was removed, along

alled out   had happened. Somebody shot her,

called himself Costello to remove

ty much   it's what we assumed. The only other

t Mr. Gettleman had arranged it after

e for an   e body—was impossible. Mr. Neale

n't thick   haps twenty minutes before this Cos-

ar. Mrs.   ough time to have arranged such a job.

ie party.   Gettleman only found out about the

iat Miss   ale called him. If, in fact, he already

opened   what simpler, although the plan would

g, Miss   Remove traces of the crime and, at the

rife left,   e who might need it an excuse to say it

rty has

Raised   " Gettleman declared. "Do you realize

caught   this sort of accusation in public?"

oowder   it's not true. Mr. Bracker sent a message

e Mrs.   the party asking him to stay, saying he

wanted to discuss the script. But, unfortunately, Mr.
of the party and went home. Unfortunately, he didn'
his house. He changed clothes and went down to
and found the body. He didn't call the police. H
friend Joe Gettleman, who'd gotten him out of scra
Mr. Gettleman told him to do nothing and sent t
studio security to the scene. The head of secu
naturally think he was sent to assess the situation. E
in fact, only sent to prevent Mr. Neale from callin
police until Costello could get there.

"So, Mr. Gettleman," Betts continued, "we'll start
And before you tell me you have nothing to say, con
all your effort to protect Mrs. Bracker will go for not
ends up downtown."

Bracker said, "This is crazy. This will stop right nov

"I'm afraid it's too late for that, sir," Betts said.

He gestured to Loomis, who opened the door and
"Sergeant."

Barty came in after a moment. "I heard pret
everything, with my ear to the wall."

"I understand a room was torn out to make a plac
extra staircase," Betts said. "It would seem the walls are
enough. No doubt the gypsum shortage during the w
Bracker overheard what happened in this study during t
She knew you were enthralled by Miss McDowell and t
McDowell was demanding marriage. That night, she
this door and found you in here with Mr. Mannin
McDowell, and Miss McDowell's mother. When your v
she promptly went into that stairwell, where Sergeant B
just confirmed you can hear most ordinary conversation
voices would have been even clearer. She was very nearly
at it, but when she heard Mrs. Atwill come out of the
room, she ran up the stairs and fell in her haste, whe

Atwill found her. But Mrs. Bracker heard enough to fear you were, in fact, going to divorce her, and then later she was pushed beyond desperation to rage. Miss McDowell enjoyed what she thought was a moment of covert cruelty when she told her hostess good night. What was it she said?" he asked me.

"She said she couldn't wait until she had a home just like this one," I replied.

"Mrs. Bracker was taken to her room by Savannah Masters, but she didn't stay there. She followed Miss McDowell into the lane, but by the time she got there, all she saw was a woman standing outside Mr. Neale's gate. She followed her, ready to confront her."

"You leave her alone!" Bracker cried. "That's crazy!"

Jean said in a dry, whispered voice, "A man's going to have his flings. I knew that. I've always known that. It's how men are."

"Jean, stop!" Bracker said.

Jean threw her hands up above her forehead, warding off his words. "But they don't rub your nose in it. And they don't leave you. That's the understanding. Movie stars get divorces. But we don't. Not us. We've raised their children, and they respect us and take care of us. They don't divorce us after all we've done so they can go and live with girls half their age. They don't throw their wives out like the trash. All her friends will turn out to be his friends. They'd be embarrassed. What do they do with her? How can they invite her to parties when he'll be there with his new wife? She'll have nothing. No friends, no home, no social standing. He gets everything! I get to spend my old age alone with the memories I made for you!" She jumped up and went for him, slapping him—wildly, viciously, her hands flailing and clawing against his upraised forearms.

"Jeannie, stop!" he cried. "I wasn't! I swear to God!"

All the other men were on their feet, but Peter got there first and threw his arm in front of Bracker, taking the blows on himself. Gettleman grabbed Jean from behind by the upper arms. "Jeannie, please. He's sorry. He knows he was wrong." He pulled her away.

"Don't touch me! You filthy *men*!" She wrenched herself free, wheeled around, and slapped him hard across the face. "Oh, Joe, I'm sorry! Oh, God, I'm so sorry!" Her hands flew over her face. "I'm so sorry." She dropped her head and began to sob, low, deep moans of agony.

"It's all right," Gettleman said softly. "I'm a tough old bird. It would take a lot more than that to hurt me." He laid a gentle hand on her arm and guided her back to her chair. He knelt before her. "He's not going to leave you, Jeannie. You're his rock. He couldn't make it without you. You know that. Not without you."

Peter put Bracker back in his chair, out of her reach, and stood in front of him so he stayed that way. Softly, Bracker began to cry, his hands dangling between his legs.

"Joe was only trying to help," Jean said. "It's my fault. Put me in jail."

"She hasn't done anything," Bracker said. "She didn't do anything."

Betts said to Gettleman, "Why don't you sit down, sir?"

I got up and gave him my chair next to Jeannie. I went and sat down on the sofa.

"Tell us what happened, ma'am," Betts said.

"Jeannie, don't talk to him," her husband said.

"She does it here or downtown."

"I took a gun out of Ben's dressing room," she said, her fists in her lap, staring at the floor. "I didn't even know if it was loaded. I really don't know what I meant to do, what I was thinking, except about how she'd stood there smiling at me, telling me how she couldn't wait to have my home. I can't imagine it now, that I might have been ready to shoot her. I saw her from my window go down the lawn toward the back gate. I put the gun into the pocket of my dress. It was really quite small, the gun. You couldn't see it. When I got to the lane, I thought it was her. I didn't even think about it. I just went after her. Just before I got to the gate, I heard something, a crack, but muffled, like a branch breaking high above. I had no idea what it was. I went in and along that little path. I didn't see her in the yard. I thought she might have gone to the cabana. She wasn't there, so I walked on around the pool. I was going to the house. Then I saw the body. I thought for a moment I'd actually done it. Then all I recall thinking was to act like nothing had happened. I'm very good at that. So I went back to the house. But when I got to my room, I fell apart. My maid found me and got Ben and Joe. I don't know what I told them, maybe that I thought I'd shot someone. Joe got the doctor, and he gave me something. The next morning, they told me it was all a vicious prank. Somebody played a horrible joke on Roland, and nobody was dead. Just a horrible joke. Joe and Ben thought I might have actually done it."

"Jeannie," Ben said, his voice shaking. "I didn't."

"You did that night. You both did. That crack must have been the gunshot, but I didn't see anyone. I don't know who killed her."

"Where's the gun you took from your husband's dressing room?" Betts asked.

Gettleman said, "I took it."

"Where is it?"

"Does it matter?" Gettleman said. "If I give it to you, you have no way of knowing it was the one Jeannie took down there."

"You're still going to give it to me. Did you go down to Mr. Neale's house yourself?"

"Yes. Long enough to see the body. I could tell it wasn't Miss

McDowell."

"Which didn't make any difference, since you were afraid Mrs. Bracker had mistaken the girls," Betts said.

"But Jeannie didn't shoot anyone. She has nothing else to say to you. None of us does. And you're not going to take us downtown and put us in the papers. That was a bluff. If you did, you'd just warn whoever did kill that girl to make sure he's gotten rid of any evidence he might still have. You have a good career, Mr. Betts. There are powerful men who like your prospects to be the next DA and, who knows, then maybe governor. You're not going to put that in jeopardy."

Betts smiled and touched his silk tie. "You're half right. You're not going downtown. But it wasn't all a bluff. It can still make the papers. It's tempting for you to think that if you all keep your mouths shut, make some calls, put on some pressure, this can be made to go away. Mrs. Bracker didn't hurt anyone. The dead girl was a nobody, and she was blackmailing a good citizen. If you don't say anything, there's no scandal. No courtroom. No disbarment.

"I don't believe in perfection; I've been a lawyer too long," Betts went on. "I was told all the evidence had vanished. But it didn't. We found traces of blood in the cabana, between the floorboards, places you can't clean easily when you're in a hurry. Oh, and we found Costello—Mr. Tallis, I believe, when he's not impersonating a detective. I can charge him with murder. We'll see if he wants to take his chances. He'll probably decide to turn you in. Even if he doesn't, the blackmail that Arky Kulpa and Ida Smoody were pulling on Mr. Neale will all come out. Shall we ask Mr. Neale what he thinks of that? You'd all end up at the center of a scandal, and that's the best you can hope for.

"But, as I said, I don't believe in perfection, so I'm going to make you a proposition. You tell Mr. Costello to talk. I want the body. I want the bullet. I want whatever else he removed from the scene. And I want straight stories from all of you. You help me nail the killer, and he stays out of prison. You get to keep practicing law, Mr. Gettleman. Mrs. Bracker stays out of the papers, and so does everybody else, as much as possible. And you might want to think about apologizing to Mrs. Atwill while you're at it."

"We can leave that to another day," I said. An apology right now wouldn't mean any of them were really sorry, and I didn't see any advantage in adding to the humiliation at the moment. "How do you know Costello?" I asked.

"Mike Tallis," Gettleman said after a pause. "We went to school together, high school, back in New York, the Upper East Side, in Yorkville, a tough neighborhood. Irish, German, Jews, some Italians just north. You didn't mix. Who would have figured a big Irish kid like Mike Tallis and I would end up friends? He joined the army; his family couldn't afford to send him to college. We kept in touch, a letter now and then. He spent twenty-two years in. He trained men out here during the war, then in the Pacific, spent some time in the military police. An honorable record. They riffed him. Is that the word? Riffed?"

"Yes," Peter said.

"He's forty-two, they have no use for him now. He called me up, asked if I knew anyone who might be hiring. He liked Los Angeles, wanted to stay here, but he couldn't live on the pension. So I gave him a job, unofficially. I'd been thinking about our security. It's going to be important now, with Congress breathing down our necks. We have to know the studio isn't going to be blindsided by allegations we've harbored communists. I needed somebody better than Mack Pace to find out what problems we have before we have them. Somebody smoother. Somebody our employees didn't know. He gave me some reports. They were excellent. He has a talent for it, for the kind of work you do, I guess, Mr. Winslow. Investigation. And then that night, the night of the party, I called him. I was desperate. I asked what I should do, what I *could* do. What he did, he did to help me, and maybe because he thought I expected him to do it to keep his job. And maybe I let him think that."

"You want to get him out of jail?" Peter said. "Get him to talk."

The next morning, Sergeants Barty and Loomis took a small party of officers who could be trusted and drove out a canyon road in the north part of the county, accompanied by the man I knew as Costello. It was not a deep grave. It had been done in a hurry. No more than three feet deep, and not long enough to lay a body out flat. They found Ida Smoody. The detectives brought her back quietly to the morgue, and the staff dutifully recorded her as a seventy-two-year-old woman who'd been found dead in her home. All routine. Nothing out of the ordinary. Nothing to arouse a reporter's interest.

They didn't record the real cause of death as a gunshot wound to the head.

They didn't record that inside her skull, they found the bullet that killed her. Or that it was a match for the one that killed Arky Kulpa.

CHAPTER 36

I got to sleep in my own bed without patrol cars circling or bodyguards lurking, which made Juanita almost as happy as my being around to eat her cooking.

Birdie Hitts had to give up his swank beach hotel room and go back home.

Peter and I were thanked for our help, encouraged to share any other ideas we might have, but on no account were we to *act* on any of those ideas on our own. With Roland now talking to the police, Peter had very little to do for Roland's attorney. His boss gave him another assignment, and he went out of town for a few days.

I went to work, too. Nothing could breed forgiveness for your sins in Hollywood like the chance to make money from you. Of course, I'd have to write a *very* good story treatment indeed to make up for turning in the head of Epic Pictures and his wife to the cops.

I made myself a new ring-binder notebook, using the copy of *The Hard Fold* Ben Bracker had given me the day I met him. Mine was not nearly as neat as the one Arky had prepared. I made notes in my sometimes glue-smeared margins and struck through subplots with a light pencil. I marked scenes I thought should be kept and samples of dialogue that captured a character's voice particularly well.

I still couldn't decide who the killer should be. People who read the book would know it was the prurient brother. Should I

313

give him a motive acceptable to the Code Office, or change the killer entirely and surprise even those who knew the book? Maybe I should create two story treatments, with alternative endings. That might even give the studio a chance for more lead-up publicity. *Two endings being considered. Who will the killer be?*

It might increase the chance I'd get to write the script and not be bounced out on my rear the second I turned in the story.

In my study, I set up my large corkboard on its sturdy easel and pinned up index cards of the major plot points and a few lines of important dialogue, then began to pin up ideas for the scenes to deliver them, and introduce characters and provide clues.

I started with how my hero would first meet my heroine, the young reporter. She'd be in the newsroom, a lion's den of desks, clattering typewriters, and cigar smoke curling around the brims of the battered hats the reporters hadn't bothered to take off. She'd be perched on the desk of one of them, pumping him for details about the murder case.

I scrawled on an index card, "She is young, eager, beautiful, bright. She is full of excitement, enthusiasm, and the future—all the things now lost to the hero. He immediately despises her."

On Friday morning, while I was chewing on a pencil and staring at the board, Harry Virdon called to invite me for afternoon tea. I took along a basket of flowers and a crate of oranges. She arranged the flowers in three vases and distributed two of them to the dining room and her private sitting room. She set one aside in the kitchen to give to Dorothea.

"She's napping," Harry explained as she carried the tea tray ahead of me into her bed-sitting room. "It's best to talk while she's asleep. Too much of what we might say would only distress her. She doesn't know all this started because she told Ida about my past. Colleen would never say anything, and none of the other girls knows. That detective, that Barty, he seems to understand. He came and asked them all some more questions a couple of days ago, but he's never told them anything. He was a gentleman to Dorothea. They didn't send that other one."

"Loomis."

"Thank God for that."

"Is Gertie still flirting with the sergeant?" I asked, as she handed me my cup.

"She changed her dress when she found out he was here. Is he married?"

"I've never asked. We're not what you'd call friends. He doesn't wear a band."

"A lot of men don't," Harry said, "and those that do sometimes know how to slip it off in a hurry."

"He's never worn one in the months I've known him. He's a bit old for her."

"He's a man with a steady job and a pension down the road. A girl could have the money to make a nice home and raise a couple of kids. She could do a lot worse."

I agreed a girl could do a lot worse than Phil Barty.

There was a timid knock on the door, and a girl peeked in, light haired with wide-set eyes and a delicate chin. She had a slip of paper in her hand. "I'm so sorry to disturb you. Is this everything you'll need from the market? Do you still want the fruit? There's a crate of oranges in the pantry."

The girl handed the list to Harry.

Harry read it over. "You can take the fruit off, thanks. Everything else is fine. If they can't deliver today, it's all right. Just bring back the bread, the eggs, and the lard. The rest can wait till Monday."

Harry handed back the list. The girl nodded, yanked a quick smile in my direction, and went out.

"That's Lizzie. She's helping with the shopping and cleaning now. I need the help, and I can give her free meals for it. I'd have introduced you, but I haven't worked out how to explain you're Lauren Atwill and not a Mrs. Tanner working for *Redbook*. Do the police have anything new, about Ida? Anything you can tell me?"

"I'm afraid they're not telling us much." I couldn't of course tell anyone Ida's body had been found. "I know you have to rent her part of the room eventually, but could I pay the rent for six months or so, give Colleen a chance to get over this, as much as will ever be possible?"

"That would be very nice," Harry said. "Thank you. I'll accept that, for her."

She told me how much, and I took my checkbook from my handbag. I went over to the small desk by the door to the kitchen and used her fountain pen to fill out the check. "Just put it under that paperweight," she said.

I did, on top of a short stack of bills waiting to be paid.

Harry had a corkboard of her own, much smaller than mine, hanging above the desk, with lists pinned to it of things to be done next week, next month: bills to be paid, repairs to be arranged, reminders about laundry pickup and delivery, birthday party plans for one of the girls.

"Is something wrong?" she asked.

"No, no. I was just admiring your lists," I said.

"I'm a dedicated list-maker. I'd never get anything done without them. Are you sure you're all right?"

"I'm . . . just a bit distracted. It's been a long two weeks, and if I don't turn in a cracker-jack story, I'm going to be fired. It's not going that well. I wish I were as organized as you."

"Have your tea and some of this cake. And talk to me about your fictional killer if you want. It would be a relief to hear about one that'll get caught. I assume the killer in your script will get caught."

"The Code Office wouldn't allow it any other way. Yes, the killer always has to be punished."

I tried to find Peter, calling him from a pay phone as soon as I left Harry's. But he wasn't at home or at his office. One of these days, somebody would invent a real Dick Tracy two-way wrist radio. I'd be the first in line to get one.

I didn't leave a message with the answering service. Peter was coming to dinner and would be at my house by six. I could wait that long. After all, it was just an idea.

When he arrived, I took his hat and coat, laid them on the hall table, and led him into the privacy of the study. I shut the door.

He reached past me and locked it, then pulled me into his arms, and before I knew it, we were on the sofa, and he was vigorously making up for his absence of the last few days. Since I didn't object, in fact quite the contrary, it took twenty minutes before we were sitting up again. And another few before we had all our clothes back on.

Being a man, he accomplished that first and mixed me a gin and tonic and poured himself a bourbon.

"You look very pleased with yourself," I said, as I finished buttoning my blouse.

"Any reason I shouldn't be?" He handed me my drink and gestured with his glass at the corkboard. "You've been working hard."

"I got distracted. Stop smirking. I meant earlier today. I had an idea about Arky's new scheme. I hope this isn't a blow to your ego, but that's why I shut the door. I was working on an alternative ending to the script. Then I went over to Harry's for tea, and I saw some lists that she made. I started thinking about Ida's list, with all the details about Harry's life. It's in Ida's handwriting, but not the way she'd say it. '*Your* mother did this,

317

your mother did that.' She scratched out the 'your' and substituted 'my,' but not until later, because 'my' is in a different color of ink. She either took it down from dictation or copied it from another list. Verbatim. If she and Arky had been creating it together, she wouldn't have written it down like that. If Arky wanted her to have a list—and didn't want his own handwriting floating around—he would have typed it. She *copied* it. From a list Arky showed her but didn't want to give her."

"An accomplice?"

"Somebody else in a position to know details of Harry's past."

"But they had Dorothea."

"Yes, but was her memory reliable? There were three people at the party who saw Ida or could have seen her, who could have followed her to Roland's or lured her. Three people that we know of who could have supplied those details: Joe Gettleman, Savannah Masters, and Kentwood Grantlin. They all knew Roland well twenty years ago. Could that be what Arky meant when he said he had dirt that had turned into gold?"

Peter sat down in the chair by the hearth, frowning, his eyes focused in the middle distance. Finally, he said, "He let her go. Arky made about three thousand tax-free off Neale, not something you give up easily. Especially not a guy like him, used to taking advantage of people. Ida broke up with him, and he let her—no threats, no pressure to keep getting money from Neale. Why would he give it up?"

"Because he found something bigger, a lot bigger."

"If he had a list worth a fortune, why did he wait to use it? He had to have had that list since before Ida Smoody ever approached Roland Neale."

"That's a long time," I conceded.

"He said, '*turned* into gold'. Something changed. What could have changed between November and two weeks ago?" Suddenly, Peter stood up. "Gold." He snatched a blank sheet of paper from my desk. "I'm your bookie. I have your marker. I've got an idea for a scheme, something that just fell into my lap. I found out Roland Neale had a bastard child, and that could be worth money. But I need help to play it. I need some reliable details about the woman he had a child with. I have your marker, but I'll give you more time to pay what you owe in return for the information. But then what happened that made *you* worth more than extorting a few thousand from Roland Neale?"

"Penelope Grantlin died."

"Exactly. She leaves a fortune to her son and his wife."

"But in trust. With Roland Neale as the executor. He has to approve all distributions above the allowance."

"If I show the list I got from you to Neale, he'll make you live on that allowance for the rest of your life. You'll never see another penny. How much would my list be worth?"

"Except, of course, the police haven't found another list, as far as I know."

Peter said, "We have to call Phil Barty. I think I might know where it is."

"This better be worth it, my first night off in two weeks," Barty grumbled, as he lumbered ahead of us into an interrogation room and shut the door. We couldn't go to his desk. Reporters were roaming the floor, looking for last-minute stories to meet deadlines. Sometimes, Peter had once told me, they even helped themselves to files left unattended on detectives' desks. We didn't need any curious eyes.

Barty laid the package he'd recovered from the evidence room on the table and yanked a chair out. He gestured me into it. "Leave your gloves on."

I did, even though I was sure it was already covered in police fingerprints. Most detectives didn't wear gloves when handling

319

items considered evidence, let alone those that had not been. I unfolded the paper wrapping. Inside was the spiral binder Arky had prepared for me and the cannibalized copy of the novel he'd used to do it. The copy's spine was broken and had only its front and back covers and a couple of pages inside: a list of other novels by the same author, a splashy advertisement for other novels from the same publisher, and a form for ordering them. I opened the notebook and thumbed through it to the end.

"It's finished," I said to Peter. As he had guessed it would be. "He should have left it in the wicker basket by my bungalow door, not put it in his car."

Barty took a step closer and looked down over my shoulder.

I flipped to the front and began turning the sheets of typing paper, examining each one.

Three-quarters of the way through, I found duplicates. There were two different sheets that contained the same pages: 275 and 276. The first of the duplicate pages looked like all the others in the notebook. The center of the sheet had been cut out in a rectangle. The page margins had been glued neatly to the sheet. The odd-numbered page faced me. When I flipped it over, I could see the even-numbered page through the rectangular cut-out. But on the second duplicate, Arky had glued a page 275 to one side of a sheet with a cut-out in it, and a separate 276 to the other side, pages he must have taken from other copies of the book.

I could feel something in the space between the pages.

"Set it down," Barty said. He closed the notebook, folded the paper wrapping back around it, tucked it under his arm, and went out to his desk. He pulled something out of the middle drawer, put it in his pocket, and returned, closing the door. He set the notebook back on the table and sat down in front of it. He opened the binder and pulled open the rings. He removed the duplicate page, laying it on the table. From his pocket, he took a small cardboard box of razor blades and removed one. He folded back just enough of the blade's thin wrapping to expose one side of the blade and carefully slit one side of page 275. Out of the space between the pages, he pulled a sheet of paper, folded in quarters. He unfolded it and laid it on the table. It was a list containing the first dozen of the entries we'd found on Ida's list—intimate details of Harry's life. It was written with a fountain pen, in a flowing, artistic hand.

I said, "Arky was taking it to the meeting with his accomplice, now his blackmail victim. If he got the money, his first installment, he could just pull that sheet out and hand it over."

From my handbag, I retrieved the card Arky had given me the day I met him, the one with the messenger-office number on it. He'd written his name on the back and a note. "CALL IF YOU NEED ANYTHING, ARKY."

I handed it to Barty. Peter looked over his shoulder as the sergeant compared the handwriting to what was on the list.

"The *R*'s are different," Peter said. "And the loops in the *Y* and the *G*."

"Is there anything you're not an expert on?" Barty snapped.

"We didn't come here to get anybody in trouble," Peter said.

"Good. Because now I got to go tell the lieutenant about this, and he likes to think his detectives know what the hell they're doing."

CHAPTER 37

Within an hour, we were all seated in Assistant DA Betts's office, along with Lieutenant Ambrusco, away from the prying eyes of reporters, who were still roaming Homicide with impunity.

Ambrusco had high-colored cheeks and dark hair arranged in a careful wave above his wide brow. After we'd all told our stories, Ambrusco raised a hand. "I think we can let Mr. Winslow and the lady go on home now."

Neither of us moved.

Betts said, "We keep telling them to butt out, and they keep turning up evidence. What do you say we let them stick around? What's our next step? There are no prints on that list. I can't get a search warrant if I can't prove whose handwriting this is. And to convince a judge, I'm going to need to show him more than a signature we dug up or a few lines off a driver's license form."

"That could take a while," Barty admitted. "To find samples, samples long enough, and not tip the killer we're doing it."

"Meanwhile," Ambrusco said, "the killer's got rid of the gun and the clothes."

"Maybe," said Barty. "But that would be two suits or two dresses, maybe a coat the night Kulpa died. Maybe you don't want your maid to notice things are gone. You don't want to call attention. You look everything over, you don't see anything, so you just get it all dry cleaned, the shoes shined. Maybe you even hang on to the gun, not under the mattress, but someplace safe, thinking you might need it, maybe to plant it on somebody else if things get hot. If we make the killer feel a little safer, maybe any evidence left won't get tossed out."

Betts said, "And how do we do that?"

"We make an arrest in the Kulpa killing," Barty said. "And we say we're looking at the guy for the disappearance of Kulpa's girlfriend. But we'll need a real suspect to show the press."

Ambrusco nodded. "We have cadets we can use, nobody would know them."

"With respect, sir," Peter spoke up, to spare Barty having to tell his boss he was full of beans, "you'll need somebody who'll stand up to a check. A phony suspect with a phony name won't work. Any decent reporter'll knock that down in an afternoon."

Barty said, "We need a guy with a record, preferably for gambling. A couple of assaults would be nice, too. He'll have to cooperate, keep his mouth shut, act like he could be guilty. We want to ask Julie Scarza to give us a guy."

"Sergeant," Ambrusco said, "under no circumstances are we asking a gangster for a favor." The indignation was almost certainly for my benefit.

"Strictly speaking, sir," Barty said, "*we* wouldn't. *She* would."

"She knows Scarza?" Ambrusco said and stared at me.

I felt I was probably more qualified to answer that than Barty. I might be a woman, but I was, after all, sitting in the room. "Yes," I said and explained how I'd met Scarza and why he might be willing to do me a favor.

"What's he going to want?" Ambrusco asked Barty.

"We offer to let a couple of his guys out early," Barty said. "He has to have a few inside, here or out in county. They could get out with time served. We don't promise him any passes for the future. Our killer might relax a little. Maybe hang on to the gun—if it's in a safe place. Maybe not decide to throw out all the clothes."

Betts said, "That's fine, except I'd still need handwriting samples. How are you going to get them for me?" He glanced at Peter. "I don't think we can rely on breaking and entering."

Peter said, evenly, "No, it might be hard to explain to a judge how you laid hands on personal notes written by Savannah Masters or doctor's records from Kentwood Grantlin. You need samples, long samples you can trust and get quickly."

"So, what do you propose?" Ambrusco said. "Another deal with a gangster?" Peter turned to Barty. Ambrusco said, "You can't be serious."

Peter said, "Why would either of the suspects be involved with Arky Kulpa? Gambling. He was a bookie. And if you have gambling debts with one bookie, you've got them with others. I might be able to get you handwriting samples you can rely on, and a judge would accept."

"From a bookie?" Ambrusco asked.

"From a businessman," Peter replied.

"And this *businessman* won't tip the killer."

"No, but you only have my word for that."

They discussed it, argued about it. In the end, Betts decided it might be worth a chance. But first Scarza had to agree to help. I called the number from the card that Eddie, Scarza's right-hand hooligan, had given me. Eddie didn't answer, so I had to leave a message with another hooligan, asking if it would be possible to arrange a meeting with Mr. Scarza. I left my home number and said I'd be there after eleven and throughout the day tomorrow.

Peter and I returned to Pasadena and ate the steak and mushrooms Juanita had planned for the dinner that was supposed to have been eaten at seven o'clock. She was now planning menus in which the meat course would not be ruined if I disappeared suddenly for hours. I'd called her before we left

City Hall. She insisted on frying the steaks when we got there, but I sent her to bed after that.

Peter and I were just finishing slices of a pecan tart when the phone rang.

It was Eddie. Mr. Scarza could see me tonight.

So, at midnight, Peter and I were back in his car.

Scarza sat at the same poker table in the same diner in which I'd last seen him when he'd terrified Birdie Hitts. He was wearing evening clothes, complete with gloves. He said hello to me, eyed Peter. He didn't offer one of his gloved hands to either of us to shake.

We sat, and Eddie and the goon who'd dragged Birdie Hitts around a few days ago took their sentry positions at the doors.

Peter laid out for Scarza the favor the police were asking for, through us.

"Who are these suspects you're after?" Scarza asked.

Peter said, "I can tell you they aren't in your employ."

"That doesn't mean it necessarily would be a good idea for me to cooperate in apprehending one of them. There are people I do business with and good customers I'd rather not send to prison. I assume that, if a phony suspect is what the police are after, they hope to find some evidence they don't want the killer to destroy. The gun that killed Arky perhaps."

"Perhaps," Peter said.

"So Arky and this girl, the Smoody girl, were both killed over this blackmail. The last time I spoke with Mrs. Atwill, she wasn't sure."

Scarza was reminding me he'd expected to hear from me if I discovered who killed Arky.

Peter said, "It's only within the last twenty-four hours that we've become certain the killings were committed by the same person. Before that, it was only instinct and a reluctance to believe in coincidence."

"Now, you are certain," Scarza said.

"Not certain of the killer," Peter said.

"What do you think of the cops' idea, Mrs. Atwill?"

I said, "A lot depends on whether the killer's smart or just believes he is."

"Yes, a very big difference. You say 'he'."

"A complication of our language," I said.

"And a complication in your investigation," Scarza said. "Women are more cautious and suspicious should the police wish to deceive the killer into revealing herself. If your killer is a woman, however, it would increase the chances of finding the gun. A woman would be more reluctant to part with a weapon that is harder for women to acquire."

"In this case," Peter said, "the killer acted brazenly. First to kill Miss Smoody with so many people not that far away, out in the open. Then to walk up to Mr. Kulpa in a public place, and not that late at night."

"Arrogance. Yes. Easier to trap, perhaps, but more dangerous if you do. I agree to speak to Mr. Betts. Eddie will arrange it." Then he raised a finger, and Eddie opened the door. Our meeting was over. "A pleasure to see you again," Scarza said to me.

The next afternoon, the police arrested a bookie named Jacky Dorf for questioning in the killing of Arky Kulpa and hinted that they suspected him in the disappearance of one of Kulpa's girlfriends, too, although they didn't release her name. Dorf had a record, including a conviction three years ago for assault on a rival bookie.

Now we had to get handwriting samples.

And so the first public date I had with Peter was to a fancy nightclub. To identify a killer.

I wore an evening gown of sapphire blue with a square neck; soft, discreet drapes in the bodice and skirt; and cathedral sleeves. My first night out at a club with Peter, I didn't feel comfortable with the idea of a strapless gown. Elegance, not innuendo, I decided.

We drove out to Ramon Elizondo's club, which was in the county on a twisty canyon side road, a gleaming hacienda built on a green-lawn oasis in the scrub grass and Manzanita. It was a Hollywood idea of a gangster's nightclub: a lobby with silk walls and beveled sconces and carpeted in plush, deep mauve accented with white magnolias. There were broad arches that led into the dining room and dance floor, and wide chrome steps up to the "members only" club where the gambling went on. And a lot of it went on, given what the club must cost to run, although the club was probably also a way for other gangsters to put in dirty money and bring it out clean, its location at once reducing the number of bribes that had to be paid and the scrutiny of those who couldn't be bought.

We didn't have to ask for the club's owner. Rudy, who greeted customers and quietly assessed them, knew Peter well and had been told to direct us upstairs. He said, "Your table is ready whenever you are." He turned and signaled to the men at the top of the stairs near the casino's brass-studded leather doors, a couple of weightlifters in a dozen yards of evening clothes.

They were there to admit "members" to the club and prevent access to anything else, unless you were approved. We were, so we turned left at the top of the stairs and continued to a door near the end of the hallway. A tall, skeletal man named Lenny opened it at Peter's knock. It was a club room for private high-stakes poker parties and meetings of the sort of people Elizondo still did business with: men who specialized in finding new ways to take money from people with money to take.

Ramon Elizondo stood by the fireplace, smiling at me, in a cashmere sports coat and a crisp shirt, the collar open along his tanned throat. He hadn't changed yet. He didn't usually begin his appearances in the club until after eight.

Elizondo was Peter's friend, the man who'd hired him as a kid to haul illegal booze and strong-arm "distributors" and anybody who tried to compete. Because he had, Peter was able to feed his brother and sisters, and keep them in school with a roof over their heads. After Prohibition ended, Elizondo sent Peter to Ed Paxton's agency. He'd figured Peter wasn't really cut out to be a gangster.

"It's good to see you again," he said warmly and took my hand, holding it a moment. He had dark, arresting eyes, full of masculine knowledge and experience, but his regard never crossed the line to appraisal, at least not of me. Even when Peter wasn't around. He was the Hollywood version of a gangster. How much of it was cultivated and how much calculated, I didn't know.

Peter trusted him.

We sat in leather armchairs. He offered refreshment, and we accepted. Lenny mixed the drinks and brought them over on a small tray. Then Elizondo nodded, and Lenny went out and shut the door.

Elizondo sat back, his elbows on the arms of his chair, his fingers lightly together. He asked what I was working on. I told him about the script.

"I liked that book," he said. "The author knew how certain men talk. Movies rarely do. The jargon they use is some producer's idea of how certain men should talk."

"Whatever's in the book will be outdated. Perhaps I could sign you on as an advisor."

He laughed. "I'd be glad to help, though perhaps we shouldn't tell the producer."

Then he turned to Peter. Peter had already explained over the phone, but now he did so again, face to face. He told Elizondo the samples were needed in a murder case. That was all. He said nothing about how important it was that no one else should find out.

Elizondo reached inside his jacket, took out several folded slips of paper, and handed them to Peter, who examined them. Elizondo explained to me, "These are markers from the last year. Some have been paid, and you may have those. Generally, we retain all the markers, even after payment. Occasionally, a guest will insist on an extension of credit, and regrettably, I will have to show them evidence that they are in fact less than prompt in their repayments and, in some cases, that they still owe us money. That's why the markers are always made in a customer's own handwriting."

Peter handed them over to me.

The language on each agreement to repay was the same, but all handwritten, and then signed and witnessed. All of the agreements were to repay the money owed within ninety days.

Four were from Kentwood Grantlin, for a total of eighty-five hundred; five came from Savannah Masters, for nearly twelve thousand.

Elizondo said, "Dr. Grantlin is fond of poker but is too often tempted to bluff or draw to a weak hand. He also likes the ponies, and I hear he's not very good at it. However, we don't take racetrack action at the club. Miss Masters likes craps, the only game of chance in which the player does not rely on anyone but himself, when he has the roll. Warm the dice, blow on the dice, talk to the dice. We give celebrities such as Miss Masters a few hundred in chips, because our other customers like to tell their friends they played next to a movie star or someone famous in Hollywood, as she is. And because more than the five hundred is almost always lost. Miss Masters brings stars here with her, and so we extend her quite a bit of credit; her husband, too, as you see. Will those help?"

I remembered enough of the peculiarities of the cursive hand on the list. "Yes," I said, with a shudder, "I think we might have the answer."

Rudy showed us to our table, along the rail of the gallery, just above the dance floor. It was a good table, but not one of the best, as those were reserved for people who wanted to be seen. Champagne appeared immediately, compliments of Mr. Elizondo. Peter told the waiter we were going to dance first. I laid my evening bag on the table and gave Peter my hand. He pulled my arm through his, and we walked together down the short steps to the dance floor. Then, for the first time in public, Peter held my body to his. The band was playing *Where or When*. There were glances at my dress, my jewelry. A few more at Peter. But no one paid much attention to us. We weren't famous. We were just a couple, dancing. I leaned my head toward him. He touched my temple with his lips.

We knew who killed Ida Smoody.

We danced and whispered about what had to be done next, and how we could get the police to go along with it.

CHAPTER 38

"It's like that Agatha Christie around here," Sergeant Barty muttered.

I was fairly sure Mrs. Christie hadn't written a crime novel in which a half dozen police officers would be watching a house from the outside, and a few more would be concealed inside. But the sergeant was setting a trap in an old house while standing in a front parlor on the hearth rug. Perhaps that's what he meant.

Perhaps he meant he had to endure the presence of amateur sleuths.

But Harry wanted me there with her and Dorothea, so Barty had agreed. And if I was there, he'd have to put up with Peter as well.

I tried to stay out of the way, sitting quietly in an armchair, my handbag primly in my lap, as the men arrived, in pairs, in mufti, up through the backyard. Harry served coffee in the kitchen. When all of them had finally gathered in the parlor, cups in hand, Harry collected me and took me into her room, where I could remove my hat and have some coffee and toasted muffins, which she'd set out on a tray. She'd put on a dress, an acorn-colored light wool with a narrow belt. She still had a figure. Sergeant Barty took some notice of it when she came to claim me.

It was eight o'clock on a Sunday morning. The street was quiet. So was the house. The girls were all gone, sent off on a weekend holiday treat in the mountains the day before. Harry had told them it was through the generosity of a former boarder, who'd made good but wanted to remain anonymous. It was, in fact, me. Colleen couldn't go; she'd had to work Saturday night. She'd been told the truth and was staying in a small hotel.

Dorothea was still sleeping. There was no way practical to get her out of the house. When she awoke, I'd take care of her upstairs in her room. If she became too agitated by the presence of the men, Harry had some sleeping pills she could give her—had given her in the past to no ill effect, she said.

We sipped coffee while listening to Barty instructing the men in the front parlor. Then some of them began to move. Loomis left first, down through the tangled undergrowth of the backyard to a nondescript sedan, one without any hint it belonged to the police. He had a search to conduct and a team standing by, waiting for the killer to begin a normal Sunday routine. It was vital the suspect saw nothing to make that routine vary. One hint of the police, and everything could fall apart.

Three more men followed, at intervals, dressed in the sort of clothes men in this neighborhood would wear. They'd do a full two-block loop on foot and come into their observation point—the house across the street—by its back door. In a few hours, two of them would take up their position on that home's front porch, with a game of checkers, ready in case the suspect tried to make a run for it. The other would be stationed inside with his binoculars in case there was a signal from the officer concealed in Harry's tower.

Later, three other men would leave to wait in the overgrown tangle behind Harry's house. Harry had no garage for them to hide in. Inside the house, besides the man in the tower, there would be one officer on the second floor. No officers on the first floor, because it was too risky they might be spotted or heard. Just Sergeant Barty in the front parlor, and if the search went well, Loomis. If it didn't go well, we'd all be on our way home.

It seemed like a lot of men to me just to prevent the flight of a suspect. But criminals had been known to disappear from under the noses of the police department. And if a suspect made it to the Mexican border—or in truth the border of most states—capture would be difficult indeed, given how hard it was to trace fugitives.

At nine, Harry woke Dorothea and brought her downstairs quietly to give her some breakfast. I was waiting in the kitchen, a friendly, familiar face. Harry reminded Dorothea who the men in the parlor were, and why they were there. And how she would have to stay out of the way upstairs with me later.

Harry made Dorothea pancakes, pouring out circles of batter she'd already prepared into a cast iron skillet.

"I do like my pancakes on Sunday," Dorothea confided in me. She wore a calf-length woolen skirt of sage green, a blouse with a sailor's collar, a thick buttoned cardigan, and, over all, her black and red shawl. She cast a worried glance at the door into the front hall. She whispered, "Is that rude man here?"

"No," I said, "but he might come back later."

"I don't like him. The other one is gruff, but a gentleman beneath. Very much the way a policeman should be. Is he here?"

"Yes, but he's busy."

"Gertie will be sorry to have missed him," she said, then giggled.

Harry poured her a cup of tea. Dorothea held the cup with both hands as if they were cold. "Do they have guns, all those men?"

"I imagine," I said.

"Guns are so noisy."

"Nobody's going to need a gun," Harry said.

"Then why do they have them? Harry has one locked in her

night table."

"And it'll stay locked up." She said to me, "I've had to wave it once or twice at some of those lowlifes down the hill. They come staggering up here on a Saturday night, come right to our front door, acting like this is a cat house."

"Do you have a gun?" Dorothea asked me.

I did, in fact, and in my handbag. I'd been carrying it since the night Costello appeared in my backyard. But I said no.

"I have to stay upstairs," Dorothea said.

"Yes, dear," Harry said. "I'm afraid so."

"Because there will be more strangers. Later," Dorothea said.

"Yes. Till then, I have some new magazines for you in my room, and we'll listen to the radio, if you'd like."

When Dorothea finished her pancakes, Harry took her into the bed-sitting room and settled her down in the larger armchair, with a lap blanket, the magazines, and the radio, tuned to a church program.

We waited.

The men still in the front room played cards, read, talked, joked, tried to do something with their energy. I read the news-paper, then another one.

Peter came in, said hello to Dorothea. She remembered him. He dropped off a couple more newspapers he'd brought with him to pass the time. "I'll be upstairs later," he said to Dorothea, to remind her there'd be men there.

"Upstairs? Oh, we don't allow men up there." Then she smiled and went back to her radio. Hymns were playing now. She hummed along. Harry glanced at us anxiously. Peter returned to the front room.

Harry made fresh tea, and we sipped. And read. And waited.

At one o'clock, she took sandwiches out of the pantry and removed the damp cloth covering them. The men ate them in the kitchen, standing up, making sure they left no traces they'd been there.

She brought some in for us, along with Dorothea's vitamins. I ate, but Dorothea was still full from her pancakes. After the church services were over, we found some music. I was running out of ways to pretend I was reading.

At two o'clock, the phone rang in the front parlor. Harry went out to answer it, then handed the call to Barty. She came back in just a minute. "It's the sergeant's partner," she said. She wouldn't say Loomis's name in front of Dorothea.

Talking began again in the front room, murmured, but with new urgency.

Peter came in, smiling, relaxed, nothing to alarm Dorothea. "Our guests will be here in about a half hour."

I nodded, thanked him. He went away.

The plan was on. Loomis had found what he was after in his search.

"It's so nice and warm in here," Dorothea said, smoothing her lap blanket. "I think I might be falling asleep."

"Why don't you take a nap then?" Harry said.

"I just got up."

"That's what Sunday afternoons are for," Harry said. "Naps. Come on, why don't you just climb into bed here? I'll wake you if anything happens."

Dorothea slipped out of her shoes and handed Harry her shawl.

"Warm enough for you?" Harry asked as Dorothea slipped under the covers. "Maybe an extra blanket on your feet?"

"Yes, please. That would be very nice."

"Would you like me to leave the radio on, down low?"

"Yes, yes, please. Your friend, the tall one. Is he still here?" she said to me.

"Mr. Winslow. In the front room. He'll be here."

335

"Of course. I forgot his name. Can he shoot?"

"The eye out of a gnat," I said. It was not all that much of an exaggeration.

"That's good," she said and chuckled softly as she drifted to sleep.

Harry carried the tray into the kitchen, and I followed her. "The 'vitamins,' " she said as she washed out the cups. "She never remembers what the pills look like, so she can't tell the difference. I want you to know I don't drug her. But she couldn't have stood up to this. It was no good thinking she could."

"You're right. She's much better off sleeping."

"I just wanted you to know. There are times when she gets scared, and there's nothing to do to get her to sleep at night but to give her something, but only when there's no other way. She'll sleep now for at least four or five hours." She slapped the kitchen towel into the drain rack. "Twenty years. It was stupid to put on this dress. That bastard is coming here, and I put on my best dress."

"You didn't do it for Roland Neale. You did it for Ida. For the role you have to play today. It doesn't hurt that you look beautiful. The men were noticing."

"Oh, for heaven's sake," she said, but she laughed.

Harry's neighbors were stirring. A few took strolls after their Sunday lunches, perhaps on their way to visit friends. A few swept sidewalks, clipped hedges, or sat out on the porch with the Sunday papers. The two officers on the porch of the house across the street bent over their checkerboard.

The men inside Harry's house made their last trips up to the bathroom. Three of them went out the back door and down into the tangled vines of the slope. Peter went upstairs with two officers. One of them took up his position in the tower with his binoculars and a set of colored flags to send signals if necessary.

When I told Barty that Dorothea would be asleep for hours, he told me to stay with him in the front parlor. He might have something for me to do, answer questions he might throw my way. He told me what he wanted. He grabbed a chair from the card table and set it beside another near the hearth.

The slipcovered sofa under the windows had been dragged forward a few feet and the best armchair arranged beside it. Two others sat opposite, but not too close.

After what seemed like a very long time, the car pulled up, Sergeant Loomis in a gleaming black Lincoln, borrowed for the occasion. It was easier to get famous people to come with you if you had an expensive car for them to ride in.

When Barty went to the door, I watched from the front window, standing well back from the net curtains. Loomis got out and opened the back door. Kentwood climbed out and offered a hand to Savannah. She laid a gloved one in it but scanned the front of the house with something like irritation before stepping out to the curb. The front-passenger door opened, and Roland Neale appeared. He paused as well, longer, looking at the tattered house Loomis had brought them to. Barty opened the front door. Loomis gestured them before him and followed the three up the front steps.

Harry took her assigned place in her chair. I remained standing beside mine because I could see the front door from there.

The three came in cautiously, glancing toward the dining room, then the parlor. Barty offered to take their coats; Savannah slipped out of hers and handed it to him. Kentwood and Roland hung up their own, on the pegs in the hall by the door.

"You know Mrs. Atwill," Barty said as they all came in. "And Miss Virdon. I think you might remember Miss Virdon." There was an edge of disapproval in his voice when he said her name. Harry straightened her back.

Roland stopped dead in the doorway. "You didn't tell me,"

he said to Loomis. "You never said—" He turned back to Harry. "I thought—"

"That I was dead," she said. "Why would you think that? You never bothered to find out *what* happened to me."

"Who are you?" Kentwood asked her abruptly.

"It's Harry Virdon," Savannah snapped at him.

"Oh, I'm sorry. Of course," Kentwood said. Nonetheless, he looked as if he still weren't quite sure who she was.

"Why don't you all sit down?" Barty said. He directed Kentwood and Savannah to the sofa, and Roland to the armchair beside it. Loomis took the chair near the door. I sat down. Barty remained standing in the middle of the large circle we'd created.

He spoke to the three guests. "We appreciate you coming here with Sergeant Loomis. We know you've been through a lot these last couple of weeks. But there are a few things we needed to talk about, and we thought it was best done in private. We didn't want to go downtown. There's no reason to put you through that."

"Yes, so this man said," Kentwood said, gesturing to Loomis. "But what are we doing *here?*"

Barty said, "The girl who masqueraded as Mr. Neale's daughter lived here."

"Masqueraded? So she *was* a little chiseler," Savannah declared.

"Savannah, please. She wasn't my daughter, no," Roland said to her, quietly.

"Of course she wasn't," Harry said. "My daughter died when she was three. I was living in New York at the time because your buddy Joe Gettleman made sure I couldn't get work out here."

"Miss Virdon," Barty said, "you said you'd be quiet." He went over to the card table in the far corner and picked up some papers from an open folder. "Mr. Neale was being

blackmailed. More accurately, a girl named Ida Smoody—who also called herself by a stage name, Mimi Delacourt—was trying to extort money from him with the help of a bookie named Arky Kulpa, a guy she met at Epic, where she did some extra work and where he ran messages when he wasn't running numbers or taking bets on the ponies. The girl had proof she was Mr. Neale's daughter. She showed him copies of some personal letters from Mr. Neale and pictures of Miss Virdon as a young woman." He laid one set of papers on the coffee table, spread them out. "We found these hidden in the girl's room. And here are some more things we found, clippings and other information about Mr. Neale's life and career." All three of the guests bent forward to look at them, but none touched them.

"Mr. Neale believed her," Barty went on. "Probably because he wanted to. But she also had details about her mother that most people wouldn't know. This list." Barty laid the list Peter had found in Ida's room in the middle of the fan of documents and clippings. "She and Kulpa used this list to create memories of things her mother had told her about life in Hollywood. Memories the girl then shared with Mr. Neale, in small doses. About a favorite pair of red dancing shoes, a favorite dress. The places her mother had liked to go. People she knew, things she did as a young woman. The list is in the girl's handwriting, but you can see she was being coached by someone who knew a lot about the woman she claimed to be her mother. Not the sort of information she or Mr. Kulpa could have come by in newspapers and public records. There was an accomplice to all this, who wanted to get money out of Mr. Neale and maybe a little revenge. And this person might be responsible for the girl's death and Mr. Kulpa's."

Savannah said, "But you arrested someone for killing that man. I saw it in the papers."

"I'm afraid not," Barty said.

"I saw it," she insisted. "And our reporters told me he did it and that he probably killed the girl, too."

"He didn't." He turned to Loomis, who got up and gave him a folded handkerchief. Barty unfolded it carefully in his palm, facing me. Against the clean white linen, there was a glow of deep lavender. He turned to the guests and held it out to Savannah. "Do you recognize this, ma'am?"

Savannah stared at it, then her eyes darted away.

"Ma'am?" Barty said.

"I don't think so. No. Why? Where did you get it?" she demanded.

"Have you seen it before?"

"There are a lot of those around these days, amethysts."

"Amethyst?" Roland said in a hushed voice and sat forward.

"Sir?" Barty stepped over to Roland's chair and showed it to him. "Do you recognize this ring? Please don't touch it."

"Oh, God. Yes. I—I gave it to her. Her birthday was in February. Amethysts are the birthstone for February. Where did you find it?"

"Was she wearing it the night of the party?" Barty asked.

"Yes," Roland said.

"Did you see it that night?" he asked the other two. "Can you help corroborate that?"

Kentwood said, "She was playing tennis. She wasn't wearing a ring. No, I'm afraid I didn't see it."

"I'm sure she wasn't," Savannah said. "You know she was playing in her slip. I took her to put her clothes back on. I was there. She didn't put on a ring. I notice jewelry. I would have noticed a ring as nice as that."

"Mrs. Atwill, how about you?" Barty asked me.

"I'm afraid I didn't notice," I said.

Roland said, "She had it on when I saw her, at the party. I was so angry with her. I told her to take it off. Someone might

recognize it, I told her. She did and put it in her bag, that little bag she was carrying. That's when she started to cry. I should never have yelled at her."

"You're sure it was this ring?" Barty said.

"It's my aunt's ring. I gave it to her, years ago. She left it to me, in her will. What have you done?" he demanded of Harry. "What have you done?"

"Nothing," Barty said. "We needed her help, and she gave it to us. We had to let you think she might be guilty. Frankly, sir, we were afraid you wouldn't tell us the truth about the ring, if you thought it would accuse a member of your family."

"What are you talking about?" Roland demanded.

"We searched your house today, while you were all at church and while you were having lunch afterward with the Brackers. They were good enough to help us out, too, by inviting all of you to lunch today."

"You searched my house again?" Roland stared at him.

"The other one. The mansion your aunt left you. That's *your* house, isn't it?"

"Well, technically, yes, but they can live there for the rest of their lives."

"Arky Kulpa had an accomplice," Barty said. "The accomplice had a fondness for gambling and a tendency to lose. Arky made a deal. The accomplice gives him some information about you, and he and the accomplice can drain some money from you. The accomplice gets more time to pay off debts, waiting for your aunt, Mrs. Grantlin, to die, when there would be a fortune. But when she died, she left money in trust instead, with you as executor. Arky now has a gold mine in his hands. A list that proves you were betrayed, Mr. Neale. How much would the accomplice pay to avoid that?"

"You said that was *her* handwriting, that girl's," Savannah pointed out.

"It is. *This* is the killer's." Barty pulled a page out of his jacket, held it up, showed it to the three of them, although he stood far enough away to prevent anyone's snatching it. "This is a copy of what we found in Arky's car, hidden inside a notebook he'd prepared for Mrs. Atwill to use in writing her script. He was on his way to meet his accomplice that night, probably for the first of some big payoffs. Unfortunately for Arky, he didn't know Ida Smoody was already dead. He didn't know her killer had found her, by accident, at the party and decided there was a chance not to pay any money at all. In all likelihood, Miss Smoody had no idea who the accomplice was, probably didn't even know there was one. But as soon as she told Miss Masters her name that night, she was in grave danger."

He turned. "So you got your gun. You're a doctor, you carry drugs with you, opiates. Doctors get robbed. You carry protection. You got your gun out of your doctor's bag, which as a doctor, you always keep in your car. You watched her, you followed her. Caught her alone, maybe in tears after Mr. Neale had yelled at her, promised to make things right with him. Lured her to his house. The body would be found in his yard. Mr. Neale would be arrested. You might even be able to break the will. Arky would believe Mr. Neale was guilty, at least long enough for you to get rid of him, too."

"That's crazy," Kentwood said. "I would never do such a thing. For God's sake."

Barty pulled another sheet of paper from his pocket. The marker from Elizondo. He showed it to Roland. "This is your cousin's handwriting. It's a match."

Kentwood jumped up. "That's a forgery. I haven't done anything. For the love of God. What are you doing? This is obviously some attempt to blackmail me, some plan that man had, that man who got shot. Some plan he had. It's a forgery. The list's a forgery. Her," he stabbed a finger at Harry. "The

two of them. Her and that man. My God, you said he was a criminal. He must have known how to forge."

"Did he know how to plant a ring under the lid of your cufflink box, doctor?" Barty said. "That's where we found it. Your mother's ring. You took it back. You took it back from a dead girl, a girl you shot in the face."

"No! I swear to God, Roland, no! They're lying."

Barty said, "We'll need to go downtown and talk about it."

"I will not. I was brought here under false pretenses. I'm talking to a lawyer first. I'm not going with you. Get away from me! I'm not going anywhere with you!" He marched toward the door. "I'm not going to jail!"

Loomis stepped in front of him. "Sir."

Kentwood's arms shot out and struck Loomis hard in the chest with an athlete's strength. Loomis staggered, slipped, and fell, right in Barty's path.

Kentwood grabbed his coat, shoved his hand into the pocket, and came out with a gun. He pointed it at Barty's face. "Stay away from me!" he screamed.

There was scrambling above, running steps. "Who's that? Who's up there? Stay back!"

Barty took a step back, lifting his hands. "Let's all calm down here."

"Tell them to stay up there!" Kentwood wheeled, pointed the gun alternately between the detectives and the top of the stairs. "Tell them to go back. Now!"

"Stay up there!" Barty called. "All right. All right, they're going to stay."

The stairs were too steep. From where Kentwood was standing, the angle was too sharp for even Peter to get off a good shot.

Barty said, "Let's talk."

There were thundering footsteps on the front steps, the

porch. Kentwood pointed the gun at me. "Tell them to stop, or I'll shoot her! Now!"

Barty shouted to the men at the door, ordering them to stop. Ordering them to stay where they were. "Nobody comes in the house! Nobody!"

Barty and Loomis glanced at each other, but there was no use telling Kentwood that if anything happened to any of us, he would die. He was beyond being rational about that. Their best hope was to try to get as many other people out of the room as they could.

Kentwood tucked himself inside the wide arch to the parlor, where he still had a view of the foyer and the front windows. "Close the drapes!" he screamed at Roland, who stood by the armchair, holding Savannah behind him. "Do it!"

Roland eased to the windows and did as he was told.

Savannah had her forearms across her chest, breathing in whimpers.

I listened for men at the back door. Would they try that, despite Barty's orders? Could they, without Kentwood hearing them?

"Winslow!" Kentwood shouted. "I know you're up there! Winslow!"

"Yes?" Peter called back. "I'll come on down, we can talk."

"Stay up there! Everybody stays up there, stays outside. I'll kill her!"

"Nobody's coming in, nobody's coming down," Peter said. "Whatever you say."

Barty said, "It can be just you and me. Send everybody else out. Just you and me. I'll give you my gun. We can talk about the forgery, get to the bottom of it. You don't need all these people here."

"She's not going anywhere!"

"Send the ladies out."

"You!" Kentwood said to Harry. "What's back there?"

She said, "The kitchen, a pantry, that's where the back door is. My bedroom, the door's closed. There's a woman in there asleep. I gave her pills. She's old, she's not well. Please don't hurt her."

"Back stairs. Where are the back stairs?"

"There aren't any. I took them out to make the pantry."

"Can I see the hall from the kitchen?"

"Yes, if the door's open. The hall, the bottom of the stairs. Yes."

"What are the windows like?"

"High," Harry said. "No one could see you."

"She stays!" He jerked his head at me. "All the rest of you, outside!"

Barty said, "We can't leave the lady. I'll stay here. Let her go."

"If you don't leave, I'll shoot you. And your partner. Then your friends will storm in here and more people will die. And she'll be first. *Her first!*"

I said, "You have to let everyone else go."

"Mrs. Atwill, no," Barty said.

I kept talking to Kentwood, trying not to look at the stairs and judge whether there was any chance Peter could get to a shooting position.

I said, "You're right. This is too many people for you to try to watch."

"Get out!" he yelled at Savannah. She didn't move. Loomis slowly raised his hand and motioned to her. She edged across the room to him. "Don't get in front of him!"

Loomis stepped forward, let her slip behind him. "The back door," he said to her, "go out through the pantry. Go on." He called out to the floor above, "Tell them she's coming!" When she'd cleared him, he gave her a little push between the shoulder blades, and then she ran, clutching herself, sobbing.

"Rolly next!"

Roland started to speak, but Barty cut him off. "Go!" he ordered. Roland went out.

"You!" Kentwood said to Harry, keeping the gun pointed at Barty. "We're going that way, to the kitchen. You're going to open that door. Make sure it stays open. No tricks. You two go out first," he said to the detectives. "Keep your hands up. Either one of you drops his hands, I shoot both of you."

There was scuffling from above, then angry grunts, a muffled blow, and a tumbled thud.

"What's going on?" Kentwood shouted.

Peter called back. "Nobody's coming down. If anybody tries it again, I'll shoot him myself."

"Get over here!" he commanded me. He grabbed me hard by the upper arm and held me close to his side, so I'd be between him and the stairs. We edged into the hall. Harry opened the swinging door full; it caught and stayed open. She backed up into the kitchen. Barty went through, then Loomis, their hands raised. Then us.

Kentwood surveyed the room. The high windows. Nobody could get a shot off from outside. The view of the bottom half of the staircase if he stood near the doorway. "Close the door to the dining room," Kentwood said, and Harry did.

"That's the pantry," Harry said. "There's a lock on it. The key's in it. I keep it locked at night, so the girls don't try to slip food out. It's my house. I can tell you about it. I should stay."

"Don't argue with me! Get out! I'm not talking anymore!"

"Go on, sergeant," I said quietly. "There's nothing to be done now but wait. We'll all just wait. Everybody needs some time. A little peace and quiet."

Harry went out, then Loomis and Barty backed toward the door. "Turn around," Kentwood commanded them. "Go out with your hands up. She's going to lock the door after you, so no ideas about shooting through the door."

They went, slowly. They were both trying to think of something else, something new, something that would keep them in the house. But there was nothing left.

They shut the pantry door after them. Then Kentwood pushed me to the door, in front of him. I locked it.

He grabbed me back, then turned, put his back against the wall, and tested the door, making sure I'd locked it.

"Sit down," he said. I did as I was told, on the far end of the kitchen table. He returned to the door to the hall, where he could see the steps and anyone trying to come down them.

He was sweating, beads at his hairline. He licked his upper lip. "We're just going to wait here, while I think. Don't do anything."

"I'm not," I said. "I'm just going to sit here." I put my hands on the table.

We were quiet. His breathing got steadier. But his eyes didn't relax.

"I didn't do anything," he said. "This is all a frame. She framed me, or that man. Both of them. They were in it together."

"It seems to me they don't have much. The ring, whether it's the same ring, that's only your word against Roland's memory. And your word against the police that they found it hidden."

I waited. The house was still, except for the hall clock's ticking.

Then I said, "The handwriting means nothing. A blackmailer had a list; who knows where he got the information on it. He forged your handwriting and planned to blackmail you, now that you'd come into money. You're a doctor. Who would a jury believe? That you'd blackmail your own cousin? And how are they going to prove gambling debts? Are they going to get gangsters to testify in court?"

He glanced out the door, toward the stairs, but his eyes narrowed. He was thinking about it.

I made a dangerous bet. Because of the size of the gun he held and the amount of blood I'd seen on the windows of Arky's car. I said, "They don't have the gun. That's not the murder weapon. You carry that one for protection. You're a doctor. You have to. You thought you were being framed. The cops have framed people before to solve a case they couldn't break. You were just protecting yourself. You panicked. It got out of hand."

He considered it. I'd said enough though. So I sat there.

"The ring. The ring. I need to explain that. It's in her will. They're not going to believe it was a different ring. I'm not going to prison. I won't do that."

And then the door to Harry's room opened. Kentwood wheeled around.

"No!" I shouted at him. "It's just Dorothea. She woke up. She's harmless."

"I had a bad dream," she said. "People were shouting. Where's Harry?" She shuffled toward me, still groggy from the pills, her shawl clutched in front of her with her fists, right over left. "I couldn't get back to sleep. Who are you?"

"Dr. Grantlin," I said. Kentwood dropped the gun to his side. I got up and collected Dorothea. "Why don't you sit down?"

"Where's Harry?"

"She's gone upstairs? Would you like to go up there? I think she's putting something away in your room."

"All right. In a minute. I need a glass of water."

"Let me get it," I said.

"No, no, I'm fine. Is someone sick? Why is there a doctor here?"

"He's a friend of mine. We were just visiting with Harry."

"That's nice. There's some cake left. Almond cake."

She shuffled to the cabinets above the counter on the far wall. "Oh, dear, I can't reach the glasses," she said. "I'd like one of those with the daisies on them. They're my favorites."

"Sure," I said and followed her. She stood beside me at the counter while I opened the cabinets.

"You know I think I will sit down. I feel a little weak."

"Of course." I pulled my chair out further, and she sat in it, angled, facing me, her back to Kentwood. "A bit of water, and then maybe I should go back to bed." She opened her shawl. Lying in her lap was my gun. "I was sleeping in Harry's room, and then I had a dream. Everybody was yelling. Such a fuss."

I knelt in front of her. "A little water, you'll feel better. Then I'm going to take you back to the bed."

"Yes, dear. Thank you. That would be nice."

I put my arms around her and hugged her. She lifted the gun under the shawl. I let my right hand slide down her arm, patting her. "You're going to lie down now," I said.

"That would be nice."

With my left hand, I grabbed her right shoulder and shoved her hard, threw her out of the chair and into the corner, onto the floor beside the refrigerator. I wheeled in the opposite direction with the momentum of the shove and fired. And kept firing. I forced myself to be still in that brief eternity as I pulled the trigger again and again, with Kentwood and his gun not ten feet away. Then I dived under the kitchen table. I pointed the gun toward him, up at him. But I couldn't see more than his legs.

He sat down in the chair against the wall, but on its edge, hard. The chair legs flipped out, and it slid away, clattering onto its side. Kentwood sat down hard again, this time on the floor.

And then there were trouser legs in the doorway beside him and Peter's shoe, kicking Kentwood's gun from his limp hand, and then Peter was under the table, his hands on me. "Are you all right? Are you all right?" I must have said yes.

He said, "Here, let me have that. Just relax your hand." He slid the gun from it. He must have handed it up to somebody because both his arms were around me then, and I could feel the palms of his hands on my back, empty.

Somebody else unlocked the pantry door. Barty and Loomis crashed in, and others. There were shouts, to get an ambulance. To get towels. Men yanked open drawers, found towels, and two of them knelt by Kentwood, holding the blood into his body.

Brusquely, Barty cleared the room of everybody who wasn't needed and everybody who wasn't sitting on the floor. Ordered somebody to make sure Savannah was kept out. And to let Harry in. In another moment, Savannah began shrieking out in the yard. Harry rushed in and dashed to Dorothea.

Out in the hallway, men gathered, stunned, their heads down, casting anxious looks back toward us, and talking to each other without looking each other in the eye, probably already trying to figure out what their explanation would be for how this had all gone wrong.

"She okay?" Barty asked.

"Yeah," Peter said. "She's fine."

Harry was sitting in the corner, by the dining room door, tucking Dorothea's shawl around her.

Peter helped me to my feet with one hand and held the other behind my head to make sure I didn't hit it on the table top. We went over to Dorothea. I knelt beside her, still holding Peter's hand.

"I didn't take those pills," she said.

"I know."

"Something was going on. All these men with guns. I didn't believe you, about not having one. Good thing you did. I don't know where Harry keeps the key to hers."

I said, "You saved my life, you know. Are you sure you're all right?"

"I used to do all my own stunts," she said. "I still got the stuff."

EPILOGUE

It turned out I was a rotten shot. Five bullets, and I only hit him twice. Enough to knock him down but not nearly enough to kill him.

The police brass were there five minutes after the ambulance. They roped off the block and proceeded to alter history. They were determined nobody with a reporter's pass would ever find out the killer was brought down by a couple of women.

Peter and I were bustled out of the house the back way. The Chief told reporters that Dr. Grantlin was being questioned about evidence they'd found in his handwriting—implying they'd found it in Ida's room and not in a notebook belonging to me. The doctor, realizing he was cornered by LA's finest, had pulled a gun and held the landlady and a resident as hostages until the police through their ingenuity figured out how to save the women. One of the men who'd been upstairs—the one Peter had punched for almost getting people killed—ended up getting credit for those two bullets in Kentwood. The reporters liked the bruises on him.

Harry had no desire to put Dorothea on display. She agreed to their tall tale as long as they agreed to keep reporters away from her house and to pay to fix the bullet holes in her kitchen.

The story was front page for weeks, of course, because of Roland. And because money, sex, and betrayal were involved. Every bit of privacy Harry had was gone. Roland paid for private guards to augment the police, to make sure no reporters

bothered her. He issued statements through the studio about what a fine lady Harriet Virdon was, and it was a shame anyone had tried to profit from such a tragedy as the death of her daughter. He told the press he was to blame, for being gullible, and he was ashamed of his behavior all those years ago. The press loved him.

He paid to have Ida's body shipped to Tennessee to be buried by her aunt. He paid for the gravesite. She wasn't the girl the press made her out to be, he said.

The press ignored that part.

Joe Gettleman kept his license. Mike Tallis, whom I could never think of as anything but Costello, was released from jail.

Kentwood spent two weeks in the hospital and pled to a deal that would give him another one thousand in prison. He stayed off Death Row because the people he killed weren't important enough to anyone. To anyone who mattered.

Savannah took a short leave of absence from the *Eagle*. As soon as her husband pled guilty and disappeared from the front pages, she was back at her desk. We never had that interview about my divorce.

Harry got pictures of herself plastered all over the papers and scandal mags. Of course, the one of her half-naked was discovered by an enterprising photographer named Birdie Hitts. Peter and I paid him the hundred dollars we still owed him for the information about Mary Ann anyway. A deal is a deal. He made plenty more covering the Roland Neale blackmail story for *Inside Scoop*. Pictures of the Parisian Gardens' bar where, according to Birdie's story, the blackmail scheme had been hatched. There was even a picture of the bar stool on which "our reporter" had last seen Arky Kulpa alive. Birdie decided to keep me out of it as long as I promised to tell him the next time I signed on to a picture. He'd decide whether to tell his editor a big story was coming or pack his bag and get the hell out of town.

Ben Bracker didn't divorce his Jean, but, business being business, Mary Ann was announced as the co-star in *The Hard Fold*. I finished my story treatment, handed it in, and it was assigned to a producer. He called me, thanked me, told me it was great, promised to be in touch.

I went back to Marathon. I waited. Then I read in the trades that the treatment was being handed over to another screenwriter at Epic, who'd written gritty pictures before.

My agent called the producer.

The producer loved the treatment, loved it.

But he said he needed a writer who really understood murder.

ABOUT THE AUTHOR

Sheila York grew up traveling, the daughter of a career army officer. She spent much of her childhood in Munich, Germany, and later studied abroad as an exchange student in both France and England. After postgraduate studies in clinical psychology, she took a sharp turn and enjoyed a long career as a radio disk jockey, with occasional assignments as a TV news anchor and sports reporter, before combining her love of mysteries, history, and the movies in the Lauren Atwill series. She serves as treasurer of the New York chapter of the Mystery Writers of America and lives in Bloomfield, New Jersey, with her husband, novelist David F. Nighbert.